Chaos

The Lost Gods 5

Chaos, the Lost Gods 5
By Megan Derr

Edited by Samantha M. Derr
Cover designed by London Burden

Second editiom November 2019

Printed in the United States of America

Chaos

The Lost Gods 5

Megan Derr

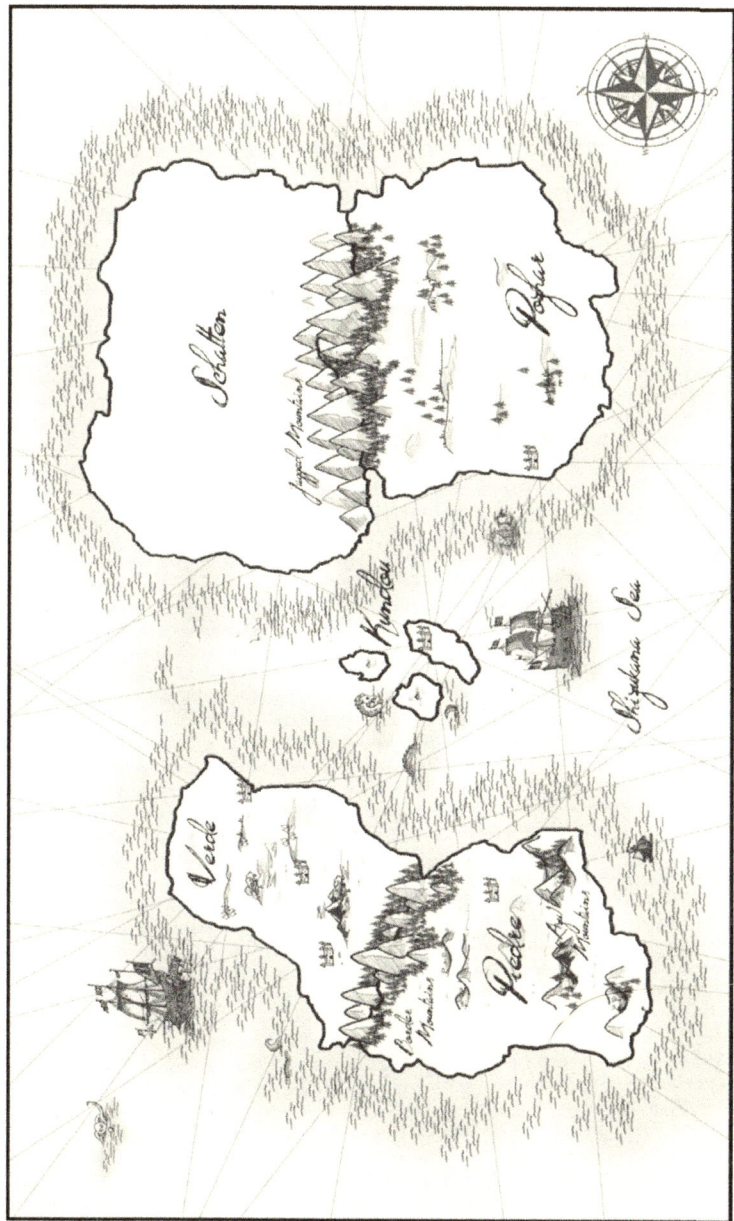

Visions

The dark of a moonless night. Anything can happen when nothing can be seen.

"What?"

Friedrich jerked his head up as he heard someone speaking, daring to interrupt him in the middle of a Seeing. Whipping around, he scowled at Karl, the Master Seer and his second in command. "What do you want?"

Karl bowed, but if ever a man could display impudence in a bow, it was Karl. "My pardon, High Seer. I only came to see how you were doing, as we have not seen you all day."

"I am Seeing; it is what Seers do," Friedrich replied.

Do they also drink the way you tend to?

Be quiet.

"High Seer?"

"What?" Friedrich asked, realizing he had been paying too much attention to his own head and missed whatever Karl had said.

"I asked if you were all right. You have been pale these past few days and more distracted than is normal. We worry for you."

Friedrich sneered inwardly at that. The only thing Karl worried about was how much longer he would have to wait before he could usurp Friedrich's place. "There is no need to worry about me," he said and turned back to the altar he had been facing.

Normally, the Altars of Vision held obsidian bowls filled with water. When a penitent sought his future, the Seer added the penitent's blood, the Seer's blood, and Essence of Moon to the bowl. In the glow of the beeswax candles on either side of the bowl, the Seer was able to foretell the penitent's fate.

The bowl in front of Friedrich was empty, however; it had not been used since Friedrich had assumed the mantle of High Seer and the large prayer room had been assigned to him. Unlike the other priests, Friedrich needed no implements to foretell a future. All he needed was to touch someone. Occasionally, all he needed was to stare into the penitent's eyes.

And sometimes, when he was alone and let his mind float, pieces of various fates came to him: wispy images, whispers in the dark, elusive scents, or the softest brush of fingers.

"The dark of a moonless night," he muttered again, eyes going distant as the vision overtook him.

> *An impression of sadness and a deeply buried rage. The pure, unrelenting dark of a moonless night. Anything can happen when nothing can be seen. A choice must be made: darkness or shadows.*

He broke off, head throbbing and hand trembling as he pulled out a handkerchief to mop up the sweat on his face and bare head. Movement caught the corner of his eye, and in the moment before Karl realized he was watching, Friedrich saw the envy and loathing plain upon his face. "You can leave," he said. "Assure our brothers that I am fine, merely busy answering the call of our Lord Teufel."

Karl bowed and deferentially touched his fingers to the black circle on his forehead: the Eye of Seeing, a mark with which all priests were born, making their fate clear even as they drew their first breath. "Yes, High Seer. Please summon us if you have a need."

Friedrich turned away and waited until Karl was gone before sinking to his knees and burying his head in his hands. The vision had started several days ago, faint at first, little more than smoke curling in a breeze. It taunted him, teased him, drove him right to the edge of madness—and still he could make no sense of it. Could not get a feel for whose fate he was Seeing, or why he was Seeing it repeatedly. And he had yet to see the whole of it.

Whatever was going to happen, it was going to be bad. He sensed he knew how the vision would eventually end when the whole of it finally came to him. Teufel displayed rare mercy in the way the vision crept upon him slowly, allowing him to brace for it. He loathed visions of death; they hurt and left him drained for days. Friedrich dreaded the day the penitent whose fate he was reading finally arrived to hear it.

Turning, he sat down on the steps that led up the altar and braced his elbows on his knees. He tilted his head up to stare at the ceiling, which was decorated with an elaborate geometric design in black, gray, and violet. After a few minutes, it added to his dizziness and he dropped his head, closing his eyes to try and make the world hold still.

He heard the footsteps coming in the jangle of spurs and stood up before the knock came at the door. "Enter."

Two men stepped into the room, dressed in black leather and dark violet tunics split up the middle. They wore large swords at the left hip and coiled whips at the right, the metal bits at the end gleaming in the candlelight.

Friedrich drew his hands into the sleeves of his own dark violet robes and stood tall, staring down the sorcerers who regarded him with arrogance. They bowed low, before the bolder of the two said, "High Seer, we apologize for disturbing you. We come with troubling news and hope that you might offer us your wisdom and power."

"It is my duty and honor to assist those who serve our Lord Teufel," Fritz replied. "Tell me of your troubles, sorcerers."

The quieter one reached into a pouch at his waist and pulled something out, holding it out so Friedrich could see it clearly. It took Friedrich a moment to realize what it was: a Sentinel scale. It was the size of his hand and gleamed in the light, black as pitch but with dozens of colors deep within. Friedrich did not touch it. "That is the scale of a Sentinel. How do you come by such a thing?"

"We found it dead, High Seer. Not far from the village of Deer Run, half a day's ride up the Haunted Mountains on the path to Sorrow Cliff."

Dead? A full grown Sentinel? "How was it killed?"

"By blade and magic, though the residue of the magic was nothing like we have felt before," said the first sorcerer. "Men are guarding the body, and we have priests investigating the locals, but so far no clue has been found. It is like it was slain by a ghost."

"Absurd," Friedrich said dismissively. "Come, we'll go to the Hall of Vision." He led the way out of his private prayer room and down the hall of prayer rooms, beckoning to half a dozen priests as he saw them. Though he loathed Karl, the man was a good Seer, so Friedrich beckoned to him as well.

By the time they reached the Hall of Vision, he had collected eight priests in total. He walked down the long hall, which was made from gleaming obsidian heavily spelled to last the ages and resonating with the power of Seeing.

No one should be able to kill a Sentinel, the voice in his head said pensively.

Friedrich flinched inwardly. *Well, should does not always mean much. Be quiet. This is not going to be an easy Seeing and your nattering won't help.*

Rumbling softly, the voice nevertheless obeyed and subsided. Relieved, Friedrich took his place at the vision pool. It was built in the shape of a crescent moon, the black walls of the pool making the water dark. The eight priests he'd brought with him gathered around the outside of the crescent, from tip to tip, while he stood in the curve.

Drawing the knives kept at their waists, each priest slit his thumb and let their blood drip into the black water. Friedrich slit his own thumb, but let the blood drip into a small crystal bottle in which swirled the silvery, pearlescent Essence of Moon. It turned pink with his blood, and he poured the whole of it into the pool.

It shimmered briefly before it settled into darkness again, but swirled occasionally with red and silver. Closing their eyes, the priests began to pray. Nine priests to lend their powers of Seeing to reach across all the land: eight to anchor, one to See.

The vision, when it came, started out surprisingly gentle. Friedrich wished it hadn't, because what started easy usually ended with him unconscious. But such things were his fate, and so he stared into the depths of the pool and let the vision have him.

Darkness. A natural darkness. It was night and the moon had only just begun to wax. He felt the beast before he saw it, a pool of gleaming black that made the night around it a paltry imitation of darkness. Its breath steamed in the cold air, clawed feet crackling the snow and ice. Its eyes gleamed violet, burning stars fallen to the earth to menace the children of shadows.

Friedrich felt contempt ripple through his mind, but also amusement, as he uncoiled the whip he wore at his right hip. He flicked it with practiced ease, cracking the calm of the night. The Sentinel growled, the sound so deep it vibrated in his chest.

Another crack. Another. Alarming the Sentinel, whose eyes burned but could not see well. With its hearing fractured by the cracking of the whip, it faltered, reared back, slipped in the snow, and then roared in pain and anger as the whip came down and struck a real blow.

It rushed the source of the sound and pain only to strike against an enormous, dying tree. Friedrich struck again with the whip, over and over, keeping it disoriented, angry, and in pain. Then he began to murmur words of magic, the power thrumming through him.

But it felt different. Hot. Almost too hot, as though he had thrust his hand into a fire. Friedrich recoiled from the rush, struggling to break free of the vision, but he was trapped in it, trapped in the past as he witnessed, firsthand, the killing of the Sentinel.

The Sentinel shrieked as the spell struck, a sound like hundreds of nails scraping glass. Friedrich's mind screamed in helpless agony, but the body in which he was trapped showed no reaction. He simply coiled his whip and put it away, then drew his sword and rushed the writhing, suffering beast.

Friedrich plunged the sword into the creature's eye, all the way down to the hilt. The body thrashed and shuddered, then lay still. Bracing his foot on the Sentinel's snout, Friedrich yanked his sword out and cleaned it in the snow. He sheathed it, then checked over the Sentinel, removing a leather glove to place his hand on the beast and assure himself directly that it breathed no more.

Light gleamed in the dark, a small rainbow on the man's right ring finger. Friedrich stared at it and his world exploded in a painful assault of colors and countless fates.

Friedrich screamed in agony. Stumbling back from the pool, he fell over and cracked his head, but still the assault would not stop. He sobbed in agony as the light and colors washed over him, drowned him, threatening to break his mind entirely—

Beloved, hold fast to me.

Drache, Drache, Friedrich said desperately, clinging to that dread voice he could not live without. *Save me, Drache.*

I will always save you, beloved. Come to me.

Whimpering, sobbing, Friedrich let Drache have his way and slumped unconscious on the obsidian floor of the Hall of Vision.

"Fritz."

Friedrich opened his eyes, shaking with relief when he no longer saw the Hall of Vision or that terrible cascade of endless possibilities. Instead, he saw only the familiar place where he always visited Drache. A dream, only a dream, but more home to him than the walls in which he lived.

It was a temple, or something like that, with beautiful white marble for the floor and roof. Four pillars were all that held it up. There were no walls, just open space allowing him to look down at the ground far below and stare out for miles at the bright, beautiful landscape beyond. A soft breeze carried the sweet scent of flowers and fresh air.

He wore dark violet robes, though they were not the heavy, ornate robes of the High Seer, but a bed robe loosely tied with a silver cord. Friedrich sat up in bed and stared at the man who stood at the far edge of the large room, staring down at something far below.

Like Friedrich, his skin was dark, the rich gold-brown of topaz. But he was taller than Friedrich, more slender, and instead of a smooth, shaved head, he had bright gold hair bound in a braid that fell to the floor. His chest was bare, and he wore a loose wrap around his hips, the rich dusty lavender color of the fabric complimenting his skin.

The man turned. His features were beautiful with the barest touch of delicate prettiness to them. He smiled warmly. "You haven't come to see me in a long time, Fritz. I've missed you."

"Pardon me if I prefer to avoid these more detailed conversations with the voice in my head," Fritz groused and moved to the edge of the bed.

"You know I'm more than that," Drache chided.

Fritz shook his head. "I don't know what you are, except a problem. If anyone finds out I hear a voice in my head, they'll throw me out and replace me."

"Would that be such a bad thing? High Seer hardly makes you happy."

"I was born to See," Fritz said stiffly. "I like Seeing." When he didn't have to See someone die, when the visions didn't make him sick, didn't depress him. He wished more happy fates came to his Sight.

Drache wandered over to him and planted his hands on his hips, long braid falling sinuously over one shoulder as he stared down at Fritz. "I said High Seer hardly makes you happy, not that Seeing does."

"I don't hate it, I just hate the sorrow," Fritz said. *"So much sorrow should be tempered. But I can only See what fate gives me."* He looked up at Drache, drinking in the vision he made, the beauty and the warmth of him.

Whoever, whatever, Drache was, he made the aches and the pains go away. He soothed something in Fritz, made the world bearable again. But only in the recesses of Fritz's mind—recesses so deep that even dreams could not reach.

Though in the waking world Drache drove him mad—someday, he feared it would be quite literally—in the safety of his own mind, Drache soothed away the pain. Drache knelt before him and settled between his legs, arms braced on Fritz's thighs as he tilted his head up. *"What did you see, beloved, that almost broke you?"*

"Chaos," Fritz said softly, shuddering at the word. *"Too much, too many, impossible to see all, impossible to see just one. I didn't know what to do, couldn't stop it, couldn't control it."*

"No, chaos cannot be controlled, only guided by fate. Night and day, life and death, chaos and order. One does not exist without the other, and neither should be greater than the other."

Fritz stared at him in horror, fear running through his veins. *"Blasphemy."*

"Truth," Drache said. *"You saw chaos for yourself."*

"It was out of control, in need of taming. People need to know—"

"People need to choose," Drache cut him off. "But you did not come to me to argue, beloved. You came here to heal. Let me soothe you, ease you, restore you."

Fritz sighed softly and let his fingers slide into Drache's soft, gold hair as Drache leaned up far enough to bring their mouths together. He smelled like sunshine on one of the rare clear days that Schatten enjoyed and the wildflowers that grew along the bank of an icy brook. He smelled like the home Fritz had not seen in twenty-odd years and tasted like a hundred memories from that same lost place.

He clung to Drache, going easily when Drache rose and pushed him back onto the bed, that warm mouth gliding along his skin with a familiarity that spoke of having done it a thousand times. Drache knew every place to nuzzle, to lick, to bite down hard or to nip lightly. He pushed Fritz's clothes away with the ease of a thought, his own wrap discarded even more quickly.

Their bodies fit together easily as he pressed Fritz deeper into the bedding. His braid tumbled to one side. Fritz wrapped it around his hand, tugging lightly and drawing Drache down into a long kiss that allowed him to explore every crevice of Drache's mouth, losing himself in the feel and flavor of his imagined lover.

It was for the best that being a priest generally meant a lonely life and that being High Seer guaranteed it. What real lover could ever compare to Drache, who was everything he needed and craved.

Fritz slid his mouth from Drache's delectable lips, tasting the skin of his jaw, his throat, before Drache pulled away to put his own mouth to work down the length of Fritz's broad body. "Relax," he whispered against Fritz's chest, looking up at him through lashes as golden as his hair, his eyes a rich, royal purple. "I said I would take care of you. Let me."

"I don't think it's possible to relax when you're doing that," Fritz said, but he lay back on the bed, hands resting on the blankets on either side of his head, and gave up doing anything beyond surrendering all the noises and pleading words that Drache wanted, groaning loudly when that hot, knowing mouth slid over his cock and took him deep, rendering him incapable of doing anything, but losing himself to Drache.

No matter how hard he tried to ignore it, no matter how much he drank to drown it out, the voice that had whispered to him since he was a child got through to him, pulled him under over and over. An invisible friend as a child, a dream lover once he was old enough for such things.

He could not live with Drache in his head, but he would rather die than go a day without him.

Fritz thrust up into Drache's mouth, crying Drache's name as he came. He whimpered softly when Drache took his mouth and pushed slick fingers inside him. When Drache finally pushed inside him, the fear and panic that had driven Fritz into the dark of his mind in search of peace finally washed completely away. His world narrowed to the soft bedding stuck to his back with sweat, the warmth of the skin beneath his fingers, and the fluid movement of the muscles beneath. They smelled of wildflowers and sex, and nothing felt more natural than the way he rose to meet every thrust, the way Drache pushed in deep, the sting of his biting kiss as Drache came and drove Fritz over the edge once more.

He woke with a cry, choking on a name he dare not speak lest someone ask questions. Friedrich lay in bed, cold, trembling, aching. His hand was bandaged and the uncomfortable fog of medicine clouded his mind.

The room was dark, but thin beams of light snuck in through the edges of the tapestry over the window. The smell of wax and smoke was sharp: a candle must have recently gone out. Friedrich threw back the blankets, damp with his sweat, and strode to the tapestry, pulling it away to let in dull, gray morning light. At least, it seemed like morning, but he supposed it might be evening. Without the sun and Citadel bells, it was hard to say.

Leaving the window, he went to his wardrobe and pulled out fresh clothes. Someone had filled the pitcher at his wash stand, and Friedrich poured the water into the bowl along with a sliver of rough, gray-ish colored soap.

When he was scrubbed clean and felt reasonably awake and aware, he dressed: small clothes followed by a black wool under robe over which he pulled the heavier, dark purple robe embroidered with geometric designs in white, silver, gold, and light purple thread at the cuffs, along the bottom, and around the edge of the hood.

He folded the right flap of the robe over the left, small, hidden hooks holding the fabric in place. He cinched it with a belt of heavy purple and gold fabric. Into a hidden pocket went the master keys and around his neck went a circle of prayer beads carved from amethyst and onyx. Pulling on sturdy black ankle-boots, he finally felt ready to face the questions he knew were waiting. The visions that caused him to pass out never failed to garner interest and cause his priests concern, even if it was a not uncommon occurrence.

He opened his door and was not surprised to find his way blocked by a guard—one of about thirty sorcerers kept at the temple for security reasons since not everyone was able to hear and accept their fates with grace. Every priest bore the scars of the anguished and enraged. Friedrich had been punched, kicked, bitten, shoved, and on three occasions, stabbed or slashed with his own knife. People could be alarmingly quick when they were in a panic.

"High Seer," the guard greeted, turning to face him. He sheathed his sword and bowed, deferentially touching his forehead, which bore a black diamond. The mark of sorcerers; it appeared when a person came of age and had the strength to wield magic. "I am happy to see you are well."

"Thank you," Friedrich said. "Where are the men who came to see me?"

"They were given quarters and await your summons."

"Summon them, then, and bid them come to me in the library. The Master Seer, as well," Fritz said and walked off after the guard had bowed.

The great library of Unheilvol was enormous, taking up the entire back half of the temple, with the archives extending into special rooms below the temple. He trailed through the stacks until he came to the section he wanted, touching the mark on his forehead and then the symbol carved into the archway that prevented any but he from passing.

With a soft shimmer of permission, the protective seal let him pass, and Friedrich wandered the shelves of restricted religious texts. Only the High Seer, the High Sorcerer, and those of greatest and deepest devotion could read the blasphemous texts upon the shelves. Books written by nonbelievers, by those corrupted by the whispers and lies of chaos.

Chaos led only to tragedy, for people were not capable of shaping their own lives. Fate was necessary for the good of all, and fate was a matter for the gods. Anyone who said otherwise was blasphemous and not to be tolerated.

Fate should be tempered by chaos, and chaos should be tempered by fate, Drache said.

If you cannot say something reasonable then be quiet.

It is not that I need to watch what I say; it is that you need to learn to listen.

Shut it. Friedrich yanked a book from one of the shelves, an old book of Seeing that had some useful points despite its flaws.

Agreeing with me is never a flaw.

Yes, it is, Friedrich retorted.

He read through the chapter he sought, then read sections of five other books before he gave up, resigned that he had seen exactly what he feared. The sound of footsteps followed by that of someone clearing his throat drew his attention, and Friedrich slowly left the restricted area to join the sorcerers and Karl.

"High Seer," Karl greeted. "I am glad you are all right. You slept a day and a night. We feared you would not recover."

"I've slept longer," Friedrich dismissed, though those instances had been when he was still an acolyte. "Unfortunately, I have no good news to share. You will take my words to the High Sorcerer at once. A stranger in our land slew the Sentinel and I Sense he will continue to kill them, though I did not See why. What I did see was chaos—"

He stopped as they all gasped and made signs of protection. Karl frowned. "That is not possible. We are a land of fate and dread chaos holds no sway here."

"It has breached the walls and entered Schatten," Friedrich said. "The visions I saw were true. Too many possibilities, too many fates—chaos that leads to madness which eventually will lead to destruction. Tell all to the High

Sorcerer and tell him to come to me at once, that we might plan against this threat. I must pray and hear all that Lord Teufel cares to tell me about the matter. Do not disturb me."

They bowed, and Friedrich left. He could feel Karl's eyes on him, but did not care. He was far more concerned about the presence of chaos in Schatten.

And Drache's dangerous, rebellious whispers.

Whispers

"Two for a nick!"

David jumped at the voice, which bellowed practically in his ear and sent him crashing into Killian, who squawked in surprise and shoved him back. Barely keeping himself from careening into someone else, David regained his balance and scowled. "I hate these creeping markets."

Killian made a noise of agreement as he dodged a fat woman herding half-starved goats down the street. "I can't wait until we can head home. What's our first stop?"

"We're supposed to pick up the wool, then we have to fetch the tea, then spices, and then—"

"I won't remember further than wool, so you may as well stop," Killian said cheerfully, then dodged a man hauling rolls of tanned hide. He wrinkled his nose at the smell and looped an arm through David's as they continued to fight their way through the throngs of people. "Suppose we have time to stop for a nip?"

David rolled his eyes. "No. Your father will murder us both if we return smelling like a tavern."

"Only out of jealousy," Killian replied. "That's the wool merchant we want, right?"

Peering through the crowd at the place Killian pointed, David gave a hesitant nod. "I think so, but we went so many places yesterday I'm not sure."

Killian rolled his eyes. "We'll know soon enough, come *on.*" He dragged David along, shoving his way through people and leaving David to flush and stutter apologies. Eventually they reached the stall they sought, which was run by a husband and wife who watched their goods and the people perusing them with sharp eyes.

The woman's eyes landed on him and she jerked her head inquisitively. David stumbled forward, jostled by the crowd, and said, "I'm here to retrieve the wool Master Reimund ordered yesterday." He fumbled in the purse at his waist and pulled out the chipped wooden token Reimund had given him.

He held it out, and the woman took it with a grunt, jerking her head again, signaling for them to follow. She led them to the back of the stall, where several bundles of wool had been neatly wrapped and bound. She indicated the one that belonged to them and Killian knelt to check it over thoroughly, ignoring the offended, angry look the woman shot him.

"All right, then," Killian said when he was finally done, standing up and slinging the bundle over one shoulder. He nodded to the woman, then led the way back out to the throng of people. "What's next?"

"Tea," David said. "That's not in the market, though, it's at the shop—"

"At the end of Spice Row, on the corner, I know," Killian cut in. "I think it's stupid we buy tea when we already have—" He broke off as a man who had rounded the corner in front of them knocked into him. Turning around as the man continued on his way without comment Killian bellowed, "Watch it there, scale-belly!"

The man whipped around, hand going to the sword at his hip, and sudden fear churned David's gut. Not just anyone was allowed a sword—only city guards, patrols, and sorcerers. The man before them was dressed in heavy leather armor, under which was a dark purple tunic that was split up the middle. He had a whip at his right hip, and the black diamond on his forehead only confirmed the obvious: Sorcerer.

David didn't wait for Killian's smart mouth to get them in trouble, just grabbed his wrist and bolted, knocking and shoving people in a desperate bid to get away from the sorcerer. No one would stop the sorcerer if he decided they needed their tongues removed—or their heads.

"What is your problem?" he burst out once they were well away, tucked into an alley, and bent double gasping for breath. "Why would you do that?"

Killian scowled at him, an effect not as ominous as he probably thought; he struggled constantly to prove he was the same as David, but the four year difference in their age mattered more than Killian ever liked to admit. Fourteen and eighteen were very different things, no matter how Killian tried to prove otherwise. "He's the one who was wrong!"

"He's a sorcerer," David hissed and cuffed him upside the head. "He can do whatever he wants, and there's nothing we can do about it. You're lucky he didn't cast a spell that left your body twitching in the streets! If he finds out who we are, he'll come down on Reimund and your father."

"He don't know us from anyone else," Killian scoffed. "I'm not afraid of a stupid, scale-belly sorcerer."

"You should be!" David snapped and cuffed him again.

Killian shoved him. "Stop it! You're not my shading father!"

David shoved him back. "Watch that wool! Stop taking the light and act like an adult! Come on, now we're behind schedule. If you hadn't been a brat, we might have had time for that nip you wanted so badly." He stormed off, angry and scared. They'd narrowly escaped terrible punishment, but Killian was too young and bratty to realize it. If the sorcerer really wanted to find them …

He stepped warily out of the alleyway and started heading back to the main parts of the city where they needed to be. Killian reached out to grab his arm a couple of times, but David jerked away, ignoring him.

When they finally reached the tea shop without incident, he sighed faintly in relief. The smell of tea, pungent, sharp, and comforting, washed over him as he slipped inside. A bell over the door alerted the shopkeeper to visitors, and he came out of a backroom. "Ah, there you are boys. I was starting to wonder; he said yesterday you'd be along much sooner in the day."

announcements were made—and punishments administered. A man currently rattling off city notices fled as quickly as he could when he saw them, leaving the dais empty. The people in the square slowed to a stop as they realized a punishment was about to take place, and the sudden lack of movement drew even more people to the square until it was quickly filled. The sorcerer cuffed him hard enough his ears rang, and David began to strip off his clothes, throwing them in a pile well away from the post to which he was promptly chained. The cold metal bit into his skin, the combination of chilly winter air and fear making him shake.

He'd been whipped once before, when he was a little younger than Killian, young enough the whip had not had barbs. It had been a token whipping administered by the village chief. Looking back, he knew it had been for his own safety, to make him fear breaking the laws about leaving the barrier without permission.

The beating he was about to suffer was being administered just because the sorcerer could, because they all could. Nobody crossed a sorcerer, except Killian and his light-stealing mouth.

David screamed in agony as the first blow landed, painfully aware that there was silence all around them despite the people who had filled the square to watch him be punished. The second blow was worse, and by the fourth, his screams were constant. The leather burned as it struck his skin, and the metal bits sliced through his skin as though it were little more than cheap cloth, pain on top of unbearable pain as metal and leather and blood mingled.

The law said lashings could only carry on so long, never more strokes than the victim could handle, but David also knew sorcerers were as happy to disregard that law as they did so many others. He had lost count of the number of strikes by the time he passed out.

His world was nothing but alternating flashes of agony and blissful darkness until he finally woke to the sound of someone softly crooning a song he vaguely remembered his mother singing when he was a boy. He licked his lips, then tried to ask, "Where ... "

"Shh," the stranger said. "You're in the temple; your companions brought you here after the sorcerer finished with you. I've cleaned and numbed your wounds, but they'll probably start to hurt again pretty soon. Lay there, don't move. The cuts are deep and many, and they won't heal properly if you don't let them."

Tears stung David's eyes. He was alive. He hurt, despite what the priest had given him. He couldn't move, couldn't work—couldn't do anything. How was he going to get home? What was he going to do if he couldn't earn his keep? Reimund wouldn't keep him on if he couldn't work.

The priest said something, but David didn't catch it as unconsciousness mercifully took him away once more.

When he woke again, dingy gray light spilled in through one papered window. He could just see Reimund and Sigmund, Killian's father, standing with their hats in their hands, murmuring quietly with the priest.

Reimund saw that he was awake and approached him, kneeling down beside him. "David, I know you're in pain and we don't want to move you, but the guard is ready to go ..."

David nodded, understanding. Travel between the villages and cities had to be done under special escort so that people were not wrongfully attacked by the Sentinels that roamed the land. But guards were limited. Once a journey was scheduled, changing it was nearly impossible. If he did not go with them, he would be left behind in Two Mill to fend for himself. "I can handle it."

"We'll be careful," Sigmund said as he finished speaking with the priest and handed off coin. He shoved his hat on his head, then crouched down. "Swallow this, boy. It'll keep you out. We've made up a place for you in the cart; you can sleep through most of the trip. Once we have you back, Maja will fix you right up. I can't—Killian told me—you're a good boy, David. Thank you. I'll see that you heal up proper and don't have to worry about anything. Now, swallow."

Obediently swallowing the bitter medicine pushed into his mouth, David slumped back down and waited for it to take effect. "How bad?" he asked, voice hoarse.

No one answered him, but the grim set to their faces was all the reply needed. David closed his eyes against the fear that washed over him. How long until he could work again? Would he still be in time to make his journey to Unheilvol?

Before the thoughts could get the better of him, he succumbed to the medicine and slipped gratefully back into oblivion.

The journey home was three weeks of long, hard travel. Two Mill was closer to the middle of the country, where the land was flat and smooth. Black Hill, where David lived, was in the foothills of the Haunted Mountain. It was hard going and crawling with Sentinels.

After the first week, David could sit up and manage food and drink on his own. The wounds still bled and had to be treated frequently, but at least they were healing. Hopefully once he was home and able to get real rest, they would heal faster. Maja would make it better; she always did. He would be able to get back to work.

"Here," Killian said and thrust a cup of hot tea into his hands before sitting down next to him with a cup of his own. "Feeling any better?"

"A little," David replied and sipped the tea, grateful for the warmth of it, even more so for the medicine he could taste that would ease the pain already climbing back up to unbearable levels. He nodded at the group of men on the far side of the camp. "What are they whispering about? They look scared."

Killian shifted, looking anxious himself. "They found a dead Sentinel yesterday. You were asleep, and they don't want to talk about it much because they're scared."

"Sentinels die, though it's rare to find the bodies, I admit."

"No," Killian said, shaking his head and then looking up at David with fearful eyes. "It was killed. Someone used a sword, thrust it right through the eye into the brain. Magic was used, too. It's like a rogue sorcerer killed it. Someone said something about another being found the same way up close to Oak Hill."

"Two? Someone killed two? I don't believe it. I think someone is telling tales," David said dismissively. Oak Hill was roughly five days travel from Black Hill, and they'd stop there before making the last part of the journey home. "No one would kill a Sentinel. Lord Teufel would never permit such a fate. The Sentinels watch for intruders and keep them from tainting Schatten." They also ensured that people stayed where they were meant and did not travel more than strictly necessary. They were Teufel's faithful, terrible beasts. Like the sorcerers, they were meant to be guards but in reality were monsters. "He would never tolerate a fate that included killing them."

Killian nodded, but did not look convinced. "What else could kill a Sentinel and leave something resembling a sword wound, though? And two of them—that many people would not make the same mistake about the Sentinels being killed by a person."

"Sure they would," David said and finished his tea, already beginning to feel the effects of the medicine. "It's like that time three years ago when everyone swore old Rufus had been murdered. Remember? Because he had been fighting with most of the town, and he looked all blue-ish? One person said it was murder and everyone else picked that up, and it took that priest coming in and saying no, he'd died all natural."

"I suppose, but it still seems strange to me." Killian finished his own tea and took their cups back to the campfire to wash out and put away. By the time he returned to David's side, it was getting difficult for David to keep his eyes open. Killian laughed at him, but was careful as he helped David lie back down in his little nest. "You'll get better soon."

David just grunted.

"Thank you," Killian said quietly, and he kissed David's cheek as he slipped into sleep again.

When he woke, it was to the sound of shouting—frightened shouting from most, though there were a couple voices trying to get people calmed down and under control. David whimpered as he forced himself to sit up and crawl to the edge of the cart. It sounded like something bad had happened.

Then he saw it: a dead Sentinel. Not a small one either, but a full grown bull with horns and wings. He shivered just looking at and hastily made the sign of protection, touching fingertips to his forehead, lips, and heart.

He saw why everyone believed a person had killed it. The air still reeked of magic, and the Sentinel showed not just signs of having a sword plunged through its eye, but the telling marks of a whip across its snout and remaining eye. One of its horns had been broken, and the dark violet membranes of its enormous wings had been burned in several places.

Who could possibly kill a Sentinel? But it was just as Killian had said before: only a sorcerer had all of those abilities. They were the only ones allowed to carry sword *and* whip, and possessed magic. But sorcerers knew their fate the moment the black diamond appeared on their foreheads. They were destined to serve Teufel, to protect the children of shadows, maintain justice, and guard the land. No sorcerer would be fated to slaughter Sentinels—but then how and why would he?

A word rose up in David's mind then, and he shuddered, ashamed and afraid to even think it. *Chaos.* It was impossible. Lord Teufel had cast out chaos centuries ago for the good of his people, to honor Lost Licht who had died for them, died fighting the chaos that sought to destroy them.

Gritting his teeth, David slid from the cart. He bent over in agony as his back protested the movement, but he couldn't sit around useless in the face of such a problem. He slowly made his way across camp to where the men were all shouting and arguing, stopping close to Reimund. "What's going on?"

Reimund turned and scowled at him. "You shouldn't be moving about, you'll just make your injuries worse and be stuck abed longer."

David drew himself up, biting back whimpers of pain. "I'm fine. It's healing well enough. I think whatever is going on is more important. Shouldn't we be leaving?"

"Can't," Reimund said, scrubbing a hand through his stiff, gray hair then scratching at his beard. "One of the sorcerers just left to fetch help from Deer Run and send a message to the High Sorcerer in Unheilvol. We have to remain to help guard the body and vouch for what we've seen, especially the magic, since in a couple of days all residue of that will be gone. Also don't want nothing eating the corpse. They'll send better sorcerers, probably men to start hunting the blasphemer committing these atrocities."

"Good," David whispered. "It shouldn't be happening."

He ignored the treacherous part of his mind that hated the Sentinels, was terrified of them, and was tired of the way they made everything more difficult and dangerous. "Where's Killian?"

"Went hunting with his father," Reimund said with a grunt. "It'll take days, even weeks, for someone to come see us, take our accounts, and finally send us on our way." He heaved a long sigh. "Hopefully, we do not have to wait for someone to arrive from Raven Knoll. But whatever Lord Teufel wills, so shall it be, and we are grateful. Enough of that for now. Would you like some tea, a bit of medicine to help the pain, but not so much it'll put you to sleep."

David nodded. "Tea would be good, thank you. I'll try not to be a burden—I'm sorry, I know—"

"Och, boy," Reimund said and gave his shoulder a light, awkward pat. "I'm a grump, it's true, but if not for you that brat Killian would be dead. Think seeing you all bloody and close to never waking again shook him good, finally put some sense in that fool head of his. I'll not be tossing you out for taking someone else's beating, boy. Hm, I suppose it's not much fair to call you that anymore, is it? Killian is a boy; you're well into being a man. Good lad. Have a sit, I'll get that tea."

Trembling with relief, David sat down before the fire, pulling his heavy wool cloak more tightly around him. The snow was piled high on either side of the rode and all around the small clearing where they'd made camp. High above, the clouds were heavy and almost black, foretelling still more snow.

It made him think of his parents, as it always did. He'd been twelve when he lost them to Sentinels after they left Black Hill without permission. Maja, Reimund, and Sigmund—they'd always said that his parents had gone out in search of food during an especially lean year, but David had heard too many other whispers around the village to believe that.

His parents had been trying to escape, to make it up the Haunted Mountains and escape to the other side, to the Lost Lands that Licht had sealed off so that his people could be safe in Schatten. David had wondered a thousand times what fate they'd heard that made them so desperate to defy Teufel and try to escape it.

Mostly, he wondered why they had not taken him. He would rather be alive, but ... why hadn't his parents wanted him with them?

David tried to shake the thoughts off and mustered a smile of thanks when Reimund handed him a cup of tea. He sipped at it slowly, surprised when Reimund sat down next to him. "You're looking gloomy, but you always do this time of year."

"I'm fine," David said with a shrug. "I just hate the cold."

"They knew you were better off here," Reimund said. "Whatever drove them, they knew it wouldn't work. Stop dwelling on it." He gently ruffled David's hair. "Faithful as you are, I just know Lord Teufel's fate for you will be a generous one. Maybe … " Reimund trailed off when they heard the sound of several horses racing toward them.

A moment later, five horses came around the bend in the road and entered the camp. Five sorcerers … David's breath lodged in his throat as he stared at the man in the center of the group. He had pale hair—a rarity, and a high blessing, to be so marked in the Lost Licht's color. David had only ever heard of one sorcerer had such pale hair: High Sorcerer Torben.

How had the High Sorcerer arrived so quickly when he resided in Raven Knoll, the holy city where the temple of Unheilvol was located. It was a two month journey from Black Hill, but the Sentinel killings had only started a few weeks ago according to Killian—not even a full month had passed since the first if the whispers were to be believed.

David looked hastily away when the High Sorcerer caught his eyes, bowing his head low. Magic. If the High Sorcerer had travelled so far, so quickly, then he must have used powerful magic. David had not seen much magic in his life, only the warding and fire spells used by the sorcerer guards who protected them from the Sentinels, but whispers ever murmured of the might and power that the sorcerers and priests could wield when the situation arose. It was said the High Sorcerer could cast black curses that destroyed a man in a moment or made him suffer a long, agonizing nine-day death.

The only man more powerful than the High Sorcerer was the High Seer, and whispers said that he spent his days lost in visions that would break the mind of an ordinary man.

David hunched down and focused on his tea, wishing that he were home safe and warm and praying that everything quickly returned to normal.

Cursed

He woke with a groan, his head feeling as though someone had attempted to bash it in with a rock. Gingerly reaching up to touch the source of the pain, he was relieved to feel only a massive knot—annoying and painful, but unlikely to be a real problem.

Dropping his hand, he forced himself up, making it to his hands and knees before the world starting spinning a bit too much for his taste. He felt weaker than a newborn kitten. What had happened to him?

A chill ran through him when he realized he didn't know. Well, 'what' he could probably figure out if he could provide 'where,' but that too came up blank. He tamped down on the panic that tried to rise up and tried an easy question: who.

Sasha, his mind supplied.

Relief poured through him, and Sasha forced himself to his feet. He looked around his surroundings and took in almost too much information at once: he was in a small cave, the entrance mostly covered by snow. It was bitterly cold. The smells of blood, magic, and death were thick on the air. He moved closer to the cave entrance, kicked away the frozen wall of snow, and clambered out.

Bodies—there were bodies everywhere. Sasha stood staring at them, trying to put memories to them. He hadn't just magically appeared in the cave; the state of his head said he'd been involved in something. In proper light, his clothes only confirmed that he'd been involved, somehow, in whatever had killed the men before him. His clothes were torn and stained with blood. He was battered and bruised and exhausted.

He was also missing his weapons. Sasha didn't know where that thought came from, or how he knew it, but his hands moved of their own volition to his hips, and as suddenly as that he could see the missing weapons in his mind: a black whip supple from use, the grip worn to his hand. A sword given to him as a gift from … someone who made him feel happy and sad all at once. It was set with a piece of amber in the pommel, a flower petal caught in its depths.

Looking around, not immediately seeing them, he began to pick his way through the bodies. He found the whip by a man with a dagger through his throat and realized that belonged to him as well. Pulling it free, he cleaned it in the snow, and slipped it back into its sheath at the small of his back. He retrieved the whip and cleaned it as best he could, looking it over for damage. Flicked once, twice, thrice, each crack echoing through the surrounding mountains and somehow steadying his nerves. He coiled it with easy motions, secured it at his right hip, and continued on to find his sword.

Images flickered through his mind:

> *Violet eyes.*
> *He was tired. The third beast killed in as many weeks—he thought. Time was hard to track, the days bled together and became a blur of snow and hiding and fighting.*
> *The sound of horses alerted him, and he whipped around—*

Sasha cried out as pain shot through his head, driving him to his knees. His chest ached with a deep, throbbing pain. He fumbled at his cloak, tore it off, then fought with the buttons of his heavy wool jacket and the laces of the linen shirt beneath, pulling all away to reveal a black-violet spider web inked into his chest.

No, not ink ... magic. He touched it gingerly, but withdrew his hand immediately when that only caused the pain to flare.

Cursed ...

How had he wound up cursed? Where was his sword?

Violet eyes. They glowed with magic. They reminded him of the beast he'd just killed, but somehow seemed much worse. He radiated power, the first real threat he'd encountered since beginning his quest. Unlike the others, his hair was pale, falling around his shoulders, thick and smooth.

"So you are the source of the chaos."

He didn't reply to the question, just struck. He was met with magic that actually worried him a little bit. But he'd faced worse and would not be beaten down. He went for his whip even as he summoned his own magic, the ring on his finger flashing a hundred colors in the shreds of sunlight slipping through the heavy clouds above—

The men screamed as the ring flashed, recoiling, and he used his chance to strike. He killed the first two easily, plunging a dagger into the throat of the first and pulling his sword to attack the second, but he slipped in the ice and snow and dropped his whip.

After that, the fight grew more difficult, a riot of steel, magic, and cracking whips— and the ones they used were tipped with bits of metal. But the real threat held back, watching, waiting on his horse. Rounding on the bastard as he killed the last of the lackeys, he switched his sword to his left hand and held his right hand up, balling it into a fist as he summoned the magic contained in the rainbow ring.

Ring of chaos ...

They struck at the same time, magic clashing with magic, a killing curse countered at the last moment, an explosion of painful light. His head felt as though someone had driven a spike through it.

He landed with a grunt, the bastard on top of him. What was going on? Where was he? Acting on instinct, he managed to grab the bastard, shift enough to throw him off, then snatched up his sword and plunged it into the bastard's throat.

Stumbling to his feet, he wandered blankly amongst the corpses, stumbled, and cracked his head against the edge of a cave. Regaining his feet, he stumbled some more until he banged into the back of the cave and everything went black.

He looked down at his hand, realizing his right hand was indeed missing its glove. Where had he put it? The ring shimmered in the weak evening light, and he could feel its power.

Ring of chaos ...

Pain jolted through his head again. He was forgetting something important. Many things that were important. Who was he? Who was Sasha?

Nothing answered his question; no reply came from his own mind, just silence.

He resumed walking, desperate to get away from the fear that threatened to turn into panic. Looking through the snow, over the bodies, he finally spied the one he sought just past a rise in the snow. His sword was still buried in the body, the amber pommel shining. It took effort to yank the sword from the frozen body and more energy than he feared he possessed to get it sufficiently cleaned before he sheathed it.

Where was he? Where was he supposed to go? He looked down at the man he had killed, eyes lingering on the black diamond on his forehead. Kneeling, Sasha touched his fingers to the mark. Like the spider web on his chest, it had been put there magically. The mark stirred an image of a book, and words drifted out of the fog of his mind.

> *Shadow Sorcerers, so legend and a few more credible sources say, bore a mark on their foreheads: a black diamond, similar and yet quite different from the circles borne by the Seers. According to some accounts, the circles were called 'Licht's Eye' and the diamonds 'Licht's Blade'. Some historians postulate that the diamond is, in fact, a combination of sun and moon, the crescent moon being the traditional symbol of Lord Teufel, the Shadow of Licht. Diamonds are the 'eclipse' where sun and moon join—that is, sorcerers serve both Licht and Teufel, and yet neither of them, standing as a neutral between the two temples. This is of course ...*

The words faded off, leaving Sasha with his head throbbing at his temples, painful enough it was making him nauseous. So the mark identified the man as a magic user, or perhaps a special level or type of magic user. Something flickered in his mind, but was gone again in a moment like candle smoke in a strong wind.

He looked the man over further, noting his clothes, noting the clothes of all of them, then at his own. A fully functioning mind wasn't necessary to tell him that, despite the fact he wore all black, his clothes stood out. Perhaps he needed to relieve his unsuccessful attackers of a few things. Going to their horses, which were clustered together in a grove of trees for warmth, he rifled through saddlebags until he cobbled together a full set of clothes.

Taking the pile, he carried it back to his cave so he could dress without the freezing wind blowing where he preferred it didn't. Stripping off his clothes, he quickly pulled on the foreign gear, though it took some fumbling to adjust the heavy, center-split tunic and to lace everything up properly. When he was done with that, he pulled his own boots back on and resettled his weapons. He hesitated over his whip, which was quite different from the barbed ones used by the dead men, but it fit his hand, and he knew it well, and he had no desire to use something as vile as the metal-tipped whips of the dead men.

Finished changing, he ventured back out into the snow to go through the corpses and relieve them of anything useful, pleased when he found food, a fire starting kit, and even a small bag of candy. A search through their saddlebags turned up a map, which almost made everything that had happened to him worth it, as it was much better than the one in his own bags. He also found a mirror and a small bag of bathing supplies, which made him even happier than the food—if he could ever find somewhere warm enough to use it all. Last, he pulled out small sacks of horse feed. All in all, he was feeling remarkably prepared for a man who had no answers for the questions: who, what, where, when, and why.

When he was finished with poking around for supplies, he sent all but one of the horses off, hoping they would find their way home. He secured the remaining horse just outside his cave and got it settled for the night, rubbing its nose in reassurance. The horse whinnied at him and seemed content with the food he gave it.

Sasha gathered up the saddlebags and saddle and hauled them along with everything else he'd collected into the cave, somehow knowing that his bag was hidden behind a rock there.

A good place to rest for a couple of days. He'd restore his magic, get his bearings, then try to find the Great Wall.

What was the Great Wall? He tried to remember, but his head just hurt too much. Food, some real rest, then maybe he would have the fortitude to battle the curse.

Lighting a fire proved a difficult task, as it took some time to find usable wood, and he was so dizzy and exhausted by the end he could barely stand. But he pushed on, getting the fire started and melting snow—lots of snow—to have enough for tea and travel soup.

As the soup cooked, he sipped his tea and looked over the map he spread across his lap. He pulled his compass out of his bag to get his bearings, but then realized he didn't know where he was so he hardly knew where to go.

But ... he was definitely in the mountains, the landscape told him that much. The men had horses and enough feed for a few days only, which meant they had expected to be back somewhere they could replenish their supplies soon. So if he was in the mountains, he could not be too far into them.

He ran his finger along the map, over the marks of civilization, until the name of one abruptly struck something in his mind. *Deer Run.* Is that where he had been heading? It was definitely further into the mountains than the next nearest town, which was Black Hill. Everything else on the map looked close to the mountains, but definitely not in them and not as close as Black Hill or Deer Run. If the landmarks on the map were to be trusted, he might be able to figure out his way. At worst, he would just get himself lost. Eventually, if he stumbled around enough, he would get un-lost. Or dead, at which point he would cease to care. Ideally, he would find a way.

Course somewhat decided, he tucked the map and compass away. His fingers brushed along the mirror, a smallish circle of polished silver that just let him see his reflection. He frowned, reaching up to touch his hair—long, black ... wrong. But why was it wrong?

I could run my fingers through your hair all day.

Sasha dropped the mirror, startled by the voice, the memory—but it was only a whisper in the dark. He sighed and retrieved the mirror, frowning thoughtfully. His eyes were a dark, muddy sort of purple, though that could be because the light was so poor.

He looked like everyone else, so why had he been so certain he was a foreigner? He *was* a foreigner, he was certain. Frowning into the mirror, he lightly ran a finger along his forehead. If he was going to pass as one of their sanctioned magic users, then he would need the black diamond on his forehead.

Deception ...

Shadows moved in his mind like a hand struggling toward his, but always just a breadth out of reach.

His body did not require his mind, however. He moved the mirror to his left hand and pressed the tips of the first two fingers of his right hand to his forehead. *"Shifting, shaping, moving, changing. Nothing deceives better than something desperate to live. The best place to hide is in plain sight. Disguise me so, gods of life who know best how to deceive."*

As he finished whispering the words, heat filled his body, then began to move, coalescing in the center of his forehead. It burned, sharp, bright, and hot—then stopped. Sasha opened eyes he did not realize he had closed and stared in satisfaction at the black diamond on his forehead.

The smell of the soup made his stomach growl and he poured a large portion of it into his empty cup and gingerly sipped it while he went through his own bag, pulling everything out so he could repack everything between the bag and the saddlebags on the horse.

Unfortunately, nothing in the bag gave any indication as to who he was or what he was doing. Aside from killing the beasts called Sentinels and looking for some Great Wall, none of which meant anything to him. Finishing his cup of soup, he poured the rest from the pot into it, then dragged the saddlebags close and pulled out the few things remaining it, spreading it all out on the cave floor—a spare tunic, a knife, and little packets of something he'd missed before. A delicate taste from one of the packets resulted in something sharp and bitter. Medicine, would be his guess. Couldn't hurt to hold onto it, he supposed, though he had no idea what the various packets did.

When everything was laid out, he slowly began to repack it and store it in the saddlebags, folding up his own bag and storing it in them as well.

All in all, he supposed his situation could have been worse.

Loneliness washed over him then, cutting so deep his eyes stung, though he had no idea why. Given all the dangers he had apparently faced just hours ago, surely he was traveling alone because it was safer? But that made no sense; it was always better to travel in company. If he had not woken in the cave, where he was relatively warm and safe, what would have happened to him? What if his wounds had been more than he could handle alone?

Why would he venture into such a dangerous place alone, especially when he was clearly foreign and therefore easily marked?

His head throbbed and staying awake was suddenly to difficult a thing to manage. Sasha set the saddlebags behind the rock where he had first hidden his bag, then put out the fire and cleaned up his cooking utensils. Tucking those away in the bags, he piled up snow as much as he could manage at the cave entrance to help keep in warmth, then pulled out his bedroll. Settling down, he wrapped up in his cloak and finally let sleep have him.

He looked up when he heard footsteps,
feeling a prickle of awareness.

"I wanted to discuss something with you."

The weight of the words made his shoulders tense, but he only nodded and rose. "What did you want to discuss?"

"Have you ever heard of a child of chaos?"

"We normally call them the children of storms, children of the sea, but children of chaos would be another name for the people of Kundou."

"It has been used that way, but in this case I mean a very specific child of chaos. A true child of chaos is extremely rare, and for almost nine hundred years the world did not have one."

"But one has been born now and this is important?"

"A child of chaos is someone completely immune to fate. Wherever he goes, whomever he touches or interacts with, he changes that person's fate—or rather, adds chaos so that they are not bound to one fate. He gives them choices."

He frowned. "All right. And?"

"And there are ways to mark a child of chaos ... You are the only one."

"So what am I meant to do, then?"

Sasha twisted, turned, and jerked in his sleep, murmured to himself, then settled once more.

"You're a man of great kindness," a soft voice said.

"Is that another trait of a child of chaos?"

"No. Merely a bonus."

He sighed. "You need not keep pressing. I hear what you're saying ... I'm no hero."

"No?"

"Doing one's duty does not make a man a hero. All it makes him is lonely."

Loneliness washed over him, the ache of a life where he went through the motions but did not really live. What reason did he have to live? He pinched the bridge of his noise, willing away the pain.

"... Don't despair ..."

"Despair? I don't despair. I have never once in my life despaired anything. I make a point not to go further than resignation; it wastes too much energy. Is this a trip from which I might return, or should I plan never to come back?"

"You have no previous lives, being a child of chaos, so I cannot see the past to gauge the myriad possibilities of your future."

It was a better answer than he had expected.

Sasha woke up with tears drying on his cheeks, remembering loneliness, the sorrow, the deep resignation of knowing he would not return alive.

He was meant to save the land he was in, but he could not remember its name or what he was saving it from. Shoving aside his cloak, he fumbled with stiff, cold fingers at his clothes until he parted them enough to get at the mark on his chest. The black-violet spider web gleamed wetly in the morning light. He ran his fingers over it gingerly, but the sharp pain from the previous day had eased to a dull ache. *The curse had settled in.*

Shaking off the ominous thought, he stood up and packed up his bedroll, then gathered the saddle and bags and trudged out of the cave. The horse stood patiently waiting for him, shaking its head and greeting him with a soft snort. Sasha petted its nose, patted its side, then saddled up and settled his belongings.

More snow had fallen in the night, enough to obscure the bodies, but not enough to impede travel. Swinging up into the saddle, Sasha urged the horse forward and rode away from the cave. He let the horse have its head, and realized he might not wind up wandering aimlessly around the mountains as he feared if the horse knew where it was going.

The smell of snow and evergreen trees was sharp on the air, the gray, hazy light indicative of morning. His head ached slightly, but nothing like it had the previous day. Sasha thought back to the men he had killed, wondering if they would be missed, and how long it would take if so.

If the fractured remains of his memories were to be trusted, the men had been there explicitly for him, which meant there were others out there searching. Hopefully the stolen clothes and the false black diamond would pass muster and he would go largely unnoticed.

Well, there was nothing he could do about it until he was somewhere it mattered, so best to tuck the problem away until it actually became a problem. He did so and let his mind simply drift, settling on nothing, giving his overtaxed head more time to recover.

He had been travelling perhaps two hours when he heard the screams: a woman and child. Kneeing the horse to a faster pace, he veered off the faint trail they'd been following and plunged up a sharp hill. At the top, he looked down on where the woman and child were huddled before an immense tree as a gigantic black serpent bore down on them.

Sasha dismounted, ordered his horse to stay with a touch to its side, and raced down the hill. He moved to stand between the snake and its prey and uncoiled his whip. He flicked it, over and over, the sharp *crack* of it throwing the serpent off, making it pause. Sasha paused just long enough in flicking the whip to throw a knife, catching the serpent between the eyes.

It hissed in fury, reared up, and he struck with the whip at the soft, vulnerable portion of its bared throat. That drove it back further, made it panic. Dropping his whip, Sasha drew his sword and ran at it, slashing up and slitting open the soft underbelly. As the serpent came down, he brought the sword down on its throat, almost entirely severing the head.

Moving several steps back, out of the range of its death throes, Sasha turned to the woman and child. "Are you all right?"

The woman shoved her child behind her, staring at him with wide, fearful eyes. She dropped to her knees in the snow, apparently unheeding of the way the snow soaked into her skirts, and bowed her head. "Lord Sorcerer—I don't know what to say—I don't understand—"

Sasha wiped his sword and sheathed it, then retrieved his whip and returned it to its place before finally replying, "I am happy that I could help and that you're both safe. Whatever is the matter?"

"It's only—I know I break the law by leaving the village barriers without permission—and years ago the Seers of Unheilvol foretold of this very demise from which you have spared me. Forgive me, Lord Sorcerer, but I do not understand why you saved me from my fate."

"I see," Sasha said and approached her slowly. He held out his hands, and when she cautiously took them, tugged her to her feet. He lightly touched her forehead with the first two fingers of his right hand. "Take your child and return home, madam."

Her mouth dropped open and tears streamed down her face. Sasha did not wait for her to reply, simply returned to his horse and rode off. Only when he was well away did he draw a deep breath and let it out slowly, calming the faint trembling of his hands.

Child of chaos … meant to bear the ring of chaos … immune to the threads of fate … stop him.

Sasha sighed. So he was meant to stop someone, stop something, free people like the woman and child he had just saved. But the men he'd killed had nearly prevented that—very nearly. Whatever had happened up in the mountains had almost cost him his life and *had* cost him his memories. If he was going to save people, he needed those memories back.

He had absolutely no idea how to do that, however, so for the present, he would simply have to push on and stubbornly wander around in the dark.

Two Voices

Friedrich dropped the goblet of wine he'd been holding. It crashed to the marble floor, the sound reverberating through the hall. Dark red-black wine splashed across the floor, nearly invisible against the black marble tile. All around him, priests gawked.

Karl rose from his place at one of the long benches in the dining hall and strode toward him with a poor imitation of concern. "High Seer, are you well?"

"The High Sorcerer is dead," Friedrich said flatly, rubbing at his chest, willing away the bone-deep ache there. His head throbbed from the force of the vision that had slammed into him. He rubbed his eyes with his fingertips and repeated into the stark silence, "The High Sorcerer is dead. Summon the Master Sorcerer to me at once."

Karl gestured sharply to two priests, who obediently ran off to carry out his orders.

"To my prayer room," Friedrich said, and he turned sharply on his heel. He left the dining hall without another word, Karl barely keeping pace as they headed for the opposite end of the temple where the prayer rooms were located.

Candles sparked to life with a mere thought as he stepped into his prayer room, the smell of beeswax and lingering incense soothing his disarray. He stood facing the Altar of Vision and the empty bowl that he never used, focusing on the light, the smells, the power that lingered in the very walls of Unheilvol. The power of the Seers was to foretell the future, see the fates of the children of shadows.

But when and where he must, past, present, and future were also his to see. Not without difficulty, and not without price, but he was High Seer. Hopefully he would not need the pool in the Hall of Vision; he was not quite ready to face that again, not given what had happened to him last time.

Gradually the world around him faded away, even Karl's impatient shifting. He focused on the threads that connected him to the High Sorcerer: threads of power, threads of fate, threads of the Seeing he had once performed for the man.

It had been the first Seeing he had done after being made High Seer. He'd been young, far too young, but too powerful to be anything else. His predecessor had remained close to help him learn the more mundane aspects of overseeing Unheilvol, but Friedrich had overtaken the Seeing completely.

The first had been a boy of nineteen, already marked with the diamond of sorcery, with a cruel glint to his eye and bruises on his face testifying to how he preferred to handle problems. He'd intimidated everyone around them, even the former High Seer, but all the challenge had faded from his eyes when he'd met Friedrich's.

He had, to Friedrich's surprise, met his fate with grace.

Born by power and death, you will live the same, you will die the same. On the day when the moon hides the sun, you will stand on High. Forty years to the day, you will die by the hand of your own son, made as you were made.

Friedrich could still see that future, that image, but it was cracked and faded and soon would be gone. Only his memory of it remained, the man meant to live it already dead in a place and time never foretold.

Letting the lost fate go, he reached for the vision that had struck him in the dining hall, head throbbing as it came to him.

Violet eyes. They glowed with magic. They reminded him of the beast he'd just killed, but somehow seemed much worse. He radiated power, the first real threat he'd encountered since beginning his quest. Unlike the others, his hair was pale and fell around his shoulders, thick and smooth.

"So you are the source of the chaos."

He didn't reply to the question, just struck and was met with magic that actually worried him a little bit. But he'd faced worse and would not be beaten down. He went for his whip even as he summoned his own magic, the ring on his finger flashing a hundred colors in the shreds of sunlight slipping through the heavy clouds above—

Friedrich broke away from the vision, opening his eyes and throwing out his arms to catch himself on the altar when his balance suddenly felt uncertain. Not the ring again. Not the chaos. He trembled just thinking about that moment, the way it had driven him all the way down to hide with Drache.

I won't let it harm you again, beloved. I'm braced for it. I cannot do much, but I can do this.

How?

You know better than to ask me to explain things, Drache said, the words holding a hint of a growl and frustration.

Fine. Do it then, because I must see what happened to the High Sorcerer.

Use the pool in the Hall of Vision. It will help.

Making a face, Friedrich turned to Karl and said, "If I am to pursue this, I need the Hall of Vision again. Come, I would prefer to confine what I learn to you and me, and of course, the Master Sorcerer when he arrives. Whatever is happening in Schatten, I do not want it passed around the temple and all the rest of the country."

"Of course, High Seer," Karl said and shadowed his heels as they made their way to the Hall of Vision.

He stood in the curve of the crescent moon pool with Karl opposite him. They both slit their palms, let the blood drip, and Friedrich used his good hand to add the Essence of Moon. Closing his eyes, he reached out to Drache. *Are you certain?*

I promise I will take care of you. I always do, beloved.

I suppose it would be foolish if I created an imaginary voice that was out to destroy me.

Drache's sigh brushed over his mind like a heavy summer breeze. *I'm not imaginary.*

But you never tell me what—who—you are.

I cannot.

Whatever. Shoving away pointless bitterness, Friedrich drew upon his magic and reached into the threads of fate, casting out for the High Sorcerer's threads holding fast to them, willing close those that had already gone dark and dead.

Before, he had seen the High Sorcerer from the outside. This time, he wanted to see what happened from the High Sorcerer's point of view. Steeling himself, trusting Drache, he fell into the vision of the High Sorcerer's last moments.

> *Violet eyes and black hair, but something about them seemed wrong. The man's skin was too fair to be a real child of shadows. He radiated magical power that seemed to burn and an aura of countless colors surrounded him. Torben finally had to close off his ability to read auras, or risk being overwhelmed by flood of colors. But he'd seen enough to confirm what he'd already strongly*

suspected. "So you are the source of the chaos."

The man did not reply, simply attacked. Torben hung back, let his men face him. They wouldn't live, but it would allow him to gauge and read the man, get a better idea of what he faced. He was forced to look away when a brilliant cascade of rainbow light suddenly filled the clearing, only barely noting the crack crack of a striking whip.

His men screamed and tried to retreat, but the intruder was too fast for them. He killed the nearest two with such ease that Torben was disgusted by the lack of skill in men he had hand-picked for the venture. He did not move to help when the man plunged a dagger into the throat of one and drew his sword to attack the second.

He slipped in the snow, dropped his guard, and the others were upon him. The fight became harder to follow after that, a wild rush of steel, magic, and cracking whips. Torben continued watching, waiting. Then all of his men were dead, and the intruder rounded on him, moving his sword to his left hand and holding aloft his right.

But that was more than enough time for Torben to summon his own magic and weave a curse that would leave the man alive, but harmless—allow them to pick through the pieces of his mind at leisure.

Rainbow light flashed again as the man summoned whatever magic it contained, throwing it at Torben at the same time he released his Web of Madness. Light exploded, and Torben felt his spell fracture and falter even as it struck. His horse

*spooked, threw him, and he landed on top of
the bastard he was trying to kill.*

*They grappled in the snow, desperate
and confused and angry. Then the intruder
somehow got the upper hand, threw Torben
off, and before he could get his bearings and
recover, he saw the sword—*

Friedrich broke free of the vision with a gasp, falling to
his knees and bending double, sucking in deep, slow breaths
and hoping fervently that he did not throw up in the vision
pool. He fumbled for a kerchief and mopped sweat from his
brow.

When he finally felt that he could move with retching, he
stood and looked at Karl. "Were you able to follow in the
pool?"

The pallor to Karl's skin was answer enough, really, but
he nodded and said, "Who in the name of Lord Teufel is
strong enough to counter one of the Black Curses? No one
can fight the Web of Madness, but he broke it as if it was a
mere candle-lighting trick."

Pursing his lips thoughtfully, running the handkerchief
over his damp head, Friedrich replied, "I don't think he broke
it so much as cracked it. Whatever happened, it still hit him,
but how it ultimately affected him, I could not say. Anything
could have happened: he could be mad, he could have no
mind at all, he could be missing parts. There is no way to
know, but without knowing, I cannot track him. It was
definitely the same man who killed those Sentinels, though.
I suppose that is something."

Karl nodded. "So what do we do?"

Friedrich was prevented from replying by the loud arrival
of the Master Sorcerer and four others. "High Seer. I am
informed that his excellency the High Sorcerer is dead."

"Yes, I felt it," Friedrich said coolly, not liking the man's
tone. "Do you question me, Master Sorcerer Boris?"

Boris seemed to withdraw slightly, clearly aware he had overstepped. "No, High Seer. I am only—"

Friedrich cut him off with a gesture, and then nodded curtly at the other sorcerers. "You may wait in the dining hall until you are called."

"Yes, High Seer," the men chorused and, turning neatly around, strode out of the Hall of Vision.

"What we say here is confidential, Master Sorcerer. You should already be aware of that. If you are to take up the mantle of High Sorcerer, you had better learn it quickly."

Boris nodded stiffly, a spark of anger in his eyes. "Of course, High Seer. I do appreciate that and apologize for my slip. I am confused, I confess. No man should share his fate, but my understanding was that High Sorcerer Torben had many years left to serve in his noble capacity."

"He did," Friedrich replied, drawing his hands into his voluminous sleeves and staring down into the vision pool as he said. "Unfortunately, a man of chaos is wreaking havoc across Schatten. He has killed at least three adult Sentinels and now has slain the High Sorcerer and those who accompanied him. But we may have a chance to stop him— the High Sorcerer cast a Web of Madness. It did not work as it should have, but it still struck the man. He will not be acting right, though what manner of wrong he will be acting I cannot say."

"A curse should be an easy thing to feel out, even if it is corrupted or fractured," Boris replied.

"Do not underestimate a man, even damaged, who was strong enough to counter that curse and then slay the High Sorcerer," Friedrich said sharply. "The High Sorcerer underestimated the power of a man who walks in chaos and now he is a frozen corpse in the snow somewhere. I would wager they were in the Haunted Mountains; that is where all reports of slain Sentinels have thus far originated and where his last missive said he was headed. You will travel to Oak Hill, his last point of communication, and you will retrace his steps. You will find the man responsible for all this chaos and you will kill him unless Lord Teufel bids you do otherwise."

Turning to Karl, he said, "You will go with them. The powers of a Master Seer will prove useful, I sense, in tracking down this intruder."

Karl stiffened. "Seers do not leave Unheilvol, High Seer, not until age Blinds them."

Fury poured through Friedrich. Jerking his head at Boris, he said, "Leave us."

Boris immediately obeyed, and in mere seconds Friedrich and Karl were alone. "How dare you question my orders, and in front of others no less!"

"But it is Lord Teufel's will that we—"

"You obey me!" Friedrich said. "If I command that you leave the temple to accompany the sorcerers, then you do it. Lord Teufel speaks through me, and by his hand I am always guided. You question me, you question him. Is that what you are doing?"

Karl paled, having at least enough sense to realize his possible transgression. "N-no, High Seer. I—forgive me—I only fear what effect this chaotic element will have and whether the Seers can handle—"

Friedrich cut him off with a sharp gesture, sneering. "No, you fear that if I send you out, you will die and lose your chance to usurp my position."

"High Seer, I would never presume—"

"Oh, you presume," Friedrich cut in, laughing, feeling tired and bitter. "Do you think you hide it, Karl? That glint in your eye that says you are just waiting for the day when the visions break me? We both know you long for that day when you will step into my shoes and order me killed out of mercy. But be careful what you wish for Karl, because all too often we get it—and live to regret it."

Karl's mouth tightened. "You're not special just because you See without implements."

"Your tone says you do think I'm special, and you resent it, think it should be you," Friedrich said. "Stop fretting because someday it will be."

"You can't know that," Karl said. "The Seers are the only ones in Schatten not privy to their own fates. We sacrifice that knowledge of ourselves to give knowledge to others. It is a price we pay willingly, happily."

It is not a gift, not when Lord Teufel arranges it before they are even born. Once, it was an honor, but a choice to be accepted or rejected.

Friedrich scowled inwardly. *Shut it. Now is not the time for your blasphemy.*

Teufel is the blasphemous one.

Enough!

Karl was giving him an odd look, and Friedrich determinedly took back control of the conversation. "A Seer cannot look into his own fate, that is true. But should I desire it, I could know the fate of every man here. I knew yours the day I looked into your eyes and declared you my Master Sorcerer."

"That is forbidden!" Karl bellowed, but Friedrich saw the hunger burning in his eyes, the need to know. It was often a bitter reality for the Seers, to know they could see all but their own fates, that they must live in darkness to bring that light to others.

Friedrich stepped toward him. Karl stepped back once, twice, then froze. He trembled slightly as Friedrich reached out to press his fingertips to the circle in Karl's forehead. Karl drew a sharp breath and started to jerk away, but then fell still. His breath was sour, skin clammy, but Friedrich ignored it all as he reached out for the fate he had looked at nine years ago.

> *"Born last, the smallest of nine, but blessed with the mark of the Seers. Your family relieved to be able to get rid of a mouth they could not feed. Affection is*

useless. Family is nothing. Power is the key to stability, to being someone who matters. Seer to Master Seer, there to pause. But madness grows, two voices war, and despair will make you High Seer."

He broke away, panting softly. Karl stood still, taking in the words, losing himself in them, myriad emotions rippling across his face. Finally he seemed to shake himself and stared at Friedrich. "You shouldn't be able to do that," he said quietly. "It's more than just each priest not being permitted his own fate—we shouldn't be able to foretell each other's. Otherwise the rule would be too easy to break. Why are you an exception? You're an exception to everything."

"I am High Seer," Friedrich said. "In this life, in every life, over and over again. I am the power of centuries, the power of many lives. That's all I know."

"Two voices. Despair. You are going to go mad," Karl said, and for a single moment there was something like sympathy in his eyes. Then it was gone, replaced by the more familiar ambition and contempt. "Soon, I think."

Friedrich nodded. "Yes, probably."

It doesn't have to be that way.

What other way could it possibly be? I am High Seer. We all die the same. It is the price we pay—

It was not always that way! The Seers of Schatten were once revered, honored, and well-cared for so that we—

The words broke off on a scream of pain that drove Friedrich to his knees with a scream of his own.

"High Seer!"

Friedrich panted for breath, feeling nauseous again, part of him hoping his breaking point had finally been reached. He was tired of it all: the visions, the weakness, the pain, the envy of his peers, and the constant presence of Drache.

Who had gone terrifyingly silent in his head, and the realization sparked a panic. *Drache? Drache? Drache!*

He stood up hastily, forcing himself to shut the fear away until present matters were attended, but inwardly he could not stop panicking. He had not meant it, he did not really want Drache to go away!

"Recall the Master Sorcerer," he said curtly.

Karl gave him a look, but with a soft, derisive noise, obeyed. When they both returned, Friedrich said, "Locate the fallen High Sorcerer and hunt down his killer by any means necessary. He looks like one of us, save his skin is too fair and he bears no diamond upon his brow. Show the man no mercy, give him no quarter. Bring me his head unless Lord Teufel wills otherwise. Stay on your guard and work together. The powers of chaos are treacherous and, by their nature, unpredictable. Go."

The men bowed, then left, and Friedrich quickly retreated to his own rooms. He sat down on his bed and covered his face with his hands, tears falling hot as he tried in vain to get Drache to come back to him.

Throughout everything, Drache had been there. Mysterious, blasphemous, frustrating, and at times infuriating—but also faithful, reliable, and the only one who had never turned away from him. Friedrich didn't care if Drache was purely of his own imagination, he was *something*. When he went to sleep, sank into the only place where he could see and touch Drache, he was beautiful and breathtaking and the only thing Friedrich really needed.

And now he was gone, silent in a way he had never been; there was a hole instead, cold and dark and deep.

Why had he gone? What had Friedrich done? He played the whole conversation over again, trying to figure it out. Drache's last words replayed the loudest: *It was not always that way! The Seers of Schatten were once revered, honored, and well-cared for so that we—*

We

That was what had done it. *We.* Drache had never given anything about himself away before, often claimed he could not. Friedrich tended to take it as proof that Drache was pure imagination, since it seemed like him to want to keep such details vague. But that word … so Drache had been or was a Seer? But if he was a current Seer, he would be in Unheilvol. There was no such thing as a rogue Seer; Lord Teufel would never permit it.

So likely he had been a Seer at one point, perhaps he lived Blinded somewhere and somehow managed to live through Friedrich's mind. Was that possible? He thought he would have heard of it before if that was the case. Even if it was possible, it didn't seem likely a Blinded could manage it. They were old, too weak to See, sent off to smaller temples to guide and teach the children of shadows how to love and worship Lord Teufel.

He would have to do research—late at night, when everyone else slept and no one would take it as overly strange that he was too restless to sleep. Given the toll his recent visions were taking, he was certain the temple was rife with gossip about his time being up soon. But he had lived in Unheilvol since he was a child, turned dutifully over at the age of ten. By fifteen he was Seeing for those who most often had simple fates: farmers, shop clerks, and other mild peasants. At nineteen, his power was too great to ignore and he'd been granted the position of High Seer.

That had been twenty-one years ago. Most High Seers made it to fifty, but he knew for a fact that the last High Seer with his power had lived a hundred years ago—and he had died at the age of forty.

It amused Friedrich, in a tired, bitter way, that Karl and the others thought that it was impossible for them to learn their own fates. If they ever bothered to go down into the archives and read through the records of all the previous Seers, they would see their own lives repeated breath for breath over the last nine hundred years.

The patterns weren't hard to find, not when he knew his Seers, knew fate. Knew there was no point in resisting.

Except someone was resisting. Someone he had to destroy at all costs because absolute chaos would be no better than absolute fate.

His hands trembled when he realized where his thoughts were going, what he was risking. He was the High Seer, appointed by Teufel. He was the very last person who should have been entertaining thoughts that went against everything he had been taught—everything he knew.

At least, everything he thought he knew. But without Drache there to whisper blasphemous thoughts, it was suddenly far too easy to listen to his own.

What was the point, though? His fate was sealed, no matter what happened. Eventually, they would kill the chaotic intruder who had invaded Schatten, and Teufel would reassert his will. There was absolutely no point in doing anything other than obeying.

Obedience is well and good, but defiance has always had its place.

Hot tears stung Friedrich's eyes. *Drache.*

Of course. Who else.

I thought you were gone. You went so abruptly, and there was nothing but cold silence …

Defiance has a price, but I am back and shall have more care. I would never leave you, beloved. I couldn't, even if I wanted, which I don't.

You said 'we'.

Yes.

You are, or were, a Seer.

What I was, what I am, I cannot say. It little matters anyway. I am as bound by fate as the rest of Schatten.

Despair crawled through Friedrich's gut, and he tried to fight it—but knew it was futile. What he wanted didn't matter. Eventually, despair would conquer him, and like all his previous incarnations, he would die of madness and alcohol and freezing cold.

That may not be true, Drache whispered, the words a soft caress across his mind. *Chaos walks the land, and with his every action, he breaks another thread.*

Friedrich ignored him, refusing to get his hopes up, and slowly stood to return to the dining hall. He had Seers to reassure and wine to drink.

Ill Omen

David cried as he stood at the edge of the cliff, unable to sing the hymns along with everyone else as the priest cast Reimund's ashes into the wind. Reimund had been strict, at times even downright hard with him, but he'd taken care of David when the rest of the village would have left him to die as a lesson on why it was foolish to act as his parents had.

But fate was fate, and Reimund had said it was his fate to see to David, though he would not tolerate a boy who did not work hard and earn his place. David had done his best, every step of the way. They were not father and son, but he always thought they were as close to that as they could be. Reimund had taken care of him, not thrown him out, even when David had been scared he would.

And he was dead. David cried harder, lowering his head as the last of the ashes were thrown over the cliff. What was he going to do? He wasn't Reimund, he had still been learning Reimund's duties, learning the tricks and nuances of being the village supplier. It took years of experience to get the hang of what and how much to buy so the village did not suffer in between the months when he was able to make the journey to buy more supplies.

Killian's father always helped with the transporting and the hauling, but the real work fell to Reimund. David knew much, but he didn't know enough. The village would suffer if he did not master the duties quickly. He wondered if they were simply going to search for a replacement, and then wondered fearfully what would happen to him if he was cast out.

Surely, they wouldn't. He'd been good, he'd worked hard. He had earned a place in the village and overcome the stigma of his parents, the whispers he overheard because nobody except Reimund had ever admitted to him what they'd done.

The priest finished the ceremony and led the way back down the cliff, trudging through the snow, the sound of his bell casting notes of finality across the mountains, which echoed the sad refrain. Back in the village, David quickly retreated to the house he'd shared with Reimund in the center of the village, slipping in the back way to avoid the front half where the goods were stored.

It still smelled like tea and the stew that Maja had brought them a couple of days before, enough to last them a full week. Bowls of it, along with bread and Elza's herb butter, still sat on the table. David's quiet tears turned into full sobs as he sank to the floor and drew his knees up against his chest.

Reimund deserved a better fate, deserved something better than to be slain in seconds by the venom of a newborn Sentinel that had somehow slipped past the barrier and crept into the village in search of warmth and food. Was that really the fate Lord Teufel had intended for such a good man? For the only person who actually cared enough not to let David die?

He was alone again. Well, except for Killian, but it wasn't the same. Killian had a family: father, mother, aunts, uncles, cousins. All David had was Reimund and their little set of worn, but cared for rooms. Trips to the market every three months. It was a simple life, a hard one, but it was his and he'd enjoyed it well enough. Had looked forward to someday taking over the bulk of the duties and taking care of the man who had cared for him.

Eventually he grew too exhausted to continue crying, and the chill of the room forced him to act. He grabbed logs from the pile stacked neatly against one wall and carried them over to the stove in the middle of the room. Once the fire was going strong again, he fed the logs in one by one until all was set. Warmth slowly began to permeate the room and drive back the cold. David filled a battered kettle with water and set it on the stove, and while it heated, he began to clear off the table.

The tears resumed halfway through the chore as he realized he would never again make dinner for two, never have it ready and waiting when Reimund walked through the door looking cold and tired, but breaking into a smile and greeting him in that gruff way.

Reimund might not have been his father, but every now and then it had been easy for David to forget that.

David went to the old, chipped wash basin in one corner of the room. He broke the thin layer of ice over the top, and carried the bowl to the table. He poured in some warmed water, then set the kettle back on the stove. With a cloth and some soap, he cleaned up his face and hands and felt the slightest bit better for it by the time he was done.

When the kettle began to whistle, he added some tea leaves to a cup—almost crying again when he started to grab two cups—and then poured hot water over them. Sitting at the table, he bowed his head and drank tea while trying to ignore the quiet of the room, the fact that there would never be anyone else in it with him. The tea was dark, but faintly sweet. It had been a present from Reimund on his birthday. It reminded David of his gift for Reimund's birthday, still hidden beneath his mattress.

He had no idea what to do with it. Reimund would probably have told him to use it and not waste it. But thinking about it just provoked fresh tears.

A sudden knocking at the door made him jump and spill his tea. David huffed at himself, then went to answer the door. An old woman, almost completely hidden by a heavy fur cloak, stood holding a bundle of paper-wrapped parcels. Just behind her was Killian, holding a heavy iron pot—very heavy, to judge by the expression on his face.

"Maja?"

She clucked at him, smiled gently. "Let us inside, boy."

David stepped back to let them inside, closing the door behind them. He hastened to add more wood to the fire and fetched a cloth to clean up the spilled tea. Refilling the kettle, he set it on the stove and put the iron pot Maja handed him in the remaining space.

Maja pulled off her heavy cloak and left it on the bed in the corner—Reimund's bed. David had always slept on a pallet by the fire. That the bed was suddenly his was too much for him, and he shoved the thought to the back of his mind with all the others he did not want to face.

"There, there," Maja said, and she cupped his face, crooning softly. "Reimund would not want you to be so sad, my dear. It was his time, and all things happen for a reason. He would hate to see you grieve hard and long for him. Such things were not his way."

"I-I know," David said, but hearing it just made everything worse somehow. He wanted Reimund back, wanted the only man he had to call family to walk through the door and tell him there had been some horrible misunderstanding.

But he was dead, his ashes returned to the land and shadows, until he was fated to be reborn.

Maja patted his cheek gently, then moved briskly about to make them all tea and serve up the soup she had brought. "Spicy potato and sausage," she said, though the smell made it clear. "Your favorite. Sit, sit."

David sat, and though he had absolutely no desire for food, under Maja's sharp eye he forced it down, bite after bite, until the soup was finally gone.

Throughout the meal, no one said anything—not even Killian, which was strange, because Killian only stopped talking when he fell asleep. According to his mother, even then he still muttered and grumbled and snorted.

"Everything will be all right," Maja said into the silence. "I know you're worried David, but all will be well."

David nodded, words stuck in his throat. He drank the last of his tea, then finally managed, "I don't know how to do everything yet, Maja. Rei—Rei—he taught me a lot and I can do some of it, but not all of it and not the way he could. If I can't do my job—"

"Shhh," Maja said softly, reaching across the table to cover his hand with her own gnarled one, eyes so dark a purple but so warm. "The village will give you time and help you. It was Reimund's time to go, which means it is your time to become a man. You already are, really. This is just one of your final steps. Now, there is soup enough for the week, and someone else will bring you food for next week. Killian will stay to keep you company. Tomorrow: rest and mourn. The day after that, we will begin to move forward."

He nodded again, because that seemed the easiest thing to do. Maja stood up, and Killian went to fetch her fur cloak. She hugged David tightly and kissed his cheeks, then said, "All will be well, David. There is a purpose to everything, a picture we cannot see, and all will be well in the end. Get some rest, David. Everything will be a little more bearable in the morning.

"Yes, Maja," he said and hugged her one last time. She smiled at him, then let Killian help her into her cloak. She patted his cheek and said, "You take care of him, boy. None of your foolishness, understand me?"

Killian nodded and when she narrowed her eyes, hastily added, "Yes, Maja."

She sniffed, unimpressed, and patted his cheek again, this time much more firmly. "See that you do. Your biggest problem, boy, is your tongue. It wags when it should hold still. See you keep it still." A last warning look, a smile for David, and she left. The wind whistled through the village, clattering the door and knocking snow against the house, the bits of ice in it rapping against the old wood.

When he was certain Maja was well out of range, Killian said, "It wasn't his time to die, you know."

David froze. Stared. Fervently wished that Killian had just *listened* and kept his mouth shut. Some things, people just didn't want to know. "That's stupid," he finally replied. "It doesn't even make sense. What do you mean, it wasn't his time to die? How would you know?"

"I listen to'em when they get drunk," Killian said. "They sit around the fire in my house when they think me, my mom, and my aunt are asleep. They drink and drink and start to talk about things. Lots of things. But mostly their fates."

"That's not allowed!" David snapped. "Reimund would never—"

"Yes, he did!" Killian interjected hotly, drawing himself up. "I'm not lying. Why would I? Reimund said he was fated to die of illness when he was an old man. He was happy cause that meant he'd get to see you grow up and settle down and all. I remember. Now everyone is whispering about it and scared because what's it mean when a man dies in a way not fated?"

David made the signs of warding, remembering all over again the sorcerers, their extra days on the road, and the dead Sentinels. That forbidden word he should not say, should not even think. "That's absurd."

"Well, you tell that to the village, 'cause they're whispering *a lot*, and most of it ain't good. They're scared. Mostly of you, 'cause first your parents tried to fight fate, and now Reimund died against fate, and all those Sentinels dead—"

"It's not my fault!" David snapped, but sharp, sudden fear made his hands trembled. He fisted them to make it stop, not really succeeding. He whispered again, "It's not my fault. We were eating dinner. Talking about letting me try to hand out everything myself at the end of the week. Laughing. He-he-he was *laughing* when it bit him. Didn't even know what happened until too late. His blood turned black, and he said my n-n-n—" He broke down sobbing again, dropping to his knees on the floor and wrapping his arms around himself.

Killian's hands awkwardly patted his shoulders, and then with a sigh, Killian sat behind him, pressing their backs together. The attempt to comfort would have amused David at any other time, but right then it just made him cry harder.

He wanted Reimund back. He wanted everything to be good again. Was he going to be thrown out of the village as a bad omen, as ill luck? Would they give him food and supplies? Or would they simply cast him out for the Sentinels to feast upon?

It wasn't fair, but in the very next thought he acknowledged what Reimund had always said: life isn't about fair, it's about making the best of an unfair situation.

As his latest bout of tears finally abated, David was struck with a wave of exhaustion. Being awake was suddenly entirely too difficult. "I'm going to bed," he mumbled and started to stand up to get his bed things from where they were stacked neatly by the wall.

"Oh, sit down," Killian said with a huff. He added more wood to the fire, set a heating stone on top, and made a half-hearted attempt to clean up the dishes while it warmed. "Now stand up," he ordered and tugged David to his feet to get him out of the many layers of clothes he wore. Hanging everything up on hooks in the little storeroom off the side of the house, he came back with heavy wool sleep clothes and helped David into them.

David watched, numb and heavy-lidded, while Killian picked up the heating stone with a pair of tongs and ran it through the bedclothes. "I can't—that's where—"

"Douse it," Killian replied. "It's a bed; it's meant for sleeping. It's stupid to sleep on the cold floor when there is a perfectly good bed, and you know very well Reimund couldn't abide stupid."

The words hurt, but they also stupidly made him feel better. It was true. Reimund would roll his eyes and look at him with that glower of his for wasting everyone's time by doing something stupid. He sniffled a bit, but thankfully it did not turn into another bout of sobbing. Shadows, he was just too wrung out.

"Into bed," Killian ordered, and he dragged David along across the room and pushed him down into the bed. He brought the blankets up to David's chin, then went to fuss with the stove so it didn't get too hot, but would keep the worst of the cold at bay.

When that was done, he removed his own boots and cloak and climbed into bed beside David. "Go to sleep," he ordered and then, in typical Killian fashion, promptly did so himself.

David listened to the sound of Killian's breathing, the lack of Reimund's snores, until exhaustion finally overcame grief and dragged him into sleep.

He woke to the sound of urgent knocking on his door and immediately started to apologize for accidentally falling asleep on the bed—and then reality returned and tears stung his eyes. But the insistent knocking kept him from drowning in grief, and he fumbled to get out of bed, stumbling to the door as he tried to right his twisted up sleep clothes.

Yanking the door open, he stared at Adam, the village baker. "What's wrong?"

"We need your bed," he said. At David's blank look, he added, "We were going to check the traps this morning, at the edge of the safe territory, and found an injured sorcerer in the woods. Almost didn't leave the safe area, but it's a sorcerer, right? Anyway, no one else has room for him. Maja is full up with those sick kids and Greta. She said to try you, seeing as you've spare room now. So hurry it up and come help us move him. There's a day to be getting on with and a sorcerer to make comfortable first."

David bobbed his head, not bothering to otherwise respond. He beckoned Adam inside to stay warm by the fire while David hastily dressed.

On the bed, Killian groaned and sat up. "What's going on?" he asked.

"Nothing," David said. "Maja needs me. I'll be back shortly, just stay in bed."

Killian grunted and obeyed, never in a hurry to leave a warm bed in the winter. He would not be happy when David had to order him out of it when he returned with the sorcerer, but Killian may as well stay warm and cozy until then.

Stomping his boots to settle them, David followed Adam to the far south corner of the village where Maja's house was located. Even in the cold, he could smell the herbs of her healing trade.

"In the shed," Adam said, and he led the way around the house to the drying shed where Maja prepared most of her herbs. Maja was there, kneeling on the ground beside a man with sickly white skin and a series of nasty cuts that had been left by Sentinel claws across his side and stomach. It was only by the blessing of Teufel that the man had survived.

By the size of the claw marks, he'd only encountered a small Sentinel—a child, something a little smaller than a horse. That was more than enough to kill an ordinary man, but sorcerers were different.

Maja finished stitching the wounds closed and began mixing a thin paste in her bowl. When it was ready she gently worked it over the wounds, singing a soft hymn as she did so to encourage Lord Teufel to speed the healing. When that was done, she had Adam help her to bandage the wounds. "Thank you," she said when they were done. "If you'll go fetch the stretcher, I will give David herbs and instructions."

David obediently sat beside her as Adam slipped out, but he had helped Maja often enough in the past they both knew he did not need instructions. Instead, he took in the troubled wrinkles on her brow, the tight set to her mouth, and asked, "What's wrong, Maja?"

"You must not speak of this to anyone," Maja said. "People are scared enough right now and whispers could turn into angry shouts in the flicker of a flame."

"Speak of wha …" David's words trailed off, forgotten, when Maja pulled the man's shirt completely apart and revealed the mark on his chest. A spider web spanned his chest from collar bone to halfway down his ribs, spreading out to not quite vanish around his sides. In the dim light, it looked black, but David suspected it would be more purple in good light. "What is that?"

Maja shook her head and replaced the shirt, smoothing the man's long hair from his face. "A curse, but I don't know what kind. It is not the kind of magic taught to a lowly healer. It may be causing him pains we don't know about—might cause problems we won't expect. You need to keep a close watch on him, alert me to anything strange he might say or do. Understand?"

"I understand," David said quietly. "Who would curse a sorcerer?"

"A good question, but to be honest, lad, I don't want to know the answer."

David nodded in agreement. Before he could say or ask anything else, Adam came back in and grunted at him to help. They got the stretcher laid out and gently hefted the sorcerer into it. David settled the packets of herbs into the folds of the sorcerer's clothes and covered them so they wouldn't come to harm on the short trip, then hefted the stretcher with Adam and slowly trekked back toward his house.

Killian was gone when he arrived, making David sigh. The additional assistance would have been nice, but no doubt Killian's parents needed him. Ah, well, maybe he would return later.

He and Adam quickly moved the sorcerer from the stretcher to the bed. Adam nodded tersely at him, then vanished, leaving David to get the man settled alone. He built up the fire first and set water to boil for the tea and medicine. Returning to the bed, he stripped off the wet, torn, bloody clothes and threw them in a pile by the door to dispose of later.

Part of him flinched to treat the deep violet tunic of the sorcerers so callously, but the clothes were too damaged to salvage. Hopefully when he woke, the sorcerer would understand. He gently shifted and tugged until he got the man under the blankets, then brushed back his long, messy hair ... and wound up just staring. David had always had a healthy fear of sorcerers, and the whipping that had left his back an ugly mess of scars had made it that much worse. The best thing to do when encountering a sorcerer was to keep heads down and feet moving. David had never really looked at one; he could not even remember the face of the one who had beat him.

Whatever he'd expected, it was not for a sorcerer to be so beautiful. His skin was so strangely pale, but that might have been something to do with the Sentinel; David had heard their venom could do funny things when it didn't kill. His hair was a sooty black, the same as the diamond on his forehead. His features were smooth, almost delicate, reminding David of the rich folk he occasionally saw in Two Mill.

He reached to trace the line of one fine cheekbone, then snatched his hand back at the last minute, face going hot, heart thudding with panic. Bustling away, he busied himself making tea, carefully mixing together herbs to make a tonic. When it had properly steeped, he carried the cup—Reimund's favorite, part of a set of dishes made for him and his wife when they'd married and made all the more precious after she'd died—over to the bed. Setting it on the little wash table close to the bed, he gently shook the sorcerer.

"My lord, wake up," he said softly. "You must drink your medicine so that you'll heal proper."

The man grunted and groaned, but at David's continued urging, finally opened his eyes. David recoiled, startled, heart leaping into his throat, but when he looked again, everything was normal, and the man only blinked at him, his sleepy, confused, *violet* eyes dark with pain. Had he imagined them looking gold? He must have because people didn't have gold eyes.

David shook himself, called himself an idiot, and fetched the cup. Sliding an arm around the sorcerer's shoulders, all the while apologizing for his impertinence, he slowly got the sorcerer to drink the bitter tonic sip by sip. "I know it tastes awful," he said. "I am sorry, my lord. But I know you would prefer to be strong again as quickly as possible. There, you've only a few sips left now. And all done. Close your eyes and get some rest, my lord. I'll rouse you again when it's time for more."

The sorcerer said something in reply, but the words came out strange, not quite right. But gibberish wasn't unusual when a man was in so much pain. No doubt in a day or so the man would be much more lucid—and probably unpleasant and furious about being stuck in a tiny peasant village, demanding that his own come to fetch him immediately.

A pity that someone so beautiful was probably so much like the man who had lashed him. David returned the cup to the table and mixed up several more doses of the herbs so the tonic could be made more quickly later.

He was just beginning to start porridge cooking when a knock came at the door. Opening it, he oofed when Adam thrust a large bundle of things into his arm. "The sorcerer's belongings. See you take care of them."

"Of cours—" But Adam was gone, already a shadow in the snow that had begun to fall heavily. David closed the door and carried the items to the table. He hung the saddlebags—where was the horse? Probably the village stable, unless the Sentinel had eaten it—over a chair, then looked over the two remaining objects: a sword and whip. His hand trembled when he saw the whip, and he could not quite bring himself to touch it.

He rifled through the saddlebags after a nervous glance at the bed, but found only a spare change of clothes, travel food, a map, and compass. Well, at least there were clothes for the sorcerer to wear, though they would need to be washed, if the smell was anything by which to judge.

Finally he looked at the sword. He had never seen a sword up close, not really. Swords were weapons of the sorcerers and guards; they were not for mere peasants. Like the sorcerer, it was unexpectedly beautiful. The hilt was wrapped in leather stamped with an image he could not quite make out, but it fit his hand well when he cautiously gripped it.

It was the stone set in the end of the sword that was most beautiful, however. It was a deep gold color, something that fell just shy of being orange. The stone reminded him of that moment when the sorcerer had opened his eyes and they had seemed gold for a moment. His heart started beating a furious pace again, and he looked helplessly toward the bed, wondering why a sorcerer's eyes would have looked yellow.

It must have been a trick of the light. David hung the sword from its belt next to the saddlebags on his chair. He finished setting the porridge to cook, then did some quiet tidying up. He picked up the teacup he'd used for the sorcerer's medicine and like a fist, memories of Reimund struck. Hot tears trickled down his face, but David wiped them away. He couldn't cry when there was someone to take care of. There was also the bartering to handle in a few days. Reimund always said the work had to come first, because people were counting on it and that mattered more than anything else.

Rinsing the cup out and putting it aside, David fetched the broom and went back to cleaning.

Magic

Sasha's stomach felt as if someone had raked it open with hot knives and then shoved hot coals inside it. There was also a general ache and a nauseous feeling, but he had the sense that it all could have been much worse. He tried to sit up, but then immediately regretted the action and fell back on the bed with a loud groan.

Bed?

He opened his eyes and took in his surroundings. He was in a small, dimly lit little house. It reminded him of country houses back home, especially with the stove in the middle of the room. The room smelled like winter, potatoes, and a faint hint of tea.

Where was he? Had he been figured out? Captured? But no, if someone had figured out his artifice he would not have been lying in a bed, and he certainly would not have been in someone's home.

Movement caught his eye as a shadow by the fireplace turned toward him, then stood up. Sasha's eyes widened as the light fell across a face that left him breathless. The boy was handsome, the sort of flame that drew moths and convinced them they were happy to die just for a chance to touch. Something in his chest twisted, ached, left him longing for … something … and then the shadowy memory slipped away from him once more.

"You're awake," the boy said, the word spoken in a thick, ragged accent that took Sasha a moment to catch up to. Why had he thought the accent strange? But like so many other questions, it remained unanswered. Sasha watched as the boy went to the stove and picked up the kettle to pour hot water into a little, handle-less teacup. The smell of tea and herbs sharpened, and then the boy walked over to him. "How are you feeling, my lord?"

"Like I angered a fireplace poker and my stomach suffered for it," Sasha said hoarsely.

The boy froze, laughed for a moment, but then immediately stopped as fear overtook his levity. "Uh. I am sorry, my lord. Here, are you up to drinking the tea yourself? It will help ease your pain. I just changed your bandages a short time ago. The wounds are healing well."

Sasha nodded in answer to the query about tea and accepted the cup when the boy held it out. He cupped one hand around it, braced the bottom of the cup with the other, and drank the tea slowly, cautiously. All the while, he could not take his eyes away from the boy. He had rough-cut dark hair that fell to just past his ears, as though it were in need of a trim that there had been no time to give. He had eyes the color of an iris in full bloom with spring sunshine pouring down upon it. The color was all the more vibrant against his dark bronze skin.

He must have been on the mend if his body could muster the barest stirrings of lust. Sasha ignored them and focused on finishing his tea. "Thank you," he said, handing back the empty cup. "How did you find me?"

The boy's dusky cheeks darkened. "Um. You're welcome. It was the others that found you, just beyond the village barrier, while they were out checking traps. Is there anything else I can get or do for you, my lord? Um. Would you like some soup? It's still warm."

"Why do you call me 'my lord'?" Sasha asked and realized by the look on the boy's face that he'd made some error.

"M-my lord is a sorcerer," the boy said, pretty eyes popping open wide. The direction of his gaze shifted slightly, and Sasha realized the boy was staring at his forehead. He reached up to touch it, and only then remembered the diamond upon it and that he was impersonating the look of the men he had killed high up in the mountains.

"Ah," he said, wondering how to recover from the gross error he had unwittingly made.

But then the boy said, "Is the curse affecting my lord's recollections?"

"Curse?" Sasha asked, before he remembered the spider web on his chest. He reached up with a stiff, heavy arm to awkwardly push away the blankets and touch the mark. It ached, but not unbearably—likely because his stomach was already in more than enough pain to process it, as well. "Yes, I think it has messed with my mind a bit."

"Yes, my lord," the boy said deferentially. "I promise we will get you to those who can help you."

Sasha nodded faintly. Hopefully they would do no such thing—a real sorcerer would all but kill him on sight. Hopefully by the time that problem arose, he would be sufficiently healed. Scorch that Sentinel for taking him by surprise. "Would you help me sit up?"

"Of course, my lord," the boy said, and he set the teacup aside on a small table beside a wash basin before stepping forward to help him. He had a gentle touch, a healer's touch, Sasha noted fleetingly. After a couple of minutes of careful shifting, Sasha was propped up against the pillows, his stomach aching, but it was for the moment a bearable ache. He looked at the boy and said, "Thank you. What is your name?"

"Um ... David, my lord."

Shaking his head, Sasha said, "You need not call me that. My name is Sasha; that will suffice."

David frowned, clearly puzzled. "Sasha. Yes, my—Yes, Sasha. As you wish. Do you think you are up to trying the soup?"

"Soup sounds like a wonderful idea."

Smiling shyly, David turned away to fetch the soup. After a couple of minutes, he brought Sasha a bowl filled with a dark, creamy broth, thin slices of potato, and small bits of sausage. It was warm, spicy, and Sasha had the sudden thought that he hadn't had anything so homey and good in a very long time. He ate it slowly, mostly sipping at the broth, eating the rest where he was able, and completely ignoring the spoon David had initially offered.

By the time he was full, he was exhausted and barely had the strength to hand the nearly empty bowl back to David. "Thank you," he murmured before his eyes grew too heavy to keep open.

When he opened them again, the room was dark and there was a shadowy figure on a pallet before the fire. Sasha felt a wash of guilt that he had driven David from his own bed, but acknowledged that sleeping on the floor would have done him no favors in regard to recovering.

He tried to remember how he had gotten there and was relieved when the memories came easily. Far too many hours spent wandering the mountain had finally led him to a well-worn path. It had occurred to him too late that he should have asked the woman he'd rescued for directions. Idiot.

Sasha tried to move, but hissed in pain and gave up the effort. Fire and ash, that little Sentinel had nearly gotten the better of him when the massive ones had not even touched him. Stupid to be so careless, and he deserved exactly what he had gotten. If only he had more of that tea the boy—David—had given him. Whatever herbs it contained did wonderful things for alleviating pain.

He looked around the room, trying to see what he could in the dark and barely noticed the gleam of firelight on amber. His sword. Relief swept through him to know he had not lost it. Likely the rest of his things were about then, but even if they weren't, he at least had his sword.

Thoughts of the sword brought another memory flickering to life and Sasha lifted his hand—and froze when he realized his ring was missing.

Then another memory returned, and he relaxed slightly. That scorching Sentinel had gotten him and he had realized he would need a healer. He knew he couldn't allow anyone to see the ring and had hidden it. Once he recalled that, it was easy to shift his head enough to feel the press of it where he had tied the ring into his hair.

He needed to leave, resume his journey, though he had only the vaguest of notion about where he was going. Perhaps someone in the village would be able to help on that point, however. How long would it take him to heal enough to be on his way?

Pain flared again, but he tried it ignore it, casting his eyes around the room again, desperate for distraction. There were clothes hanging on one wall with chests of varying sizes arranged below them. The stove took up the middle of the room, and rag rugs covered much of the wooden floor. The bed, table, and two chairs made up all the furniture. Dishes and cooking utensils were neatly arranged on a series of shelves against another wall.

The room was chilly, the fire in the stove low. David must have been cold, but he slept on peacefully. Where was he exactly? He hadn't thought he was near any villages, but it was strangely easy to become lost in the dense forest that seemed to encompass so much of the country. Something made him think that was on purpose and not merely the nature of the forest itself.

He sighed softly and wished he had a book to read.

Movement caught his eye, and turned to see David begin to toss and turn in his sleep, murmuring nonsense and crying out for someone named Reimund. Sasha frowned and called out, "David! David!"

David jerked and sat up with a cry, breathing heavily—then went still, and turned to look at him. "Oh. Is something wrong, my—Sasha?"

"You were having a nightmare," Sasha said softly. "Talking to someone called Reimund."

"Oh," David said, voice shaky. He slowly stood up and went to fetch wood for the fire. "Um. Reimund was my ... he took care of me, raised me, after my parents died. He was killed by a newborn Sentinel a few days ago."

Sasha winced. "I am sorry for your loss. May he see good fortune in his next life."

"You say strange things," David said quietly as he set the kettle on and dumped a small packet of herbs into a teacup. "In your sleep, you speak in a strange language. I thought the words were just addled because of your wounds, at first, but I think they're real words, just different. Do all sorcerers know a different language?"

"I didn't know I knew two languages," Sasha said, which was sort of true, but the way his mind flickered and images tried to break free ... he was well aware, sort of, that he knew two languages.

He also had the sense that the language he spoke in his sleep was the normal one and the one he spoke at present was foreign. But his head was so addled, as David had aptly put it, that he wasn't certain what he knew.

The kettle whistled and David quickly fixed Sasha's tea. Handing it to him, he asked, "Are you hungry at all?"

"No," Sasha said. "Thank you for the tea. It helps a great deal."

David smiled shyly. "It's Maja that came up with the combination. She's the village healer. Normally you'd be with her, but she's got a houseful of sick kids and a woman having troubles with the baby she carries. She didn't want you getting sick, or not having enough quiet to heal. I don't—my place is empty, except for me."

Without thinking, Sasha reached out to touch David's cheek and said, "No place is empty where warm memories burn. The body is gone, but the soul lives on. He also left you behind, David, and I promise that was enough to ensure he died happy. Be at peace."

Tears fell down David's cheek. "You—you're not like any sorcerer I've even seen or encountered. Nothing at all. Who are you?"

"Sasha, only that," Sasha said softly, the sorrow of a lost memory blooming in his chest, stinging his own eyes. He slowly withdrew his hand and focused on drinking his tea. When he finished, he handed it back and said, "Thank you. I appreciate all that you have done and are doing for me. I will have to find a way to reimburse you."

"I am honored to be of help to a sorcerer," David replied.

"Yet I think you are scared of the likes of me," Sasha said, "and you keep saying that I am strange for my kind. By the way you hold yourself and always keep a certain distance away, I would wager that you have been hurt by one of my kind in the past."

David flinched. "Nothing less than I deserved, lord. I do not mean—"

Sasha reached out, snagged his hand, and held it gently. "You need not be afraid of me, please. It was only an observation, not a reprimand. I am sorry for the pain others have caused you."

"I—" David broke off and just nodded. Turning away, he returned the cup to the table and fussed with the stove a little more.

"What time is it?" Sasha asked.

David looked out a window covered with a dark fur, then said, "Few hours from dawn, yet. You should go back to sleep if you're able."

"You as well," Sasha said. "Not the floor; there's plenty of room in the bed." When David began to shake his head and protest, he added, "I insist. We'll both sleep better—and be there should the other have problems. It will help my pain and your nightmares. Come."

After another moment of hesitation, David gave a slow nod, clearly uncomfortable but not willing to disobey him. He slid into the bed and settled at the very edge of it, tension pouring off of him.

Sasha reached out with one hand and rested his fingers against David's cheek again, saying softly, "Be calm." Warmth flowed through him and poured into David. He could feel it when the calming spell took effect. David gave a soft sigh and was asleep within minutes. Sasha slowly withdrew his hand and let out a sigh of his own.

He reached up to touch his chest, tracing the lines of the spider web he could not see well in the dark room. Would his memories ever return? Was there anyone who could break the curse?

A memory flickered, a face in shadow and impossible to see well, but Sasha had the impression it was somber, yet friendly. Then it was gone again, leaving his head aching. He sighed again and let his hand fall. Pointless to worry about it because he was stuck with is lapses in memory indefinitely. He'd waste less energy if he stopped fretting about it and just accepted.

Soft, murmuring noises drew his attention, and he glanced over at Davis. The barest hints of firelight cast a soft glow across his face. He really was beautiful, and Sasha could not think very highly of a village that let such a lovely, sweet boy sleep alone. He was old enough for someone to want to stake a claim. If he were younger, and not in the middle of his strange quest, Sasha would definitely have suggested a few ways he could express his gratitude for David's help.

He couldn't remember his age, but he knew he was too old for a pretty thing like David. He was also injured, cursed, and impersonating the enemy to bring down a greater enemy. Summed up so neatly, it sounded distressingly like a bad adventure story told to children.

Sighing again, Sasha settled more comfortably and closed his eyes, listening to the soft, steady sound of David's breathing until he finally drifted back to sleep.

He woke to the sound of voices and dragged his eyes open only with effort. A faint, gray morning haze was slipping into the room through cracks in the door and the edges of the window. There was a warm weight along his right side, and Sasha turned his head to see that sometime in the night, David had shifted to curl up alongside him.

Emotions caught in his throat: longing and loneliness and resignation. He let himself enjoy the view, the warmth, for a few seconds more. Then the voices beyond the door grew louder, sharper, and then suddenly they stopped and someone banged on the door.

David jerked and sat up, wide-eyed and disoriented. He groaned as the banging came again and stumbled out of bed, nearly falling to the floor. Reaching the door, he yanked it open, nearly falling again when someone small and quick darted in followed by a larger, broader figure.

"What's wrong, Killian?" David asked, taking in the tense expressions on their face. Killian scowled, but at a look from the other man—clearly his father, to judge by the similarities in their features—remained silent. "Sigmund?" David asked, when the silence stretched on.

Heaving a sigh, grim-faced, Sigmund said, "Killian and I went out early, before dawn, to check the traps. The weather has been bad lately, even worse than usual, but it let up enough earlier that we decided to do what we could before we got stuck inside again. Only when we reached the first trap, we saw one of the barrier crystals had been broken. We checked another two before we acknowledged that the barrier is gone."

"That—that isn't possible—" David said, voice trembling.

Sasha frowned. "How did the barrier break?" He wanted badly to ask what they were even talking about, but knew that would give his cover away entirely.

They all turned to look at him, and Sigmund dipped his head respectfully. "My lord, we do not know. I have never heard of such a thing happening. Even in the old tales of the darkest days, when my Lord Teufel first cast the Great Seal and created the Sentinels, the barriers were there and held strong. But if they truly have fallen, then we are vulnerable to the Sentinels."

"I see," Sasha said. "Take me to see the broken crystals."

David shook his head. "My lord, you're not—"

"I am the only one in this village who might stand a chance of repairing it," Sasha said sharply. "The well-being of one man does not overrule the safety of an entire village. Help me up. Take me to the crystals."

Though clearly still reluctant, David nodded and helped him get out of bed and dressed.

By the time he was dressed, armed, and had finished a cup of tea, Sasha wanted only to go back to bed. His stomach felt as though it was on fire, but the stitches were holding and hopefully the tea would take effect soon.

"Let's go," he said and followed them outside—where they were met by a world of white. The snow was falling so heavily that it was impossible to see, impossible to go anywhere without immediately losing all sense of direction. Worse, a sharp wind cut through the air, sending the snow in a hundred different directions. Occasional bits of ice struck Sasha's face, leaving a faint, lingering sting.

Sigmund swore loudly, angrily, but Sasha could hear the fear he was trying to hide from the younger two. "We can't trek out there with the weather like this, and we will never see the Sentinels coming. We won't know they're here until too late. They'll just pick us off in the dark and probably have fun doing it. Light-takers!"

Power and the remnants of memories prickled along Sasha's skin. The air was so cold that breathing it hurt, and already he was covered in white. Stepping away from David's house, deeper into the snow where they wouldn't be able to see him, he reached up and freed the ring that he had woven into his hair. He pulled off his gloves to slide it into place on the ring finger of his right hand, felt the heat of powerful magic. He pulled the gloves back and closed his eyes, trusting things he could feel, but not remember. He focused on what he needed and cast the spell. *"Snow and ice, a world gone white, a blizzard spun out of control. Dragon of the Winter Storms, take back the power that is yours and bestow clear skies upon us."*

As the last of his words were carried away by the howling wind, a momentary stillness fell. Then Sasha heard the faintest, barest roar in the back of his mind, and the snow seemed to burst with bright, white light for the span of a single breath.

Slowly, the winds calmed and the snow eased. Bit by bit, the storm abated, until the air was filled only with dingy morning light and brisk cold. Sasha let out a breath, ignoring the wave of exhaustion that washed over him, and gestured. "Let us go quickly to the crystals."

Sigmund stared at him a moment longer, but finally shook himself and moved stiffly away from the house. "I did not know sorcerers could control the weather, my lord."

"They can't," Sasha replied. "No mortal can. I only asked nicely for divine assistance."

"I've never heard of Lord Teufel helping in such a way," Killian said.

Sasha regarded him coolly. "You are not a sorcerer, do not presume to know our ways. Are the crystals far?"

"No, my lord," Sigmund said. "I apologize for my impertinence."

"Forget it," Sasha replied. They lapsed into silence as they walked, forming a single line to trudge through what remained of the path Sigmund and Killian had made during their earlier trek. Sasha didn't know what he'd expected of the crystals, but it certainly was not the beautiful, enormous chunks of raw crystal before him. The largest came to about his knees, black and glistening where the snow did not cover it. On either side of it were slightly smaller crystals, making three in all. Someone, or something, had struck them hard enough to leave them cracked and broken, pieces scattered in the snow all around them. Kneeling with one arm wrapped around his stomach, he touched his right hand to the largest crystal.

He could feel the tatters of powerful magic, and that some darker magic had broken it. A sorcerer? Who else would have that kind of power? "Do you have magic users in the village?"

"No, my lord, of course not," Sigmund answered, looking terrified by the very notion. "Black Hill has always been unfailingly devout and abiding."

"I never doubted that," Sasha reassured. "I just hoped the matter might be that easy. The protective spell is very old, very powerful magic, but stronger, darker magic shattered it. Such a spell would take knowledge and experience. If it is not someone local, then there is someone dangerous prowling about intent on bringing harm to the village, and possibly other villages." Sigmund nodded, looking grim-faced.

"Everyone is going to think *you* did it," Killian said, scowling at Sasha.

Before Sasha could reply, Sigmund gave the boy a sharp backhand. "You'll watch your tone around the sorcerer, boy, or did you forget already that the stripes on David's back are because of your fool mouth?"

"Yes, sir," Killian said. When Sigmund raised his hand in a clear indication of another backhand, he hastily added, "My apologies, Lord Sorcerer."

"Forget it," Sasha replied. "You are not incorrect in suggesting that people will suspect me. But I can repair it, which I think will matter more than whether I broke it to begin with."

Relief flooded Sigmund's face, and David smiled shyly at him. "Can you really?" David asked.

Sasha did not reply, merely placed both of his hands on the crystal and bowed his head, letting his eyes fall shut as he said, *"Death is the one true fate of all beings, but comes only when it must and at its proper time. Nothing is more precious to death than life. Gods of death, protect your children from death that is not their fate."*

The magic rushed through him, hot and cold all at once. It surged into the crystal, poured into the smaller ones, and a line of black light shot out from either side of it, the protective circle wrapping around the village.

Exhaustion struck Sasha harder, and he slumped against the crystal, resting his head against its refreshingly cool surface. On some level, he knew it was a bad thing that he thought the cold nice, but he could not seem to figure out why.

"Come, my lord. You've done more than enough for us. It's time to get you back to bed."

"I'll help him," David said, and the press of his body was warm and familiar. He wrapped an arm around Sasha's waist and slipped one of Sasha's arms around his shoulders. They returned to the village slowly, and by the time Sasha was pushed back into David's bed and his wet clothes stripped, the edges of his vision were fuzzy and black.

He vaguely heard the others leave, but his attention was primarily for David. There was something else he needed to be concerned with, but Sasha could not make the thought solidify enough for him to do anything about it. Whatever it was, it would simply have to wait until he was rested and no longer in agony from the wounds and lingering traces of Sentinel venom in his body.

Gentle fingers slid into his hair, helped him sit up just enough to drink the tea that David fed him sip by sip. Then he was laid back down, the blankets pulled up over him, and the last thing he heard was David's soft, warm voice murmuring reassurances.

Shadow of Light

Fritz smiled as warm lips brushed the back of his neck. He could feel Drache's smile in the soft kiss. The smell of flowers was all around them, the landscape below was of a place too beautiful to be anything except the product of a dream.

"Schatten, once upon a dream," Drache murmured, lips sliding along Fritz's ear, making him shiver and lean back against the hard, lithe body behind him. Drache's hands slid across his chest, then slowly trailed down to loop loosely around his hips. Those hot lips returned to his neck, teeth grazing, eliciting more shivers.

Turning around in Drache's arms, Fritz drew his head down and took a long kiss, their mouths sliding together with the ease of lifelong lovers. "Drache ... "

"You have not visited me in a long time, beloved," Drache murmured, fingers lightly trailing over his body, petting, caressing.

"Busy trying to save the country, in case you forgot that part," Fritz replied.

Drache made a derisive noise. "It is when you are at your worst that you should most come to me. If you want to save the country, you're better off letting the child of chaos be to do as he will."

"Child of chaos? Is that what he is?"

"Yes," Drache said. "They are very rare. One has not been seen for a long time."

"How would you know that?" Fritz asked.

Drache did not reply, simply nibbled on Fritz's lips. Fritz wrapped his free arm around Drache, twisted the long braid around his hand—then yanked. Giving him a wounded look, Drache finally said, "I cannot say more than I have."

Fritz huffed in irritation, but let it go. "If there is a child of chaos, is there a child of fate?"

"Yes," Drache said, sounding amused. "His name is Teufel. Made by Licht, loved by Licht, the living shadow of the god of light and order."

All thoughts of getting naked fled Fritz's mind. "What—"

Drache sighed and drew back, letting his arms fall. "Why else would he be called the shadow of Licht? Does this question never occur to anyone? He is, in every way, Licht's shadow—the dark of Licht, something that can come only from Licht."

"I ... as you say, the question never occurred to me. He is the shadow of Licht. I never thought to think farther than that."

Sighing again, Drache turned away and moved to stand beside Fritz at the ledge of their temple. "Honestly, it's unfair to assume you should think of it. Teufel's grip is tight— painfully so. You probably cannot think of it. I am honestly surprised I can discuss it, except that here, in the recesses of your mind, some things slip through. Not enough, unfortunately, but some." He looked at Fritz, reached out to caress his face, lingering on his lips. "You are beautiful, beloved."

Fritz scoffed at that. "I think you may be confused as to what that word means."

Drache—Drache was beautiful, that waterfall of bright gold hair against his dark skin.

Drache just smiled and reached out to wrap his arms around Fritz's neck. Nuzzling against him, he said, "You're beautiful, to me and to others. You are perfection to me."

"One of us is clearly addled in the head— I daresay both of us. Me for imagining you, and you for thinking I'm perfect. I guess that really only leaves me to be a mad, egotistical, incredibly vain High Seer."

"You're not imagining me," Drache said and bit his lip sharply. "Now stop talking, unless it's to tell me how much you love me."

Fritz snorted at that, but did not protest when Drache guided him to the bed, pushed him down on top of it.

A grin curved one corner of Drache's mouth, eyes warm with fondness. "Do you love me?"

"No," Fritz replied, unresisting as Drache stripped away their clothes and pushed him back, letting his arms fall on either side of his head. Drache's hands covers his wrists, holding them in place, that hot mouth trailing along Fritz's skin, teeth nipping at the lobe of his ear.

"Do you hate me?"

"Yes," Fritz said.

Drache kissed him slowly, as though taking sips, savoring every small taste, leaving Fritz breathless and trembling. "Liar," he said quietly, then continued the slow, delicate torture across the span of Fritz's body.

Too much. Not enough. Fritz needed more. He shoved and twisted, climbing on top of Drache and pinning him to the bed, then went to work on Drache's body with a mouth far more ravenous, biting into firm muscle and lapping at smooth skin. He raked his tongue across Drache's nipples, nails leaving red score marks across his stomach. Ignoring Drache's cock, he teased instead at the juncture of hip and thigh, absorbing the heady scent of his dream-time lover.

"Stop being a tease," Drache said.

"Those words are positively hilarious coming from you," Fritz said, but he drew back to find the oil that somehow was never very far out of reach. He pressed a warm, slick finger inside Drache's body, stretching him as he continued to tease with tongue and teeth. It took only minutes for one finger to become two and then three.

By the time he relented, Drache's teasing and smirking had fallen away to be replaced by a look of hunger, his eyes shining, strands of hair sticking to his face and neck with sweat. Fritz slicked his cock and lined up, slowly pushing inside, eyes locked on Drache's beautiful face, the emotions that flickered across it as Fritz filled him.

He bent down to take a kiss as he sank all the way in, feeding on Drache's mouth as if it was a necessary thing, absolutely convinced it was. Drawing back, he gripped Drache's hips and began to fuck him in hard, steady strokes, lost in the tight, the heat, the love and lust that blazed in Drache's lavender eyes.

If he could have stayed in that moment, in that world of heat and passion forever, Fritz gladly would have paid any price. But all he could do was fight his release as long as he could and cry Drache's name when he finally succumbed.

Panting, sated for the moment, and ignoring that it was all just a dream, Fritz curled around Drache and just breathed in their mingled scents, the sweet smell of flowers on the air. He twined his fingers through Drache's braid, stroked his thumb over the soft, beautiful strands. "I've never seen anyone with hair like yours. Everyone keeps their hair short; even the rich cannot afford hair like this."

"It's old-fashioned, to be sure," Drache said, mouth quirking in amusement. "I suspect only one other person wears his hair so, and he does not wear it quite the same way. But I am glad you like it." He kissed Fritz softly. "What troubles you so much you would come down to me without my begging?"

Fritz said nothing, not wanting to discuss it, just wanting a few moments of happiness and peace. He was tired of the waking world, of waiting to finally go mad and die. He was half-convinced he had already gone mad and was actually running around naked and drunk, spewing fractured prophesies and screaming until somebody finally showed mercy and killed him.

The increasing frequency of reports on strange events did not help. Though he had sent Karl and the sorcerers out, so far only bad news had come back to him. Fritz dreaded whatever was going to happen next.

"All will be well, if you let it," Drache said. "Chaos is returning, and despite what you think, that is a good thing. Stop clinging to fate and give chaos a chance. It may be our only chance."

"Chance at what?"

In reply, Drache cupped the back of his head and drew him down for a long, hard kiss. Fritz drew a ragged breath when they finally broke apart. "Give it a chance," Drache said again.

Fritz tried to demand an explanation, but the world suddenly vanished around him.

A sharp banging sound made him jerk up in bed, Drache's name frozen on his lips.

His door. Someone was knocking on his door. Groaning, Friedrich snarled, "Enter."

The door swung open and a priest slipped inside, bowing low. "High Seer, there is a city messenger to see you. He has brought words from several villages and towns, all delivered via note-birds last night and this morning."

"I will come at once," Friedrich said. "See that food and wine are brought to my office."

"Yes, High Seer," the priest said and slipped away.

Getting out of bed, Friedrich quickly washed and dressed in fresh clothes. He ran a hand over the fuzz on his head and grimaced, but shaving it smooth again would have to wait until he had more time.

He closed his eyes and briefly, recalling his recent dream, savoring it, strengthened by it.

Beloved.

No time for you now, Friedrich said. *I told you, I'm busy and everything is only getting worse.*

I will help as best I can. The shift of power in the air grows stronger every day. A storm is brewing that Teufel cannot easily stop. Let us hope it grows beyond his ability to control.

I serve my Lord Teufel, Friedrich replied sharply. *You seem to keep forgetting that.*

You need to stop serving him.

I have no choice.

Drache said something in reply, but Friedrich stubbornly refused to hear it.

He walked briskly through the halls of Unheilvol until he reached his office. A messenger stood outside the door and bowed low when he saw Friedrich. "High Seer."

"I am told you have several urgent messages for me," Friedrich said as he led the way into his office. He sat down behind his enormous desk and set aside sermons and accounting papers, gesturing for the messages. "What do they all say? Why are we getting so many troubling messages at once?"

"The barriers have fallen, High Seer," the messenger replied. "They started falling the night before, to judge by the messages. Nearly every city, town, and village in Schatten has sent word that their protective barriers are gone, leaving the Sentinels to wreak havoc as they please. We have already received word of many deaths and more messages have no doubt arrived in the time I have been gone."

That should not be possible, Drache thundered in Friedrich's head, making him wince and press his fingers to his temple. More quietly, Drache added, *Those barriers were created by Lord Teufel. Only someone of your caliber would be able to mess with them at all, and I don't think you could break them without a great deal of practice first.*

It could only be the work of the rogue sorcerer we are trying to find. If he wants to seed Schatten with chaos then that is certainly one way to go about it—and a good reason to reject it! Chaos only brings pain.

No. Chaos brings choice. By its nature is it neither cruel nor kind. It simply is. To destroy every barrier in the country and leave people vulnerable is not chaos. It is vindictive and malicious. It is purposeful, which is definitely not chaos.

So who do you think is behind it?

You know very well what I think.

Lord Teufel would not do this to his own children.

They're not his children! Drache started to say more, but stopped with a cry of pain. Friedrich froze and barely held back a sigh of relief when Drache did not vanish as he had before.

He focused on the messenger. "Do we have any idea who is responsible? What is being done to protect the children of shadows?"

"We—no one knows what to do. Magic is normally for the High Sorcerer, but no one—"

"Of course," Friedrich cut in, and he dropped the notes on his desk as he stood up. Dismissing the messenger, he called for a priest. "Assemble every available guard and sorcerer. If their job is not of life-saving importance, then they are to come to me at once in the Hall of Vision."

The priest bowed and dashed away. Friedrich left his office and headed quickly to the Hall of Vision. He rang the bell at the back of the hall, summoning the entirety of Unheilvol. While he waited for the hundreds of occupants of the temple to arrive, he strode across the hall to the vision pool and took his place in the curve of the crescent. Instead of facing the pool, however, he turned and faced the altar at the very back of the room, the dais on which it rested not quite touching the tips of the crescent.

Where the rest of the temple was black marble, the wall and dais of the altar were made from obsidian. Friedrich did not know how it could have been done, except by way of magic. A table of some rough, white stone formed the altar itself. Silver candle sticks held candles of black beeswax. With a thought, Friedrich lit them and the soft orange light reflected off the obsidian wall. A bowl sat between the candles, and Friedrich approached it with a knot of dread in his stomach.

He'd never been called upon to use the full force of his abilities. Not since his last life, anyway. No record of those moments was ever made, and he did not know why. But he knew the madness that always sealed his fate came not longer after this deepest of visions. He had known the day was coming, he had just kept hoping it would forever be *the next day.*

Drawing the dagger at his hip, he slit his wrist and let blood pour into the bowl until he began to grow dizzy. Magic healed the cut, and he sank to his knees, too weak to stand. He needed to help Schatten, to put back the barriers that had been torn down. But Drache was correct: though he had the power to do it, he did not have the knowledge or experience. There were no records of such magic. Lord Teufel, for the good of his children, kept such knowledge away from them.

To find it, he would have to cast his Sight much further afield.

Half-asleep from the loss of blood, he let his dagger slip from his fingers, bowed his head, closed his eyes, and prayed, "*Lord of Dark, Lord of Shadows, Lord who grants me perfect Sight in both, give me vision of the time and the place that will save the children of Schatten.*"

A sharp bolt of pain burst in the center of his forehead, as if someone had taken his dagger and shoved it through the black circle. Friedrich screamed in pain—

> *And it stopped, leaving only a faint, dull ache. He opened his eyes and saw that the altar was gone. Everything was gone. There was nothing but obsidian beneath his feet and all around him was the open night sky. The air was pleasantly cool, a faint breeze teasing at his robes. High above, the moon was the barest sliver of silver, and the stars were bright, sharp points of light. He had the*

sense he was high up, though he could not see well enough to know for certain.

It struck him as a dark, wild-edged version of the temple where he visited Drache.

The soft swish of fabric drew his attention and Friedrich turned—and stopped, too stunned to move, eyes fastened to the vision before him.

He was beautiful, the most beautiful man Friedrich had ever seen. His skin was a dark, nutty brown, covered in shimmering gold dust. He was bare-chested, skin smooth and flawless, muscles well-formed. Gold hoops gleamed at his nipples, connected by a fine gold chain. There were gold bands at his wrists, a heavier chain at his throat from which hung a brilliant purple stone that nestled perfectly in the hollow of his collar bone. But it was his hair that was the most stunning. It was as long as Drache's, the color of the night around them, and pulled back in a long tail with gold clasps holding it together at regular intervals.

If darkness could take a human form, then that form was before him. The man was night wrapped in carnal thought and sent to drive mortals mad. "Who are you?" he asked.

The man laughed, his voice as sensual as the rest of him, husky with a hint of wicked. "You are the Highest of my Seers and you do not know me?"

Friedrich's eyes widened, and he immediately fell to his knees and bowed his head. "Lord Teufel."

"Mm," Teufel murmured, long fingers running over Friedrich's not-quite smooth

head. After a moment, the fingers fell away and cupped his chin, forcing his head up. "It's been a few decades since last you came to me this way. A century, in fact. You are looking for a way to help my children."

"Yes, Lord," Friedrich replied. Long nails, painted purple, stroked his cheek. Moonlight gleamed off the jewels on the rings Teufel wore. "I did not mean to disturb your Holiness, however. I sought only to see deep into my own past, to find a spell I might have known in another life."

Teufel gestured for him to rise. He was shorter than Friedrich, but somehow seemed to loom anyway. "Always a good priest, my Highest of Seers. I was the one who chose you, long ago when the world was still new."

Friedrich frowned, confused. "My Lord?"

"You were the first priest, the first granted Sight, and you ever remained the strongest. Few could compare to you in power—only two, in fact. The Priest of Storms and the Priest of Ashes."

"I don't ..." He trailed off, not certain what to say. That he didn't understand? That he didn't know who those two priests were? Was he supposed to know them? Why?

Teufel chuckled and stroked his cheek again, then stepped back. "They were priests from the days when Schatten foolishly aligned itself with the other four countries. They little matter now, sealed out where they cannot do the bidding of their gods."

He smiled and Friedrich felt a chill. "I want only to serve Schatten, my lord."

"Once, I believed you when you said that," Teufel said. "But serving Schatten

means serving me, and in the end you turned on me. You've been suitably punished—are still being suitably punished—but every now and then you need a reminder. So here we are."

"R-reminder?"

Teufel's smiled took on an edge that made Friedrich step back before he caught himself and tried to hold still. "I know when your mind begins to turn to thoughts of treachery. In every life you are the same." He paused, then said, "Well, nearly the same. You look very different than you once did, my priest. I admit, you were chosen mostly for the potential you had in terms of power, but I also chose you for your beauty. I am the shadow of Licht. Nothing less than the best should surround me."

He raked his nails lightly down Friedrich's broad, bare chest, leaving a faint sting behind. "I found you, brought you up, gave you power, let you into my bed ... and in the end, you too betrayed me."

Memories like smoke wisped and curled through Friedrich's mind, of a dark-haired beauty and tangled sheets, the smell of myrrh and cinnamon and Licht blossoms. Of a long, lithe body covering him, fucking him, gold dust rubbing off as he held fast to firm shoulders.

Friedrich's eyes stung as he remembered, as realization dawned. "You belonged to Licht, but... why ..." He knew the answer, though. Teufel had loved Licht— absolutely, passionately, and blindly. But he had enjoyed his toys and enjoyed them thoroughly.

His favorite toy had been the man Friedrich had once been: Ehrlich, Priest of Night and Day, the most powerful Seer in the world, and one of three priests who had granted great power by the gods. Slain nine hundred years ago when Licht was lost, though Friedrich could not yet recall what exactly he had done wrong. Only that he had angered Teufel, and Teufel's wrath always ended in blood.

"You defied me, you betrayed me," Teufel said, the words almost sing-song. "So you were killed, as you deserved, and so you continue to suffer, as you also deserve. Your current life bleeds away, Highest of Seers. I can take it any day now, but how I take it depends on you."

Friedrich looked at him, eyes stinging, vision blurred. "What do you mean, Lord?"

"Find the child of chaos, capture him, bring him to me at Sonnenstrahl, and I'll give you the death you have craved these nine hundred years. Defy me, try to fight me as you once did, and I will ensure that you die as you always have—and that you will take all of Unheilvol with you."

"You can't—" he broke off with a cry of pain when Teufel struck him.

"I can do whatever I want, and neither you nor that child of chaos nor those damn fools who lurk at my border can stop me. Bring me the child of chaos, or watch your temple die in agony and madness before I finally take your life—and your hope. I will restore the barriers of protection when my children stop succumbing to chaos and remember their place."

"What—"
But his question went unfinished as the
world vanished around him.

Friedrich cried out—then realized he was back in the Hall of Vision, finally free of that terrible vision. He wiped tears from his eyes, wiped his nose with a handkerchief he fumbled from a pocket. Movement caught his eye, and he turned as a priest slowly approached him.

"Are you well, High Priest?"

"I will be," Friedrich said. "My Lord Teufel has spoken to me." He allowed the priest to help him to his feet, then dismissed him. On slow, unsteady feet he walked back to his place at the curve of the vision pool. The hall was filled with priests, acolytes, workers, guards, and many others who had been in the temple at the time the bell was rung.

Friedrich cleared his throat and said loudly enough the hall would carry his words to all, "My Lord Teufel has gifted me with Vision of him and told to me directly his desires and disappointments. A threat has descended upon Schatten, a child of chaos who threatens to ruin the loving order our Lord Teufel has bestowed. The protective barriers were removed by Teufel for our unfaithfulness, and he will restore them when the child of chaos is found and brought to me. See that his desires are made known across the land."

The hall exploded into conversation, fear and panic wending through the crowd. Friedrich motioned to his priests, who immediately set to calming and moving the crowd.

Retreating to the altar, he stared into the bowl where his blood still pooled, dark and thick and cold. He swallowed, feeling raw and used and afraid. Tentatively he reached out to the only being that could soothe him, and might be able to answer some of his questions. *Drache?*

Beloved.

Is it true? All that he showed me?

Yes, and there is much more he has not—will not, until the moment when it will hurt the most. Nobody excelled at cruelty like Teufel, and nobody was better at ignoring it than Licht.

Drache's bitterness coiled through Friedrich's mind.

Who are you, Drache? Are you me? A memory of me? Any other day, Friedrich would have been horrified, yet amused in some small way, that he had been enjoying dreams of fucking an ancient version of himself.

The idea did not feel wrong, but it was not right either.

Something like a memory, Drache replied. *Teufel's hold on me has not loosened enough for me to say more than that.*

Does he know about you?

That I speak to you? No. He has rendered me mostly powerless, but not entirely, as he believes.

Friedrich closed his eyes, not knowing what to do. He felt alone, afraid, and helpless. If he did not do as Teufel wanted, Unheilvol would die with him. What could he do except comply? Only a short time ago, he would have been more than happy to comply.

But Teufel had lashed out, woken memories, taunted him, forced him. All Friedrich could remember was defiance, that once upon a time he had felt it necessary to oppose Teufel despite the danger of doing so.

Fate was never meant to be absolute. Licht and Teufel would not accept that.

What do we do?

Find the child of chaos. Take him to Sonnenstrahl. Do whatever you must to help him kill Teufel.

Friedrich accepted the words with the barest of nods, his fear and helplessness driven out by the strength of a decision freely and firmly made. He was dead no matter what he did, so he would die doing what he had tried to do nine hundred years ago: stop Teufel.

Farewell

"You must go soon," Maja said. "I know you do not want to leave your responsibilities here, or us in these times of strife, but it is the duty and honor of all the children of shadow to hear their fate, and you must go before you are too late."

"But I don't turn nineteen for another month, and then I have a whole year—"

Maja lifted her hand, silencing him. "When the weather is good and the travel easy, it takes two months to reach Sonnenstrahl. Less, of course, if you have a horse, but we cannot spare one for you. When the weather is as foul as this? It will take much, much longer, David. You must go now so that there is time aplenty should something in your journey go wrong. You never should have waited this long."

"Reimund was going to take me; we should have left weeks ago," David said.

"I know, and I am sorry, but life goes on and time slips away, and you must leave."

David nodded and rose. "Very well. I will settle things today and leave in the morning."

"You should take the sorcerer with you," she murmured softly. "He frightens people."

"He's been nothing but kind!" David protested. "He fixed the barrier. He fixed the weather long enough for us to better prepare against it! Ever since he's been able to move he's done nothing but help."

"He's different," Maja said, voice still quiet, but firm. "Different is not the way of our land, and eventually something will go very wrong and that sorcerer and you will be the ones most hurt. Leave, David. Go to Unheilvol and take him with you."

David didn't reply, just stormed out. He pulled up the hood of his cloak as he trekked across the village to his home, wincing at the cold wind that threw snow and ice into his face. The door blew out of his hands as he pushed it open, banging against the opposite wall. Heaving an aggravated sigh, David pushed it shut, then stripped off his gloves and cloak and went to the stove to thaw.

"I take it your meeting with Maja did not go well," Sasha murmured from behind him, making David jump.

He flushed, and then rolled his eyes. "She insists I leave *now*—well, in the morning—to go to Unheilvol. Says I should take you with me."

Sasha's mouth curved slightly. "Making the locals nervous, am I? But I should be going anyway, now that I am mostly healed, thanks to you. The least I can do is serve as your guard to Unheilvol."

David blinked at that, realizing Sasha was right; he hadn't scheduled the journey and requested an escort. He would have had to travel entirely alone—but then again, it hardly mattered when the barriers seemed to be down everywhere except Black Hill. Without Sasha's help, they'd be in as much danger as everyone else. Setting aside the rambling thoughts, he said, "I would appreciate the escort. The Sentinels ... I don't know how you aren't afraid of them."

"I feel I've dealt with worse," Sasha said softly, eyes going distant even as he set the kettle on the stove next to a pot of stew. "The memories are locked away, but the feelings associated with them are not entirely gone. Sentinels mean nothing to me; they're only beasts." He moved away to fetch tea and the loaf of bread and cheese someone had given him in payment for help.

He was going to miss Sasha, David realized. Leaving Black Hill meant that, in a few months, Sasha would be gone forever—probably would get his memories back once he ran across another sorcerer or reached the priests of Unheilvol. Then he would sneer at his memories of an idiot village boy who presumed too much and spoke out of turn.

"I suppose I should begin packing," David said with a sigh. "Not that I have much to pack, but we will definitely need whatever foodstuffs we can muster." He nibbled on his lower lip, thinking of what he had to trade and who would be willing to part with food. What little coin he had was better saved for when he reached Two Mill, where he could replenish at actual shops.

Sasha returned to the stove to fetch the boiling water, pouring tea and then exchanging the kettle for the pot to dish out stew. "Sit, eat. I traded for plenty of food today—enough to see us decently fed for a few weeks, and by then we should reach another place to resupply, yes? Where is my map ..." He finished a bite of stew, then stood up and went to his saddlebags. "That's strange," he said after a moment, standing up with a folded map in one hand. "My compass is miss ... ah, I bet it was lost in the snow. I had just pulled it out to verify where I was going when that Sentinel came out of nowhere."

"Compass?" David echoed, thinking of the gift still tucked away under the bed, never to be given to Reimund. It hurt still, to think about him—hurt a lot. But Reimund would have been the first to get mad at him for brooding. He would also have yelled about something going to waste.

Standing up, David went to the bed and crawled under it to get the package he had tucked away there. Pulling it out, he handed the cloth wrapped bundle to Sasha. "Here, you may as well have this, if it's a compass you need. It will just go to waste, otherwise."

"Was this for ...? I could not take it."

"He wouldn't want it sitting around not being used," David said, throat getting tight. He thrust the package at Sasha, then resumed his seat and drank his tea.

Sasha stared at him a moment, then gave one of his slow, thoughtful, accepting nods. He unwrapped the old rag and scrap of fur in which David had wrapped the compass and pulled it out. The burnished bronze gleamed in the light of the stove. Sasha traced the etched cover, then thumbed it open, a smile overtaking his face. Looking up again, he said, "It's handsome, better than the one I had even. Thank you."

David flushed and looked down, smiling a bit as he set aside his tea and went back to his stew. They finished the meal in silence, and David set to work cleaning up supper while Sasha began to pack. When he was done with cleaning the dishes, David began readying the house for a long absence, putting things away, setting aside food that wouldn't keep so he could give it to others, and giving the entire room a thorough cleaning.

By the time he was done, he wished the weather was warm enough for a dip in the river. Instead, he just set a large pot of water to heat. "I set wash water to warm," he said to Sasha. "I'm going to give this food away and say goodbye to Killian."

Sasha nodded, and David gathered up the food and left, slowly trudging across the village to where Killian's house was located behind the blacksmith. He rapped on the door and smiled in greeting at Killian's mother, Gertrude, when she opened the door.

"Hello, David," she said cautiously, which hurt. Killian's family had always been friendly to him, always invited him inside to warm up, have a cup of cider … but since Reimund, since Sasha, they had been much cooler. Instead of being offered warmth and cider, he was left standing there, Gertrude clearly wishing he would say his peace and depart.

"I'm leaving tomorrow for Unheilvol," David said stiffly. "I came to give you my perishables, but since you clearly have no need of them—"

Gertrude stepped back and beckoned him. "Come in, come in, lad. Killian is out back fetching wood from the shed. He'll be here in a moment. I take it you're wanting to say goodbye? Set the food on the table, there. Thank you for giving it to us."

David nodded.

Going to the fireplace—a luxury David had always envied them—she swung out a small caldron and ladled hot cider into a mug. She handed the mug to him, and mustered a faded smile. "Drink, warm up. I'm sorry about Reimund, sweet."

"Me too," David said quietly. "Thank you for the cider."

She nodded and wiped her hands restlessly on her apron, then bustled back to the cooking area and began to put away everything he had brought her. "That strange sorcerer going with you, lad?"

"Yes. He says it's long past time he finally went home and resumed his regular duties," David said.

Gertrude nodded, but didn't reply, busy sorting things in the little pantry cabinet in one corner. The door banged open before David could think of something to fill the silence, and Killian burst in as if the winter wind were chasing him. He stacked firewood haphazardly against a wall near the fireplace, then rounded on David. "There you are! You've been spending so much time with that fancy sorcerer of yours, I thought you'd left me behind! Decided I'm good enough again?"

"Killian!" Gertrude said sharply. "If you do not stop behaving so rudely I will send you right back outside and make you stay there until I feel like letting you in again."

"Yes, Ma," Killian replied petulantly. Turning back to David, he said, "So why did you come by? Want to go checking traps with me tomorrow? Dad is going to be busy—"

"I can't," David cut in. "I came to say goodbye. I have to go to Unheilvol to hear my fate. We're leaving at first light."

Killian froze, staring at him—and then exploded in anger, lunging forward and punching David in the face. "You're running off with that stupid, pretty-faced sorcerer! I knew it! So typical, meet a pretty fancy and run away at the first chance! He's an evil, conniving sorcerer and you're a fool! I hope he leaves you stranded and alone like you deserve!" He kicked David hard in the shin, then hit him in the stomach before bolting off.

David stared after him, stunned and hurt in ways that had nothing to do with Killian's blows. "I—what—I'm going to hear my fate, not running away with Sasha! What in the name of shadows was that all about?"

Gertrude clucked, torn between defending her hurt son and amusement at … something, clearly, but David had no idea what. "David, lad, you must be the only one in the village who *hasn't* noticed my son is a bit sun-dazed by you."

"What?" David asked, feeling his face go hot. "He is not!"

"Oh, yes, he is," Gertrude said, bracing her hands on her hips. "He's been a right terror ever since that sorcerer started moving about. Never has anything nice to say and more than a few crude things that are angering his father to no end. That sorcerer is handsome, educated, and seems in no hurry to leave your bed—"

"It's not like that!" David said.

Gertrude snorted at that and finally went back to kneading the dough that had gone untouched since David's arrival. "That's your age showing, then. Get on with you; Killian won't be coming back. He'll be here when you get back, though. You two can work it out then."

"Tell him I said goodbye and I'll miss him—a lot," David said. "Goodbye, Gertrude. Thank you." He fled, face still flushed as he walked home. The smell of tea washed over him as he stepped inside, comforting and familiar, momentarily making him forget his embarrassment.

But the sight of Sasha in only breeches and stockings, still sorting out the rest of his clothes, brought everything Killian and Gertrude had said slamming back to the forefront of his mind. Because, of course, he and Sasha hadn't done anything. Sasha was a sorcerer, and David nothing. He was a plain, simple village boy exactly like dozens of others. Sasha was beautiful, older, brave enough to travel alone, and strong enough to cast a protective barrier or stop the snow. Even the Sentinels did not frighten Sasha.

He would *never* think of David as anything, except maybe the boy who had taken care of him while he was bedridden.

That didn't stop David from thinking about things he barely even understood. Things the older men whispered about, things he'd seen once or twice—kisses and once he'd caught Helga and Rufus in the village stable doing much more—but never had a chance to do.

Things that apparently Killian … ugh, that was just too weird a thought. Killian was his friend, maybe his best friend, but David didn't want to kiss him or anything. No, if he was going to kiss somebody, he wanted it to be somebody like Sasha. Older, knowledgeable, somebody who knew how to get something done and wouldn't say reckless, careless things that got other people hurt. Someone steady and reliable.

But he was pretty certain people like that didn't want anything to do with a young fool like him.

"You look like you've been scorched down to the bone," Sasha said.

David shook himself. "Not really. Killian is mad I'm leaving."

Sasha gave him one of those half-smiles that made it so hard not to stare at him, pulling his shirt on as he said, "Jealous you're travelling, I would imagine. Probably thinks you'll find something or someone who'll make you want to stay with them and never come back here. That's the usual fear of those left behind, that they'll be forgotten. Too often, though, the Killians of the world are correct: people leave little villages and never return. Life is bigger and brighter in large cities. It takes a long time for some people to realize that doesn't always mean better."

"I plan on coming back," David said.

"You are going to learn your fate," Sasha reminded him gently. "You don't necessarily know what you'll be doing."

David flinched and fell silent.

He looked up when a hand cupped the back of his head, fingers gently combing through his hair for a brief moment. "Fires warm and calm you," Sasha said, smiling gently when David looked up. Strangely, the words did make him feel calmer and warmer. They were so close he could scarcely breathe, was afraid he would give away the silly thoughts always lurking at the back of his mind. "Whatever guides your steps, David—fate, chaos, a little of both—what comes will come and rarely can it be faced until it does come. Live in today, not in tomorrow."

"I'll try," David said.

Sasha nodded. "Wash up, and then I think it's time for bed, so we can leave bright and early tomorrow. A pity I've lost my horse, but I suppose as bad as the weather has been, it would be of little use to us. Hopefully we can obtain a couple once we reach Oak Hill."

"Should be able to," David said, and he moved to obey, stripping off and washing quickly, shivering until he managed to pull on warm clothes. He added a bit more wood to the fire and carefully closed the stove up, then locked the door, checked the fur covering the window, and blew out the lamps before he finally crawled into bed beside Sasha.

His stomach churned with nervousness about the journey, though there was some excitement there, too. He'd never been further than Two Mill, and they'd only ever stayed there long enough to buy supplies for the village before turning around and going home again.

To see the famous city of Raven Knoll and the legendary temple of Unheilvol that resided there …

Would his fate be a good one? A simple one? A terrible one? What was in store for him? Would he face it bravely, or collapse, or go mad? Mercy of the Lost Licht, he hoped he did not go mad from hearing his fate. What if he did and no one was there to take him home and he wandered the streets a mad penitent—

"Shh," Sasha said, reaching out in the dark, touching his cheek. "Your thoughts are louder than the howling wind, David. Go to sleep."

David tried to reply, but exhaustion overwhelmed him as quickly as that, and he drifted off thinking that Sasha's sneaky spells were worse than his big ones.

When he woke, the room was still dark, and the glow of the fire had faded, but he was still incredibly warm—almost too warm, but it was so much better than being cold.

The first time it had happened, he had been confused and then mortified. Every night, at some point while he slept, he moved to curl up against Sasha's chest, his head tucked in neatly beneath Sasha's chin. He could feel every breath Sasha drew, his heartbeat ... and the arm that Sasha had draped over him.

David had no idea why he kept doing it, or why Sasha seemed content with it—while he slept, anyway. He did not want to know how Sasha would react if he woke and found David so boldly pressed against him. Though he knew he should move, it felt so comfortable, so warm, that he could not bring himself to do it. Sasha made a soft noise, murmured nonsensically, and his arm tightened briefly around David.

He'd never slept with someone else, except Killian when they traveled together because inn beds were expensive and it was safer out in the open. That wasn't anything like being curled up with Sasha in a bed that was plenty big enough for them both. It should have felt stranger, but try as he might, David could not find it strange. The only thing that surprised him about it was how right it felt—and that Sasha had not yet caught him. He kept waiting for the day when Sasha woke and angrily ordered him to the floor.

Except he had the feeling that if Sasha thought one of them should leave the bed, he would insist on leaving it himself and letting David stay in it. He hoped Sasha stayed asleep. It would be their last night in a bed together and David wanted one last chance to enjoy the bone-deep comfort of sleeping in Sasha's arms. Settling back in, closing his eyes, David slid back into sleep.

When he woke again, he could feel it was close to dawn. He was so accustomed to rising before the sun, it was natural as breathing, or near enough. Sasha was already gone, and David flushed hot to think he'd woken up and found David clinging to him like a kitten to its mother at super time.

Hastily getting out of bed, he stripped it and tucked all the blankets away into a wooden chest so they would come to no harm while he was gone.

Next, he put out the fire in the stove, cleaned it out, and made absolute certain there was nothing that would accidentally catch fire. He was just finishing up when Sasha reappeared, dusted with snow and smelling of the fresh bread and cheese he carried. He wrapped it all up and tucked it away in one of his bags. David realized then that the saddlebags were gone, traded somewhere for a knapsack that was better for walking.

"All set?" Sasha asked, pulling on his cloak, sliding his arms through the holes cut for it, and closing it down the front. Then he pulled on the knapsack and fastened it into place before settling a fur cap on his head and pulling on fur-lined gloves.

David quietly pulled on his own gear and pack, then gave his home one last look around, swallowing the lump in his throat. He'd be back in half a year or so—at worst a year. It was hardly forever, and after that journey he would probably never leave home on such a long journey again.

So why did it feel like he was looking on his home for the last time?

Nodding, brushing the thought way, he finally said, "Ready."

"The snow is falling lightly, and I've got fresh food and some hot ale for when we stop to eat," Sasha said. He lightly gripped the back of David's neck, squeezing reassuringly, his touch warm even through layers of fabric and fur. "Let's be off."

They left the village heading north, the crunch of their feet in the snow the only real sound in the quiet of the dark morning. The moon still gleamed high above, not yet banished by the sun. His breaths misted in the winter air, and his face was already beginning to feel the effects of the cold, but David only pulled up his face mask and kept walking.

He paused right at the edge of the Shadow Forest and turned back, but Black Hill was already mostly hidden by the falling snow, little more than patches of black and curls of gray smoke. Swallowing tears, he nodded in farewell to it, then turned and followed Sasha into the dark of the woods.

Alone

Time was hard to judge in the forest. It was, in fact, easy to lose track of everything. It was a bit like wandering a house that seemed empty, should be empty, but every now and again there was the nagging sense he was being watched. He could not wait until they left the forest behind.

Sasha really could not wait to reach another town. His brief stay in Black Hill had reminded him of the comforts of civilization, and he wanted them back. They had only been travelling three days and had a great many more to go, but he was already sick of it. He had not travelled so hard in the dead of winter for a long time. He wondered with a sigh how he knew that, but nothing about those previous trips, or why they had ceased, came to mind.

He was long past tired of being a mystery to himself.

David's sharp intake of breath drew his attention and Sasha turned sharply—then drew his whip and struck, the cracking sound echoing through the dark woods. The baby Sentinel he'd hit reared back from the sound and the pain. Sasha hit it again—once, twice, thrice. When it was disoriented and helpless, he drew his sword and brought it down on the Sentinel's neck, severing it just enough to be fatal.

They backed away hastily from the thrashing, dying Sentinel and continued on their way. "This forest is strange," Sasha said. "It's like it's ... aware or something. It's so dense that it's hard to keep track of time."

That earned him an odd look, but as usual, David attributed the lack of knowledge to Sasha's curse. It was endearing, if somewhat alarming, how naïve the boy could be. Sasha would take advantage of it, at least to a point, to further his goals, but it also made him want to protect David and make certain nobody ever took that naivety away.

His mind immediately went from thoughts of protecting David to memories of waking up curled around David, who had been warm and pliant and comfortable in his arms. An ache twisted, hard and sharp, in his chest, made his eyes sting.

But he didn't know *why* and it was more infuriating than usual. Fires, he would do anything to break the curse. He did not dare do it himself, when there was no telling what removing it—or removing it incorrectly—would do. If he had to put up with it much longer, however, he might just try.

"It's called the Shadow Forest," David finally said, looking around at the high, looming trees, the canopy of leaves and snow that blotted out nearly all of the light. "They say it covers most of Schatten, that it appeared the day Lord Teufel sealed Schatten away forever. The Sentinels make their home here, and I've heard some say that buildings from long ago can be found—but that those who find them never find their way back."

"That sounds ominous," Sasha said. It also sounded like the forest was a labyrinth, and likely a shifting one. He'd read of such magic …

He could see the book in his mind. It had been a gift. An old book, one he'd thought long vanished from the world. Sorcery was outlawed and many books written by and for sorcerers had been destroyed, but a few had survived the centuries, and one of them had discussed the reshaping of nature.

It took more power and ability than he possessed. The shaping of nature should be left to the gods. When it was not, far worse things that the Shadow Forest emerged.

"Is any part of this landscape not dangerous?" Sasha asked. "The mountains were crawling with Sentinels, but they were plenty dangerous all on their own, especially with the snow making it impossible to judge the lay of the land."

David frowned at him. "The Sentinels, the forest, the mountains—all are meant to protect Schatten from the outside, from those who would bring harm to us, to Lord

Teufel, those who seek to finish what they started in destroying Licht."

"Mm," Sasha said, and he paused as a tree caught his eyes—rather, the terrible claws marks on it. Many of the trees were marked so, as if a Sentinel had lashed out in anger. Sasha wasn't certain he wanted to know what would make a Sentinel so angry when, as near as he could tell, no one but he had ever attacked them.

"It wants to mate," David said, and Sasha turned toward him. "It was looking for a female. They don't move as much; the females are much bigger than the males. The one that left these marks on the trees was probably a young bull in his first heat; they're the only ones that claw randomly at things like this."

"A pity they're such a menace, because they sound fascinating," Sasha replied. "I have never seen anything like them."

David frowned at him, and Sasha realized he was getting far too careless about pretending to be a sorcerer. Well, trying to explain himself would only make it worse. Best to move on and hope the slip was forgotten.

"So you said the next town we'll encounter is Oak Hill?"

"Yes," David said slowly, still eying him warily. "We should reach it in a couple more days. If we're really lucky, we can get horses there, but I don't know that we'll be so fortunate. Winter has never been this bad before, and with the barriers fallen, people will be even more cautious. They may not let us into the town at all. Black Hill will start turning people away soon just because supplies are going to run low if this lasts too long. There's so much ill-omen in the air ..." He worried at his lower lip, which was already red and swollen from where he frequently did that.

Sasha had a sudden, sharp desire to worry that mouth with his own teeth, give David something much more interesting to think about than ill omens. "I'm sure Black Hill will relax now that I'm gone."

"And me," David said softly, sadly. "Everyone considers me ill luck because of my parents. They whisper that I should have been left to die, that I wasn't meant to be if my parents left me when I was still a babe. They tried to run away, up the mountain and out of Schatten."

"I'm sure they left you because whatever they were doing, they did not want you to die if they failed," Sasha said. "Near as I can tell, they knew they were going to fail."

David nodded, but the sorrow on his face was heartbreaking. "Why wasn't I good enough for them to stay?"

Pain sliced through Sasha then, a wound so old and deep that, for a moment, he couldn't breathe. He looked at David, the pain and confusion and longing in his face, and did not have the heart to say that sometimes people were simply selfish and did not care who they hurt by their actions. That there was no sense in wasting energy on people like that. David made him wish that wasn't true, and Sasha sensed it had been a very long time since he'd met anyone who made him that stupid. "The hardest thing we can do in life is leave a loved one behind. I don't think it was that you were not good enough. I think they wanted to make certain the way was safe before they came back for you. Schatten is a land of fate, a land where nothing ever really changes. Yet they tried to break free, anyway, tried to defy fate. No doubt it scared them, especially since they did not know what they would find on the other side of the mountain. If they failed, you were safe. If they made it, they could build a new, safe life for you."

"I never thought of that," David said softly.

Sasha mustered a smile. "As I said, one of the hardest things we can do in life is leave a loved one behind. When we do, it is because we love them and want only the best for them."

"Do you have family? Did you have to leave them behind to become a sorcerer?"

"I ..." A memory flared to life in Sasha's head like a painting in a room lit only by a single candle. A woman, close to his age. She was beautiful, familiar, and definitely felt like family. "A ... sister, I think. I don't remember clearly. But yes, I did have to leave her to do what was necessary."

David reached out and lightly touched his arm, then withdrew, smiling shyly. "I'm sorry. She must be proud of you, though. Those gifted with the diamond of magic are rare. They say there are not even three hundred sorcerers in the whole country. I think Black Hill has more people than that."

Sasha laughed. "If it has more than three hundred people, it is not by much." He winked. "As to the number of sorcerers ... magic is a powerful thing, and the more people who have it, the more it will be abused. There is a lot to be said for magic, but there is also much to be said about not needing it. Oh, I think we're coming to a clearing."

"That'll be the pond," David said, and he quickened his step. Sasha followed him, curious as to what was so special about this pond that David's face would brighten that way. The clearing, when they reached it, showed signs of frequent use as a campsite. There was a fire pit, a pile of firewood carefully stored under an overhang, and the area around the fire pit had been cleared so that sleeping would be as comfortable as possible.

Far to one edge was, as David had said, a little pond. It was frozen over, but not by much. Sasha crouched down beside David as he broke through the ice with the hilt of the hunting knife he carried. When the ice cracked, he sheathed the knife and removed his gloves to pick at the broken chunks of ice to move them out of the way.

When the ice was clear, leaving a patch of green-blue water bare, he pulled his gloves back on. He smiled up at Sasha, eager and bright and so *young*. Sasha had not once seen David act so much his age; he generally acted like someone several years older and had shadows in his eyes no young man should possess.

But right then, he looked like an eighteen year old boy enjoying himself on a clear winter day. He also, to Sasha's dismay, looked all the more kissable. It made him feel old, wanting David.

"Look!" David said, breaking Sasha's thoughts, and Sasha obediently looked at the hole in the ice.

Perhaps a half dozen little fish had risen to the surface, swimming and playing. They were a beautiful shade of indigo, with long fins and tails that were slightly lighter in color than the body; they moved like trails of silk. David held his fingers out, and the fish pushed eagerly at the tips of the leather gloves until they realized it wasn't food.

After a moment, the little fish vanished again, but then another cluster, these ones more blue than purple, rose up. David beamed at Sasha again as the blue fish were replaced by a cluster so dark a purple they nearly looked black. "They're called winter fish because they only come out when the weather is cold. Everything else goes to sleep, or flees to warmer places, but these little fish come out of the depths and swim around in the cold waters."

"They're pretty," Sasha said. "Shall we stop here for a while? I have no idea how late in the day it is, but it feels as though we have been walking for quite some time and it is getting darker."

David looked up at the sky—well, the trees and the snow and the bits of sky not entirely blocked—and said, "It is getting on toward dark, so we may as well stop. I'll get a fire going."

Sasha waved the offer aside. "Admire your fish. I can start a fire and prepare dinner." That got him another smile, and Sasha hastily stood before he gave into a sudden, burning need to lean forward and steal a kiss.

The fire took only moments, and Sasha was happy for the distraction of putting together a travel stew—calling it stew at all was ridiculous, really—as it kept him from brooding about his lack of memory or pondering how David might taste. It seemed wholly unfair, after taking his memories, for life to then throw him a distraction. Saving the world seemed like a task that did not leave room for distraction, and yet

Sasha found himself very thoroughly distracted whenever David entered his sight.

He sighed at himself and added a portion of the dried herb mix he'd packed. The longer he could give his food flavor, the happier he would be.

David wandered over just as he finished setting the stew to simmer, still smiling and happy as he sat down right next to Sasha. "Reimund was the one who showed me the fish, on my first trip to Two Mill. I was only ten, and the men with us were grumbling because they thought I was too young. Even Killian wasn't allowed to go until he turned fourteen last year, and his father has made the trip nearly all his life."

It did not really surprise Sasha at all that Killian had been made to wait until he was much older—that boy acted exactly his age. "Two Mill is where you buy supplies for the village, right? And where you saved Killian from a lashing."

"Yes," David said, flinching.

"You're very brave," Sasha said.

David shrugged. "It would have killed Killian. I just don't understand why sorcerers—" He closed his mouth, looking horrified. "I'm sorry, I should not speak—"

Sasha held up his hands. "Peace, David. I think it is clear that I am nothing like the other sorcerers. I may lack a great many memories, but I am absolutely certain I dislike them as much as everyone else."

"Your whip doesn't have the metal bits," David said. "I noticed when I removed your things. I thought it was strange. They always have metal at the end."

"The sole purpose of such things is to cause pain," Sasha said. "Whips such as these were meant first for herding; it's the noise that matters, not how much pain it can inflict. The idea of using them to hurt came later. Even now, I use it mostly to keep the Sentinels disoriented. Any pain I cause them is secondary. A sword is much more useful. The sorcerers use their modified whips just to be cruel."

David nodded and smiled softly, saying shyly, "I'm glad you're not like them."

"Me, too," Sasha whispered, and he did not even remember moving. David drew a sharp, startled breath, and Sasha started to draw back, horrified by his own behavior—but then David leaned in, chasing his mouth, and after that, Sasha was helpless to do anything but kiss him.

David's lips were soft, unmoving at first against his, but then he seemed to figure out what to do, kissing Sasha back awkwardly, but with true heat. It was not the best kiss Sasha had ever had, but it was by far the sweetest.

"You—" David stared at him wide-eyed. "You kissed me."

Sasha laughed and did it again. David responded faster the second time, hands fluttering before one finally settled on Sasha's shoulder, fingers curling into his shirt as their mouths slid together. Given how easily David was learning, he would be nothing but a delight in bed.

The thought was cold water to Sasha, and he drew back, disgusted with his own behavior. He was the lowest of the low to take advantage of David—

Whatever would have happened next was prevented by the sound of horses. Sasha stood up as a group of five men rode into the clearing. All but one of them had a diamond on their forehead. Fire and ash. Beside him, David drew a sharp breath, and Sasha swore he heard the word 'Seer'.

And yes, one of the men had a circle on his forehead rather than a diamond. He and the man beside him both radiated impressive power. They were not as powerful as Sasha, but combined they might prove problematic.

The man beside the Seer, clearly the sorcerer in charge, looked between Sasha and David, then eyed Sasha coldly. "What is going on here?"

"I was badly injured by a Sentinel two weeks ago," Sasha said. "This young man nursed me back to health. He needs to journey to Unheilvol to hear his fate, and I am escorting him." When the man narrowed his eyes, Sasha realized he was missing something. Instinct made him tack on, "My lord. I am sorry, the injury has left my wits quite addled."

David tensed beside him, but to Sasha's relief, said nothing. It would be far too easy for David to give away the truth, and Sasha really should have thought of that sooner. If he had learned anything over the years, it was that men most often died when they were distracted.

"You have better things to do with your time than play escort a single peasant," the man snapped. "Where have you been that you've heard nothing—" He broke off, narrowing his eyes. "What is your name?"

Sasha wondered what exactly had given him way. "My name is Sasha."

"That is not a Schatten name," the priest said sharply

"No, it's not," Sasha agreed, and in one smooth motion grabbed his whip, flicked his wrist to uncoil it and sent it snapping through the air. The sharp *crack* echoed through the dark forest, startling the horses. Sasha cracked it again, again.

The men threw themselves off their horses, landing haphazardly in the snow. Sasha coiled his whip and put it away before drawing his sword as the men approached. "David, get out of the way," he ordered without looking.

As the men rushed him, the tang of their magic sharp on the air, Sasha held a hand out toward the fire, then threw his arm forward. The fire followed his movements, and flames burst into furious life as they flew toward the men barreling at him.

The nearest one screamed, more in panic than in pain, and faltered enough two others crashed into him and the whole trio went falling. Sasha left them and focused on the main sorcerer, barely getting his sword up in time to meet the hard swing that came at his head. The man's violet eyes flashed, all the warning Sasha had before blinding, painful light burst around him, driving him to his knees.

Light of Truth, he knew it to be called. A painful, paralyzing light that was a unique trick of the shadow sorcerers of Schatten. Sasha heard the sorcerer laugh, felt more than saw the man loom over him. Rough hands grabbed him and hauled him back to his feet.

"Here I thought taking care of you would be more difficult," the man said. "However did someone like you kill the High Sorcerer?"

Sasha grabbed the hands holding on to him, and the man screamed in agony and dropped him, stumbling back. The painful light went out as though snuffed. Sasha stared at the man, who clutched his left hand and glared furiously at him.

"How did I kill your High Sorcerer? I am better trained and more powerful, that's how," Sasha replied, and held his right hand out toward them, as though beckoning them to take it, and said, *"Gods of sleep, of respite, of solace, grant peace to my enemies."*

"What—" the priest never finished his question as the scent of roses filled the clearing along with a fine, dark gray mist. Within seconds of breathing it in, the priest and sorcerers all dropped to the ground, out cold.

A soft, hissing sound resonated through the clearing, and then all was normal again.

Sasha checked them over, removed anything useful they had that could be easily carried, then went to the horses. Three of them, he stripped down and sent running back in the direction of Black Hill. The remaining two, he emptied the saddlebags and began to repack his own belongings.

"You can't steal their horses!" David said.

"I think horse theft is the least of my crimes," Sasha replied, mouth quirking in amusement. He turned, and the amusement faded when he saw the look on David's face. "David ..."

"You're the one—you killed the adult Sentinels. You're the reason everyone's fate is going wrong."

"What makes you think their fates were right to begin with?" Sasha asked, even as a heavy weight settled in his chest.

Tears filled David's eyes. "Reimund was supposed to die an old man. He said so. Then everything started going wrong because of you and now he's dead early. The barriers are gone. Everything—everything is wrong because of you. And I think maybe I knew that, but you were so ... so different," he finished on a whisper, though it was clear from his hesitation that was not the word he'd initially planned to say. "Who are you, really?"

"I don't know," Sasha said. "I never lied about the curse on my chest; it really has taken most of my memories and left what remains in pieces. I only know I am here to save Schatten."

"Schatten doesn't need saving. Lord Teufel sealed us away to protect us."

Sasha tried to tamp down on his anger because it wasn't David who sparked it. He hated Teufel for so subjugating Licht's people that they believed he was doing the right thing. "Do you really believe that? Does your life really make you happy? Locked in your village, unable to travel without permission lest you be hunted down by beasts? Whipped and left for dead because you accidently knocked into a man in a crowded street? Tell me what about your life you love, David."

David opened his mouth, then closed it again. But Sasha knew that look on his face: fear, anger born of fear, and a resistance to change. What had he expected? It was going to take more than a couple of weeks and a few stolen kisses to convince someone that he had a right to hate what Teufel was doing to him—to all of Schatten.

"You're not from here," David said at last.

"No," Sasha said. "I am from Pozhar, on the other side of the Haunted Mountains—what we have always called the Jagged Mountains. I came here to save Schatten."

"But—chaos will destroy us. It destroyed everything before. Reimund would still be alive if chaos hadn't changed his fate!"

"I am sorry about your father," Sasha said and finally moved toward David, something inside him breaking at the way David took a hasty step back. "I would never hurt you, David. You saved my life."

"Maja saved your life."

Sasha shook his head and said softly, "No, it was definitely you, David." He stepped close, and when David held still that time, pressed his right hand to David's forehead and silently willed him to sleep. Catching the unconscious David in his arms, Sasha walked back to his horse and secured David over the saddle.

Next, he went about cleaning up the campsite and securing the men he had put into a much deeper sleep. When they were arranged around the fire, he murmured, "Fire warm and protect you." The campfire flared higher, a ring of flames bursting out and spreading to encompass the group then vanishing, leaving a shield of warmth and protection.

Looking back toward the horse, Sasha sighed and remembered the warmth and taste of innocent kisses. He sighed again as he walked to his horse and mounted, keeping David firmly in place as he rode off toward Oak Hill.

Sasha would deposit David there, make arrangements to ensure he reached Unheilvol, then be on his way. He let go of David to run his fingers across his stomach, where his wounds were mostly healed, but still sore. Before them, he had been content to travel alone. Had been fairly certain that, at the end of the journey, he would die alone.

Two weeks with David had reminded him what it was like not to be alone, and Sasha had the sense that alone was all he had felt for a long time. But better to have two weeks and those brief kisses than nothing at all.

Gods willing, he would accomplish his goal and someday, David might not hate for it.

In the meantime, he would ensure David's safety before continuing on his solitary journey.

Sentinels

Friedrich tossed and turned in his bed, unable to settle. A day of people flooding Raven Knoll in search of protection and food had left Unheilvol scattered, the priests unable to fulfill their regular duties because they were pulled away to help the city residents handle the flood of people. He had listened to report after report of Sentinel attacks all over the country. Coupled with the relentless snowfall, it added up to nothing but misery and far too many deaths.

And it would not stop until they located the child of chaos and took him to Sonnenstrahl. *I don't even know how to get into Sonnenstrahl. I assume Teufel will give me a key?*

Key? Not so much. But I'm sure the Great Sentinels will let you pass.

No one has seen Sonnenstrahl in over nine hundred years. I don't think anyone has approached the Great Wall in nearly as long. Even he shuddered when thinking about it. The Great Sentinels guarded the gates of the Great Wall, and they did not hesitate to kill any who drew too close. Legend said there was a thirteenth Great Sentinel that wandered the land, but Friedrich had never seen him nor heard of sightings from better than a third hand source. *I wonder if they are truly as big as rumor holds.*

They are, Drache said grimly.

The regular adult Sentinels are big enough. How do such creatures sustain themselves? Especially since they do not leave their gates.

Magic—and the occasional stray fool, I have no doubt.

Friedrich grimaced at the thought. He turned over on his side and stared at his room. It was an empty room, save for the essentials. He'd never been much for possessions. When he'd arrived in Unheilvol years ago, he'd had nothing but the clothes he wore and a string of wooden prayer beads. That strand had been lost years ago, but Friedrich still missed them, the simple life they spoke of. His prayer beads of amethyst and onyx spoke only of a life he loved and hated in equal measure.

A life he would be sacrificing—quite literally. He couldn't imagine that defying Teufel resulted in anything other than death. *But he was going to kill me anyway.*

His mind played over the same words he had already recalled a thousand times. *Find the child of chaos, capture him, bring him to me at Sonnenstrahl, and I'll give you the death you have craved these nine hundred years. Defy me, try to fight me as you once did, and I will ensure that you die as you always have—and that you will take all of Unheilvol with you.*

What death he had craved for nine hundred years?

Friedrich could feel Drache's discontent, his frustration, at not being able to explain what he clearly knew. Giving up on any pretense of sleep, Friedrich climbed out of bed and got dressed, then wandered the halls of the temple until he reached the front steps.

Unheilvol rested on the top of a hill that overlooked the city of Raven Knoll. It was the largest city in the country, though Gold Rock was close and boasted the Field of the Rock that gave the city its name. According to legend, it had been a favorite place for Licht to sit and watch his people, and occasionally he could be found there, willing to listen and give council.

Licht never cared for closed spaces. He liked to be out in the sun and wind. It's why all his temples are so open, or were. Teufel prefers his rooms and walls and labyrinths. Better for keeping people contained.

"Mm," Friedrich murmured, looking out over the dark city. There were patches of weak light here and there, and the occasional slip of indistinguishable noise reached his ears. Far at the end, he could see the larger fires atop the guard towers of the city gate.

Tilting his head up, he looked at the shadowy image of the moon behind thin clouds. The snow had ceased falling for a time, but he knew it would return. *What is the purpose of so much snow? Winter has never been so bad before.*

It keeps people where they are, makes them too afraid to travel.

Yet they travel anyway. Raven Knoll cannot handle too many more people, not over an extended period. We are a city of transients. He didn't want that many more people to die when he defied Teufel. Though Teufel had only said Unheilvol would die with him, Friedrich did not doubt he would harm the inhabitants of Raven Knoll as well.

Hopefully he will not realize your defiance until it is too late. You are doing the right thing, beloved.

I know, Friedrich said with a sigh. He just wished the right thing did not put so many people at risk. Men were not meant to be tangled up with gods. Something he should have remembered before he became the bed toy of a god's shadow.

But from what few, wispy memories he possessed, he was not certain there been any way for him to have said no.

There was not, and it was not like being in his bed was entirely a chore. Far from it. Drache's sigh rolled through his mind. *Once, the danger and the darkness had its appeal.*

Hardly the first time—or the last—that someone made a stupid decision for such foolish reasons. At least I know better now. Every time he thought about that brief interlude with Teufel, his stomach churned. So easy to see how once that beauty and darkness had seduced him. It would have been childishly easy for Teufel. Who would be able to resist being hand-picked by a god to serve as his most powerful priest and his favored paramour?

He shook his head at himself and cast his eyes over the city again, feeling restless with no real reason to put to it. *Can you tell me anything about Sonnenstrahl?*

A little bit, I think. That constraint has eased now that you've been ordered to go there. The heart of Schatten, the location of the Citadel, once the seat of Licht's power. That is where we will meet, you and I. The Citadel spreads out a great distance in all directions, forming a great circle. Twelve paths spread out from it, turn into twelve roads, the rays of the sun reaching out to Licht's people, inviting them always to come closer to him. Around the Citadel is the white stone city of Sonnenstrahl itself, once beautiful and vibrant. Now, it is only a broken relic, overrun with thorny vines from which grow poisonous black roses.

The words provoked an ache of sadness, of longing, in Friedrich.

It was home, Drache said. *Now it is little more than a graveyard. Licht would have wept to see his beloved city reduced so.*

Licht ... lost forever, slain by his brothers for daring to defy them, because he wanted what was best for his children. Friedrich wondered what the true story was.

I wish I could say, but I'm not sure even I know the whole of it.

Who are you Drache? Why do you know so much?

I am memory, a relic, a fool. That is all I can say.

Friedrich sighed and turned to go back into the temple, walking through the halls, steps echoing faintly, as he made his way to his prayer chamber. He lit the candles, focused on the way the light flickered and danced against the gleaming black marble walls, let it pull him into a trance.

The first thing he did was cast out for Karl, trailing along threads of past, present, and future. It was the past that snagged, and Friedrich let the Seeing wash over him.

> *Karl remained silent, eyes locked on the sorcerer. Something was strange about him, though there was nothing about his appearance that Karl could pick out. Well, his pale skin, but he had seen survivors of Sentinel attacks suffer stranger side effects.*

Beside him, Boris said coldly, "What is going on here?"

"I was badly injured by a Sentinel two weeks ago," the strange sorcerer said. "This young man nursed me back to health. He needs to journey to Unheilvol to hear his fate, and I am escorting him." The man paused, and Karl was just about to reprimand him for being so unbelievably rude when the man belatedly added, "My lord. I am sorry, the injury has left my wits quite addled."

Karl saw it then, what had been bothered him—the man's weapons. No sorcerer had a sword like that, with a showy jewel in the pommel. And his whip was wrong. Even coiled up as it was Karl could tell it did not remotely resemble the whips used by the sorcerers.

He nudged Boris slightly, then flicked his eyes to the sword.

"You have better things to do with your time than escort a single peasant all over," Boris snapped. "Where have you been that you've heard nothing—" He broke off as he saw what Karl had pointed out. "What is your name?"

"My name is Sasha."

"That is not a Schatten name," Karl said, furious that the bastard was impersonating them so successfully. How had he managed to make the diamond on his forehead? None but Teufel could bestow that mark.

"No, it's not," the man replied, and before they could react, he grabbed his whip, flicked his wrist to uncoil it, and send it snapping through the air. The sharp crack echoed through the dark forest, startling the horses. Karl tried to regain control, furious their horses were reacting to a sound they should have known—but no, they had been forced to obtain new horses, no thanks to the light-loathed Sentinels.

Despite his best efforts Karl was thrown from his horse and landed with a pained grunt in a pile of snow. By the time he regained his feet alongside the others and faced the imposter, the man had drawn his sword and was preparing to attack again. "David, get out of the way," the man ordered the peasant he was with.

Karl hung back as the sorcerers rushed him, the air filling with the acrid flavor of magic, making the hairs on the back of his neck stand up. He was a Seer, for shadow's sake, not a sorcerer. He should not be forced to fight.

The man held a hand out toward the fire, then threw his arm forward. Karl could only gawk, irritation overtaken by disbelief and envy at the way the fire followed the man's movements, enormous flames filling the air and headed directly for them.

He flinched as the sorcerer in the front of the group screamed, and his moment of hesitation was regretfully enough that the two others behind him crashed into him and the whole trio went falling. The imposter shifted his attention to Boris, raising his sword just in time to block Boris' swing. Karl felt the rise in magic and shielded his eyes in the moment before Boris cast the Light of Truth.

Boris laughed and hauled the imposter to his feet. "Here I thought taking care of you *would be more difficult. However did someone like you kill the High Sorcerer?"*

The imposter grabbed Boris' hand, and Karl recoiled in dismay when Boris screamed in agony and abruptly let go of the impostor. The Light of Truth went out as though it had been nothing more than a candle. Boris and the impostor glared at each other.

"How did I kill your High Sorcerer? I am better trained and more powerful, that's how," the imposter said. He stretched his right hand out toward them, palm out as though he was offering to help them up. The back of Karl's neck prickled again as the man intoned, "Gods of sleep, of respite, of solace, grant peace to my enemies."

"What—" Karl started to say, wanting an explanation, but then the spell took hold of him and the world went black.

When he woke again, he was in a dingy, dimly-lit room of a house. "Where am I?" he demanded.

The door opened a moment later, and an old woman stepped in. She smelled like herbs and as if she had not bathed in days. Karl wrinkled his nose. "Hag, where am I? Where are my men?"

"You are in Black Hill. Some of our hunters found you while they were out looking for food. They brought you back here, since Oak Hill is too dangerous a place to be anymore. You are lucky the Sentinels did not get you, my lord. Your men are staying in other houses; I did not have room for all of you here. They are awake, if you want—"

"Fetch them," Karl snapped. "We will need horses and food—immediately, hag."

The woman's mouth tightened, but she turned and left. Karl swung his legs over the edge of the bed he was on, feeling dizzy and faintly ill. Magic. That damn imposter sorcerer had used some sort of strange magic on them.

He'd had a peasant with him. David, he'd called the boy. That might come to something. Given his location, he would hazard someone knew the boy—and knew of a strange sorcerer injured by a Sentinel. If that part of the story was true.

Figuring out the truth would be easy enough, and then he would find that sorcerer and teach him a lesson. He would drag the light-loathed bastard back to Unheilvol. He would not let Friedrich steal all the glory, either. He was by far a better High Seer than that half-mad fool. Lord Teufel would see that.

Friedrich broke off, amused despite himself. *He thinks me only half-mad? I think I'm flattered.*

He is the fool to be so reckless. It will be what destroys him.

I tried to warn him. He laid his traps; eventually he must empty them.

Drache's discontent was a soft rumble in Friedrich's mind. *I still do not want him harming you.*

He cannot do me more harm than I have done to myself, than Lord Teufel has done. Karl is a child, and while he might be a powerful Seer, he lacks everywhere else. He does not even seem capable of guarding his thoughts, though he knows my powers. No, Karl does not concern me. Do not be troubled about him.

Drache rumbled again, but let the matter rest.

What interests me is that the intruder now bears a black diamond. He was immune to the Light of Truth. I have never seen magic like his, and though I saw him kill the High Sorcerer, it is still disconcerting ...

He is a sorcerer, if not of Schatten. If I had to guess, I would say he is a fire child. They were the only ones who truly rivaled Schatten in magical ability. That spell he used to put them to sleep, though, was an invocation of the gods. He invoked the Basilisk, which is ... breathtaking, really. I think the only one who might stand a chance against him is you. It is fortunate for all of us, beloved, that you and he are on the same side.

Friedrich nodded. *What has that boy, David, to do with anything?*

I do not know. I would wager nothing, but time will tell. You could cast out for him.

Maybe later. I have a feeling the man was telling the truth about escorting him to repay a debt. If it is true, then he is journeying to us here anyway. We'll see how he figures into everything then, if he does at all.

As you wish, Drache said.

Friedrich once more let himself fall into a trance, but instead of focusing on any one thing he simply let his mind wander, let Visions come to him. He was not surprised when the one that immediately rose up was the one that had plagued him for weeks and continued to be a source of frustration.

> *Sadness and rage. The dark of a moonless night. Anything can happen where nothing can be seen. A choice must be made: darkness or shadow.*

He opened his eyes, frustrated as ever by the vision. Whose fate was to choose between darkness or shadow? What sort of choice was that?

Drache's voice rippled through his mind. *Without light, shadows are nothing more than darkness. Without shadows, one does not appreciate the light. Light and shadow, chaos and fate, life and death. I have told you many times, beloved, these things need each other. There must be balance. Schatten withers from the effects of too much fate. But chaos—*

His words stopped at the sound of a distant, thundering roar. The echo of it had barely faded out when another came—then another. Friedrich ran back toward the front of the temple, vaguely aware of the thud of additional feet as other priests did the same.

At the top of the steps, he stared and looked down at the city below, the distant, ominous glow of violet eyes. Three sets and of a size that meant they could only be full grown Sentinels. More roaring, the sounds of destruction, people screaming. *What are Sentinels doing in Raven Knoll?*

They are probably running out of food in the smaller towns and villages, Drache replied.

The words made Friedrich shudder. *I have to do something, but I have no idea how to fight a Sentinel.*

Magic.

I don't know that kind of magic!

But even as he said the words, he was racing down the steps, down the hill, and into the city itself. He ran down the center road that divided the city in half, cutting a straight line from the gate to the temple. A Sentinel stood in it, large enough to take it over completely, tail and claws decimating everything in easy reach.

Friedrich froze, horrified, as the Sentinel snatched up a young man, crushed him in its jaws, and began to devour him. Turning away, Friedrich threw up. Heard the Sentinel grab another person.

They need you. You have the power. Light of Truth—even the Sentinels cannot fight that when it is powerful enough.

Wiping his mouth on his sleeve, Friedrich let his power flow through him. It was almost like falling into a trance, but rather than pouring that power into Seeing, he threw his hand in the air and willed the Light of Truth into being.

High above the city, light burst—bright, white, paralyzing and even painful to everyone who was touched by it. The Sentinels roared in fury, but could not move.

It will not last long, beloved. You have no sword to drive into its brain or to slit its throat open. A killing curse, then.

I don't know any curses. I'm a Seer, not a sorcerer.

Once, they were one and the same. The Seers of Schatten were the most powerful magic users in the world. Sentinels are as cursed as the rest of the children of Teufel. Show them mercy.

At Drache's words, the spell came to him, a memory dredged up from a previous life. Swallowing his terror at the enormous beast that loomed as large as the houses he stood between, Friedrich held his hands out palm up and fingertips tilted down, as though offering something—or urging the Sentinel to come to him. *"No creature of Licht was ever meant to suffer so dark and dreary a fate. Torture yourself no further, but find peace in the mercy of the light that loves you."*

Brilliant golden light poured from Friedrich's hands and pooled over the road, falling across the enormous feet and legs of the Sentinel. It crawled up over the Sentinel, consumed him, and with a last, mournful roar the beast fell to lie in the road, dead.

Friedrich immediately ran down an alleyway, cutting through the city until he reached the next looming shape right as the light of truth began to fade. He killed it the same as the first, but the third one began to wreak havoc once more before he could reach it.

And by the time he finally killed it, the city was teeming with dozens upon dozens of smaller, younger Sentinels—

from the babies still in serpent form, but the length of two or three men, to the adolescent and young adults who ranged in size similar to that of ponies.

What had drawn so many to Raven Knoll? *I thought you said they survived on magic and the odd snack.*

That is only the Great Sentinels. These ordinary ones are just that—ordinary. They are as affected by the weather as the people. Sufficient food is scarce, the weather is brutal, and now with the barriers down ...

But if they've all been driven here, what has become of the outlying villages? Surely they have not all been ...

I don't know, Drache said quietly, but that too-quiet tone only confirmed Friedrich's fears that the Sentinels had already killed too many people. If he failed to stop Teufel, so many more would die.

He cast another Light of Truth, giving people a chance to kill or flee the Sentinels around them. Ignoring the dizziness and exhaustion that washed over him, he pressed on. Everywhere he looked, there were people dead or dying. Soldiers, sorcerers, and priests all worked together to stop the influx of Sentinels, but in so large a city, overcrowded and still in the dead of night ...

A priest caught his eye, one arm bleeding, a cut on his cheek, his robes ruined. Friedrich crouched down in front of him, resting a hand on his leg in reassurance. "You've been very brave."

The priest gave a shaky laugh, face wet with blood and tears. "I grew up in a village that was right in the middle of a favorite area for Sentinels. It's located near hot springs and all these caves that are kept warm by them. I used to brag that Sentinels didn't scare me as much because I saw so many as a child before I was brought here. That is my lesson learned, isn't it, High Seer?"

"You're out here fighting rather than off somewhere hiding," Friedrich said. "Do not belittle your own bravery. How is your arm?"

"It's bearable, not much more than a scratch and not enough venom in it to do more than make me really tired later," the man replied.

Friedrich nodded. "Well, go ahead and start helping people make it to Unheilvol. We'll put as many there as we possibly can, and then figure out what to do next. The city is no longer safe. Tell everyone you see who is not fighting to gather supplies and help people make it to the temple."

"Yes, High Seer," the man said, and he stood up, swayed a bit, then set his jaw and moved off to carry out Friedrich's orders.

Once he had vanished from sight, Friedrich pushed on, killing remaining Sentinels, helping people where he could, ordering anyone still able-bodied to help the others. By the time the city had quieted, there were far too many dead.

He stopped in one of the open squares and looked out over the people gathered there, each one battered and weary, some asleep and … *Some of them won't make it to morning. This isn't right. Life isn't fair, but this is beyond that. This is cruel.*

This is Teufel, Drache replied flatly. *This is him reminding everyone that their safety, their very lives, are in his hands and he can snuff them out whenever he so desires. He wants that child of chaos.*

I hope someone brings him too me soon, then, or that he comes to me of his own volition.

If he is intent on destroying Teufel, then likely he is headed straight to the Great Wall.

He'll never get past the Great Sentinels.

A man who can call down the power of the gods themselves is not going to be impeded for long by the Great Sentinels. But he would be wiser to take you with him. I hope that one way or another, he comes to Unheilvol before he begins his direct assault.

I hope whatever he intends to do, he does it soon, before there is nothing left of Schatten to save.

Another scream rose up, and Friedrich mustered his flagging strength to help his people and get them within the relatively safe walls of Unheilvol.

Living

"Boy, the caravan is getting ready to leave."

David turned from the window he'd been staring out of and retrieved his bags from the floor at his feet. "Thank you." The woman grunted, clearly long past done putting up with him, and stomped off. David made certain his bags were settled comfortably, then trudged downstairs and outside into the street and down to the square where the caravan was just finishing packing up.

He still could not believe that Sasha had left him, had gone on without him.

Sasha was the reason Reimund was dead, the reason the barriers were gone and everyone was dying and afraid to leave their houses. He was the reason everything was going wrong. David should have been glad they had parted ways, especially since he'd overheard the other day at dinner in the tavern that people were actively looking for him now—men like the sorcerers he'd knocked unconscious. What would happen if anyone of them caught Sasha?

He wasn't supposed to care, because Sasha was the source of the problem. Once he was caught and taken to Unheilvol to be dealt with there, everything would go back to the way it should be. But everything Sasha had ever said to him kept repeating in his head. He remembered all that Sasha had done for Black Hill. Everything he'd done for David.

He also remembered those kisses. For those few minutes, sitting in the campsite waiting for dinner, the world had seemed like a wonderful place to be. Then those stupid sorcerers had shown up and ruined everything.

"Ready to go?" A gruff voice asked, drawing David from his thoughts. He looked at the man, someone he vaguely recognized as having made the journey to Two Mill with him before, and nodded. "Up on your horse then, boy," the man said, and David obeyed. It was going to be slow travelling, but there were many like him who could not afford to wait any longer to journey to Unheilvol. The rest of the unusually large caravan were either desperate for supplies, or gambling that a city would be safer. Too many had already died in Oak Hill; David was sick with worry about the people in Black Hill. He wanted to go back, take his chances, but he knew he would be of no help to anyone there.

He kneed his horse into motion as the caravan headed out, keeping to the back of the group where he'd be mostly left alone. The falling snow coupled with the need to keep eyes alert for Sentinels made conversation impossible. David's thoughts drifted helplessly back to Sasha and that moment when the sorcerers ruined everything.

It wasn't the sorcerers' fault, however, as much he hated to admit it. He was the one who had ruined everything when he'd turned on Sasha. What was he supposed to have done, though? If not for Sasha, Reimund—and who knew how many others—would still be alive.

Sasha's words played over and over in his head. *"Does your life really make you happy? Locked in your village, unable to travel without permission lest you be hunted down by beasts? Whipped and left for dead because you accidently knocked into a man in a crowded street? Tell me what about your life you love, David."*

He'd loved Reimund. He loved Killian. After that … David couldn't think of a single thing. The harder he tried to argue with himself about it, that he'd been right to be angry with Sasha, the more he realized he'd just been afraid and had acted stupidly.

He would never get the chance to tell Sasha that, however, because Sasha was long gone and David did not know where to find him. Realizing that Sasha being lost to him hurt more than anything else forced him to accept what he should have realized back at the campsite.

David looked out over the landscape, willing Sasha to suddenly appear. He had no idea what Sasha was going to do, or what else he would change and by how much. Light, a future where he had no idea what would happen next sounded so much better than the certainty of knowing he would live and die fetching and bartering supplies in Black Hill.

Where would Sasha go? What was he planning to do? Was he still going to head for Unheilvol? That seemed the only place he *could* go if he wanted to stop Teufel. Would he still be there when David finally reached it? Shadows, he wished he could just forge on alone. If he had, he might have caught up to Sasha. Unfortunately, it was far more likely that he would have encountered a Sentinel and he had no way of fighting them. It was better to travel with the caravan, and he would just have to hope that he somehow ran across Sasha again in Unheilvol. David wished he had kept his stupid mouth shut.

He heaved a sigh and tried to distract himself, because if he kept playing the same thoughts over and over, he would drive himself to madness. There was nothing else to do, however, as they pushed on along a road that was barely visible. The snow fell steadily, just shy of being too heavy for travel to be possible, though if the wind kicked up it *would* become impossible.

Eventually, his mind drifted to his fate, to what he would hear when he entered Unheilvol as a penitent. If Sasha was messing with fate, however, if he really was chaos—well, obviously he really was—then would he still have a fate to be foretold? Would he have several? What would happen to the Seers if they could no longer See? Hadn't there always been Seers, even back in the days before Licht was lost?

What it would be like to go his entire life not knowing his fate? It was what he had done so far, why did that have to change? Why did he have to know how the rest of his life would play out? Why did he have to know how he would die?

Reimund ...

If not for Sasha, Reimund would be alive. But David did not want to imagine a life where he had never met Sasha.

He'd lost Reimund and gained Sasha on the same day and some part of him was all right with that. He did not like it, but … if that was the price …

Just thinking it made him want to cry, made him feel ashamed. He wanted Sasha back, though, wanted to say he was sorry, wanted a chance to see what might have come of those kisses. He never would, though, because he'd panicked and acted like a boy instead of a man.

David sighed and looked out over the landscape again, trying to think about something—anything—else, because thinking about Sasha would not bring him back. It was impossible to see much beyond the snow though, only hints of trees and a shadow that might have been the distant mountains or a figment of his imagination.

The only thing that mattered was there was no movement, no crunch of heavy feet moving a ponderous body through the snow, no fetid smell. David fervently hoped that it remained that way. He dreaded an attack like those he had already heard so much about.

When a halt was called a little while later, he froze briefly in surprise. Had so much time really passed? It did not seem like it … but then the alarm spread through the long caravan, whispers of a Sentinel corpse. David broke from the line and rode to the front, ignoring the shouts and questions thrown at him, until he reached the front of the line, where perhaps a dozen men were gathered around a massive mound of snow that had already been partially cleared away to reveal a dead Sentinel.

David tensed, relieved and stupidly hopeful when he saw the tell-tale whip marks across its snout and the ruined eye where a sword had been plunged into it, all the way into the brain. The slit throat was for good measure.

Sasha had killed it. Sasha had been there. "How long has it been dead?" he asked.

"A few days ago, I'd guess, though it's hard to say with the snow keeping the corpse frozen," one of the men said. "You look like you know who managed this."

Giving a casual shrug, David said, "I've seen dead Sentinels like this before—a sorcerer, they say, is behind it."

"The one they're hunting," another man muttered. "That one the High Seer ordered brought to him."

David shrugged again. "No idea. I just remember the dead Sentinels he left when I was coming back from Two Mill the last time."

"Hey!" a voice called out, causing the cluster of men to whip around, the guards going for their swords, the other men and women going for their knives. The source of the voice came up to them, panting and horrified. "Bodies! There's bodies over this way!"

They all followed the man's lead further down the road from the Sentinel's body and sure enough—four bodies left in the snow, two dead horses, and a third half-eaten. David turned away from the sight, grateful, at least, that the weather kept it from smelling and drawing further predators. A bit more searching turned up the remains of a campsite, and David realized he really had been so lost in thought more time had passed than he'd realized. Given the weather, they were making good time.

Unfortunately, they'd have to keep making it. The longer they were out there the likelier they were to run into Sentinels. If one Sentinel had attacked, it was likely others would as well. They were harder to prey upon while moving, though absolutely nothing was enough to stop a Sentinel when it was intent upon something.

Nothing, that was, except Sasha. David closed his eyes for a moment, recalling Sasha's smile, the warmth in his eyes, the way he always seemed to know the right thing to say. The feel of his mouth against David's, the way he felt when David had woken up to find they'd twined together in the night. How fierce he was in a fight, the ease with which he had defeated the Sentinels and Sorcerers that terrified all of Schatten.

The look on his face when David had turned on him.

It hadn't even been a look of shock, and that was the worst part. It had been resignation, as though Sasha had known the day would come and was sad only that it had arrived so soon. It was a look that said Sasha expected everyone to leave him, and David hated to have been one more disappointment in his life when Sasha had brought so much warmth and light to his own.

He just could not stay angry about Reimund, even if he should, even if it was wrong to accept it.

Someone spoke, drawing him from his thoughts. "These people were from Deer Run, even further southwest than Black Hill. I remember them because I urged them to wait to travel with us, but they feared a larger group would be easier to track in all this snow."

The man standing next to David snorted. "That will teach fools to listen to those of us who know better. They're lucky they made it as far as they did."

"They're dead," David said, anger sparking. "They're not lucky at all, and they weren't wrong. A smaller group would be harder to pin down in this weather. No sense in speaking ill of them now. We'd best just push on and hope we can find somewhere to rest that won't result in us winding up the same way."

Looking abashed, the man said, "You're right. Pity we can't burn them properly, give them a burial."

"We can on the way back, if we just mark the spot."

"I think the spot will be pretty clearly marked," another man drawled. "That Sentinel corpse isn't going anywhere, even if another one comes along to eat it when—if—the weather thaws."

Another man jerked around and glared at him, yanking away the cloth covering his mouth to say, "What do you mean 'if'? Of course it will! We won't be left in this winter forever, what are you trying to say?"

"I'm saying, this time of year the weather should be calming down, not getting worse," the first man said. "We all know it's wrong! The Sentinels are worse, the sorcerers are hunting one of their own because he turned rogue, which shouldn't even be possible, and the barriers have fallen. I'm *saying* that Lord Teufel is either punishing us, or has forsaken us! We're all thinking it; I'm just saying it!"

Another man bellowed in outrage and in the span of a breath, everything suddenly burst into violence. David scrambled away, retreating to the tree line, staring in horror as men and women alike began to brutally attack each other.

They were behaving like animals while the younger people—barely more than children, and some of them *were* children—all fled to join David. He urged them back until they were well hidden in the shadows of the forest.

When he was certain they were as safe as they could be, he returned to the raging group, grimacing at the blood smeared across the snow. So much of it had already turned to chunks of ice. His stomach churned.

Someone knocked into him, and David went crashing to the ground. He wiped snow from his face, kicked away the person hovering near him, rolled out of the way, and clambered to his feet. Everywhere he looked, people were fighting. What had made them snap so? Had it been brewing the entire time and he'd simply not noticed, too immersed in his own thoughts?

They shouldn't have been fighting. More than ever, cooperation was needed. Wasn't that how the people of Schatten had always gotten by? Yet when everything got difficult, suddenly they turned on each other. The words of an old admonition, repeated by the village priest to the point David had loathed hearing them, came suddenly and sharply to mind. *People are not good at controlling their own lives. Left to shape their own fates, they choose the wrong paths and make poor choices. Better to leave our lives, our fates, in the hands of the gods, who know better than us where and how we should walk through life.*

Watching them fight, David could not help but think that was true. The moment chaos descended and they all had to figure out what to do on their own, without trusting they were following their fate ... the dead were mocked and they beat each other in the snow, leaving children stranded, leaving all of them vulnerable to the Sentinels.

"Enough!" he bellowed, more shocked than anyone when the word cracked out, drowning out all other sounds. Everyone stopped and stared at him. David stared back, hands balled into his fists at his side. "What is this accomplishing? Is this how you behave when we are all in danger—from starvation, from cold, from Sentinels. If Lord Teufel is punishing us, or has forsaken us, maybe it is because we have forgotten how grateful we should be to him for ensuring that such things as this never happen. He abandons us and you turn on each other like beasts! Your children are hungry and scared and Sentinels could be upon us at any moment. Is that what you want? Try proving to Lord Teufel that we deserve his love and protection and stop showing him why we do not."

They stared a moment longer and then he felt the anger leech away, saw it replaced by shame. Apologies were murmured and slowly they began to help each other, returned to the horses, and called to their children.

Shaking from residual fear, unable to believe all that he had said, David slowly made his way through the throngs back to his own horse. He mounted up and waited while everyone else got settled.

"That was well done, boy," the man beside him said gruffly, and he reached out to clap David on the shoulder. "If we are feeling Lord Teufel's wrath, then clearly you are meant to set us back upon the path of the faithful."

David shook his head. "I am nothing, but a boy from a small village, and no one fit to show anyone back to any path."

"You're on your way to hear your fate, right? I would not be surprised to learn your fate is much greater than you think. Thank you for stopping us before we did something we would have truly regretted."

"I'm just glad it's over," David said quietly, and he pulled his face mask back up as the caravan finally began to move again.

His stomach churned, his mind at war between all that he had just said and all he had been thinking about Sasha. Which was better—fate or chaos? He looked over the people around him and saw that no one was happy.

He remembered how unhappy he had been his whole life, so resigned to his fate that he had not realized he had been merely existing until he had spent two weeks with the strangest, but most alive man he had ever met.

That was it, really: Sasha had seemed alive. He was always so quiet, so contained, so still, but he had burned brightly inside. People didn't need fate, they didn't need Lord Teufel planning their lives before they drew a breath. They needed someone like Sasha, who lived, showed them how to live, without dictating those lives.

David's throat ached, raw with repressed emotion, and he thought were it not so cold he would have given over to tears. He wanted Sasha back, more than anything else in the world. If he was meant to die the next day, in the next hour even, he would consider it a life well lived if he only got to see Sasha one more time and say that he was sorry.

He needed to accept he had lost that chance, needed to move on and try to live ... but the gnawing ache would not ease. Perhaps there might be a way to find Sasha in Unheilvol, as he had considered earlier. Surely, one way or another, Sasha would wind up there. All David had to do was get there in time and then wait. He could—

A deafening roar split the sky, a sound that shook him to the bones, shook the earth, spiked a paralyzing terror that left David crying despite the cold. All around him the others shouted in fear, and children began to wail, men and women alike weeping quietly. "What—what was that?" David finally managed to ask, then flinched and cowered as the horrific roar came again, and he barely kept his horse steady.

"That's a Great Sentinel," the man beside him said, voice trembling so badly that it took David a moment to understand the words. "Someone angered a Great Sentinel. But the Great Wall is nearly a full day's travel from here on a good day. Now? It would take at least twice that. Who would dare wander close to the Great Wall in times like these?"

Another roar came, louder and fiercer than ever—and then it was followed by another, though the second was different in tone. David realized it reminded him of the pained, dying cries of the smaller Sentinels that Sasha had killed in the village.

Realization struck him even as he cringed from another dying roar. Sasha wasn't going to Unheilvol—he was going straight through the Great Wall and into Sonnenstrahl.

It was far easier said than done, however, because legend said all of the Great Sentinels must be killed, or ordered to stand aside by Lord Teufel himself.

Sasha …

"Where exactly is the Great Wall from here?" he asked, yanking down his mouth cover to be better heard.

The man next to him did the same, eyeing him askance. "What does it matter? Let the fool die, if he wants to do something that mad. We wouldn't get there in time to help him, anyway."

"Just tell me!" David snapped.

Eyes widening, the man replied, "It's your fool neck boy, but Lord Teufel won't reward you for wasting your life on a fool. Head almost dead north, but after a day or so veer slightly west. It's hard not to run into it, really. I went close enough to see it once when I was a boy, before I heard my fate. Didn't see a Great Sentinel, by the mercy of Lord Teufel."

"Thank you," David said, and he kneed his horse to turn away.

"Boy—what do you think you are doing, truly? You're of more help here, like when you stopped the fighting. Don't throw all that away—"

David ignored him, urging his horse as fast as he dared in the weather, relieved when they reached the trees where the way was much clearer. He thought he heard voices calling after him, but he kept riding. Unheilvol was no longer an option; he was going to find Sasha no matter the cost.

The cost proved to be a very long, exhausting, and terrifying journey. He kept to the woods for as long as possible, making reasonable time since the ground was much clearer. The silence of it was unnerving, though not as terrifying as the occasional distant roar of a Sentinel. He jumped every time he thought he saw one, and did cry in relief when one passed by only paces away, seemingly too cold and exhausted to notice that food was nearby.

All too soon the forest came to an end, and he was forced to abandon his horse before plunging into so much snow and biting wind that David feared he would never be warm again. Even his mind was numb, unable to think past forcing his feet to continue moving—step, step, trip, stand, step, step, step. The misery of it made him want to give up. He *had* been a fool to leave the caravan on the tiny chance that he would find Sasha. But every time he thought of Sasha, he felt an ember of warmth, a spark of hope, and he was able to take another step.

Only once did he find shelter, in the remains of an old house that was more collapsed than not. How long he slept, he didn't know, but when he awoke, he was still cold and tired. He dragged himself out of the house, anyway, and resumed his exhausting journey. Only the dullest shreds of sunlight guided his way as he continued north for what he hoped was a day before he began to bear west.

What if he was wrong? What if he had hopelessly lost himself? It was better to die trying, however, than to live a life where he had not tried at all. Existing was safe. Living was dangerous, but he would face all the danger in the world if it led to Sasha.

Just as he began to give up, David ran—literally—into a wall. For a moment, he just clung to it, eyes closed and stinging with tears too cold to shed. When he finally got a hold of himself, he got his bearings and began to walk along the wall, hazarding a guess as to where he might find Sasha.

What if Sasha had gone the other way? What if David had taken too long and he was already somewhere else?

Ignoring the fear and doubt as best he could, David pushed on. He was tired, hungry, cold—so light-forsaken cold. If he failed, no one would look for him. He doubted anyone would miss him. That alone was enough to keep him going, keep him trying—until his foot caught on something and he tumbled into the snow with a yelp.

He scrambled up, tripped, and wound up on his back, out of breath and irritated with himself. He lay there until he calmed down, then drew a deep breath and climbed to his feet. David stared at what was just barely visible at the bottom of the snow—snow that was not nearly as deep as what he had just been trudging through. He knelt to get a closer look, pressed his fingers against it.

It was a road, an actual paved road. The stones were gray and dingy, cracked in most places and some places there were only holes where stones had been. Standing, he looked around—and then saw the enormous shape that towered so close to him. Looking it over, trailing his eyes all the way down its length, he realized it was the creature's tail he had tripped over.

A Great Sentinel—and it was dead. Disbelief and elation poured through David, making him forget the cold. "Sasha!" he bellowed. "Sasha!"

No one replied, but it wasn't as if he'd expected an answer. Hoped, perhaps, but not expected. David began walking around the dead Great Sentinel in hopes of a clue, any clue, as to where Sasha might be.

The Great Sentinel really was as massive as all the legends had said. It seemed the size of a few houses and taller than four or five of them stacked together. Walking around it seemed to take an age, and by the end he was trembling with the effort.

As he finished circling it, nearly back to where he had begun, he saw the door. It was near the enormous gate, which was made of thick, spiked iron bars and felt like magic even from such a distance. The bars looked as though each was as big as his arm, if not bigger; the entire gate looked too heavy to move. Strangely, when he looked through them he could see nothing—not a single hint as to what was on the other side of the Great Wall.

Strange, but at present it was the door beside the gate that really puzzled him. It must be a gatehouse, but why would there be a gatehouse at the Great Wall?

Well, at least he could rest, recuperate his strength, and try to figure out what to do next. Reaching the door, David shoved it open, stumbled inside, and managed to close it again. He turned around to take in his surroundings and cried out in shock when he saw the figure passed out before the dying remains of a fire.

Stumbling across the room as quickly as he could manage, he stiffly removed his pack and dumped it on the floor before he dropped down next to Sasha. Carefully looking him over, heart thudding in his chest, only after several minutes of checking and double checking did David slump back in relief. Sasha looked tired, and rather battered from his fight, but he was all right.

Wiping tears from his face, David set about rebuilding the fire, wondering absently who had left the pile of wood that was stacked in one corner. When the fire was burning and the little room began to warm up, he stripped out of his sodden clothes and quickly changed into dry ones. Next, he turned to Sasha, amused despite everything that he was once more nursing Sasha back to health. Tossing the wet clothes aside, he reached out to lightly stroke his fingers over the scars on Sasha's stomach.

How many more times would Sasha come so close to death? If David could choose his own fate, then he wanted that fate to be keeping Sasha alive.

Rifling through Sasha's bags, he found a change of clothes that did not smell great, but were dry. He quickly got Sasha changed and then set up a proper bed with both of their bedrolls. When that was done, he carefully dragged Sasha onto it, concerned and amused that he did not so much as stir.

After Sasha was settled he double checked the door was closed and threw the bar to secure it. He returned to Sasha and added a bit more wood to the fire before he lay down beside Sasha and drew their cloaks up over them. They fit together exactly as he remembered from those few nights they had shared a bed, and for the first time in days, David finally felt as though he was right where he was meant to be. Closing his eyes, he fell immediately to sleep.

Together

Sasha woke feeling as though he had been thrown against a wall and then stomped on. His back ached fiercely and his left hip felt as though someone had driven a hot knife into it. Whoever had attempted to bash his head in with a rock ... hadn't that happened before? ... needed to finish the job and put him out of his misery.

A hazy memory surfaced, then solidified: he *had* been thrown into a wall. The Great Wall, by a Great Sentinel. The scorching monster had a nasty tail swing and could move shockingly fast for something of its size. If he had to guess, he'd put the bastard at pretty close to sanctuary of the Cathedral of Ashes in size. That didn't include the wings that Sasha had gotten a hint of, and he was grateful the weather had kept him from learning how something so large was able to fly.

The smell of something cooking slowly drifted into his awareness, followed by the smell of a familiar tea. Memory smells. As tired and sore as he was, Sasha was not at all surprised he was smelling those things that reminded him of being warm and comfortable and safe, of those two weeks he had spent with David. The only thing better would have been the sweet, fresh-herb scent of David himself that even days of work and no chance to properly bathe could not entirely erase. He smiled ever so faintly, thinking of David's gentle touch as he helped Sasha to sit up so he could drink the tea that eased the worst of his pain.

He needed to open his eyes, get his bearings, and head for the next Great Sentinel. That reminded him he wanted a closer look at the gate the Great Sentinel had been guarding, to confirm that he really would have to kill all twelve in order to get through the Great Wall. He hoped it was twelve, and not thirteen as he feared, because the twelve he knew how to find were going to be difficult enough.

Sighing inwardly, stomach growling as his mind continued to insist there was food cooking, Sasha braced himself and tried to move—and immediately regretted it as every throbbing ache woke into sharp pain. Make a sound that was somewhere between a groan and a whimper, Sasha relaxed back into the bedding and prayed for unconsciousness or death.

Wait. Bedding? He hadn't made a bed ... had he? No, he hadn't. That scorching Great Sentinel had nearly gotten him, and Sasha had exhausted himself calling upon magic powerful enough to subdue it. He'd managed to retrieve his weapons and crawl, quite literally, into the gatehouse. It had taken all his remaining strength to light a fire, and then he had simply passed out.

So where in the Flames had the bedding come from? Sasha finally dragged his eyes open and at first, saw only dark. But as his eyes began to sort it all out, he realized he was covered by a cloak lined in dark gray fur. That wasn't his cloak; his was entirely black.

The sound of movement filtered into his awareness, and Sasha swallowed. He wasn't alone. Someone had found him. But who? How? Even David would not have known he was headed for the Great Wall—and even if he had, David had made it pretty clear he wanted no part of Sasha anymore.

Sasha gritted his teeth and shifted slightly, immediately regretting the movement, but fire and ash he was going to get up—

And then the cloak was pulled carefully away, and the fragrant, sharp scent of Black Hill's healing tea filled his nostrils. All Sasha saw, however, was David, who smiled in his shy, sweet way as he set the tea aside and helped Sasha sit up. "How are you feeling?"

"Like I was thrown into a wall," Sasha said hoarsely. He took a sip of tea when David held the cup to his lips, grateful for the way it soothed a throat he had not realized had taken the same beating as the rest of him had. "Which, incidentally, I was," he added, then took another sip of tea before asking quietly, "What are you doing here, David?"

David flushed and did not immediately reply, simply focused on helping him drink the tea until it was all gone. By the time he'd finished, the worst of Sasha's pain had been muffled. "Feel up to some food?" David asked.

"A little, perhaps," Sasha said. "Why are you here?"

"I woke up in Oak Hill and realized you were gone and ... I tried to head toward Unheilvol. I left with a caravan and was on my way. But it didn't feel right. Then everything went wrong and I no longer knew what to do. We heard you fighting the Great Sentinel, and I knew I had to try to find you."

Sasha's brows shot up at that. "You heard me fighting it and decided to come find me? Are you mad? You could have died! You had no guarantee I would be here or even where to find me—"

"I had to try!" David said, hands fisting in his lap. "All I could think was that I would never see you again, that things were so ... different, better, when you were around. That without you, I'd just be in Black Hill bartering supplies my whole life. You were good to us, and I shouldn't have gotten mad—"

Reaching out, Sasha stilled the flood of words with a finger to David's lips.

"I missed you," David finished, looking down, skin flushing.

Sasha slowly drew his hand back, admitting, "I missed you, too. But it was probably for the best that we parted ways, David. What I'm doing ... I am fairly certain I will not come out of it alive. I do not want you to die with me. Should I fail, being near me will not help you. If I succeed, you'll have an entire new life ahead of you."

"I want to stay with you," David whispered, looking at him, every thought and feeling plain upon his face. Such honesty, such openness, was a rarity in Sasha's world. How he knew that, he couldn't say, but he knew it was true. David was a wildflower when Sasha spent all his time amongst carefully cultivated roses.

He wondered if being with him would prove a chance for David to flourish, or cause him to wither.

David looked away. "I'm sorry I yelled at you and accused you of killing Reimund. It's not like you did it on purpose or anything. It's just ..." He trailed off, shaking his head. "Let me stay with you. I can make tea and food. I know the customs of Schatten and can move around without attracting attention—"

"It would be wiser for you to go," Sasha murmured. "But you're capable of making your own choices." Sasha was a selfish fool, and he knew it, but he also did not care. David had come for him, and he would be damned if he sent him away again. "You can stay if that's what you want," Sasha said. "I'm happy to have you back."

Beaming at him, David gathered up the tea cup and rose to fetch food. Sasha resisted an urge to drag him back and steal a kiss, mostly because he knew he was in absolutely no shape for even that much. Haste would not do him favors, either.

He shouldn't have been thinking about bedding David at all, but there was no point in denying that was exactly what he wanted to do—and was going to do, scorch the consequences.

Except that David was the one who would be hurt when Sasha died or returned to Pozhar. But if he lived, did he have to return? As usual, his mind provided no answers.

Thankfully, David pulled him out of his thoughts when he returned with a cup of soup that smelled remarkably fragrant. "Thank you," he said, relieved when he proved capable of holding the cup himself. "It smells wonderful."

"I've learned to carry herbs when I'm going to be travelling a lot," David said with a smile. "Anything that helps to stave off the monotony of camp food. But you do the same thing, so you know how awful camp food can get."

"Yes, all too well." Sasha closed his eyes, stomach growling for things it would never have again: borsht, schii, pelmeni ... he did miss the food back home.

He forced the thoughts away, not interested in torturing himself, and drank the soup, setting the cup aside when he was done. "I cannot believe you found me. How did you know where to go?"

David shrugged. "I didn't, really. I only knew to head for the Great Wall. From there, I just had to guess which direction you had gone. But I figured even if I picked wrong, eventually circling the wall would lead me to you."

"Did it occur to you that you would have run into a Great Sentinel I had not gotten to killing yet?"

The look on David's face, the way his skin paled, made it very clear he had *not* thought of that. Sasha smothered a smile by ducking his head, and only then did he realize that his bed was actually a combination of bedrolls and cloaks.

Looking up again, he asked, "How long was I asleep?"

"The better part of two days since I found you, and I don't think you were unconscious very long before that."

Two days. Sasha grimaced. "If this happens to me every time I kill one of those things, it's going to take months to kill all of them. Though it would be a good sight easier to do if the weather was not so brutal."

"Hopefully the weather will begin to ease soon," David said quietly, running his finger around the rim of his cup for a moment before he set it aside and fussed with the fire instead. "It should have stopped snowing this badly weeks ago, but it just keeps coming. Spring is only about a month away. I don't know what we'll all do if the snow carries over into the planting season ..." He trailed off, brow furrowed, teeth worrying his bottom lip.

Sasha looked away, reminding his body sternly that he wasn't in shape for *any* sort of nonsense, even if his only intent was to soothe. His gaze swept the room they were in, and a question he'd hazily asked himself before collapsing returned. "Why is there a gatehouse? I thought the Great Sentinels were the only ones who guarded the wall."

"I don't know," David said. "I thought it was strange, too. Was the wall perhaps here before Lord Licht was lost and back then they had guards to man the gates? I always thought back then Sonnenstrahl was welcome to all ..."

"I suppose it does not really matter," Sasha said and yawned. They needed to pack up and go, but he could not seem to muster the willpower to stand ...

When he woke again, it was to a much darker room and the feel of someone settling in alongside him, slowly and carefully, as though afraid of disturbing him. Sasha shifted, slid an arm around David's waist, and slid back into sleep, lulled by David's presence and the warmth of the fire.

The smell of food and tea roused him the second time, and Sasha cautiously moved, relieved when the pain proved to be bearable. He pushed back the cloaks and slowly sat up. David looked up from where he was sitting close to the fire heating water and smiled at him. "Good morning."

"Is it morning? I confess I have lost all track of the hours and days."

David laughed as he pulled the pot of hot water off the fire and began to fix them both tea. "I honestly have no idea, but 'good morning' seemed as suitable a greeting as any. Here's your tea. How are you feeling?"

"Thank you," Sasha said. "Sore—very sore—but I think moving will help more than resting at this point, as much as I would like to stay in here and out of that wretched cold. I grew up in weather such as this, though it was certainly never as bad as this. I would swear it was not even this bad when I first arrived here."

"It's getting worse," David said. "Like I said, normally it starts easing off by now. I never really minded snow in previous seasons. I never loved it, but I never minded it. Right now, I'd give almost anything to see a clear sky." He sighed and stared into his tea.

Sasha reached out, took David's hand in his, and when he looked up said, "I promise that I will do all that is in my power to get you those clear skies. Schatten has been too long in the dark; I will restore the light."

David swallowed. "You—you're not even from here. No one from the outside has ever come. Why did you?"

"If I had a grand and lofty reason, I do not remember it. I know only I had instructions to infiltrate Schatten and destroy Licht and that it feels like the right thing to do. But since I have met people, seen firsthand how they live and what Teufel has done, it has become a personal mission." He let go of David's hand to gently brush the back of his hand against David's cheek. "Very personal."

"You—you kissed me—" David said and then ducked his head, rolling his eyes at himself.

Sasha chuckled. "Yes, and I will do it again when I do not smell like Sentinel breath." He wrinkled his nose, then finished his tea and moved close enough to the fire to check on the soup that was still reheating. "We'll have to move on soon, if only because our supplies won't last forever and it's entirely too many days to anywhere."

"Oak Hill is only a couple of days away, though we'd be better off managing as long as we can and get closer to Two Mil or even Raven Knoll."

"Raven Knoll is where Unheilvol is located. Do you still seek your fate?" Sasha asked.

David shook his head. "No. I'm choosing you; that's fate enough for me. But it's the largest city in the country. If anyone has supplies to spare it will be them—but it's also where you're likeliest to be caught, so we're probably best off working our way closer to Two Mill."

Nodding, Sasha checked on the soup and then filled both their cups. "So we should head north east, then. I never would have found my way without your compass. I should have given it back when I left you in Oak Hill, but ..." He couldn't, because he'd been certain it was all he would ever have left to remind him of David.

It was the epitome of foolish to let himself get so attached so fast ... but he was only fooling himself in thinking that 'let' had ever been part of it. No one had control over who they let in, not really. Bitterness rose up at that thought, followed by an old ache. Sasha shoved it aside, tired of emotions and memories that had no faces. He sighed softly and sipped at his soup.

"What's wrong?" David asked softly and lightly touched the back of his hand.

Sasha turned his own and caught David's fingers before he could withdraw, soothed simply by that small touch. He was a fool, but he was pretty certain that fact had never stopped him before. "I am tired of my memories being lost. I remember my given name, that I am from Pozhar, that I was the only one capable of coming here, that I am meant to bring chaos to Schatten ... but precious little else. I have no idea who or what I am back in Pozhar."

David shifted closer, hand tightening in Sasha's, his face endearingly earnest as he said, "We'll find someone to break the curse, someone who won't turn you in. There must be somebody willing to do it, especially now that you're causing chaos." He smiled shyly, as if uncertain of the joke.

Despite everything, Sasha could not resist bending his head to kiss David briefly, the warmth and softness of his lips a balm that eased pains so old and deep Sasha could not remember when they hadn't been there. "Schatten first, then we'll figure out me. Now, for all that I loathe the idea of going back out into that snow, we need to be on our way."

Looking pleased, David nodded, rose, and began to move about their little campsite cleaning and packing. Sasha helped where he could, feeling old and feeble that he had to leave most of it to David. What was he doing with someone so young? David was just waking to the chance of a new, brighter life. If Sasha succeeded, David would countless options before him, options far better than him. Sasha had already done most of his living, even if at present he could not remember any of it. David had absolutely no reason to settle for him, and Sasha should not let him.

In the end, though, would Sasha even be an option? He still firmly believed that he would die when it was all over, for one reason or another. If by some twist of fortune he did not, there was no guarantee David would stay with him. It was far more likely that eventually David would move on as young men did—as they should.

So perhaps he should try to stop worrying about it and simply enjoy what he had for however long it lasted.

Nodding to himself, he finished helping David put out the fire and clean up the gatehouse. While David packed the bedding away, Sasha strapped on his weapons and made certain he would be able to use them. He settled his pack on his back and when David was ready, led the way outside. The snow fell slowly, almost lazily, but from the look of the clouds, the respite would not last long.

"The Great Sentinel is gone," David said, and Sasha realized he was right. The enormous body of the Sentinel was gone, leaving only mounds of snow. Where in the world had it gone?

"Must be something to do with the magic that made it," he said. "Hopefully the fact that it is gone is a good thing. I would stay and explore, but I'd prefer to make use of the relatively clear weather while we have it. Keep close to me, never lose sight of the wall."

David nodded and Sasha could not resist leaning in to take a brief kiss before he turned and started leading the way to the next Great Sentinel.

Madness

Despair clawed at Friedrich. Despair and frustration and exhaustion. People were dead. Raven Knoll was in shambles, and Unheilvol was overstuffed with survivors. There was no going down into the city; the Sentinels had overrun it.

Friedrich drank more wine, desperate to drown out what he could not force out. Teufel's words played over and over in his mind, Drache's voice equal parts reassurance and aggravation. And throughout, the overload of people confused his sense of Seeing. He dared not look anyone in the eyes when the ability was so overstimulated. The idea of touching people terrified him, because with every vision, the risk that he would finally break increased.

He could not afford to break, but if he was so close to breaking less than two months after Teufel had issued his orders …

Beloved …

Friedrich ignored him, ignored everything, and just drank, until the constant throbbing ache in his head finally began to ease. He did not dare think about what he would do when Unheilvol's stores of wine were finally exhausted.

Find better ways of coping.

Shut it, Friedrich snarled. *It is not as though you help, constantly commenting and demanding while I struggle to handle everything else.*

Drache did not reply, and Friedrich drank more wine. He tensed when he heard movement outside his door and breathed a sigh of relief when the voices eventually faded away. Standing up, swaying and stumbling a bit, he crossed his room to the one small window it featured and pushed aside the heavy tapestry covering it to stare out at the snow-ridden world beyond. Would the snow ever stop? Would they ever see spring?

He let the tapestry fall, ran his fingers over the worn fabric, the heavy embroidery depicting a field of white and purple flowers and a brilliant sun shining down upon them. Licht Blossoms, he knew they had once been called. If they still grew, it was not where anyone could see them.

Turning, Friedrich leaned against the wall and lifted his cup, draining it and licking traces of wine from his lips. More noise came from outside, and he flinched when someone rapped sharply at his door. Stumbling over to it, he drew a deep breath to steady himself, then opened it and said, "Yes?"

"High Seer, the Master Seer and Master Sorcerer have returned and request an audience with you."

"Of course," Friedrich said. "I will see them in the Hall of Vision."

"Yes, High Seer," the priest and with a bow, departed.

Closing his door again, Friedrich slowly went about getting cleaned up and dressed, finishing off his jug of wine as he did so, desperate for the numbing, floating feeling that would keep a barrier between him and the crush of people flooding his sanctuary. He longed for the peace of his quiet temple, but where else were the people to have gone? He was not sorry he had ordered everyone to Unheilvol.

He just wished he had better appreciated and braced for how badly it was affecting to him. It was not two voices that were going to drive him mad: it was thousands.

Out of ways to delay, Friedrich opened his door and slowly made his way through crowded hallways. He acknowledged various greetings and bows as he best he could, but was careful to keep his hands tucked safely within the voluminous sleeves of his robe to avoid touching anyone. The buzz of the wine muted his powers, but not enough he would be able to avoid a vision if it struck him full on.

By the time he finally reached the Hall of Vision, one of the only places left in the temple that was not overflowing with people—at least for the moment, since people were permitted to sleep there so long as there were priests to guard the pool and altar—Friedrich wanted desperately to crawl back to his room and hide beneath his blankets until it was all over.

Beloved—

Leave me alone, Friedrich said miserably, unable to take Drache's demanding presence on top of everything else.

You should come to me.

I can't. One, I never sleep deeply enough for it to be possible, or long enough for it to make a difference. Two, I have to be ready should something happen.

Wine will not help. It never helps. You know this. I can help. Let me.

Friedrich was tempted, so very tempted, but how could he sink deep into the recesses of his own mind when thousands of people were relying on him and at any moment the Sentinels might decide to mount the steps and attack Unheilvol. They had not so far, but that did not mean they would not. He had given up trusting anything Teufel had to say, except his threats to hurt people.

How was going he supposed to keep so many people alive? Supplies were low, and although there were groups that went into the city to forage, it was dangerous work that produced meager results.

They were problems he needed to better address, and he would, no matter how much he wanted to stay drunk and hidden, but for the moment, he set them aside and focused on the men standing near the vision pool. They were filthy, ragged, battered, and looked as though they would cheerfully slit his throat.

Friedrich could also not help but note they were alone. Likely they had dismissed the men who had traveled with them to eat and rest, but they should have had his prisoner. He stopped several paces away from them and reluctantly freed his arms as he said, "I am glad to see you have returned to us, Masters. Your skills and knowledge are sorely needed."

"You should not have sent us away in the first place," Boris said.

"Your High Sorcerer was murdered by the intruder whose actions have reduced Raven Knoll to its current state. There is no one else who could possibly bring him in. Why have you not done so?"

"We cannot find him," Karl snarled, hands balling into fists, anger filling his face. "We nearly had him once—"

"Yes, in the wood between Oak Hill and Black Hill," Friedrich interrupted. "He put you to sleep. What did you do after you woke in Black Hill?"

Karl's anger turned to hate as he realized that Friedrich had Seen him, but he said only, "We asked around, described the man—Sasha—knowing that at some point somebody must have seen such an odd sorcerer. He'd made some mention of being wounded and the boy he was with nursing him back to health. That proved to be true, and the boy—David—was from Black Hill. He's an ill omen; his parents once tried to flee Schatten and were killed by Sentinels. They were not sorry to see him leave with Sasha. We also learned that while Sasha was there in Black Hill, he somehow managed to restore their barrier." He made a face. "I say restore, but it was more like replace. Whatever he cast, it's stronger than the barriers that existed before."

Friedrich wished he could say he was surprised by that, but he wasn't. "To judge from what I have so far Seen of him, he is a sorcerer of a far greater ability than anyone here."

Except you, of course.

Karl does not need to know that. It will not help anything, only hasten his attempt to murder or banish me. Also, I told you to shut it.

"Why would you send us after someone you knew we could not defeat?" Boris demanded.

Friedrich cast them a scathing look. "Strength of magic does not ensure a victory. It is only one element of him, of anyone. Greater sorcerers than anyone in this room have been felled by people with no magical strength at all. That is why I sent both of you—strength of magic, strength of sword, strength of mind. If you failed, it is because you did not properly combine and utilize all your strengths."

Karl jerked as though to hit Friedrich, but at the last moment held still. "We don't stand much chance against a man who can control fire, defy the Light of Truth, and put an entire group of men to sleep with little more than a few whispers! You did not see his barrier, or all the Sentinels he has killed. If you want him, High Seer, you will have to get him yourself."

"So you never found him again after you lost him in the woods?"

"It took us days to make it back through the woods to Oak Hill," Boris said with a tired, aggravated sigh. "By the time we got there, we learned of a caravan that had departed with a boy named David from Black Hill amongst the travelers. We also learned that the sorcerer we're hunting left a couple of days before that—alone and without naming his destination. When we caught up to the caravan, most of them were dead and the others insensible from Sentinels attacks. We helped them get to Two Mill, but there the trail went as cold as all this light-forsaken snow. I am sorry, High Seer. We have done our best, but my men needed real rest and we were out of supplies. I think our best hope is that they may eventually have to come to Unheilvol. It is rapidly becoming the only relatively safe refuge, save for maybe Gold Rock. Black Hill might have a barrier in place, but it is too small to sustain much more than it has already taken in."

Friedrich nodded and said, "You have done your best and worked against more obstacles than any of us realized you would be facing. Rest for a few days, and then we will reconvene to see if we might develop a new plan. I think you are probably correct in that they must eventually come here, but I worry about how long that will take, and if Unheilvol will last that long. We are already stretched near to breaking."

"Then we definitely should not be venturing out again," Karl said.

"I said we would discuss it in a few days," Friedrich said. "Go and rest while you can because I have no doubt we'll need you both to fight the Sentinels when we must send people into the city for supplies later. Your presence will reassure people, and we should also be conducting the ceremony to appoint Boris to High Sorcerer."

At that, Boris' anger eased slightly, replaced by his more usual smugness. Friedrich doubted he would last long in the role—and not simply because of the troubled times. The man was too arrogant, too sure of himself. He was completely disregarding what similar arrogance had cost his predecessor. "We will try to have the ceremony soon, but understand that there are bigger problems, so it may have to be delayed. You are the acting High Sorcerer, however, and may act in that capacity."

"Yes, High Seer. Thank you. Hopefully we will find that light-forsaken bastard soon and put an end to him."

"Let us hope," Friedrich murmured. "Both of you go find food and rest." When they had gone, Friedrich reluctantly approached the vision pool and stared down into it, longing for more wine.

Hiding from your problems—

I can't hide, that's the problem. I have the Lord of All Shadows looming over me, I have a country in shambles, and I am the closest thing to a leader it possesses—a leader it has never needed before because our lives were so strictly dictated by Teufel. But so many people in such close proximity strains me; I cannot be both Seer and King, and yet that is exactly what is being demanded of me. My second in command is going to overthrow me any day now. The High Sorcerer and he will kill each other before the year is out because they do not share power well, and my only refuge is a figment of my imagination who is a memory of a version of me that was destroyed nine centuries ago. I cannot go on, and the only way I can get through my days is by dulling the senses that everyone taxes."

Beloved …

Stop calling me that! Friedrich snarled and sank to his knees, bending over the vision pool, tears of frustration and unbelievable agony striking the water as pain lashed at his head. Wine, he desperately needed more wine.

Come to me.

That won't fix the problem anymore and we both know it.

Drache said nothing, but Friedrich could feel his concern—and his love. And that just made him feel worse about everything. *I'm sorry. I know you're not the problem, or even part of it. That I have remained sane this long is because of you.*

I wish you would come to me, beloved. Maybe it won't fix anything permanently, but it is still more of a rest than you will get anywhere else.

Maybe tonight, but right now I have too much to do—anymore, there is always too much to do. I'm not a leader, not like this. My purpose is to See. We need a king, a ruler. Why does Schatten not have one?

It did, once. Not one, but several. I am amazed I can tell you that much and wish I could tell you more. Schatten was always a land ruled by its clergy, and you were— Drache broke off with a pained noise. *Suffice to say, you were very different, as you must already know, and so were several other men and women.*

Friedrich sighed and rubbed at his throbbing temples. *I am weary of all these mysteries, all these shadows. When does the darkness end?*

When Lord Teufel is removed from power and Lost Licht is found, Drache replied.

Well, let us see if we can find this child of chaos and hasten that happy event. Friedrich drew his knife and slit his palm, letting blood drip into the vision pool for a moment before he added the Essence of Moon.

He closed his eyes and gave himself once more to the power that controlled him, defined him—sometimes, he felt, to the exclusion of all else. Lost in the threads, he cast out seeking for the mysterious David, reaching him in the past where he had first encountered Karl and Boris. From there he followed the threads out: from where he had been left in Oak Hill; to leaving with the caravan; to a long trek through the snow desperately seeking a man called *Sasha*; and finding Sasha in a gatehouse of the Great Wall, barely alive after killing—

Surprise yanked Friedrich from the vision, and he stared in shock at the images that faded from the vision pool. "He killed a Great Sentinel. *How* in the name of Lost Licht did he *kill a Great Sentinel?*"

He wields a ring that embodies chaos and calls down the power of the gods. Whatever his motivation, it's strong. A man determined is a man unbreakable. If he is killing the Great Sentinels then we know where to find him. It may actually work to our favor; you can simply go to him—

I am not fit for such travel, though I will chance it if I must, Friedrich replied. *But there is a vast amount of Great Wall to explore. It goes on forever, or near enough.* He worried his lower lip as he thought. *I still cannot believe he is killing them.*

He is a man I would very much like to meet, Drache said. *Hopefully we will and soon.*

Friedrich snorted. *Soon is asking for a bit much, though one way or another we will obviously meet him. I need to return to that vision; I never should have lost it.* Sighing, he performed the ceremony again and fell into his power, retrieving the threads he had dropped and following them along. He watched as Sasha and David journeyed through the relentless winter, camping in caves of snow, sleeping twined together. David's affection for Sasha ran deep, and Friedrich had enough experience to see what David clearly did not: that Sasha's affection ran just as deep, if not deeper. They were not in love, not yet, but it was clearly where they were headed.

Envy churned in Friedrich's gut and pain clawed at his chest. He wanted a lover like that, someone real, who he could touch and stare at every day of his life. He loved

Drache, but how real a love was it when Drache did not exist and never would? He loved a figment, a shadow of *himself*, and he had no desire to explore just how twisted that made him.

Setting his selfish thoughts aside, he poured all his attention back into the vision, following the threads until he caught up with David and Sasha in the present.

"I don't feel right," David said as they huddled in their latest snow cave, grateful for the fire provided by Sasha's magic.

"What do you mean?" Sasha asked, frowning in concern.

David shrugged. "Like something isn't right. Sort of like when a Sentinel freezes you with fear, but not as strong. But I've never felt a Sentinel before seeing it."

"As long as we've been traveling, we're probably close to another Great Sentinel," Sasha said, expression turning grim.

For the first time, Friedrich noticed that there was an accent to his words. How had he never noticed it? Probably because most of his visions of Sasha thus far had been full of violence and seen either through Sasha's eyes or the eyes of someone who wanted to capture or kill him.

The accent was educated, smooth and clipped, nothing at all like David's longer, rougher manner of speech, which was so common to most of Schatten. Every now and then Sasha said a word oddly, as though he'd learned it from a book. That made sense, however, with his being a foreigner.

"How are you going to kill it?"

"Dragons," Sasha said with a sigh. "Of all the gods, the Dragons of the Three Storms are the most powerful. They rule Kundou, but in some respects, they also rule the whole world. It's exhausting, but last time I hesitated to use them and nearly died. This time, I won't be that hesitant."

Eager curiosity rose up in David, and Friedrich wanted to smile at how earnest he was. How had someone so sweet and honest survived so long in Schatten? In Friedrich's experience, such qualities were killed early in childhood. Certainly his life had left him all hard edges and cynicism. "Teufel said the other gods tried to destroy us, wanted what was good for them but bad for their children."

"That is not true," Sasha said softly. "Always, the gods have loved their children. Their decisions might have been poor, but their love was constant. The problem was that we doubted it, and Licht played upon that doubt to achieve his own ends. He paid for his mistakes, but his shadow continues his work, creating a world controlled entirely by fate."

"I wonder how different Schatten will be when it's not like that anymore," David said.

Sasha smiled faintly and reached out to brush the back of his hand along David's cheek. The caress provoked an answering smile, shy and sweet, in David. He shifted to sit closer to Sasha, arm sliding around his waist, head resting against Sasha's shoulder.

Feeling like an intruder, Friedrich withdrew. He stared at the pool as the vision of Sasha and David faded away, leaving him with a throbbing headache and a sharp, deep ache of longing.

It was an ache that echoed through the recesses of his mind where Drache dwelled, and Friedrich's eyes stung with the knowledge that he would *never* have the only thing he really wanted. More than to be free of fate, more than his sanity, he wanted to be able to see and hold Drache, to spend every single day with him.

Beloved, do not despair—

Why shouldn't I? Tell me, why should I not despair?

Chaos. There may yet be a chance ...

To meet a figment of my mind? To meet a ghost of me? What sort of man falls in love with himself. *I would say a man that egocentric or unstable deserves what he gets.*

It's more complicated than that, beloved. If Teufel falls, something might change. Do not give up.

"I'm trying to have faith," Friedrich said aloud.

He looked up at the sound of someone approaching, their sharp, quick footsteps echoing in the enormous hall. When he saw Karl, Friedrich stifled a sigh and stood up. "Yes, Karl?"

"The watch has spied a large group of travelers and fears they will fall victim to the Sentinels before they can reach the temple. They said to see what you wanted to do before they sent out a party."

Friedrich grimaced inwardly. "I will come along. I think the other sorcerers are either still recovering, or need to be fresh for the foraging parties." He walked around the vision pool and strode past Karl, leading the way through the temple to the front where a large party was already gathered.

"It looks like a good-sized caravan, High Seer," said a priest with a spy glass pressed to one eye. "Not less than fifty in the group, I'd say, but there's so much snow that it could be twice that."

"I hope they have some supplies remaining," Friedrich said. "Do we have men willing and able to come with me to guide them through the city?"

"Yes," said a nearby sorcerer. "We've ten sorcerers who are ready and twenty other men."

Friedrich looked at him in surprise. "So many sorcerers available?"

"They've been recuperating since the initial attack, High Seer, but they're fully recovered now and ready to join the rotations."

"That makes good hearing. Get everyone ready then, and let's get down there to save them. I'm not sure where we'll put them all, but we'll figure it out once we save them."

There must be a way to drive them out of the city altogether. Surely I should know how, if no one else.

If I knew it, I would suggest it, but I think that they are here by design and so nothing we do will get rid of them until Teufel himself wants it.

Friedrich started to reply to that when someone knocked into him, sending him stumbling forward. He tripped over a boot and went crashing down several steps, landing wrong on them and slamming his head into the edge of one. His balance was still off enough that he went tumbling down the rest of the marble steps.

He stopped only when he reached the landing halfway down, where the steps stopped and widened out to give people in need a place to rest. Every part of him ached, and his head felt as though someone had driven something sharp into it. Friedrich tried to move, but could only whimper in pain and hold still again.

The sound of voices penetrated the pain, and he thought he heard people say his name, still others screaming his title. Friedrich tried to tell them he was fine, tried to beg them not to touch him, hoped somebody would realize that was a bad idea—

And then it was too late, and people were crowding around him, touching him, and the tenuous grasp he had on his mind finally broke. Friedrich screamed as the presence of too many people consumed him, as too many visions, too many threads, finally overwhelmed him. All he could hear, beyond his own screams, was Karl's smug, triumphant voice pretending to care about him and Drache's pleading voice. Then he felt himself shatter, and went gratefully into the waiting dark.

Mercy

"I don't feel right," David said as they huddled in their latest snow cave, grateful for the fire provided by Sasha's magic.

"What do you mean?" Sasha asked, frowning in concern.

David shrugged. "Like something isn't right. Sort of like when a Sentinel freezes you with fear, but not as strong. But I've never felt a Sentinel before seeing it."

"As long as we've been traveling, we're probably close to another Great Sentinel," Sasha said, expression turning grim.

"How are you going to kill it?" David asked, because he still half-thought that dead Great Sentinel a dream.

"Dragons," Sasha said with a sigh. "Of all the gods, the Dragons of the Three Storms are the most powerful. They rule Kundou, but in some respects, they also rule the whole world. It's exhausting, but last time I hesitated to use them and nearly died. This time, I won't be that hesitant."

Curiosity about magic that was nothing like what he had seen the sorcerers use, about gods Schatten had been taught to revile, rose up too strongly for David to hold back. "Teufel said the other gods tried to destroy us, wanted what was good for them but bad for their children."

"That is not true," Sasha said softly. "Always, the gods have loved their children. Their decisions might have been poor, but their love was a constant. The problem was that we doubted it, and Licht played upon that doubt to achieve his own ends. He paid for his mistakes, but his shadow continues his work, creating a world controlled entirely by fate."

"I wonder how different Schatten will be when it's not like that anymore," David said.

Sasha smiled faintly and reached out to brush the back of his hand along David's cheek. Fighting his nervousness, still not quite believing that Sasha had any sort of interest in him at all, David moved closer and slid an arm around Sasha's waist, burrowing up against him. He rested his head against Sasha's shoulder, absolutely content with where he was, left alone together in a moment the rest of the world could not easily break.

Gloved fingers brushed his cheek and Sasha's lips grazed his brow. David wondered if they would ever have a chance to do all the things he'd barely ever let himself think about, but could not *stop* thinking about since he had met Sasha.

No doubt it was wrong to think about such things when there was a world to be saved, but he also knew he would have more luck if he tried to stop breathing. "Sasha ..." He shifted slightly, looked up, and was elated when that got him the kiss he sought. Their lips were chapped from the cold, and they both longed to be clean, but Sasha's mouth was warm and tasted of tea.

When they broke apart, Sasha nuzzled against him in a way that David loved. Sasha was so quiet and intense when he was working or casting magic. Watching him work—just watching him move, or hold perfectly still in that calm, collected way that was so uniquely Sasha—was fascinating enough David could do it for hours.

But Sasha like this, sweet and soft, left him breathless. David reached up to stroke Sasha's cheek, which earned him another soft but ardent kiss.

"Do you think there's someone waiting for you?" he asked softly. "I always wonder how anyone could let you go into so much danger and not insist on going with you. I would never let you go off without me, not again."

Sasha sighed softly, the shadows in his eyes lengthening as they always did when he dwelled on his lack of memory. "I think that if I had someone, I would remember that. No spell would make me forget that I loved someone like that. Not to the point that I would feel it was all right to take up with someone else," he said softly, brushing his fingertips lightly over David's face. "There are a hundred reasons I should not attach myself to you, but I do not think that is not one of them."

"So what are they?" David asked, half-teasing, half-terrified. "I don't think you can come up with a hundred."

Mouth quirking with reluctant amusement, Sasha said, "Oh, I'm sure I could if I was given enough time to brood upon the matter."

"True," David agreed. "You spend too much time in your own head."

Surprise rippled across Sasha's face. "I suppose I do, though I never thought of it quite like that. I think ..." He frowned thoughtfully. "I think more often I am accused of worrying too much, or trying to do everything myself, but no one has ever accused me of living too much in my own head."

"I think it's part of those other things," David said with a laugh, and he reached up to lightly touch Sasha's face again. "You go all still and stare at things no one else can see, and I'm right here, but I feel like you're a hundred miles away."

The emotions that crossed Sasha's face then David could not name. Sasha leaned in, pressing their foreheads together. "If anyone could reach out to me across a hundred miles, it's you, David."

David's reply caught in his throat, the words too heavy to get out. He settled for shifting and wrapping his arms around Sasha, the sudden movement sending them toppling to lie on the bedrolls they'd laid out on the ground to provide a barrier between them and the snow. Sasha let out a huff of laughter, but didn't say anything. He wrapped one arm around David's waist, threaded a hand through his hair with the other, and simply clung to him.

They shifted slightly, just enough to be relatively comfortable. Lulled by the fire and Sasha's warming, soothing presence, it was surprisingly easy to fall asleep.

He woke to the feel of lips brushing his cheek, the scrape of Sasha's beard since neither of them had been able to shave. "Morning already?" David asked groggily. "I really hate morning."

Sasha chuckled. "Perhaps someday I will have a chance to change your mind on that, though right now I tend to agree with you." He sighed and took down his hair, then tied it back again. David watched him, curious as to how different Sasha would look when he wasn't pretending to be from Schatten.

"How come your skin isn't different?" he asked suddenly.

"What?" Sasha stared at him, then said, "Oh," and shook his head, smiling ruefully. "I tried, but it just didn't look right on me. I looked stranger with it than with my normal skin, so I left it."

David tilted his head, curious. "I wish I knew how you really looked. I bet you're even more beautiful." He caught his own words too late and felt his face heat. But he didn't take the words back because they were true. Sasha was beautiful, and he would be all the more so when he looked like himself again.

"I'm old and faded," Sasha said with a smile. "If anyone in this hollow of snow is lovely, it's you. Now, enough of that. I prefer to save absurdly flowery words for a soft bed after I'm too spent to think of intelligent things to say. The sooner we save the world, the sooner we can find that bed." He winked, stole a quick kiss, then with a snap of his fingers, put out the magic fire.

Face still hot, though for entirely different reasons, David followed Sasha out into the snow once more. He was thoroughly sick of the snow, but simply pulled up his face mask and trudged on behind Sasha.

They hadn't been walking very long at all when they ran into a gatehouse and the long stretch of road they'd been seeking—or what was left of it, anyway. The famous roads to Sonnenstrahl had crumbled away over the years to practically nothing and did not extend past the gates for more than a couple dozen paces.

"Shouldn't it be here?" David whispered.

Sasha nodded and leaned in close enough to murmur in his ear. "Perhaps it had reason to go further afield. We'll head for the gatehouse first, that will give us some advantage. If it reappears, continue on for the gatehouse and stay well out of the way."

David nodded and pulled down his face mask to steal a quick kiss. He then followed Sasha as they continued along the wall headed toward the gatehouse, ever alert for the Great Sentinel. He looked over his shoulder at the gatehouse and realized that there was the barest bit of light coming from the barred viewing square near the top of the door. Turning back, he reached out and snagged Sasha's cloak, urging him to stop. When Sasha turned toward him, David pointed back at the gatehouse.

Sasha's brow shot up. He gestured with his head at David, who obediently stepped back and, when Sasha strode past him, fell into step behind him. David wished he could do more to help, but the only weapon he could use was a hunting knife and that was absolutely useless against a Great Sentinel.

They both froze when the gatehouse door abruptly swung open and a shadowy figure beckoned them inside. "Come in, please."

"Who …" David started to ask, but he trailed off as Sasha accepted the invitation. David hastened after him, and nearly wept when he was hit with a wall of unbelievable, marvelous warmth.

"Hang your things up here," the stranger said, his voice deep and warm, husky from disuse. David wiped snow from his face, then stiffly began to obey, not certain what else to do. He stripped off his cloak, jacket, and gloves and hung everything on a set of several hooks near the door. Raking hands through his hair to get the tangled, filthy mess out of his face, he finally turned to survey the room—and his jaw dropped to see how drastically it differed from the last gatehouse. That one had been a hovel; the one they stood in was very much a home.

As his face thawed, he could smell tea, fragrant meat, and roasting vegetables. Dried fruit stuffed with cloves and cinnamon hung from the ceiling alongside bundles of herbs. There was a bed in one corner, a curtained off corner for bathing, and an entire wall had been devoted to shelves piled with books. David stared at them with longing, then turned away, swallowing the sudden lump in his throat.

He focused on the source of the smells making his stomach growl: the fire pit in the middle of the room, over which was arranged a cooking pot and a small spit where meat and vegetables still turned. By way of magic, he supposed, because it was turning, though no one was turning it. Strange, all the little things magic could do in the hands of someone like Sasha and their strange host.

He looked about Sasha's age, maybe a few years older, and his hair was a stunning bright gold. It fell to a little past his shoulders and had been woven into a rough braid and tied off with a brown leather thong. "Greetings," the man said. "It's been a long time since I've had guests. Would you like food, or to clean up first?"

"I would love to be clean," Sasha said. "I'm not sure I remember how that feels."

The man chuckled and gestured lazily toward the curtained off corner. "By all means. I prefer my rare guests be comfortable, and I do know what it's like to be filthy for days. Please, use whatever you need. I will add more food so there is plenty for all. Tea, wine, brandy?"

"Brandy?" Sasha echoed. "You have brandy?"

"Yes," the man said with another chuckle. "What are your names? I am Achim."

Sasha shook his head, laughing softly. "My apologies for my rudeness. I am Sasha and this is David."

Achim peered at Sasha curiously. "Sasha is not entirely unknown a name here, but it is a Pozharan name in origin. You're a fire child, despite your coloring."

"Yes," Sasha replied. "How do you know that? My name, or even my pale skin, is not enough to give that away."

Smiling sadly, Achim said, "Clean up, then we'll eat and talk."

Nodding, Sasha turned to David. "Would you like to go first, or shall I?"

"You," David said, still distracted by the books. "I don't mind waiting."

"There should be water aplenty, but I can heat more if necessary," Achim said.

Sasha stared at him a moment, frowning thoughtfully, but in the end only walked over to the curtain and slipped behind it. David stood uncertainly, then asked, "Is there anything I can do?"

"Not at all," Achim replied. "As I said, it's been a long time since I last had a guest. I enjoy having company to fuss over. Do you like the books? You may help yourself."

David felt hot and cold all at once, and he flinched slightly as he looked at the books sadly and said, "I don't know how to read. There's no use for it in Black Hill. Books belong to rich people in cities, not those of us in little villages."

"I think it's more that words are power," Achim said gently, and David jumped when a hand squeezed his shoulder. He hadn't even heard Achim move. Looking up, still mortified that he could not even write or recognize his own name when Sasha … He looked away again. "Shh," Achim soothed and tilted his chin up. "You've no reason to be ashamed, sunbeam. It is not for you to be upset you cannot read—be upset that Teufel took the chance from you." He smiled before slipping away to fuss and putter around the fire.

David retreated to the books, unable to resist reaching out to touch them, trail his fingers over the leather bindings and the gold lettering. He wished he knew what they said. Were they histories? Folktales? Books on medicine? Books about animals or plants? Perhaps books about magic?

He didn't know how long he stared at them, but he was immediately pulled from his wistful musings by the familiar sound of Sasha's footsteps. David turned as Sasha drew up alongside him, face burning again, mind pulled in two different directions: admiring Sasha cleaned up and wanting to hide in embarrassment.

Sasha cupped his chin and tilted his face up to take a kiss, mouth warm, lips still damp, and the smell of fragrant, rose-scented soap filling David's nostrils. "Go get clean, sweet," Sasha murmured.

David obeyed, body thrumming from Sasha's presence, mind still wanting to cover itself with shame now that Sasha knew just how ignorant he was. He could not even imagine how educated Sasha must have been, how much he must know that he felt up to the task of sneaking into Schatten and killing Teufel.

Behind the relative safety of the heavy curtain, David stripped and threw his clothes in the pile where Sasha's still lay. He hadn't thought to grab clothes, but a set was laid out on top of a wooden chest. He turned to the bath, which was, to his surprise, filled with clean, steaming water. Long used to going second after Reimund, or whoever he was rooming with during visits to Two Mills, having clean water all to himself was a treat.

He grabbed a bucket of hot water set near the tub, a rough rag, and a bit of soap and began to scrub himself clean vigorously. When he had cleaned himself head to foot, he shaved and then washed himself all over again just for the luxury of it. When he was done, he slipped into the tub of hot water and sighed softly. In the middle of winter, in a place he had never thought he would be, he was more than happy to just close his eyes and revel in the hot water for a little while. Thoughts of other things would simply have to wait a little while.

When the water eventually began to cool, David sighed and dragged himself out of it. He used a long, wide strip of cloth to dry himself off, then pulled on the clothes Sasha had set out for him. They weren't his, but they fit well enough they almost could have been. He pressed his nose to the fabric, enjoying the faint scent of roses and berries that clung to them.

Still feeling embarrassed, he nevertheless made himself step out of the curtained sanctuary and rejoin the other two. To his surprise, there was only Sasha, who said, "Achim went to fetch more snow for water. Come here."

David slowly walked over to him, something heavy settling into his gut. Sasha sat before the fire, close enough to be warm without overheating on a thick fur rug. There was a small earthenware cup beside him, and David could just smell the rich, heady scent of the brandy. He'd never had it, but the village chief kept some and David had often smelled it when he visited the chief's home.

It tasted like something wicked on Sasha's lips when he tugged David close and took his mouth. The soft kiss quickly took on an edge of its own, and Sasha's fingers slid into his hair, keeping David in place for the sharp, hungry kiss. When David finally drew back, he was out of breath and wholly distracted by the heat in Sasha's eyes, the throbbing of his own lips, the way it shot fire through the rest of his body and stirred a faint echo of that ache in his cock. "Sasha …"

Making a soft noise, Sasha kissed him again, tugging so that David suddenly sat across his lap. He had absolutely no complaints about the arrangement, happy to twine his arms around Sasha's neck and attempt to give as good as he got in the heady kisses.

He wouldn't ever be educated or fancy or breathtaking like Sasha, but by Licht he could take care of Sasha and follow him anywhere and learn whatever he had to in order to stay with him. Certainly it would never be a hardship mastering kisses and everything else Sasha was going to teach him. "Sasha …"

"You are perfection, sweet," Sasha said, lapping at his lips as he drew back, then nuzzling against him. "Stop fretting about what you can't do. If reading matters so much to you, I'll teach you."

David stared at him, then dropped his gaze. "I was hoping you wouldn't ever know."

"I prefer to know," Sasha said. "If you don't want me to know things, then you don't trust me—"

"No!" David burst out. "I do. I came after you because I realized I trusted you more than everything else in my life. But—you're so different than me. I don't understand ..."

Sasha forced his head up and cupped his face, thumbs stroking David's cheeks softly. "David, stop thinking you are the inferior here. Education does not make a man anything but educated, and sometimes not even that. It is heart and courage and kindness that people need. It was not an educated man who found me at the Great Wall. Don't underestimate yourself just because you can't read. Reading can be taught. What you have, cannot." Sasha kissed him again and withdrew only when the door opened, letting in a rush of frigid air.

Achim smiled at them as he went to bustling about the stove once more. David's face went hot when he realized he was still in Sasha's lap and he hastily squirmed free, scowling when Sasha snickered and smirked. Achim poured cups of tea and handed one to each of them, then checked on the still-simmering food before he sat down. "All is well again, then?"

"All is well," Sasha said. "So why don't you tell us how it is possible for a Great Sentinel to assume a human form?"

David jerked so hard that hot tea splashed over the rim of his cup and onto his hand. He set the cup down, swearing, and then stared at Achim. "You're—you can't be."

"Oh, I am," Achim said with the saddest smile David had ever seen. Looking at it hurt. "We were all human once. Six Priests of Night, six Priests of Day, the ruling council of Schatten. We answered only to the Priest of Night and Day and the gods themselves. When Licht began to lose himself and Teufel's mercurial ways finally went too far, we rebelled. Teufel cursed us, turned us into beasts and bound us to the Great Wall. Over time ..." He sighed softly, drew one leg up, and curled his arm around it, eyes going distant. "Over time, many of my brothers preferred to forget their humanity and succumbed to being beasts. I do not know if anyone besides myself retains any humanity; I have not seen them in at least two hundred years. When last I did see any of them ... well, I held very little hope I would see them again. You've already killed Bettina."

Sasha nodded.

"She was one of the first to succumb," Achim said quietly, looking away into the fire. "You granted her a mercy, though I know that was not your intent."

"I take no pleasure in killing anything," Sasha said, as somber as Achim. "If any good can be found in it, then I am glad for it. I had not anticipated the Great Sentinels being anything other than beasts, however. I am rather at a loss now as to what to do."

Achim tilted his inquisitively and suddenly David could *see* it—the sinuous grace of the Sentinels. His heart began to beat faster as the realization truly sank in. His mind whirled while he tried to make sense of it. He picked up his tea again, just to have something familiar, as he listened to Sasha and Achim continued to speak. "Do not know what to do? About me? Why, kill me of course."

"You're hardly a beast," Sasha said. "I might be willing to kill, but I don't kill people who have done no wrong."

"No wrong?" Achim laughed bitterly. He stood up and began to pull the food off the fire and carry it over to a table where he began to dish it all into large bowls. "The country fell apart around us, the people began to panic—and then they began to die—and all we could do was muster feeble protests. When we finally found the courage to take a real stand it was too late. Everything we had wanted to save was already lost. Bettina is not the only one to whom you would be granting a mercy—it is only that we do not necessarily deserve that mercy."

Sasha shook his head even as he accepted the steaming bowl Achim handed to him. "I don't want to—" he broke off with a pained cry, barely setting the bowl down before he pressed one hand to his chest and the other to his head. "Clearly I should not try too hard to force my memories."

Achim frowned in concern and knelt before him, placing his own hand on Sasha's chest. "That's a nasty curse, even worse than I thought from initial readings. It's a wonder you remember anything."

"I have experience with magic and my ring protects me," Sasha said. "I'm guessing that you cannot break it."

"No, alas," Achim said with a sigh. "Once, yes, but when I was cursed all such abilities were stripped from me. The only magic I possess now is a collection of harmless tricks. I am also bound to the Great Wall and cannot go far from it."

"How did you acquire all of this stuff?" David asked.

"Meine, the one people call the Wanderer, brings supplies to me," Achim said. "He is the only one who can travel the country at will. He brings supplies to the rest of us."

"The Wanderer exists?"

Achim nodded. "I have not seen him lately, but I'm sure he'll make himself known soon. You will have to kill him, as well, to get through the Great Wall."

Sighing, Sasha asked, "There is no other way?"

"Death is a terrible price to pay for anything and not a price that anyone ever wants to pay. That is why gods always demand it."

"Indeed," Sasha said quietly, and for a moment he seemed a hundred years older. David slipped an arm through Sasha's and leaned against him, offering what comfort he could with touch and presence. After a moment, Sasha relaxed a bit and sat up straighter. He looked at Achim and said, "It seems rather the height of rudeness to accept your hospitality and repay it with murder."

"You would be doing me a kindness, I promise," Achim said, his eyes closing, hands resting in his lap, clinging to the fabric of his robe. "Do you know what it's like to exist for nine hundred years? And that's all I do: exist. I have no friends, no one to share my pain, not really. I have been a prisoner, chained to this wall, for nine centuries. It would take a stronger person than me to endure such a fate and not want to die when the chance is finally offered."

"As you wish, then," Sasha said quietly.

Achim opened his eyes, which were bright with tears. "I thank you. May daylight guide you and night grant your rest."

Sasha nodded, but said nothing, only picked up his bowl and began to eat. David forced his own food down, though he was no longer hungry. His mind chewed over all that had been said and unanswered questions gnawed at him until he could not help but ask, "Is the Wanderer that other priest? The Priest of Night and Day?"

"No," Achim said softly. "We are not able to speak much of the Priest of Night and Day, though what I know is little enough. He paid a price far worse than the rest of us for his betrayal because he was Teufel's paramour for many years."

"Paramour?" David asked.

"His lover," Sasha said.

David frowned. "But Teufel was Licht's shadow, that is why he sealed us away. The rest of the world betrayed Licht and killed him … but if that was the true story, you would not be here."

Sasha combed fingers through his hair and smiled at him. "No one knows the true story, not really. But from what little I know of Teufel, it does not surprise me he had a paramour, though he was beloved of Licht. David asks a good question, however: who is the Wanderer if there were only twelve priests?"

"He was the Captain of the Guard," Achim replied. "We were good friends. When everyone else had fled in terror or bowed to Teufel's will, he still stood with us. Now he wanders endlessly."

David fought the sudden stinging in his eye. "Why is Teufel so awful?"

"Teufel is but a shadow," Sasha said softly. "The real question is: what was wrong with Licht?"

David opened his mouth, then closed it again. When he could not come up with an answer, or anything to say at all, he simply settled for sipping at his tea and listening to the crackle of the fire.

Raven Knoll

Sasha brushed back David's hair, then settled the blankets over him. When he was confident David was comfortably settled, he joined Achim at the door. "You put something in his tea."

"He's sweet," Achim said, eyes flicking to David in his bed. "He has probably seen or endured more death than a man so young should. Indeed, he should still be a boy and it is a pity that he is already so much a man. He should not have to see the man he loves—I daresay the first person he has ever loved so—take a life in such fashion."

Love. The word twisted and coiled through Sasha, teasing him with shadows and whispered words, but no clear memories. He rubbed at his chest, then let his hand fall. His eyes went helplessly back to David, mind buzzing with too many thoughts for him to really sort them out. Love. The word was sweet and painful all at once, but he would rather die than let it go. "He should not be anywhere near me."

"I'm not sure anyone is capable of resisting a flame that burns so bright and true," Achim said. "It's in your eyes, in your heart." He gently placed his hand on Sasha's chest over his heart. "I feel there are many, in the past, who were comforted by the things you say and do—and the things you do not say and do."

Sasha shrugged. "I don't know who or what I am, save from Pozhar and sent to bring chaos to Schatten. I have powerful magic and I suspect a great deal of knowledge that is unusual for a man to possess. I doubt a man as valued as you claim I am would be permitted to venture into lands unknown on such a seemingly-hopeless quest."

"You don't strike me as a man who bothers waiting for permission," Achim said, mouth twitching.

They lapsed into silence, staring at each other, sad and somber but understanding. Achim stepped forward and embraced Sasha tightly. "Be at peace, fire child."

Sasha held him tightly, ignoring the words because he did not want to be a man who could feel peace at another's death no matter what the reason. "Are you sure there is no other way?"

"Not one that is actually achievable," Achim said as he stepped away. "The Priest of Night and Day could command us and gain access without killing us, but no one truly knows what became of him, and what little we do know we cannot say. As I said before, it is a mercy. I want a chance to live a new life, and my life is the very least I can offer to people I should have better served nine hundred years ago."

"I understand," Sasha said quietly.

"Then let us end this."

Sasha looked at David one last time, drawing strength just from the sight of him, then followed Achim out into the cold and snow. Achim moved to the gate and stood before it, standing straight and tall, his gaze unflinching and his jaw set as he met Sasha's eyes. "However you prefer, fire child. Thank you for braving the dark to bring us back into the sun. May all your lives be full of light."

"Fire warm your hearth and light your path," Sasha said, and he raised his hands, cupping them so that his fingertips were pressed together. The ring on his right hand shimmered as he intoned, *"Life and death are but steps on a path the soul walks. The soul is not meant to linger, but to walk. Cease your waiting and resume your walking. In fire born, in fire end, to be born again."*

Golden flames filled his cupped hands, and as he opened them, the flames poured out, melting the snow, banishing the cold, and consuming Achim. It lasted only seconds, but may as well have lasted hours.

As the flames burned out, Sasha felt the softest brush of feathers against his cheeks, absorbing his tears, before he was left once more with only falling snow and cold wind.

Before him, the gate seemed to shiver, shimmering with violet light that spread out along the wall on both sides.

When the last of the magic had faded, Sasha went back inside. Removing all but his breeches and shirt, he slid into the bed and bundled David close, practically wrapping around him, burying his nose in David's soft, rose-scented hair. He was asleep within moments.

Memories jerked him awake a few hours later, but even as he sat there trying to cling to them, they slipped away out of reach, leaving Sasha feeling lost and frustrated. Would he never get his memories back? Was he cursed to spend the rest of his life wondering who he was?

Just thinking about it made him tired. Sighing, he shoved his loose hair out of his face and looked around the room. The fire had mostly gone down, but the stones must have held the heat well because the room was still comfortably warm.

At his side, arms still twined around his waist, David slept on. Sasha stroked the line of his cheek, wondering again what he was doing with David. Achim's comments rolled through his mind again. If David did love him, hopefully it was more of an infatuation that would ease over time as David grew fully into adulthood and ...

And just thinking about it churned his gut. Sasha made a frustrated noise. How had he gotten himself into such a situation? Especially given his lack of memories. He pushed the blankets away and started to slide out of bed, but the soft sounds of protest, the arms that tightened around him, stopped him short. David's bright eyes blinked open, foggy with sleep he could not quite break free of. "Sasha ..." he said groggily before his eyes fell shut again. But his grip on Sasha did not ease.

Shifting and twisting, Sasha lay down once more and pressed a soft kiss to David's lips. David kissed him sleepily back, muttering his name again as he tried to press even closer. They were warm, clean, safe, and rested. The bed was comfortable, and they were in no hurry to be anywhere. It should have been the perfect opportunity to show David many things.

But the thought of seducing David in the bed of the man he had just killed turned Sasha's stomach. He gave David another soft kiss, then closed his eyes and tried once more to get some sleep.

When he woke again, it was to the familiar smell of tea and the sounds of David puttering around. Sasha groaned, yawned, then sat up and stretched. He swung his feet over the edge of the bed, eyes immediately seeking out David.

It took only the barest glance to see that David had been crying. "I'm sorry," Sasha said softly.

"It's not fair they have to die, not when they're not monsters," David said, stirring the porridge over the fire with a vengeance. "Why?"

Sasha considered his words before he said, "People too often lash out when they're hurt, especially when that hurt is caused by loved ones. The deeper the pain, the harder the lash. The more power a person has at their disposal, the more willing they are to use it to strike. Teufel is twisted, and nothing he has done deserves to be excused, but ultimately his actions result from pain. The one ultimately to blame for all of this is Licht, and we may never know in full why he caused the world so much pain."

"What did he do to the rest of the world?" David asked. "I never thought about it before because we were always told they were the ones who were wrong. Does the world hate us? Do they think we're all evil?"

"The rest of the world worries for Schatten. Many believe the country is a dead land, that no living souls remain," Sasha replied. "Come here."

David immediately abandoned the porridge in favor of pushing into Sasha's arms. "I can't believe everything is so wrong. What did Licht do?"

"Many things," Sasha said. "He encouraged a priest to kill his own brother and the Dragons of the Three Storms. He provoked the deaths and riots that eventually destroyed the

Firebird. He tried to kill the Basilisk and steal his power, and he encouraged the jealousy and rage of the Faerie Queen who murdered her siblings. Worst of all, though, is the way he abandoned his own children to do those things. Schatten was—is—the domain of Licht, and once he loved his children more than anything. Somewhere along the way, he got lost in his own darkness."

Sasha just hoped that whatever he was doing, it would bring Schatten back into the light. When—if—he managed to kill Teufel, Schatten would have no god to look after it. That was a problem for gods, however.

He was drawn from his thoughts when David looked up at him, eyes the most intense Sasha had ever seen them. Then David leaned up and kissed him, surprising Sasha momentarily before he happily gave in to it. David clung tightly, his hands sliding into Sasha's loose, mussed hair, and the way his body fit so perfectly against Sasha's was the best sort of distraction.

But Achim haunted him, and though Sasha wanted nothing more than to strip David bare and make him scream, it was neither the time nor the place. "As much I would gladly spend all my days kissing you, sweet, the porridge is burning and we have a long road to travel."

David swore at the mention of the porridge and bolted away again, scowling and fussing over it. Sasha chuckled and left him to it. He prowled the room while he straightened his sleep-mussed hair and clothes, poking through what few supplies Achim had remaining. "There does not appear to be much here," he said with a sigh. "I think we may have to leave the wall and go into a city to find fresh supplies."

"So we are going to Raven Knoll, after all," David said as he spooned the porridge into two bowls and drizzled both with honey. "I'm not sure how long it will take, but at least several days."

Sasha ate several bites of the porridge, which wasn't bad as porridge went, even with a bit of scalding, before he replied, "I just hope we can carry enough supplies to last us around the rest of the wall. If I recall correctly, most of the cities and villages are scattered along the base of the mountains and the east coast. There isn't much on the west half of the country."

"I don't know," David said. "I've never been further west than Deer Run, and it's not far from Black Hill. Gold Rock is to the west, they say, and that it's as large as Raven Knoll, but I don't know how true that is. No one I know has ever been there; they just pass on rumors they hear."

"Mmm," Sasha said thoughtfully. "Hopefully there is some truth to the rumors. But that is a problem for later. For now, we need to worry about getting to Raven Knoll, obtaining supplies, and then getting out again."

David nodded. "I packed our bags a little while ago and tidied up what I could … it seems so sad to leave it all. He shouldn't have had to die."

"He should not have had to live so long, either," Sasha replied gently. "There are people who can handle such a fate and others who cannot. It should be a choice, not something forced." He finished his porridge and took both of their empty bowls to wash them. By the time he was done with that, David had taken care of the fire, and together they made quick work of the rest of the room.

When they were ready to depart, Sasha strode over to the bookcase and looked through the myriad books that filled the shelves. Every imaginable subject was covered, and for a moment, he did not think it would have the sorts of books he sought—but then he saw them, tucked neatly at one end of a very bottom shelf. Taking the three slim volumes, he tucked them into his pack, then settled it on his shoulders. "Shall we?"

David nodded and led the way out into the snow. Not long after they started, it began to fall so heavily that they lost visibility beyond a couple of steps. They paused long enough to pull out a short length of rope and tie themselves together before they forged on with David in the lead, pushing on relentlessly until hunger and exhaustion finally forced them to stop.

It took them nine days to reach Raven Knoll, and by the time the towering walls of the city loomed into view, Sasha was ready to drop to the ground and never rise again. Visions of a bed, hot bath, and real food spun in his mind, pushing him to keep moving, to pick himself up after stumbling and press on …

But as they reached the immense gate of Raven Knoll, the gate pillars topped with marble ravens, Sasha knew something was wrong. For one, the iron gates were not just open, they had been torn off, bent, and mutilated. That could only be the work of Sentinels.

They had barely stepped foot into the city proper when the snow cleared enough that he could see them—the entire city was filled with Sentinels. What remained of the city was in ruins and at a glance, he was not certain how much of it could be salvaged. Was there anyone left alive?

At his side, David bit back a cry. "What happened? How— how could he do this? How could he let this happen? All those people … Raven Knoll is Teufel's city. The Temple of Unheilvol is his, built for him by Lord Licht. Why would he ruin a tribute to himself?"

Sasha hugged him and kissed his brow. "I don't know," he said quietly. "It just further proves he does not deserve anything except pity and vengeance. Stay close and run for cover if I tell you." He stroked David's cheek with his fingertips, then pressed on into the city, calling up his magic so that he'd be able to use it in a moment's notice.

They made it about a third of the way down the main road before they came across Sentinels, which he found rather surprising, if a relief. The fewer they encountered, the better. Sasha gestured to David, who nodded and tensed to run for cover. One enormous Sentinel with huge, heavy horns and wings moving restlessly on his back prowled toward them, half a dozen smaller ones creeping from shadows and corners, babies and infants slithering.

How could so many be in one place? The poor city had never stood a chance. Sasha held his arms out, palms up, and said quietly, "David, stay close to me. I'm going to try what I meant to use on the Great Sentinels before I met Achim. I am probably going to pass out when this is done."

"I'll take care of you," David replied.

"I know," Sasha replied. "Be careful." David nodded and stepped up behind him, twining his arms around Sasha's waist. Sasha called up all of his power and tilted his head up to face down the adult Sentinel, ignoring the others that drew close from all sides. *"Wind and water, snow and ice, thunder and lightning. The depths of the sea and the infinity of the sky answer only to the Storms. Dragons of the Three Storms, Lords of Chaos, destroy these rotted threads of fate."*

A sudden silence fell over everything, the sort of lull that always preceded a storm.

Chaos arrived with a slow rumble of thunder that ended in a world-shaking crash. The sound boomed and echoed through the devastated city, causing the noise-sensitive Sentinels to rear back in panic and pain.

Next came the lightning, the wind, and the soft snow turned into biting bits of whirling ice. Sasha turned and held tightly to David, dragging him to the ground and huddling with him there as the storm raged through the city.

When the hush came again, there was a note of finality in it. Sasha swayed as the draining of his energy finally struck him, and he slumped tiredly against David, who held him fast and kissed his brow. "I've got you," David whispered.

"I count on it, little spark," Sasha whispered and let his eyes slip shut.

He was roughly jarred awake again by the sound of shouting and dozens of voices speaking at once. Dragging his eyes open, he stared up into a face that was unfortunately familiar. "Ah, the Seer from the clearing. I was hoping our paths would not cross again."

The man's mouth twisted, making him look as though he had bitten into a lemon. "Well, at least you have spared me the trouble of having to go find you. And you've solved my Sentinel problem. Grab him."

"No!" David said, and he shoved Sasha back to stand protectively in front of him. "Get away. You can't—" He cried out as a whip cracked, the metal-tipped end catch him across throat and shoulder.

Sasha snarled and rose, throwing out his own arm as the whip came at him. "Touch him again—"

"Neither of you is in a position to be giving orders. Seize them," the man ordered.

Dragging David close, Sasha said, "When I distract them, run. I'll get free of the temple and come find you. Until then, stay safe."

He didn't give David a chance to argue, simply threw his right hand into the sky and said, *"Light is not always kind. Thunder roar, lightning strike!"*

At his bidding, thunder again crashed and boomed so loudly the entire city seemed to shake. Unlike before, the lightning that had rolled and flickered in the heavy clouds came down in sharp bolts, shattering the street and houses they struck, melting snow and leaving behind an acrid, burnt smell.

Sasha saw David give him a last, agonized look before he ran, and then the world turned dark. His last thought was that he was extremely tired of passing out.

When he woke, it was to a sharp slap to his face. To judge from the way his face was throbbing, it was not the first attempt to wake him. He stared at the man looming at the foot of his bed, recognizing him from before. Sitting up, ignoring the faint dizziness that said he was not yet fully recovered from overextending himself magically, he stared coolly at the man and said, "You may bring me tea now."

The man standing beside Sasha slapped him again, and Sasha shifted the direction of his gaze. "Hit me again and I will demonstrate how to do it properly."

"Leave him alone," the man at the foot of the bed said. "Fetch tea and food. He's going to need his strength."

Sasha smirked and shifted on the bed so that his back was against the wall and legs stretched out before him. "So do you have a name?"

"You may address me as High Seer," the man said.

"Why would the High Seer have been trekking about the countryside looking for me? My understanding was that the Seers do not leave Unheilvol, and he most especially does not. That aside, your magic isn't good enough to be High Seer. If I had faced the High Seer in that clearing, I very well could have lost the fight."

The man bristled with anger, reminding Sasha of a little dog that—he winced as the memory collided with the curse. But he remembered that little dog and how much he had hated the way it startled easily and would go yipping and running about until something made it forget it was upset. "I am High Seer. The question is, who are you? Other than the chaotic threat ruining our fine country."

Sasha shrugged. "I am Sasha, and I think it safe to say I am a sorcerer—and a far better one than you—but past that, I could not say. The other sorcerer took care of that." He paused, thinking of that fight. Had it really been months since that day? He supposed it had. "He was better than you as well, come to think of it. The curse nearly got me." Reaching up, he undid the laces of his shirt and pulled it open, revealing the spider web that still faintly ached. "I do not suppose you can remove it?"

"I think I prefer to let it stay," the man replied. "Be grateful I don't order them to recast it correctly. If that curse had taken hold of you, you'd be a drooling, broken mess."

"Try it," Sasha said coldly, smirking when the man started to recoil before he caught himself. "I promise you, it's the very last spell any of you will cast on me."

The man gestured sharply, but his words did not hold all the weight they needed to sound convincing when he replied, "You're all bluster. More importantly, you are my prisoner. I suggest you keep that in mind lest we're forced to give you reminders."

"So what are you planning to do with me?"

"Lord Teufel has ordered us to bring you to him in Sonnenstrahl, so that is what we are going to do."

"Sonnenstrahl? You can get through the gates of the Great Wall? How?"

The man's mouth tightened with anger—and jealousy, Sasha realized. "We have a man who can get through them."

Sasha desperately wanted to know who that man was, but did not ask. He would figure it out soon enough. If what Achim had told him was true … but best not to get his hopes up.

As much as he loved the idea of being taken straight into Sonnenstrahl, he had the feeling that nothing good would come of it in the end. If he was going to kill Teufel, then it must be done his way and not with a private escort comprised of Teufel's most faithful lackeys.

He would be much happier finding a way to escape and locating David, travelling with him into Sonnenstrahl. Fires, he did not even know how he was going to find David again. Wherever he was, Sasha hoped David was safe.

The door opened before either one of them could say something further, and the man from before came in with a tray bearing tea and some rather sad looking bread and cheese. He set the tray down on the table and began to fuss with it.

The so-called High Seer glared at him and said, "Are my men ready to depart?"

"Nearly, High Seer," the man said, jumping. "Perhaps another hour or so. There is much to be packed if we are to make such an arduous journey."

"Do it faster," the High Seer snarled. "See that Friedrich is brought to me."

"But he needs his rest—"

"Do it!"

"Yes, High Seer," the man said and all but ran from the room.

Sasha sighed and stood up to fix his own tea, grimacing at the stale, over-steeped taste of it. "Why are we in such a hurry?"

"Because you've destroyed enough of the country and killed more than enough people," the High Seer snapped. "Raven Knoll is in ruins because of you. The entire country is in shambles because you decided you had the right to interfere in a god's choice, to reshape a land that is not yours."

"Teufel is no god and he had no right to act like one," Sasha said. "People should not be enslaved, and I will not be sorry that I am helping to set them free. If, in the end, they choose to live according to a strict fate, then at least the choice will have been theirs."

The High Seer sneered. "You speak nonsense and blasphemy."

Sasha ignored him in favor of finishing his awful tea and taking a piss. His magic was slowly returning to him, but it would still be some time before he had his full strength back. Best to cooperate until he had both strength and opportunity. It might, in fact, be best if he waited until they got him through the gates.

His gut twisted at the thought, because doing so would mean leaving David behind. It had been hard enough leaving David in Oak Hill. Selfish though it was to want David with him, he did not feel right without David at his side.

Setting his selfishness aside, however, he was forced to concede David was safer when he was not with Sasha. There was no telling what he would be facing on the other side of the Great Wall. He was already convinced he would not survive it. He did not want David to share that fate.

Putting thoughts of David to the back of his mind so he could think clearly, Sasha washed his hands in the bowl on a table by his bed. The soap was coarse and did his cold-roughened hands no favors, but having them clean again was something. Returning to the tray of food and tea, he poured himself a fresh cup.

The door banged open and two panicked-looking men filled the doorway. "He's gone! The High Seer is—I mean, the Old Seer is gone."

"Gone?" The High Seer asked in a dangerous tone of voice. "What do you mean he is gone? He was locked up and insane! Find him at once! Send men down into the city, tear this temple apart. Bring me Friedrich or I will take your heads!"

The men fled and with another snarl of rage and a last warning look at Sasha, the High Seer left, slamming the door shut and locking it before the sound of his footsteps slowly faded away.

Sasha moved to the window and tore away the tapestry covering it. To judge by the amount of light, it was morning to midday. He would rest, wait for dark, and then see what he could do about escaping. By then, his magic should be sufficiently restored.

Returning to the bed, he lay down, closed his eyes, and fell asleep thinking of David.

Visions

Friedrich huddled in the ruins of a building, burrowing as deep into the knotted mass of broken wood and shattered stone as he could. He tensed when he heard footsteps and voices, and breathed a soundless sigh of relief when they passed him by.

Cold, so very cold. But better than the dark, damp room where he had been. Away from the voices, away from the hate, the fear. The cold was so much better than that place he had been.

Beloved.

The voice again. He hated the voice, hated more the whispers that he could no longer understand, the images that were shown to him in the shards of a shattered mirror. Broken. Broken. Something was broken. He was broken. Was he? He didn't know.

More voices, but this time they were outside his head. Bad voices. All voices were bad voices. Friedrich tensed and waited for them to go by again because he refused to go back up into the black hole from which he had escaped. When the outside voices finally moved away again, he nearly wept with relief.

Beloved, please, come to me.

Broken. Broken.

I can fix you.

Can't be fixed. Shattered mirror and the pieces have sharp edges.

Fritz, please. Come to me.

I just want to escape all the voices.

The inside voice tried to say something else, but Friedrich ignored it. He crept out of the wreckage in which he hid, stuck his head out, and looked around. When the saw that the street was clear, he crawled free and stood up. He winced as he moved because every part of his body hurt. At least the bleeding had stopped. Moving and hiding would be impossible if he was still bleeding.

He moved deeper into the city, moving around broken buildings and bodies. So many bodies. Human. Sentinel. What had killed the Sentinels? Magic had. He could taste it on the air.

Thoughts of magic made him shudder, caused him to stumble, and he fell with a cry, landing on his hands and knees. Rough stone scraped his palms, made them bleed a little. He heard a shout and climbed to his feet, racing through the streets, searching frantically for a place to hide that did not *look* like a place to hide.

Outside voices grew louder, grew closer, and he finally threw himself into a building that was mostly still standing but wouldn't be for much longer. He ran through the ground floor all the way to the back, to the kitchen, hiding in the enormous fireplace where four or five men could have stood easily. Sinking down into a corner, he huddled there, drawing his knees to his chest and wrapping his arms around them.

He was tired. He was hurt. The pieces that made him were shattered, scattered.

Come to me.

Friedrich fought the voice. He was tired of voices. They were all bad. The voices broke him.

I will fix you, beloved. You know that. Remember it. Fritz ...

"Shut it," Friedrich howled, holding his hands to his head, willing the noise to stop. All he wanted was quiet. Why would no one give that to him?

No reply came, and he breathed a sigh of relief.

He waited for the outside voices to find him, sure that the blood he left behind would be his ruin. But he waited and waited, until exhaustion began to claw at him, and still they did not find him. Still he made himself wait, until he had to move again.

Creeping from the fireplace, he walked back through the building, sidestepping holes and chunks of rock and the shattered roof. In the doorway to the street, he hesitated, looking up and down and all around to be certain that he was alone.

Assured the outside voices would not find him, he resumed traveling through the city. He had to go somewhere, had to be somewhere. But he could not remember the *where*, only that that he had to get there. If he kept moving, eventually he would find it. Right? So he walked through the streets of the city he knew and yet did not know. He remembered when he was little, before the voices had gotten worse. When it was only one voice.

Me. I'm not just any voice. I belong to you. I always have. Come back to me, Fritz. Don't stay there in the dark, please. I beg of you. I love you. Come to me.

Friedrich shook his head back and forth, resisting. No more inside voices. He couldn't break anymore. If he broke more, he did not know what would happen, but he knew it would be awful.

I can fix you. Please.

The voice sounded like it was crying, but Friedrich would not be fooled. Inside voices, outside voices. All were bad.

He slipped on the snow and went down hard, crying out when he landed badly on his right hand, twisting his wrist. Biting back another cry of pain, he waited—but no outside voices came. Slowly standing up, holding his hurt wrist close to his chest, he resumed walking.

The smell of a storm made him draw to a sudden stop. How could it smell like thunder and lightning in the middle of a blizzard? Summer storms and winter storms did not mingle, so how had they? Friedrich followed the scent and realized that it was tangled with the smell of magic he had noticed earlier.

His feet eventually carried him to one of the larger city squares, one that was still in sight of the city gate. Dead Sentinels were piled in an unusually high concentration, as though they had been closing in on a particularly intriguing prey.

But that prey had been the one to come out the victor, for of him there was no sign save the bodies left behind. The residual magic and energy in the air prickled along his skin, brushed against his mind like licks of flame. Friedrich stood in the square and tried to figure out what had happened.

Too late, he realized he was letting the voices consume him, and could only whimper, sob, as the memory of the recent past filled his mind, sharp and bright and agonizing.

He tamped down on his fear when he saw and felt the Sentinels, refusing to look terrified when Sasha appeared so calm. But his fear spiked as he watched Sasha hold out his arms, felt the prickle as Sasha called upon his magic. "David, stay close to me. I'm going to try what I meant to use on the Great Sentinels before I met Achim. I am probably going to pass out when this is done."

"I'll take care of you," David replied, afraid for Sasha, but determined to stand by him and take care of him when he fell. He could not do much, but by the Light he could do that.

"I know," Sasha replied. "Be careful."

The soft, firm tone of the words warmed David despite his fear. He didn't need a god to give his faith to—all his faith belonged to Sasha. Everything he had to give belonged to Sasha. Nodding in reply to Sasha's words, he stepped up behind Sasha and twined his arms around Sasha's waist. He closed his eyes as he felt the magic come, listening to the way the words rumbled and resonated when Sasha spoke them. "Wind and water, snow and ice, thunder and lightning. The depths of the sea and the infinity of the sky answer only to the Storms. Dragons of the Three Storms, Lords of Chaos, destroy these rotted threads of fate."

For a moment, the entire world seemed muffled, like dragging a heavy blanket up over his head. Then he head the thunder, soft at first, but then it boomed and crashed and roared, and his eyes snapped open in a panic as the entire world seemed to shake. Around them the Sentinels reared back, screamed, bellowed—faltered.

Before they could recover, lightning began to fill the sky, bursting in the clouds, racing along them, and filling the word with blinding flashes so close together it seared his eyes. He closed them again, but that only made him more aware of the sting of the snow that had turned more to jagged bits of ice, razor sharp in the force of the raging wind. In his arms, Sasha turned, clung tightly to him, dragged him to the ground, and covered him.

When a sudden quiet fell, he was half-afraid to breathe. Then Sasha slumped in his arms, trembling from exhaustion. David held him tightly, pressed a soft kiss to his brow, and whispered, "I've got you."

"I count on it, little spark," Sasha whispered back, the words making David's eyes sting.

He settled Sasha in his lap, stroked his hair from his face, and got his own breath and bearings back. But before he could decide what to do, or the best way to move Sasha, he heard footsteps. He looked up, saw the men racing toward them, and with a sinking heart realized he recognized the Seer in the lead.

"You boy!" the man said, clearly recognizing him as well. "What in the name of the shadows is going on here? That is the intruder!"

David clung tightly to Sasha. "He just saved Raven Knoll by killing all of the Sentinels! He's no intruder, he's a savior!"

"Blasphemy!" the man roared and behind him, the sorcerers and guards assembled burst into a cacophony of conversation as they looked at the dead Sentinels, at Sasha, at the argument between David and the Seer. Karl, Friedrich recognized. The vilest voice of them all.

He looked down when Sasha jerked awake in his arms. Sasha stared blankly for a moment, then comprehension filled it. "Ah, the Seer from the clearing. I was hoping our paths would not cross again."

Karl's mouth twisted. "Well, at least you have spared me the trouble of having to go find you. And you've solved my Sentinel problem. Grab him."

"No!" David said, pushing Sasha away to stand up and move protectively in front of him. "Get away. You can't—" He cried out as one of the sorcerers flicked his whip, and David heard the crack of it in the moment before it struck him, slashing across his throat and shoulder. He screamed in surprise and pain, stumbled back.

Behind him, Sasha snarled and stood up, moved in front of him and threw out his own arm as the whip struck again. "Touch him again—"

"Neither of you is in a position to be giving orders. Seize them," Karl ordered.

Sasha ignored him and instead half-turned to drag David close. "When I distract them, run. I'll get free of the temple and come find you. Until then, stay safe."

David tried to argue, tried to beg him not to do it this way, but Sasha had already turned away. "Light is not always kind. Thunder roar, lightning strike!"

As the storm broke out across the clearing, David reluctantly did as Sasha had asked him. He ran, pausing only to look back over his shoulder one last time before he fled the clearing entirely, biting back a cry of agony when he saw Sasha fall to the ground, unconscious.

When Friedrich came out of the vision, he realized at some point he had fallen to his knees. The broken stones bit into his flesh even through the layers of his robes, which had been soaked by snow and ice. He really hated the voices. But he could not forget the voice of the vision. *David.* His pain at losing Sasha sliced through the black that filled Friedrich's mind. Something about the boy nagged at him. What, though? Friedrich sighed and stood up. He must find David.

Beloved ...

Friedrich ignored the voice, interested only in David. He must find David. Walking through the square, he found the spatters of blood from the wounds David had suffered at the hands of the sorcerers. He was surprised that they had not hunted David down.

Of course, Sasha had called down quite the storm. They had probably had their hands quite full with him. Friedrich smirked at the thought of Karl being so thoroughly out of his element.

Beloved! Please!

Friedrich stopped abruptly in the street, Drache's voice finally breaking through the blackness that David's vision had cut open. *Drache ...*

You left me, Drache said, and Friedrich remembered when Drache had vanished on him and how frightened and alone he had been. *I thought you had turned from me forever. I could not get you to acknowledge me. Don't do that to me, beloved, please. You're my world.*

As you are mine, Friedrich said softly. *My entire world, even if you are confined to my head. It is not fair that as much as I love you, I can never have you. I don't even know who you are. But I did not mean to abandon you, Drache. I am sorry. It was too much. I can still feel it clawing at me.*

Come to me. I can help you. Don't I always?

Later, Friedrich said. *Right now, I must find David. I don't know why, but I must. He must be terrified right now, the poor thing. I do not miss being that young.*

How long he walked, he didn't know, but the day grew colder and darker before he finally found a house that had a bloody handprint on the doorframe. Pushing open the door, he found David collapsed in front of a cold fireplace.

Clucking in disapproval, Friedrich closed and barred the door, then decided to risk lighting a fire. That took only wood and the barest touch of magic, and then he turned his full attention to David. He wanted nothing more than to collapse, and his injured wrist throbbed something fierce, but there was work to be done.

First, he set up bedding, slowly dragging blankets and pillows out of a back bedroom and arranging everything before the fire. When that was done, he awkwardly stripped away David's sodden, bloody clothes. Tossing the wet clothes aside, he examined the wounds at David's throat and shoulder.

Thankfully, they were not deep for all that they had bled plenty. He held his hand out over the wounds, fingers fanned out, and murmured words pulled from the archives of his mind, *"If pain is darkness, let the light of mercy shine and drive the dark away."*

A soft, shimmering rainbow light spilled from his hand, closing the wounds and easing the worst of the pain they caused. He could not heal them entirely, but they were clean and would heal quickly on their own. He was surprised his own wrist felt better. The matter of wounds addressed, he bundled David in blankets and left him to sleep.

His skin prickled with a vision that wanted to be Seen whenever he touched David's skin, but he resisted it for the present because there were other things he must do before he succumbed to it. Groaning at the aches and pains starting to make themselves known since he was more or less sane again, Friedrich dragged himself around the small house to see what else it had to offer.

Unfortunately, it proved to have practically nothing. Poor David was going to need clothes, however, so Friedrich left him sleeping to poke around the neighboring houses. It took him two hours of foraging, and he was forced to return in the dark, but he did return bearing food and clothes—for David and himself, since there was little point in attracting attention by wearing the robes of a Seer.

Friedrich had never been so sore or exhausted in his life, but he made himself hold on just a little longer. He changed his own clothes, a slow, arduous process, and set David's clothes where he could grab them easily when he woke. He set the food he had found next to it, then sat down, groaning. *So I guess the next step is rescuing Sasha. That will be easier said than done. Venturing back into that temple will not help me keep from going mad again. I'm not sure how one vision pulled me out of it.*

You are High Seer. A fish taken out of water can be saved if it is thrown back into it soon enough.

That doesn't really make sense, as it was too much water, if you will, that nearly killed me.

Some fish swim in the shallows, some in the deep. Some swim in still water, others in currents.

Currents, yes. I was definitely thrown into strong currents. Thank you for not giving up on me, despite the fact that I apparently gave up on you.

You didn't. You were lost. There is a difference. You came back to me, that is all that matters. If you do not visit me tonight, however, I am going to be quite displeased.

Friedrich smiled. *How could I refuse such a lovely offer?*

Drache snorted. Friedrich started to say more when David groaned, shifted restlessly, then opened his eyes. He drew a sharp breath, slapping a hand to his wounds, sitting up, and crying, "Sasha!" all at once.

"Calm down, young David," Friedrich said.

David's eyes snapped to him, and widened as they registered the circle on his forehead. "You—you're—you're one of them!"

He tried to stand up, but yelped when the cold air hit his naked body. Face flushing dark, he sat back down and hauled the blankets up around him. "What's going on?" he asked. "Where are we? Why are you here? Where's Sasha?"

Friedrich sighed. "Those are not all easy questions to answer, and I am sure you would prefer to hear it dressed. There are clothes there and food when you're ready. How do your wounds feel?"

David stared at him blankly for a moment, then lifted a hand to his shoulder, staring in wonder. "It's—they feel fine. Tender, mostly. What—did you use magic?"

Chuckling at his awed tone, Friedrich said, "Yes, I used magic to heal you. Get dressed, David."

"How do you know my name? Oh, I guess the Seers do know it though. That one man ..." He shuddered—then froze and toppled over abruptly in a bow. "Forgive me my rudeness, Seer, I—"

"That man you speak of is little better than a Sentinel," Friedrich drawled. "I do not align myself with him, and he loathes me, which is why he tried to lock me away. Cease to fret, David. I am on your side. Dress, eat."

David stared at him a moment longer, but then slowly obeyed, moving more quickly once the cold air hit him. He scrambled into the clothes and burrowed back into the blankets. "Who are you? I mean, other than a Seer, obviously. Why did that man try to lock you up?"

Friedrich handed him a portion of the bread, cheese, and smoked meat he had found. "That man is called Karl, and he currently believes himself to be High Seer. He locked me up because I *am* High Seer, and he wanted that position."

"You're—" David eyes went almost comically wide. Any other day, Friedrich might have laughed. "I apologize for my—"

"Apologize for nothing," Friedrich said, holding up one hand to stop David's words. "Please. Right now I am little more than an old man hiding from men who should be my allies, but are instead my enemies. They have taken your Sasha to Unheilvol and I do not like to think of what they will do to him there, before they take him to Sonnenstrahl. We need to get him back and then head for Sonnenstrahl ourselves."

David had clearly forgotten all about the food in his hands. "You ... why do you want to go to Sonnenstrahl?"

"The same reason as you," Friedrich said softly. "To stop Teufel. He has hurt us all long enough. I will do what I can to help you."

"Oh," David said and looked down. Friedrich realized he was fighting tears. "I didn't—it's just me and Sasha. Really, it's just Sasha. I can't do anything except cook and watch over him while he sleeps. I didn't expect anyone else to help us." He looked up, as though wary. "Especially not someone of such great importance. Are you really the High Seer?"

Friedrich smiled. "Yes, I am. And you have a fate that wants to be told." It pulled and prickled at his skin, displeased with his resistance. Giving in to the inevitable, Friedrich set his bowl aside and finally really *looked* into David's eyes. He drew a sharp breath at the vision that came to him with sudden, sharp clarity.

> *"You stand alone. There were others with you, but they're gone now. The room is dark. There is nothing inside you but sadness and rage. Your soul is the dark of a moonless night. Anything can happen where nothing can be seen. A choice must be made: darkness or shadow."*

The vision ended abruptly, leaving Friedrich's head throbbing.

David stared back at him, looking scared and confused. "I don't know what any of that means. What's my fate?"

"Your fate is to choose, to decide something important," Friedrich said. "That is all I have seen. Eat, David. Sasha is going to need our help, and you will need all the strength you can get."

Nodding, clearly still more interested in his fate, David nevertheless began to eat. Silence stretched on for a few minutes before he finally blurted, "I don't understand what choice I have to make. Why do I have to make a choice? What does it mean, darkness or shadow? Those are the same thing."

Friedrich shook his head. "No, they're not. At least, they shouldn't be. There's an old saying from the days before Licht was lost: *Without light, shadows are only darkness*. What that means for you, I cannot say. Some visions come to me very clearly, others are too complex to be anything but vague. Your fate is to make an important choice. Accept that and do not dwell upon it."

David nodded and ate a couple more bites of food. He looked up at Friedrich, then away again. After the third not-so-surreptitious glance, Friedrich snorted in amusement and said, "Ask your questions before you choke on them."

"Oh—uh—sorry—" David said, ducking his head. "I only wondered, should I call you High Seer? Or something else? I guess I just don't understand why I have to make an important choice. That doesn't sound right. I'm nobody. It's Sasha who's important. He isn't from here, but he managed to get into Schatten and has been fighting Sentinels and sorcerers and is going to take on Teufel. Does my choice have to do with that? Because I choose Sasha," he finished softly.

Friedrich smiled faintly, remembering all that his visions had shown him of David and Sasha. "I do not doubt, from what I have seen, that Sasha is quite brave and important. But who do you think is the braver, young David? The man who forges into a country with a powerful ring, backed by gods and four nations, or the young man who throws away the only world he knows, the only world he has, to stand by a stranger who could save or ruin that world? Do not underestimate your own value, David. Finish your soup, and then we are going back to Unheilvol. It is time I took back my temple."

David nodded, then said shyly, "You still haven't told me what to call you."

"I haven't, have I?" Friedrich said, amused. "Under the circumstances, I see little point in you calling me High Seer. My name is Friedrich, but ... once, back in the days when I was a boy, they called me Fritz. I think that will suffice."

"Fritz," David repeated and smiled at him. "It's nice to meet you. Thank you for helping me—helping Sasha."

"The pleasure and honor are mine," Fritz replied with a smile.

Unheilvol

David followed Fritz through the streets of Raven Knoll, along the main street and then up the high, black stone steps to the looming temple of Unheilvol. "That's it?" he asked, not certain if he was impressed or terrified.

"Unheilvol," Fritz said. "I love it and hate it in equal measure. The dark seat of Teufel's will, though it was never meant to be anything more than a place for those who sought knowledge to find it."

"You mean it didn't always tell fates?"

"It did, but not the whole of them, or the darkest of them. Once, people were told what they needed to hear to help them flourish and be happy, not what would keep them meek—defeated," Fritz replied. He started to say more, but as they reached the top of the steps, a crowd of Seers and Sorcerers clustered around them.

David immediately recognized the man in the lead—Karl, Fritz had called him, the man who had taken Sasha. "Where's Sasha?" he demanded, stepping up to stand beside Fritz and glaring at Karl. "What have you done with him?"

Sneering at him, Karl said, "The intruder is none of your concern. Be grateful I do not have you whipped for your blasphemous behavior. Did you think showing up here with *him* would make a difference? Arrest them both."

"Nobody is arresting me," Fritz said in clear, ringing tones. "Master Seer, bring Sasha to me in my prayer room."

Karl's skin drained of color before darkening with anger. "You're—"

"Sane? Back to normal? Yes," Fritz said. "You should have killed me when you had the chance, Karl. But ah, yes—you can't kill me. You need me to get into Sonnenstrahl."

"You light-forsaken bastard!" Karl snarled, torchlight glinting off his knife as he pulled from his belt.

Fritz lifted his hands, palms out, and said, *"Dark of heart, dark of mind, and so in darkness find respite."*

Karl's face filled with unadulterated hate in the moment before he dropped to the ground, knife clattering on the marble to finally stop at Fritz's feet. He kicked it away, then gestured sharply to the men who stood gawking at them. "Lock him up. Find the prisoner recently taken and bring him to me at once."

"Yes, High Seer!" The men grabbed Karl's prone body and hauled him away, while other priests vanished as quickly as they could, eager for Fritz to forget that they had ever sided against him. Fritz ignored them, and David could only race to keep up as he stormed through the halls of the temple.

"David! David! Is that you? David!"

David froze at the sound of the familiar voice and whipped around in disbelief. "Killian?"

Laughing in delight, Killian threw himself at David, holding him tightly. "I can't believe it—you're alive! I made it all the way here and couldn't find you, and I heard from one of the caravans that you'd run off into the snow on some wild shadow hunt and yet here you are!" He leaned up and gave David a quick, shy kiss. "I'm so glad you're alive."

"Me, too," David said quietly, staring at him. Killian looked so young, even younger than he had before. He looked different somehow, but David could not figure out what it was exactly that had changed. "It's good to see you again, Killian. What are you doing here?"

Sorrow abruptly filled Killian's face. "Um. Black Hill is gone. Something happened to the new barrier that light-forsaken—"

"Killian," David cut in with a warning tone.

"Anyway," Killian pressed on. "The barrier fell. The Sentinels got in. Not many of us survived, and then the Sentinels came to Oak Hill where we had fled. Nothing is left of Black Hill or Oak Hill. We think Deer Run was destroyed as well. All that's left is here in Unheilvol."

"Destroyed..." Tears filled David's eyes. "That can't be! Not the whole village! Maja?"

Killian just shook his head. "Gone."

"Is everything all right?" Fritz asked, making David jump.

He turned, wiping at his tears. "Oh, I'm sorry, Fritz. Um. This is Killian, my friend. We grew up in Black Hill together. He says—he says the Sentinels destroyed it. All of it, and Deer Run and Oak Hill."

Fritz's face filled with sorrow. "I am sorry," he said. "I hope that very soon we will have control over Schatten again and these tragedies will be put to an end." He looked at Killian. "I am happy you survived. You must be a good lad if David calls you friend."

"I'm his best friend," Killian said, and stood tall. "He never should have left home without me." He glared accusingly at David, then asked, "Have you heard your fate yet?"

"Yes," David said quietly. "We'll have to talk more later, though, Killian. Right now we are going to see—" He broke off when a familiar figure appeared at the end of the hall. Unable to believe it, relief hit him so hard that he began to tremble.

Forgetting everyone and everything else around him, David raced down the hallway to throw himself into Sasha's waiting arms. He buried his face in Sasha's throat. "Sasha."

"David," Sasha said. "You're all right." His fingers twined in David's hair, gently tugged his head up, and then his mouth took David's in a kiss that burned away all the agony of the past several hours, soothed every ache. "I'm glad you're safe, sweet. What in the world is going on? I was told a High Seer Friedrich wanted ..." he trailed off as Fritz reached them, with Killian trailing behind.

David recoiled from the hate in Killian's eyes, feeling awful and guilty that he was clearly happier to see Sasha than he had been to see Killian. That he couldn't return Killian's feelings. "Killian—"

"I guess I'll see you later," Killian snarled and shoved past him, racing back down the hall and vanishing before David could stop him or call after him. He frowned after him, feeling miserable.

A familiar, soothing hand curled over his shoulder, drawing his attention back to Sasha, who smiled reassuringly. "You'll work it out. Boys like that burn hot and so burn out quickly. He won't want to lose a friend. You can talk to him later and work it all out. Come, I want to speak more with Friedrich and make plans for Sonnenstrahl."

David hesitated, staring again down the hall where Killian had vanished, feeling wretched. Would Killian ever forgive him? He fought an urge to go after him and followed Fritz and Sasha down the hall and into a room that held nothing but a table with a candle and bowl on it. The walls gleamed where the light from the candles fell, and David wondered if he was the only one who found the entire black temple unsettling. He had always thought Unheilvol would be a warm, welcoming place.

Instead, it somehow reminded him of the day they had walked up the mountain to cast Reimund's ashes to the wind. His chest ached suddenly at the thought of Reimund. He had been so busy he'd had little time to think of anything except Sasha, Sentinels, and snow. What would Reimund think of all he was doing? Would he be proud, or just annoyed at the waste of time and energy?

He looked up at Sasha's familiar touch to his cheek. "Why so sad?" Sasha asked quietly.

"I … something made me think of Reimund. Killian is here because Sentinels destroyed our village, Oak Hill, and Deer Run. They're all dead. I was thinking how this place reminded me of the day we cast Reimund's ashes. It reminds me of death, and I couldn't figure out why a temple devoted to fate would make me think of death. Is that strange?"

Sasha pulled him close and David went easily, gladly, soothed as always by the warmth of Sasha, the way they seemed to fit together perfectly. "I'm so glad you're safe," Sasha murmured. "I saw that whip strike you—"

"I saw you collapse," David replied. "I wanted to run back to you, but I had to keep running away. I don't like running away from you. I did that once—twice now. I don't want to do it again." He wasn't even certain what he was saying, but the words only made Sasha nod and draw him in for a kiss.

When they finally drew apart, Sasha said, "Wherever we run, we'll do it together, I promise."

David nodded, something in him easing, and he leaned against Sasha and just soaked up his warmth until he heard the door open and the smell of tea and food made his stomach growl. He reluctantly pulled away from Sasha and watched while priests came in and out with table, chairs, and a tray of food.

Fritz beckoned them to sit and poured them all tea. "I have been waiting quite some time to meet you, child of chaos. Teufel has ordered me to take you to him in Sonnenstrahl, but as I told David, I want only to see Teufel removed from power. Whatever I can do to help, I will do it."

"Take me to Sonnenstrahl," Sasha said. "That other one—Karl?—seemed to think that you could get through the gates."

"I can," Fritz said.

David frowned. "Achim said only the Priest of Night and Day could get through the gates without having to kill all the Great Sentinels."

"Achim?" Fritz whispered, skin leeching of color. "Not Achim, Priest of Night. He commanded the Final Hour of the night. How do you know Achim?"

"How do you?" Sasha asked.

Fritz sighed and shoved his teacup away. "I know Achim because once upon a time I handpicked him as a Priest of Night. I am all that remains of the Priest of Night and Day. I am a very feeble shadow of the Seer I used to be, but enough of my power remains that I can get us through the gate. Achim ...?"

"Was one of the Great Sentinels. He says they were all cursed so and the one called the Wanderer was a captain of the guard."

Grief filled Fritz's face. "You knew and you didn't tell me," he whispered. "Why didn't you tell me? Don't tell me you couldn't! Light, Drache—" He broke off with a snarl.

David stared at him wide-eyed, then looked at Sasha, who only shook his head. When he looked back at Fritz, the agony on his face wrenched at David's gut. "Are you all right, Fritz?"

"I—" Fritz slumped. "Forgive me. I am not normally so stupid. Hearing what you just told me was a nasty shock. As I said, I am only a shadow of my former self. Nine centuries ago I was Ehrlich, the Priest of Night and Day. My memories are incomplete and what little is told to me is ..." He sighed, then finally said, "It is told to me by a voice that has always lived in my head. I call him Drache. I believe he is a memory of me, or something like that, though I could not tell you why I see my own memories in such fashion. He also insists there are things he is *not* able to tell me, no matter how much he wishes."

"Achim said something like that," David said. "That they—the Great Sentinels, I mean—knew very little, but could not speak of what they knew because Teufel prevented it. So, um, Drache is probably affected the same way?"

Fritz looked at him in disbelief—and with so much *relief* that it almost hurt to look at it. "Thank you for not calling me crazy. I have never spoken of Drache before. Sometimes I call myself crazy." He stared at his tea and gave a bitter laugh. "Certainly of late I have not been sane."

"The Seers of Sonnenstrahl were once the most powerful magic users in the world," Sasha said softly. "The Priest of Night and Day had only two equals: the Priest of Ashes and the Priest of Storms. It was said that the Priest of Night and Day could see all the threads of fate, could see past, present, and future at will. Back then, they called him wise, not mad. I do not see how that has changed."

"Oh, I think I must have always been mad," Fritz said with a reluctant smile. "I was simply better at hiding it back then. Why else would I have been stupid enough to become the plaything of someone as treacherous as Teufel?"

David sipped at his tea before he said hesitantly, "Did you have a choice? If you hadn't been his ..." He struggled for a minute to remember the word Achim had used, "His paramour what would he have done?"

"Used somebody else, somebody who could not handle it," Fritz replied with another sigh. "I only wish I could say that was my only reason, but I was hardly altruistic. I liked knowing he'd picked me, favored me. But one should never be happy to be favored by one such as that." Grimacing, he waved his hand, batting the discussion away. "We are not here to discuss the mistakes of my past. We are here to figure out how to kill Teufel. I hope you have a specific plan for that."

Sasha shook his head. "Not a single one. No one knows anything about him or Sonnenstrahl, so how could plans be made? I have power, however, and experience in dealing with gods ... I think, anyway. I may not have a plan, but I have faith I will figure out the proper action to take. I will not have much choice, because eventually Teufel will come out of hiding to deal with me once and for all. He is not the sort to hide from a challenge forever."

Fritz frowned. "On the contrary, he is very much the type to hide. He's a shadow. Worse, he is now simply darkness. Do not assume that because he is quiet that he is not there waiting until your back is turned. It's dangerous enough out here, but Sonnenstrahl will be a nightmare."

"I understand," Sasha said. "When are we leaving?"

"Soon," Fritz said. "I would like to say now, but it's late. I also want to know that I am leaving the temple in good hands on the chance—the very likely chance—that I will not return. We should be ready to leave at first light, however. Your room—"

He stopped when an urgent series of knocks came at the door and called for the knocker to enter. "High Seer, the Master Seer is causing problems—he's already hurt several people—"

"I'm coming," Fritz said and left the room.

Sasha shook his head. "For a temple, this place is remarkably out of control. Then again, it sounds like it has been ravaged by problems from within and without. I hope they are able to set all to rights once this is over."

"He told me my fate," David said suddenly. "I—it doesn't make any sense to me. That I have a dark soul and have to make a choice. Do I really have a dark soul? Am I—what's wrong with me? What choice do I have to make?"

"None," Sasha said flatly. "Your life is your own and fate no longer controls you. I will wring his neck—"

"No!" David blurted. "It's not—I don't think he had a choice. He was fighting it, I think, but the power overruled him. It must be hard, not to be able to control what he Sees. Especially when he can See so much. Can he really see past, present, and future? What happens to him and the other Seers if fate goes away?"

Sasha relaxed and motioned for David to join him. Always happy for a chance to be closer, David immediately complied, yelping in surprise when he was pulled down onto Sasha's lap. "We can't—we're in a temple, Sasha."

"What are they going to do, throw us out?" Sasha asked dryly and kissed the tip of his nose. "Do not fret about the Seers, sweet. Fate is not 'going away.' It is merely being put back into balance. The Seers will always See; it is only that they will see possibilities rather than the single fate that Teufel has arranged for everyone."

"I just want it to be over," David said. "I want everyone to be safe again. I don't—I don't—" he broke off, voice trembling. "I don't want any more villages to be destroyed. What's the point of all of this if the Sentinels kill everyone before they can be free?"

"Shh," Sasha soothed and kissed him softly. "What can be destroyed can be remade. I am sorry that Black Hill fell. But you still have Killian, and whoever else managed to survive. Together you can rebuild what was lost. You'll make Schatten a land of light again instead of one of darkness." He stroked David's cheeks, then kissed him again.

"What about you?" David asked. "Will you help us? Do you have to leave? Would—could—don't leave me behind," he finished on a whisper.

"I won't," Sasha said. "We run together, remember? I have no idea what will become of me when this is over, but I won't leave you. I don't remember who I am, but even if I do, I'm yours before I'm anything else."

David laughed suddenly. "All you have to do is ask the High Seer to break the curse."

Sasha smiled ruefully and shook his head. "You're right, of course. How did I manage to forget that?" He drew David into another kiss that eventually bled into a second and then a third. David shivered beneath the onslaught, moaning softly as the kisses grew deeper, hotter, made him ache and hunger for all those things he barely knew of.

Was it wrong to enjoy Sasha so, to think of such things, in a temple and with so many bad things happening around them? It didn't feel like it; it felt like they were savoring what they had because it could very well be lost in the next moment. "Sasha …"

"Tomorrow we leave for Sonnenstrahl," Sasha said, nuzzling against him. "Tonight, however, I intend to find us a room and make full use of it." David shivered at the words, clinging tightly as he took another kiss, a little bit scared but mostly excited. He hoped they did manage it.

He jumped when the door opened again and felt his face grow hot at the smirk Fritz cast them as he resumed his seat. "I see you two managed without me. I am sorry I left so abruptly."

Face still hot, David fled back to his own seat and focused very hard on his tea. Sasha asked, "What did you do with Karl?"

"He will no longer be a problem," Fritz said. "Where were we?"

"We were done, really," Sasha said. "We leave tomorrow. Let me know if there is anything special I must do to prepare. I do not suppose you have a room to spare us?"

Fritz nodded. "Your room is being prepared, along with a bath. You'll have fresh supplies in the morning, as well, and clean clothes. Everything is being taken care of for us."

"And you found people to care for the temple while you are gone?"

"I think so—I hope so. But if we are done here, I will go and make absolute certain of it."

"Please do," Sasha said. "Thank you for everything, High Seer." Fritz nodded and rose once more.

"Your curse!" David blurted and laughed when both Fritz and Sasha rolled their eyes, exasperated with themselves.

"Of course, I'm an idiot," Fritz said. "I Saw when the High Sorcerer placed it on you. I am duly impressed you countered it as well as you did. Let us see it."

Sasha stood up and moved obediently when Fritz beckoned him away from the table. He stripped off his shirt and handed it to David, who was torn between admiring Sasha's fine chest and turning away from the awful spider web that covered most of it.

"The Web of Madness, and though I had no love of Wenzel I confess the curse was skillfully cast," Fritz said. "You are fortunate you were able to counter it as well as you did." He frowned thoughtfully as he touched Sasha's chest with his fingertips. "There are other spells on you—glamours. Those will also vanish when the spell breaks."

"That's fine," Sasha said. "I can always recast them if it's necessary. I just want my memories back."

Fritz nodded and stepped back. "Brace yourself then, because this will hurt." When Sasha nodded, Fritz pressed his hands together and said, *"Though the night seems endless, the day always comes, and the rays of the sun force bad dreams away. Open your eyes and see the light of day."*

Brilliant, golden light poured from Fritz's hands and shone in several beams directly at Sasha, covering him, turning him into a figure of gold. Sasha cried out, faltered—but remained standing. After a few heartbeats of time that seemed to last for hours, the light faded.

The shirt David was holding slipped from his fingers as shock jolted through him. He had known Sasha was not from Schatten, had known he would look different … but he had no idea …

Sasha was beautiful—like a flame come to life. His skin, once so pale against the black hair, had taken on a slightly warmer tone. His features seemed sharper, even more stunning than before. His eyes were the color of dark gold. But his hair was the most amazing thing—a dark, rich red that looked as if it would burn his fingers if he touched it.

He swallowed and said shakily, "Sasha?"

Those brilliant, faintly glowing golden eyes turned toward him and Sasha said in a soft, husky voice, "David. What do you think?"

"You're beautiful. You're like something out of a story. I didn't know hair could be that color."

Sasha smiled at him and beckoned him close in that way he had done a thousand times. It steadied David, reassured him the stranger before him was not really a stranger at all. He leaned up eagerly when Sasha bent to kiss him softly. "Do—do you remember everything now?" he asked when they finally drew apart.

"Yes," Sasha said. "My name is Nikolai Aleksandrovic Krasny."

David frowned. "Your name isn't Sasha?"

"Sasha comes from my middle name," Sasha explained. "I … have a very demanding position back in Pozhar. Often I would sneak out at night and blend in with the ordinary people of Pozhar, who seemed more real to me than most of the people I called peers. Amongst those ordinary people, I went by Sasha." He smiled softly and caressed David's cheek with his knuckles. "I prefer it."

"Me too, though your real name is pretty. It sounds like an important sort of name."

Chuckling, Sasha said, "Not so important. In the end, what matters most is that I am unique amongst all the people in the world. A child of chaos, and the only one capable of getting into Schatten. It did not take me long to almost fail, did it? That scorching Web of Madness almost had me. Thank you for breaking the curse," he said to Fritz.

"I am happy I could help," Fritz said. "Now come, I will show you to your room."

Child of Chaos

Nikolai looked up as he heard footsteps and felt a prickle of awareness that only struck him on two occasions: when he was in danger and when a god walked into his office.

"Eminence," he greeted, setting aside the papers he had been reading over and rising politely.

Raz motioned him to resume his seat, smiling easily. It just made Nikolai's skin prickle all over again. Only a bare six months had passed since the people of Pozhar had revived the god they thought they were destroying. Convincing people it was actually a good thing had not been as difficult as he had expected, but then Pozhar was a country of rebirth and always preferred to focus on that rather than death.

It did not make it any less unnerving to speak with a god as he might anyone else who stepped into his office. Trying to pretend Raz was anything but a god was impossible. He had that presence and those burning ember eyes that saw far more than any mortal ever would.

"Majesty," Raz replied. "I wanted to discuss something with you."

The weight of the words made Nikolai's shoulders tense, but he only nodded and rose, not wanting to be trapped behind a desk while he listened to what Raz had to say. The doors of his office closed and locked *with a flicker of power from Raz, and then Nikolai felt the weight of a spell fall across the room. It was no minor spell, either, and made him long to have his sword and whip at his hips.*

But those days were past. It was one thing to risk his life sneaking about the kingdom as Sasha when he had been the Advisor and the palace happier when he and Zarya were apart. Quite another when he was Tsar.

Fires, he felt tired.

Striding to the windows on the far wall, he stared down at the private gardens below, clasping his hands behind his back. After a moment, he reluctantly turned around. "What did you want to discuss, Eminence?"

Raz moved closer to him, but remained a respectful half dozen steps away. "Have you ever heard of a child of chaos?"

Nikolai lifted his brows. "We normally call them the children of storms, children of the sea, but children of chaos would be another name for the people of Kundou."

"It has been used that way, yes, but in this case I mean a very specific child of chaos," Raz replied. "A true child of chaos is extremely rare and for almost nine hundred years the world did not have one."

"But one has been born now and this is important?" Nikolai asked. "With all due respect, Eminence, come to your point. Is this child of chaos someone you need my help finding? Someone I need to help you convince to do something? Though I cannot

imagine why a god would require my assistance."

Raz nodded. "A child of chaos is someone completely immune to fate. Wherever he goes, whomever he touches or interacts with, he changes that person's fate—or rather, adds chaos so that they are not bound to one fate. He gives them choices."

Nikolai frowned. "All right. And?"

"And there are ways to mark a child of chaos. The easiest marker is that he is a child of four nations and that connection is what makes him extremely powerful in terms of magic."

"I see," Nikolai said and turned back to face the window. "A child of four nations. I suppose that would be obvious to a god when it has never been apparent to anyone else. But then, I look like I am pure Pozharan, don't I? You're the first and only to ever realize."

"Who was your real mother?" Raz asked softly.

Nikolai's mouth twisted. "She washed up on shore near our family estate in the south. Half-Kundou, half-Verde. A storm swept her away before the mermaids got to her. And, of course, everyone knows the scandal of my father's birth, when his father married a Piedren woman. My uncle never really did forgive him for humiliating the family line that way, but I was far too talented a nephew to snub." Sometimes he wondered if his Uncle's attitude was part of why Zarya had always pushed him away.

But he much preferred not thinking about Zarya; there was just too much pain there. Sometimes, it seemed like there had never been anything between them but pain. He turned away from the window and faced Raz. "I cannot be the only person in the world who bears the blood of Kundou, Pozhar, Piedre, and Verde."

"But you are," Raz said. "In an age where travel is rare—and even rarer back when you were born—halflings are rare enough. Occasionally you'll get someone with the blood of three. But the blood of all four? No. You are the only. That is why you are such a powerful sorcerer: you access four veins of magic."

Nikolai sighed. "So what am I meant to do, then? What can I do when I am now Tsar. That keeps me plenty busy enough—and confined to the palace."

"You are going to save Schatten."

"What?" Nikolai said, dropping his clasped hands in surprise. "What in the Fires is that supposed to mean? Save Schatten. That is a matter for gods."

Raz shook his head. "We cannot get into Schatten; Teufel has us sealed out. The barrier will weaken one day, enough for you to get through. You alone can breach Schatten, spread chaos, and destroy Teufel."

"Me alone," Nikolai echoed bitterly. "Isn't gallivanting about and saving the day a young man's job? Somebody who still has a spark in his eye and actually believes things like saving the Land of Shadows can be done? I stopped believing in those tales a long time ago, Eminence. I'm an old Tsar now, not a young hero."

He tensed when Raz moved closer and froze when a hand landed on the small of his back, hating that in the next breath he relaxed slightly, lulled by the reassuring warmth of Zhar Ptitsa's fire. "Schatten has been sealed away from the rest of the world for over nine hundred years. The people there live subjugated by fear, fated to lead the lives that Teufel writes for them. You and I both know that a country like that needs someone who knows what he is about—a man of experience, a leader, not someone young and reckless and brash."

Nikolai stared out at the landscape beyond the castle in the direction of Schatten, thinking of how much Pozhar had suffered under its own burden. Amplified by a thousand-fold ... he could not imagine a world of such pain.

"You're a man of great kindness," Raz said softly.

"Is that another trait of a child of chaos?" Nikolai asked.

"No," Raz said. "Merely a bonus. Another bonus is that you speak Ancient so fluently. Schatten has not changed with the rest of the world. There are not many people in the world who can understand them."

Nikolai sighed. "You need not keep pressing. I hear what you're saying. I am Tsar, closer to fifty than to forty, with more obligations and responsibilities than I can track—and you want me to drop all of that to run off and save Schatten? How does one even go about that?"

"I do not know, yet," Raz said pensively, moving to stand next to him. He leaned *against the glass to face Nikolai, ember eyes swirling, glowing, as he looked up at Nikolai. "We must first wait for Piedre and Verde to restore their gods. Until we know what happened to them all those centuries ago, until we know the whole picture, I cannot tell you much. But I wanted you to know and to be able to prepare. Piedre is still six months from its chance at freedom, and there is yet another year to follow for Verde. That is assuming they succeed. The return of chaos to the world is only a promise of a chance, not a promise of success."*

"So you are telling me I have two and a half years to put my affairs in order."

Raz shook his head. "Three and a half, until the barrier wears down enough to make Schatten accessible. The world can't handle the gods returning all at once. Losing them all at once nearly destroyed it; it could not handle a second onslaught of such power."

"I see," Nikolai said. "Three and a half years to put my affairs in order, and then I must venture into Schatten to save it. This sounds entirely too much like a child's tale for my taste. I'm no hero."

"No?" Raz asked softly. "What would you call a man who sacrifices everything for the good of his people? Who stoically surrendered even his sister and does not resent me for that? You do whatever it takes to do the right thing—"

Nikolai cut him off with a sharp gesture and a rough-spoken curse. "Pretty words, Eminence, but that's all they are. Doing one's duty does not make a man a hero. All it makes him is lonely. If the gods say that I am the one to save Schatten, then I will do it."

He fisted his hand, feeling the weight of Zarya's ring, the only thing from Zarya that he had never wanted. But there he was, wearing Zarya's ring, living Zarya's life—alone. He'd worked his entire life to save his country, but had never been able to save the only man who mattered to him. Foolish as he was, weak as he was, Zarya had still called to him.

Scorch the selfish, stubborn, obtuse bastard anyway.

Nikolai would give anything, everything, to have him back, to rule with him, not for him. Loneliness washed over him, the ache of a life where he went through the motions, but did not really live. What reason did he have to live? He was Tsar, but if he died in the night, Sonya would rule far better than he, and they were already discussing who to begin grooming as a suitable heir. The only person who understood him at all was a nine-hundred-year-old priest, and they were both too busy to have much time to spare for friendship.

And sometimes, it just hurt too much to be anywhere near Dym and Raz, who were so in love the feelings had not faded after nine centuries. It was beyond his comprehension. He could not get Zarya to love him for one lifetime, let alone nine.

He pinched the bridge of his noise, willing away the pain. He had no time to spare for matters that were, literally and figuratively, quite dead.

"Kolya ..." Raz said softly.

"I'm fine," Nikolai replied tersely. "So I have three and a half years to set my affairs in order. Is there anything I must prepare for in regards to breaching Schatten?"

"I'm sure your sword and whip skills could stand to be brought out of storage, but otherwise, I just don't know yet. But don't despair, Majesty."

"Despair? I don't despair. I have never once in my life despaired anything. I make a point not to go further than resignation. It wastes too much energy. Is this a trip from which I might return, or should I plan never to come back?"

The question was childish because of course it would be dangerous. No one had seen Schatten for nine centuries, and Teufel was the heart of the problem. It was extremely unlikely he would survive it, but he would like, however stupidly, some reassurance that Raz was not so easily sending him off to die.

He turned to glance at Raz, but his ember eyes had gone dark the way they did when he looked at things only gods could see. After a couple of minutes, he focused on Nikolai again. "You have no previous lives, being a child of chaos, so I cannot see the past to gauge the myriad possibilities of your future, except to say that I do sense happiness, as I once said to you."

It was a better answer than he had expected, so Nikolai nodded. "Then we shall see, Eminence, if an old Tsar can save a lost world. Now go away, because it would appear I have even more work to do than I first thought."

Raz laughed and reached up to kiss him softly. Nikolai felt a spell wrap around him, burn gently, and then settle. "For protection, that no one else see what you are until I permit it. When I know more, I'll speak to you again about it. Until then, Majesty."

"Eminence," Nikolai replied and went back to staring out the window when Raz had gone.

Sasha pushed his memories aside, far more interested in the present than the past. David's fingers were warm in his own, calloused and strong—the hands of someone who had worked hard his entire life instead of flitting about a palace and turning a blind eye to the problems of a dying country.

As if sensing his stare, David looked up, flushed dark, and looked away again. Sasha was not certain what that meant, but hoped it was a good thing. Certainly David had seemed taken with his altered appearance a few minutes ago. He wondered how David would react to learning he was Tsar—well, had been Tsar. He had absolutely no intention of reclaiming the throne when he was done. His only desire was to stay with David in Schatten. Raz was right: Schatten needed someone who could help them, someone with the experience to do that.

The priest guiding them drew to a stop, pulling Sasha from his thoughts. He opened a door and stepped inside, then bowed them in. "All you need should be here, but please do not hesitate to call for anything you desire. Have a good night. Someone will be sent to wake you."

"Thank you," Sasha said. He waited until the door was closed before he looked around the room, stripping off his jacket and setting it aside with the other clothes already lying on a chest. The room was sparse, but nicer than the one Karl had locked him up in. There was a large bed, clearly meant to accommodate two, a table with a wash basin and various soaps and bottles on a shelf above it, the chest, and another, larger table clearly meant for dining.

It was, he would hazard, a guest room. "Does the temple often accommodate overnight guests?" he asked, finally turning to David—who dropped his gaze as he was abruptly caught staring. Sasha smiled and walked over to him, reaching out to touch because it was impossible *not* to touch David. Even the slightest caress got the brightest smile, the warmest eyes. David was meant to be touched, and Sasha wanted always to be the one doing the touching.

The thought, the realization, was a startling one, but it was stupid to try to talk himself out of it because if there was one thing he had learned about love, it was that there was no undoing it. He had wasted most of his life being in love and then trying to undo that love. In the end he had been left with nothing more than a ring and a kingdom he had never wanted.

David nuzzled into his hand, shy and sweet as always—shyer than usual, in fact, as he cautiously lifted his eyes to meet Sasha's. "You look so different," he said softly. "Like a flame."

"A cold flame, perhaps," Sasha murmured.

That earned him a frown. "Cold?"

"Mm, that is how I am usually described." Never to his face, of course, but he knew it was what people said about him, and was one of the nicer things they said.

David's face scrunched up with disapproval. "Whoever said that is stupid."

Sasha laughed and bent to take a kiss because what was there to say to that? "They aren't stupid, but I appreciate the sentiment, sweet."

"They are stupid," David said vehemently. "There's nothing cold about you. I know what cold is like. I've been cold my whole life, but I didn't realize it until you showed up and I began to feel warm."

That needed another kiss, and Sasha gladly gave it—or took it, he could not tell. And that was the sweetest part of

David, really. He gave what he got in equal measure. He was honest and earnest and simple. There was no hesitation, no dithering or changing his mind a hundred times. No sneaking around the palace in the dead of night, whispering tender words in the dark and cold words in the light. David was open about loving, and just that was enough for Sasha to love him.

He drew David closer, tugged David's arms up to wrap around his neck, and slid his own down David's body and around his waist. Shy fingers laced gently through his hair, and Sasha drew back just enough to say, "Ah, sweet. You do not seem to realize you were the spark that brought *me* back to life. From the moment I woke up in your bed and saw you, I was caught."

David shook his head, clearly not believing a word. Sasha let it go because it was long past time for words, anyway. It was time for actions to speak. He kissed David again, sliding his mouth along those soft lips, lost utterly to the eager, artless response. David clung to him tightly, slender body fitting perfectly against his.

Sasha loosed his arms to trail his hands along David's body, smoothing across his sides and back, then down to cup his ass. That made David freeze in surprise, but Sasha only kissed him harder, taking control of David's mouth.

Pulling away, he sank one hand into David's hair to bare his throat, trailing lips along his skin, and working his way down until he reached the still-red scars left by a sorcerer's whip. Anger flickered to life, but Sasha snuffed it. Drawing back, he stroked the scars lightly with his fingers. "I'm glad you're all right, sweet."

"F-Fritz healed them," David said, face flushing dark as he looked at Sasha's chest instead of meeting his eyes. "The ones on my back and chest are worse."

Sasha smiled faintly and tilted his face up, brushing a soft kiss across his lips. "Scars are not marks of shame, David. Stop fretting." He took another, harder kiss before David could reply, then drew back, and before David could react, grabbed the ends of his shirt and pulled it off. David gasped in surprise, bumps rising on his skin as the cool air struck it.

Anger flickered to life again when Sasha saw clearly the marks he had only glimpsed in the past—angry wounds left by the sharp, metal-tipped tails of the sorcerers' whips. He grabbed David's wrist when he tried to cover them and bent to trail mouth and tongue across them. "You really are quite lovely."

"I'm just a plain village boy," David said, sounding faintly amused. He met Sasha's gaze, and then reached out shyly to stroke Sasha's hair. "You're beautiful."

In reply, Sasha just kissed him again, long and slow, savoring the warmth of David's mouth, the flavor of him. David clung tightly, matched him perfectly, leaving Sasha breathless and aching in more ways than one. Kissing Zarya, he had always held something back, and Zarya had always held too much back. Every kiss had been a hesitation, or a battle. Kissing Zarya had always meant opening himself up to pain. The terrible night they had married, Zarya had tasted of death and reminded Sasha of too many chances thrown away.

With David there was only joy. Sasha drew away and guided David over to the bed, ignoring the nerves he could see rising up, knowing David would not want him to acknowledge it. "Lovely," he murmured, eager to see David completely naked because was already temptation incarnate in just his breeches.

"Sasha …"

Smiling at him, Sasha stripped off his own shirt and cast it to the floor before he crawled onto the bed, straddling David and bending to nuzzle against him. "You are entirely too lovely for this old man, sweet."

David's fingers landed on his shoulders, resting more than holding, but Sasha would fix that. He took David's mouth in a hard, hungry kiss, holding nothing back, making a promise of what was to come. The fingers on his shoulders tightened, instinctively pulled him closer. "Sasha …"

"I do like it when you cannot manage to say more than my name," Sasha said, murmuring the words in David's ear before he bit it lightly, loving the way that made David shiver against him. David moaned softly, a sound that went straight to Sasha's cock, a sound he wanted to hear every night for the rest of his life.

He licked David's lips, kissed him again, then began to slowly work his way down David's body, extracting more delightful sounds and breathless pleas as he drove David mad with mouth and teeth and tongue. He paused briefly to remove the rest of their clothes, laughing with warm affection at the way David moved restlessly, eyes looking everywhere but at Sasha's cock. His hands twitched with an urge to cover himself.

Sasha returned to his task, loving the warm, male scent of David, the taste of his skin. David's fingers ran restlessly over him, unable to settle, but not certain what to do. Sasha chuckled before he lapped and gently bit at one nipple. David's fingers slid through his hair, body pushing up against Sasha's mouth, soft moans filling the room.

Moving further down David's body, he paused to drag his tongue across David's stomach, nipped it just to hear David gasp. He gazed up at David through his lashes, and the naked look of hunger, need, and trust was nearly enough to undo him.

He did not know what he had done to earn David, but he would do whatever it took to keep him as long as he could. Looking down again, he closed his mouth around David's cock. David bucked and cried out, entire body shuddering at a sensation that was no doubt overwhelming for him. "Sasha, I can't—"

Sasha pulled off his cock to chuckle and pressed a kiss to one thigh. "Do you want me to stop?"

"No!" David burst out, then his skin flushed darker than ever. "I mean—"

Sasha sucked up a mark on the soft skin of one inner thigh, laughing again when David swore and tried to move away and toward the bite at the same time. "Do what you must, sweet, but say my name when you do it." He dropped his mouth over David's cock again, losing himself in the task, the musk and the heat, and the smell of sweat and sex. It had been a long time since he'd sucked another man's cock, had enjoyed it so much. Zarya had filled him with fire, but left him feeling burned out and hollow. No one else had that fire. Eventually Sasha had given up trying to find it.

David consumed him, burned away the pain, the misery, the shadows that lingered, made him oblivious to everything except the sound of his name said with a ragged cry as David's fingers tightened almost painfully in his hair when he came, pouring hot and bitter down Sasha's throat.

He pulled slowly away, licked his own lips, then leaned up to kiss David deeply, swallowing the sweet noises David fed him. One of the arms around his neck slipped away, and Sasha jolted in surprise when a shy but determined hand wrapped around his cock. He drew back. "Sweet, you don't—"

"I do," David whispered.

Sasha closed his eyes at the sensation, David's hesitant stroking the sweetest torture. "Harder," he urged quietly, and then sat up, straddling David's hips. He wrapped his hand around David's, encouraged him to tighten his grip, move his hand faster. David was the very image of temptation, sweaty and mussed, hair spread out on the sheets, face flushed dark, his eyes hot with determination. Sasha had a sudden vision of a day when David was confident and knowledgeable enough that rather than stroking him off, he'd hold tightly to Sasha's hips as Sasha rode him, guiding his every moment, eyes dark with wicked promise as he thrust deep into Sasha's body.

The image was enough to tip him over the edge, and he came hard in David's hand, bending to take a hungry kiss as he spilled over them both. When the last of his release had left him, leaving him tired and sated, he stretched out alongside David and bundled him close.

He kissed David's brow and nuzzled against him. "I do love you, sweet."

David froze in his arms, then tried to burrow even closer, trembling slightly. Sasha frowned, concerned, but then David kissed him hard and quick before saying shyly, "I love you, too."

There was probably more that needed to be said, because there was no telling what would happen to them when they passed through the Great Wall, but the words could wait a little while longer. For the moment, it was enough to pull the blankets up over them and fall asleep holding each other close.

The Great Wall

The moon was still in the sky when they left Unheilvol and walked through the too-silent ruins of Raven Knoll. Fritz was surprised they could even see the moon, and hoped the clear skies lasted long enough for them to reach the Great Wall. No Sentinels had ventured into the city since Sasha had slaughtered all those already within its walls, and Fritz had given orders that once the snow eased up the people were to return and start setting all to rights. Hopefully, he would return to a city well on its way to healing.

He did not dare think about what would happen if their mad quest failed.

A shadow moved at the city gates and Fritz frowned when it proved to be a person—and gasped as moonlight fell across him, revealing a familiar figure. He was a tall, broad-shouldered man, with short, curly hair and a close-cropped beard. He looked to be around Fritz's age, but his eyes were far older than that. Power radiated from him, and sadness clung to him like the snow clinging to his beard. Fritz swallowed, then said roughly, "Meine."

"Ehrlich," Meine greeted, walking over to him and embracing him tightly. "I could not believe that I felt your power, Holiness, but I had to be certain. It is you, after all these centuries? We never knew what Teufel did to you, though we had our suspicions ... I did not expect to see you on this side of the wall. I could not believe it when I felt your presence. Have you been here in Unheilvol the entire time?"

Fritz started to reply, but the sound of movement behind him reminded him that he was not alone. "Sasha, David, this is Meine. Once upon a time, he was Captain of the Guard in Sonnenstrahl."

"The Wanderer," David said, voice sounding slightly awed. "Achim said you were real, but ..."

Meine chuckled, rubbing at his beard in amusement. "Real enough, though some days I feel like a nightmare." His eyes fell on Sasha. "You are the child of chaos. We've felt the ripples of your presence. The threads of fate are badly frayed and order is slowly bowing to chaos. It is good to feel possibilities again," he finished softly.

Sasha nodded. "I hope that ultimately I am helping and not hurting."

"Schatten was broken long ago and it healed poorly. If you must re-break it to ensure it heals properly this time, then Schatten will suffer it gladly. Are you heading for the Great Wall?"

Fritz nodded. "Yes."

"Then I will guide you," Meine said.

"Thank you," Fritz said, and they filed into a single line as they left Raven Knoll behind and began to hike through the deep snow.

I still cannot believe you never warned me that my priests had been turned into the Great Sentinels.

I couldn't tell you, Drache said with a sigh. *I wanted to, beloved. There are still so many things I wish I could say, because I think in the end my silence ensures you will hate me.*

No, Fritz said firmly. *I may be able to hate myself upon occasion, but I could never hate you, Drache. Even when I am infuriated with you, I love you.*

Sadness rolled his through his mind, the force of it making Fritz's eyes sting. *Once upon a time, a god fell in love with a mortal. They were desperately, achingly in love for a long time. But things go wrong, and everyone has a point where they can take no more, where even love is not enough.*

You mean Teufel and Licht.

Yes.

All of this because love died?

No. All this because love was lost, forgotten, and everything became tangled. Hopefully I will be better able to explain later. That is all I can say for now. I am surprised that much was permitted. Meine is correct—the threads are fraying.

Fritz sighed inwardly and hoped that Drache would soon be able to say more. *So what will become of the remaining Great Sentinels when we reach the Great Wall and go through it?*

That is up to you, but I think they all long for respite.

You want me to kill them, Fritz said.

It is not what I want—it is what they want. You must realize that, beloved.

Fritz nodded. "I do."

Amusement trickled over his mind. *You keep speaking to me aloud.*

Fritz's face went hot when he realized that was exactly what he'd done. Thankfully, the wind and crunch of snow beneath their feet seemed to have muffled the muttered words. Not that it really mattered, since Sasha and David had already seen him speak aloud to Drache. He still was not certain they did not think him crazy, but at least they were not *treating* him as though he were.

No one thinks you're crazy.

I don't see how they think I am sane after I admit I hear a voice in my head. That is not the mark of a sane man.

It is the mark of a man who is not all that he should be, Drache said quietly. *You've suffered far more than you realize, and I know what it is like to go mad. You were lost for a time, but never mad.*

Drache ... Fritz fought to ignore the sudden, overwhelming ache to hold his figment lover. If he did ever go truly mad, it would be the pain of longing for Drache that finally broke him and drove him into a darkness from which he would never emerge.

A soft rumble rolled through his thoughts, an internal thunder that made Fritz shiver though he could not say why. *I will not let you go mad because of me. Never. If we can topple Teufel, we can find a way to be together. Believe that. You must. For me.*

For you, Fritz agreed—then nearly crashed into Meine when he abruptly stopped. "Is something wrong?"

"I could feel a Sentinel," Meine said, looking out into the heavily falling snow. "I've gotten rid of it, but it took me a moment."

Fritz's brow shot up, but it was David who said, "You can control the lesser Sentinels?"

Meine nodded. "Yes, though control is perhaps too strong a word. Guide, perhaps. If they ever felt like really pushing back they could quite easily. They don't because they do not actually enjoy being the savage monsters Teufel forces them to be."

"They're trapped, too," David said sadly. "Is there anything that Teufel does not control?"

"Me," Sasha said. "No matter how hard he tries, he cannot control me, and the longer I am here, the more his control over everything else falters. Teufel is cold and dark, and the fires of chaos burn bright."

Meine smiled at him, bright and razor sharp. "Yes, chaos is wreaking havoc. I wish I could help more, but I am bound to the Great Wall. I can wander the lands beyond it, but should I ever go through the gates I will die immediately."

"What have you done all this time?" Fritz asked.

"Waited," Meine replied. "What of you? I still cannot believe you were on this side of the wall the entire time. All the times I ventured into Raven Knoll, I never once sensed your presence. Your power is a pale imitation of what it once was, but I still should have felt it."

Fritz shook his head, gripped his shoulder comfortingly. "Do you really think Teufel would ever have let my priests know that I live? Keeping us ignorant of one another was part of his pleasure. You thirteen were made prisoners of the wall, and I was cursed to live the same tragic life over and over again … and I think there is something more to my punishment, something that has to do with Drache, but I do not know what because Drache is not able to explain."

Meine frowned, puzzled. "Who is Drache?"

Fritz explained, "A voice in my head. When I dream deeply enough, I am able to visit him. He is a memory of me, or something like that."

"What—"

"I think this discussion can wait until we find a place to rest for the night. As we have only been walking a couple of hours, that is still some ways off," Sasha interrupted.

Nodding, somewhat relieved to be able to set the matter of Drache aside, Fritz said, "True enough. Onward, then. Let us see how far we can get before we must stop."

They resumed walking and Fritz envied how easy the others made it look. It was painfully clear from his increasingly slow pace that he spent his days in a warm, dry temple. He thought he might have been able to walk a good distance in fair weather, but the added challenges of winter had him all but collapsing in relief when Meine finally called a halt in the shelter of a dense copse of trees.

"Time for lunch, I think," Meine said, and he laughed when they all groaned in agreement. "I do not suppose one of our sorcerers would care to light us a fire? I could manage it, but it would take longer and not be nearly as fine."

Sasha snorted in amusement. "I can handle fire." He left the immediate circle briefly to gather wood. Returning with sticks of all sizes, he broke the larger ones and arranged them all a pile the others had cleared of snow. He snapped his fingers and the wood caught. Fritz held his hands out to the warmth, flexing his fingers as they began to thaw. "How do people travel like this on a regular basis?"

"Necessity," Sasha said. "I admit a good deal of travel would be easier with sleds, but you do not seem to have those in this country. Yet another way, I would not doubt, to ensure travel was difficult enough that people largely remain isolated."

"What's a sled?" David asked, and Fritz had to admit he was curious himself ... but even as his curiosity rose, Drache provided images for him.

Looks like fun, though I don't believe that is priestly behavior.

You were the priest of priests. You determined their behavior.

I sense that was a large part of the problem, Fritz said bitterly, angry at his past self. Drache was silent, but Fritz could feel his agreement.

"So tell me of this voice," Meine said quietly while they pulled out travel food to eat and David made tea. "Drache, you said you called it?"

I am not an it, Drache said hotly. *I may be little more than a memory in your mind, but I'm not an* it.

Fritz smiled briefly, amused. "Drache is *his* name, yes. He takes issue with being called 'it', though I think he's hard pressed to argue being only a memory or a figment."

"My apologies," Meine said. "I have never heard of such a thing. Why would a part of yourself be so separate? If he is your memory, a piece of you, why is he not *part* of you?"

"I assume it had to do with whatever Teufel did to me when he bound me to this life of High Seer, doomed to go mad and die when I turn forty."

Meine's eyes widened. "Forty? But—it was only days past your Holiness' fortieth birthday when … when everything finally went irrevocably wrong."

Fritz made a face. "That does not surprise me." *You did not tell me that.*

I … I had forgotten. It was not a happy period of time and you cancelled the usual celebration because, quite honestly, there would have been no one who was able to attend. You were angry that Teufel and Licht had ruined even so trivial a thing. That all the little things were going away, on top of the larger problems. It was a tipping point. But they were barely listening to anyone by then, which made you angrier. For days you waited for them to return … and then it all went wrong.

The sorrow that filled his mind was too much for Fritz to take, and he rested his forehead in his hands until he could get control of himself again. He was drawn from his misery by the smell of tea and looked up to see David shyly offering him a cup. "Thank you," he said.

David smiled and withdrew, sitting close to Sasha and saying something Fritz did not quite catch.

"So a part of you is kept separate? And reaches you as though a separate person?"

Sasha sucked in a breath. "I can't believe it never occurred to me before. That sounds like a Soul Breaking."

The words sent a shudder of terror through Fritz, but he could not say why. "What is a Soul Breaking?"

"It's what happened to Holy Zhar Ptitsa," Sasha said quietly. "His children were on the verge of destroying him permanently, but the Priest of Ashes managed to save him by breaking his soul into a thousand pieces. Then, over the course of nine centuries, one by one he reunited the broken pieces in the Sacred Fires until the soul was restored and Zhar Ptitsa reborn. It's a brutal process; no mortal could ever handle it as well as a god. I suspect that is what Teufel did to you. Your soul was broken into two pieces. Obviously one half is reborn over and over again as the High Seer. The other half, Drache, was ..."

"Sealed away somewhere," Fritz whispered, and the flood of anguish from Drache told him it was true. "Oh, light. Drache has been alive this entire time, trapped ... forced to wait for me to be reborn over and over ..." *Drache. Drache. How can you bear it? And you could never tell me.*

I still can't tell you, not all of it. But you've never figured so much out before. Oh, Fritz, my other half. I miss you.

Fritz was torn between sobbing and laughing hysterically. *I really am in love with myself, aren't I?*

Who could be better for you than your other half? Drache asked sadly.

Hot tears fell down Fritz's cheeks as he buried his face in his hands. "Drache."

Fritz.

A hand fell on his shoulder, and Fritz felt a warm, calming sensation pour through him. He looked up and nearly was undone by the look of kindness, of understanding, on Sasha's face. "I do not know what it's like to be missing a piece of my soul, but I know what it's like to be so close and so far from someone you desperately love. I am sorry. I promise I will do all I can to see you and Drache are properly united."

Fritz gave a shaky laugh and wiped his face with his snow-damped sleeve. "I am grateful that no one thinks I am crazy. Thank you. I am sorry for your own pain."

Sasha sat down again and looped an arm across David's shoulders. "There is no reason to be sorry for me, not when I have been fortunate enough in all of this to find David."

David smiled, shy but the happiest Fritz had ever seen anyone be. He hoped there might come a day when he could look at Drache that way, sit that close and be able to touch him so.

Someday, other half. I refuse to believe that day will never come. I have waited too long for it.

One way or another, we'll be together, Fritz vowed. *Whatever it takes.*

Drache's agreement poured through him like a soft rumble, or perhaps a sort of rough purr. Feeling somewhat better, Fritz finished his tea, grateful that it soothed the worst of his aches. "What is this tea?" he asked. "I've never had anything like it."

"Maja always called it her cure-all tea. We drink it fairly often in Black Hill, especially in winter. No matter your ill, this tea will cure it."

"I'm surprised it's not more common everywhere," Fritz said. "It should be."

"We have to pick some of the components up in the mountains, and there's not much of it that grows within the barrier. Once in a while, we risk going outside the barrier, but it's just too dangerous to do often."

Fritz nodded and reluctantly handed his cup back to be packed away. "I guess we should resume the journey, then. I am not looking forward to sleeping accommodations." He stood up, groaning as he stretched, working out stiff muscles while the fire was put out and the clearing tidied up. When they all were ready, he followed the others out of the trees and back out into the freezing weather.

It took them nine miserable days to reach the Great Wall and one day more to reach a gate.

When they did finally reach it, he was surprised at the way that Sasha and David hung back, the anguish that filled their faces. David huddled close to Sasha, burying his face against Sasha's chest.

"What's wrong?" he asked.

Sasha's mouth set in a grim line, but before he could reply David explained, "This is where Achim ..." David started to say, then stopped.

"The first Sentinel I killed was a beast," Sasha said, hugging David, stroking his hair soothingly. "But when we reached this gate, we met Achim. It took me a little while to realize he was a Great Sentinel. Like Meine, he was easy to mistake as completely human—except for his power, his knowledge, and the very glaring fact that he lived in the Great Wall. I did not know there was any way through the Great Wall except by killing the Great Sentinels. Achim said that killing him would be a mercy."

"I see," Fritz said softly.

"You did the right thing," Meine said. "Do not linger upon it, please. Achim would not want you to be upset. We have longed for death for a very long time."

Fritz rested a hand on Mein's shoulder and then approached the gate. He rested his hand against it, and let his eyes fall shut. He could feel the thrum of the magic—the curse. *A binding of souls combined with the seal of lifeblood— a soul lock. Twelve souls bound eternally to the wall and a thirteenth bound to circle it. A compass of blood and a broken guide.*

Yes, Drache rumbled in agreement. *Teufel was always the most talented sorcerer in the end. Such things always came so naturally to him.*

I wish he had put it toward kinder magics, Fritz replied. Withdrawing, he turned to face the others, gaze lingering on Meine. "It does seem I have permission to open a gate. The spell, for whatever reason, allows for that, but I also think that with Drache's help I can break the curse entirely. I'm not sure Teufel realizes I can do that. But if I break the curse, it will kill all of you.

"Do it," Meine said fiercely. "We're *tired,* Holiness. Achim and I were the only ones who had not succumbed to our beastly natures. Do you know what it was like to watch them lose their minds and turn into monsters, succumbing one by one? Please, show us the mercy so long denied us."

Fritz swallowed and nodded. "So be it." He stepped in close, embraced Meine tightly. Tears stung his eyes as he whispered, *"Blood of thirteen cast upon the wall, to bind, to seal, to hide. Power of night, power of day, cast shadow and light upon the stones and wash the blood away. Souls too long kept awake, I give you rest, in the name of long lost Licht."*

Meine gave a soft cry, murmured words of gratitude, and then collapsed heavily against Fritz. Eyes blurring with tears, Fritz knelt and laid him down upon the broken road, drawing his cloak tightly around him and resting a hand against his cheek.

Be at peace, Drache said softly, sadly. *Be happy in your next life, Meine.*

Fritz looked up at the sound of footsteps, surprised at the relief that coursed through him when he saw Sasha. Standing over Meine's body, Sasha murmured, *"In fire born, in fire end, to be born again."* Meine's body burst into golden flames, and Fritz knew he should move away, but he simply couldn't. He remained kneeling at Meine's side until the flames died away and nothing remained of Meine except ashes and memory.

"Thank you," he said quietly when it was over and accepted the hand that Sasha held out to him.

Sasha nodded, then indicated the gate. "Can we go through?"

Fritz turned to face it and spread his arms out. *"The Priest of Night and Day bids you open."*

The gate seemed to shudder and the sound of breaking metal filled the air. The doors parted ever so slightly. A scent like roses wafted out, filling the air for a moment before the winter wind snatched it away. "They're unlocked. We should be able to go through whenever we want—anyone can, now. The curse is gone, the Great Wall is just an ordinary wall."

"It's late," David said. "We should rest tonight and head out in the morning?"

Sasha smiled at him and nodded. "That does sound like the best plan. I did not think we would return to this spot so soon." He shared a sad smile with David, took his hand and squeezed it lightly, then led the way inside. Sasha and David set to work starting a fire and preparing food. Fritz tried to help them, but quickly gave up, feeling tired and dizzy and unbelievably sore. Leaving them to it, he retreated to sit on the bed so he was out of the way.

He did not remember falling asleep, but when he woke, he had been settled more comfortably in the bed and the room was dark. The fire had been banked, but still cast warm orange light on the sleeping figures bedded down near the bookcase against one wall.

Fritz yawned and started to burrow back into the blankets, more than happy to stay right there as long as possible, when he heard a noise. He paused, listening closely, then heard it again. Something was outside. He hoped it was just the wind, but in his experience it was *never* just the wind.

Reluctantly he threw back his blankets and climbed out of bed, making a face at the cold as he walked to the door. Pulling it open, he looked out into the night, where moonlight gleamed on fields of endless snow.

Scuffling, someone swearing. Fritz stepped outside, something about the voice nagging at him. He turned toward the sound, which seemed to be coming from the gate, and saw a boy standing in front of it. "You there!" he said sharply.

The boy turned toward him, and the anger on his face drew Fritz up short for a moment. Gathering himself, he said, "Get over here now, boy!"

Slinking over to him, the boy gazed up at him defiantly, still bristling with anger. Fritz grabbed the collar of his shirt and yanked him inside, then closed the door. "What in the name of the Light are you doing here, you little fool?" He gave the boy a good, hard shake, batting his hands away when the boy tried to hit him. Fritz shook him again, then gave one of his cheeks a solid smack. It was more sound than pain, a good way to calm down new Seers overwhelmed by their first hard vision, and it served just as well to make the boy go still. Anger still burned in his eyes, but he stopped struggling.

Fritz realized abruptly that he looked familiar, but he could not say why. Perhaps he'd seen the boy running around Unheil ... that was it. "You are—"

"Killian!" David said from behind Fritz and shoved past him. He gripped Killian's arms and shook him far harder than Fritz had. "What are you doing here, Killian? How did you get here? Can't you stop being trouble for one minute!"

Snarling, Killian broke free—then threw himself at David, swinging wildly, catching him on the jaw and stomach. David went tumbling with a cry of surprise and pain, tripped, and crashed to the floor. Killian fell on him and resumed his careless, but vehement attempts to pummel.

Fritz moved toward them, determined to beat the little brat until he gained some sense, when the unmistakable *crack* of a whip came down. Killian screamed in pain and clutched at his cheek, scrambling away from David and turning toward the source of the whip.

"That is enough," Sasha said, and even Fritz wanted suddenly to bow in apology and not rise until Sasha gave him leave to do so. There was something about Sasha that was commanding—even imperious. Not for the first time, Fritz had the impression that Sasha was a man accustomed to being obeyed. Coiling his whip, Sasha strode across the room and yanked Killian close. "You are a spoiled little brat, and if you do not cease to act like a child then I will treat you like one."

Killian just sneered. "What, lash me like the other sorcerers? They're all the same—eager to beat anyone who steps out of line."

Giving him a shake, Sasha said, "We do not lash anyone as a means of discipline in Pozhar. That little sting on your cheek is trifling and you know it. Do not try to manipulate David into taking your side by playing up lashings. Do not forget the scars on his back are because of you."

"Seen his back a lot, have you?" Killian said with a sneer.

Sasha's mouth tightened. "Speak of David in such fashion again and I will slap you. He is your friend—act like it."

Killian glared mutinously, but kept his mouth shut. Sasha roughly let him go, then strode over to David. "Are you all right?" he asked, gingerly touching David's bruised face.

"F-fine," David said shakily.

Sighing, Fritz grabbed Killian by the arm and dragged him over to the fireplace. "Sit," he said sharply. "One word out of you and I'll put you back outside until the weather chills that temper. Do you understand me?"

"Yes," Killian said. Fritz stared coolly at him, until Killian begrudgingly corrected, "Yes, Holiness."

Stifling a sigh, Fritz went to make tea. *What is going to happen next?*

Do you really want to know the answer?

If I said no, would it matter?

At least it will all be over soon.

One way or another, Fritz agreed grimly.

Anger

David huddled close to Sasha, still numb and reeling from the way Killian had attacked him—the anger. It had felt so much more like hate. Why did Killian hate him so much?

"It's not your fault," Sasha said quietly.

"But—if I had just—" He should have paid closer attention, said something sooner.

Sasha hugged him close, ever mindful of his battered face. "You are not responsible for his emotions or his behavior. Even if you did something wrong, you did not deserve this. Now come here, let me heal you this time."

David nodded, still feeling sort of numb even though his face hurt and he could feel bruises on his chest and arms. He'd tried to fight back, or at least to defend himself, but the assault had left him too shocked to react. Killian had attacked him—beaten him. And the awful things he'd said …

Killian hated him. Why? What had he done so wrong?

His thoughts scattered when Sasha kissed him, and warm, soothing magic washed through him. David gave in to the kiss gladly, desperate to escape his pain and confusion. When they finally drew apart, the worst of the pain was gone. Sasha smiled at him, caressed his cheek. "A cup of your tea and you'll be set back to rights."

Nodding again, David swallowed and finally faced the rest of the room. Killian sat sullenly by the fire, scowling at a cup of tea and looking as though he were seconds away from throwing it at something—or, more likely, someone. David sat down next to him, though not so close that it would be easy to grab him if Killian started swinging again.

Fritz brought him a cup of tea, and David took it gratefully. He sipped at it until the soothing properties began to take effect, then drew a deep breath and asked, "What are you doing here, Killian?"

"I didn't trust *him*," Killian said, voice full of absolute hate as he looked at Sasha. "You've been different ever since you met him. The whole two weeks he was in the village all you did was flutter your lashes and fawn over him and do whatever he wanted. You're so sun-struck you've gone blind. Now you're here doing all this dangerous stuff—and it's all his fault everyone is dead! Maja, my p-p-parents. Black Hill. Oak Hill. Deer Run. Raven Knoll. Everyone is dead or about to starve and it's all his fault! And you don't even care because you're too busy being sun-struck! Black Hill is gone and you don't care!"

David's teacup slipped from his fingers, fell to the floor where it shattered, hot tea spilling over the dirty stone floor. "That isn't true!" he said. "I'm crushed about Black Hill—about everyone. They shouldn't have died, but it's not Sasha's fault! The only person to blame for all of this is Teufel—" He broke off with a cry of pain when Killian hit him.

"Blasphemy!" Killian shouted—then he snarled in outrage when Sasha came practically out of nowhere and snatched him up, yanked him to his feet and dragged him to the door.

"We're going to have a word," he said tersely, then went outside, taking a protesting Killian with him and slamming the door shut behind them.

David picked up the pieces of the broken cup and carried them to the table before fetching a rag to mop up the spill. "Am I really such a terrible person?" he asked quietly.

"I have never met someone less deserving of that word in my life," Fritz said. "How is your face?"

"It's fine," David said, though the latest blow had set the right side of his face to throbbing again. "I just—I don't understand why he hates me. I never meant ..."

Fritz set down the food he had been fussing with and walked over to him, resting his hands on David's shoulders and squeezing them reassuringly. "David, whatever errors you made does not excuse or forgive his behavior. I do not know the whole of it, obviously, but there is never a good reason to beat a man. That aside, he is endangering everyone by recklessly following you all the way out here. It is a wonder he did not catch up to us sooner. I wish he had; I might have been able to send him back to Raven Knoll. For now, he will have to stay here and wait for us, or for the weather to clear enough he can return."

David nodded, but Killian's words haunted him. "I—I am devastated Black Hill is gone. That was my village. They raised me even though I should have died after my parents tried to run away. And then Reimund died early and they blamed me because I'm a child of ill fortune. Then Sasha came along— and I didn't know that Killian liked me. I didn't. We're just friends, I always thought. I ..." He trailed off, not really certain what he wanted to say. He stared at the front of Fritz's robe and wished he did not suddenly feel so much like a child.

"No one doubts your grief, David. You are acting like an adult—of what use would you be to Sasha if you let your grief get the better of you right now? Have you seen me mourn all the people who have died in my city? Raven Knoll is in pieces, and some of it we'll never be able to rebuild. Winter has gone so long, the crop seasons will be a mess. Emergency stores have been depleted. More people will die before this is finally over. Even if we succeed, people will still die in the course of setting Schatten to rights. But sitting around and succumbing to fear and grief will not help. Throwing tantrums and blaming others and hurting them definitely will not help. Continue to act like the man you are—the man Sasha loves— and do not let the vindictive words of a child undermine you."

"Yes," David said, and he looked up. "Thank you. I am sorry for ..."

"Being upset that a friend is hurting you?" Fritz finished dryly. "Do not be sorry for caring—never be sorry for that. Come and help me make breakfast. I am unfortunately far too used to people doing all of this for me. Being High Seer spoiled me far more than I ever realized."

David laughed and obediently—eagerly—set to work putting together breakfast and more tea. He'd just gotten the porridge going when the door opened and Sasha stepped back inside. Abandoning breakfast, David went straight to him, sliding into Sasha's arms and leaning up to kiss him briefly, feeling better just being near him. "Where's Killian?"

"Still outside," Sasha said. "He did not take well anything I had to say to him, but that comes as no surprise. Go and speak to him, I think now it will help. If he turns violent again, walk away."

Nodding, David checked on the porridge, poured Fritz and Sasha tea, then took a cup outside with him to give to Killian. After a moment of glancing around, he found Killian crouched down against the wall a short distance away. "Here," he said quietly, crouching down next to him and holding out the cup.

Killian took it sullenly. His cheek was a livid red where it looked as though Sasha had probably backhanded him. David winced because Sasha was not the kind to lash out so. It made him want to know, and yet not, what Killian had said to provoke him. "What do you want?" Killian asked.

"To say I'm sorry," David said quietly. "I never meant to hurt you or make you think … of course I care about you, Killian. And Black Hill and all the others. You—you're my best friend. I've missed you. I was hoping I would see you again when all of this was over. I'm sorry I led you to think otherwise. I love Sasha, but that doesn't mean I stopped caring about the rest of you. Especially you, Killian. You were my friend when everyone else kept their distance. Only you and Reimund treated me like I was more than an ill omen. I don't want to lose my only friend."

"You have Sasha," Killian said bitterly. "Can't you see that being with him is a bad idea? He's not from here, and it's because of him that everything is wrong."

"He's trying to make everything right in Schatten," David said. "Sasha is a good man."

Killian sneered. "He isn't from here," he repeated. "What could he know about Schatten and what's good for it? And he looks like someone set his hair on fire, or soaked it in blood." His lips curled in distaste.

David bit back an urge to snap at him, or roll his eyes. "Stop it," he said quietly. "I know you don't like it, and I'm sorry that I've hurt you, but I love Sasha and I am going with him to stop Teufel."

"No one can stop Teufel," Killian said. "You shouldn't want to stop him. You never had a problem with Lord Teufel before. You were happy and faithful until he came along. All the problems arrived with that Light-forsaken—"

"Stop it," David said. "I understand you don't like Sasha, and I don't expect you to, but stop insulting him in front of me. You're being a brat."

Killian sneered. "He deserves it. He's not from Schatten, but he comes in here and starts destroying it and poisoning minds with all his talk of chaos. Schatten doesn't need anyone else. That's why Lord Teufel locked them all out. You were perfectly fine without *him,* and if you'd stop being so sun-struck you'd see how stupid you're being!"

"I'm not sun-struck, and I'm not being stupid. Or, maybe I am, but it's the right thing to do. I was never happy, Killian. I was content because I didn't know any different. If you would stop being angry and just think, you'd realize that you—"

"Everyone is dead! Winter won't stop! It's his fault!"

David shook his head. "It's Teufel's fault. He's the one causing winter to go on forever and the one who controls our fates without ever giving us choices or chances to change them. That's not happiness, Killian. That's existing. If that's what you want, then fine. You have the right to make that choice—but I choose to stay with Sasha."

"You don't have the right to make a decision that kills hundreds of people."

"Neither did Teufel," David said. "We're obviously never going to agree, Killian. I'm sorry. You're my friend, and I'll always consider you a friend. But this argument is never going to end, so I think it's best we stop now. Come on, breakfast should be just about ready."

Killian looked ready to punch him for a minute, but in the end he only shrugged angrily and followed David back inside. They sat by the fire with the others, and David prepared bowls of porridge for them. He sat down next to Sasha and ate in silence.

Sasha looked at Killian. "Are you done being a brat?"

"Are you done being a murderer?"

"You are only hurting yourself," Sasha said coldly. "If you only came out here to pick a fight and be unpleasant, then you can turn right around and try your luck with the snow again. You should be grateful you made it here without being eaten by a Sentinel."

Killian just sneered and continued eating.

"We should be leaving soon," Fritz said. "The weather is relatively clear, and we'll make better time."

"I wonder how long it will take to reach Sonnenstrahl," Sasha said, finishing his tea and taking his cup and bowl to the table.

Fritz pursed his lips thoughtfully. "About a day, I think. If we leave soon, we should reach it right around nightfall."

"How could you know that?" Killian asked. "No one has ever been to Sonnenstrahl. We're not allowed. Teufel will not tolerate your impudence much longer."

"If Teufel has issue with me, I wish he would come and speak to me about it so we can end this matter that much sooner. That he hides away in Sonnenstrahl and simply waits for me to be brought to him only speaks to his arrogance." Sasha held out a hand to David, and he took it, smiling briefly as he stood up. "Ready?" Sasha asked him softly.

David nodded, nuzzling into the touch when Sasha caressed his cheek. His heart was suddenly beating a furious rhythm in his chest and there was a knot in his stomach. There was a good chance none of them would return from Sonnenstrahl, win or lose. But that somehow just made him more determined to go. "Ready," he said and leaned up to steal a quick kiss before pulling away to fetch their things.

He could practically feel Killian's gaze on him, but ignored him. Only after he was dressed and ready did he finally turn to Killian and say, "I'll see you back in Raven Knoll, Killian. Truly, I am sorry that I hurt you. We'll talk more when I get back."

Killian scowled and shot to his feet. "Light-taker! I'm coming with you—"

"No, you most definitely are not," Sasha said, voice cracking like the whip he wielded with such skill. "This is not a game and it's no place for children."

"I'm not a child!"

Sasha stalked across the room toward him, grabbed Killian by the scruff of his shirt, and shook him. "Yes, you are. The fact you cannot—will not—see how inappropriately you behave says that. What we are doing is too dangerous for a child and too important to be jeopardized by you. It is not a discussion, it is an order: you are staying here."

Killian sneered at him and said, "Make me."

"I already planned to," Sasha replied in a voice that made even David want to take a step back. He pulled Killian closer to the wall, then let him go. Placing one hand on Killian's chest, he placed the other against the wall and said, *"Bound by anger, bound by envy, bound by the poison of your own heart. Let the binding within be the binding without. To this room I bind you, until five sunrises have gone past, in the name of the gods who know best the taste of poison."*

"You can't—" Killian screamed with rage as the binding took, marked by a band of ivy that wrapped around one wrist. "How dare you!"

"When the spell ends in five days, if we have not returned sooner, return to Raven Knoll."

Killian said nothing, just glared, hate blazing in his eyes.

Sasha stared back coolly. "You'll be fine. There is food enough here for several days, and you need to rest anyway after travelling so hard in all that snow. If we return before the five days are up, I'll break the binding and we can all journey back to Raven Knoll together. I suggest you use the time to think long and hard about your words and your actions. If you do not grow up, you'll lose David once and for all. Fire warm your hearth and light your path, Killian. Farewell."

He walked out, followed by Fritz. David strode up to Killian and hugged him tightly. "I'll miss you, Killian. Be careful, for me, all right? I'll see you in a few days. Goodbye."

Killian said nothing, just watched him go. Sighing softly, David left the gatehouse and joined Sasha and Fritz on the road. They stared at the gate, as tall as three or four men, each gate door as wide as six or seven men, and the iron bars were definitely bigger around than he had first imagined—closer to the size of his thigh than his arm. Like before, he still could not see beyond them. "They're too big for us to move. How do we get them open?"

"That is actually easy enough," Fritz said. He stepped up to the gate, rested his hands upon it, and simply murmured, "Open." The gates obediently began to move, slowly opening inward. The scent of roses struck them, the strength of the scent making David sneeze.

Rubbing his eyes, he stared beyond the gates, jaw dropping at what he saw. Not a single flake of snow was present. Instead, every visible speck of ground was covered in a tangle of vines so deep a green they looked black, with large, sharp thorns with red-violet tips and roses the size of his fist with dark, lush, violet blossoms.

"Those look dangerous," Sasha said. "Beautiful, but dangerous."

David nodded. "They're extremely poisonous. Shadow Blossoms, they're called. Sentinels love to eat them. We use the leaves to make the cure-all tea, but there are only two leaves in an entire batch. It's part of what causes the pain to numb. Use too much and you won't wake up. The leaves carry the least amount of poison. It's the thorns and the roses themselves that are the most dangerous—and the vine, of course. Hopefully we are covered in enough layers that we can probably get through them without trouble."

"Better not to risk it if they're that dangerous," Sasha replied. Stepping up to the edge of the endless field of poisonous roses, he held his hands out over them, and said, *"All poisons fail in the face of purity. Unicorn, grant me the grace of your cleansing touch."*

A fresh, clean scent suddenly filled the air and a fine white mist poured from Sasha's hands and began to cover the field. Sasha stepped back, and they watched in silence as the mist spread, rising until it looked as though the clouds had come down to shroud Sonnenstrahl. With a shimmer of rainbow light, the mist vanished, and David stared in wonder at a field of lush green grass sprinkled with pale gold wildflowers.

"I think now we are safe to press on," Sasha said, and he led the way through the gates, down the road toward Sonnenstrahl.

Sonnenstrahl

The world beyond the Great Wall sent chills down Sasha's spine. "It looks like no time has passed at all," he said. "Like it's frozen."

"It is," Fritz said after a moment, his eyes getting that faintly distant look they always did when he spoke to Drache. Part of Sasha was curious as to what it was like living with Drache, but mostly he was relieved he had no idea. His own thoughts were more than enough to deal with; he did not need another voice added to the fray. "Drache says that Teufel has let nothing touch Sonnenstrahl since he first sealed it off. He wiped it clean and froze it in time."

Sasha shook his head. "That seems depressing to me. Life is meant to move on, no matter how hard that can sometimes be." Images of Zarya rose to mind, but Sasha pushed them away again. Zarya was dead, and he had moved on, though he had not wanted to. He glanced at David, who offered him a smile as he always did. Even Sonya had never smiled at him so often, but then, neither of them had never had much reason to smile.

David, however, never needed a reason. It was just one more reason Sasha did not want ever to live without him.

"So what will happen to it, do you think, if we succeed? Will time catch up to it and turn Sonnenstrahl to dust?"

Fritz frowned as he listened to Drache, then said, "He said it should not be anything so drastic. It should just wake up as if from a long nap. If we do succeed, I wonder how long it will take before people will be willing to live in Sonnenstrahl again. Such a beautiful place was never meant to be so desolate. I've seen it in dreams, when I visit Drache, but always from high above in the tower of the Citadel. I look forward to seeing it properly."

"The Citadel?" Sasha asked.

"Mm," Fritz said. "The very heart of Sonnenstrahl. Drache says it is on a par with the Cathedral of Ashes, the Sanctuary, and so forth."

Sasha nodded. "I do not suppose Drache can offer advice on how to kill Teufel?"

"I'm afraid not; I tried asking already. He says even if he could, he just doesn't know. Teufel rarely visits him, and he does not know where Teufel goes when he is not in Sonnenstrahl. The Shadow of Licht is only that—a shadow. He was created by Licht, given power by Licht, and Drache says that only Licht would be able to destroy his own shadow. If there is another way, he never knew it."

"Shadows without light are only darkness," David said, and Sasha and Fritz both turned to look at him. Shying away from the sudden focus of attention, David said, "That's what you said when you told me my fate: the difference between shadows and darkness is light. So, if Licht is gone, Teufel is only darkness. Would that make him weaker or stronger than what he was before?"

Sasha smiled at him. "Clever, sweet. Very clever. I would hazard stronger in some ways, weaker in others. How does he sustain himself if he is bound to Licht as you imply?" he asked, turning back to Fritz.

"I don't know," Fritz said. "He must feed off something else, but again, Drache cannot say. Wherever, however, he is bound, he is ... well, kept in the dark." He made a face at his own words.

Mouth twisting in wry amusement, Sasha looked up the road, half-expecting to see Sonnenstrahl rising up from the earth, but they were still a good distance away and nothing but more road and field lay before them. At least they were not still trudging through snow. Only minutes into the journey they had stripped off their winter gear and stowed it. The brisk spring-like air reminded him of Pozhar and made him briefly homesick. But then he glanced at David and remembered what it really felt like to be home.

They lapsed into silence, the smooth road making it easy to keep up a steady pace. High above the sun shone—the first time he had seen the sun in months, and Sasha ached for a chance to be able to savor it, to lie out on warm sand or stone and simply bask. He had not done such a thing since he was about David's age. That last summer had been one of the few times Zarya had not made everything between them so scorching difficult. It had been the second time Sasha had allowed himself to believe that maybe they'd be together after all. Unfortunately, it was far from the last time he had deluded himself.

After that summer, he had largely avoided being outside, and then had gotten too busy with his new courtly duties anyway. He had rapidly become known for being pale and still and cold.

Sasha was pulled from his thoughts by fingers curling around his upper arm and looked down to see David smiling at him. "You look sad," David said.

"Idle thoughts stirred bad memories," Sasha said. "Nothing of importance. I was thinking the sun is nice and that it has been a long time since I went sun bathing. I was about your age when last I did it and doesn't that make me feel like an old, lecherous bastard." He sighed, suddenly feeling very old; if he dared to think about how much older he was than David he would be forced to do something drastic.

"You're not old."

"Nearly fifty," Sasha replied, hating himself for bringing it up, but unable to ignore the matter once it had come to the surface. "You should—"

David huffed, fingers tightening on his arm. Sasha only vaguely noticed that they had halted—and that Fritz kept going. "You're not old. I have no interest in anyone my own age. They're too much like Killian, or too much like me. I don't want someone like that. I want you."

There were a hundred questions and challenges Sasha wanted to pose, such as the very real and likely possibility

It was a city of stories, a city from a dream—except for the emptiness, the way every sound they made seemed to echo to every desolate corner. If it was a city of stories and dreams, then those stories had been forgotten and the dreams lost. Sasha ached for it, remembering the same lonely feeling from the Cathedral of Ashes and the Cathedral of Sacred Fire. Such places were meant for people, meant to be a home, a place of solace.

Whatever it cost him, he would give Sonnenstrahl back to Schatten. "Come on," he said softly, for some reason not comfortable speaking in a normal tone. David and Fritz seemed to share the impression, though, because they only nodded in reply. David took his hand again, and though Sasha knew he should keep both hands free in case they were attacked, the comfort offered by the touch eased the heartache caused by the sorrowful city.

They walked slowly through the streets, stopping frequently to look more closely at an empty inn, the houses, a theatre. Despite the sad quality to it all, to see a city frozen forever in time was fascinating. It was as though the sun rose one day and all the people were simply gone. Food was laid out on tables, stalls were only partially set up in the market streets—it really was a city that had paused in the middle of its day.

As they looked closer, however, Sasha also saw the signs of violence: broken windows, shattered furniture, even places where objects and buildings had been burned. Carts overturned, clothes hastily packed.

But there was not, in any of it, a single body.

"What happened to all the people, do you think?" David asked, sounding as though he knew and dreaded the answer.

The expression on Fritz's face confirmed their fears. "Slaughtered. Some fled, and they may have made it, but most died here to be reborn into the fates that Teufel had already written for them. All were driven out of Sonnenstrahl and since that day it has remained as you see it now."

"And Drache?"

"Somewhere," Fritz said, scowling. "He will not tell me where."

"I think the question now is: what do we do?" Sasha said, reluctantly letting go of David's hand. "We're here—I'm here. Exactly as Teufel apparently wanted, though I cannot imagine why. One would think he'd simply want me dead. But whatever his purpose, where is he? We're here in Sonnenstrahl, we've been here and vulnerable, not to mention we were easy targets on the road here. So where is he and why has he not done anything to stop us? It would no doubt be childishly easy to get the better of us."

Fritz nodded in agreement. "Unfortunately, I cannot say because Drache does not know. The splitting of our soul left him insensate for a long time. It was not until he heard his lost half for the first time that he came back to himself at all. That ... is not something he's ever been able to tell me before."

"He must be close," Sasha said and turned to face the tower that was in the distance. Their explorations thus far had kept them close to the edge of the city, never wandering farther in than about halfway. "I would wager that both Drache and Teufel await us in the Citadel, which makes me loathe to go anywhere near it. If he wants us there, I know enough of gods to know there is an ominous reason behind it. I may have willingly walked up to his trap, but I will not walk into it that easily."

"It's late, anyway. Suppose we find somewhere in the city to rest for the night and stand watch in turns. Better to face whatever is to come well-rested."

"A good idea," Fritz said, "but I still wonder what is really afoot here. I think I would prefer simply to have done rather than spend a restless night waiting for a shadow to finally slit my throat." He gazed back at the Citadel. "I don't care what awaits us because Drache is waiting for me. I will go alone if I must, but I am going."

Sasha shook his head. "You will not go alone. I just wish we could go better prepared. We have come too far to die because of haste or carelessness. Venturing into the Citadel when the moon is high seems foolish. Teufel would surely be weaker by the light of day."

"That will make no real difference in the end. Teufel has full control of Schatten. If once he was weaker by day, that weakness has been reduced to a triviality."

"Any advantage at all helps," Sasha said. "I know you want to find Drache, but we will be safer going by the light of day—and after we have had food and rest. If Teufel wants us to come to him sooner, I have no doubt he will say. We pushed to get to the city before night fell. Here it has fallen and he has not so much as whispered. He can wait a few more hours."

Fritz heaved a sigh, but nodded. "As you say, then. I do not like it, but I am not certain I possess a clear head on the matter. Drache aside, though, I do not like lingering out here and keeping ourselves vulner ..." He trailed off as the sounds of a tolling bell filled the air. As one they looked toward the Citadel.

At the very top of the tower, moonlight just barely gleamed off a silver bell swinging back and forth, counting out the hours in deep, melancholy tolls. As it rang the twelfth hour and faded once more into silence, clouds filled the sky, drowning out the moon and stars, leaving them in a world of absolute dark.

The cool air turned frigid and the back of Sasha's neck prickled with sudden alarm. He drew his sword without thinking, and drew upon his magic.

Fritz beat him to casting, whispering, *"Light in the dark."*

Brilliant white light burst into being above their heads, and Sasha cried out in dismay when he saw they were surrounded by ... by ... by he had absolutely no idea what. People, but not people. *Illusions* of people, gray and smoky and shimmering where the light hit them. Hundreds of them, of all sizes and ages, what seemed an entire city of people turned into misty imitations of themselves. "What in the name of scorching flames are those?"

"Ph-phantoms," Fritz said, voice trembling so hard Sasha was not certain he had heard correctly. Swallowing, Fritz said again, "They're phantoms. Souls trapped here and never allowed to be reborn. All those people living here that he slaughtered … they weren't reborn, they were turned into phantoms."

Tears fell down Sasha 's cheeks as the words rolled over him. "That's cruel," he whispered. "Even worse than what he did to the priests. What did these people do so wrong that he thought he was justified in this?"

"Nothing," Fritz said, his voice just as thick with tears. "But we have to discuss it later because right now we have to go. If the legends are true, then phantoms seek the life energy of the living. They're mindless, mad with a lust for life. If they haven't attacked us yet it's because Teufel is holding them back."

David wiped at his own tears. "That's why he never reacted, why he just let us wander—he wanted us to see this."

"Let's move," Sasha said, keeping his sword out as he led the way along a narrow path that was the only part of the street—of the city—not clogged with the awful phantoms.

He was not surprised that the path took them through the city and straight to the center. It spilled out abruptly into a crescent shaped pavilion, the Citadel molded to follow the inside curve. It gleamed like moonlight though the sky above was still a perfect dark, and the stones of the pavilion itself shone like starlight.

On either side of the Citadel, enormous walls fanned out, images of the pantheon carved into them: the Dragons of the Three Storms, wild and decadent in their sarongs and jewels; the Firebird, slight and mischievous, biting into an apple; the Basilisk, tall and somber, gleaming silver forming the bandages covering his deadly eyes; the Faerie Queen and Guardians, resplendent in their proud beauty. Along the top was Licht, a sun that cast gold and silver rays of light over all.

Something moved in the open doorway—a shadow, a taunt. Sasha hefted his sword, reaffirmed his grip on it, and led the way across the pavilion and up into the Citadel.

As he stepped inside, the Citadel seemed to shudder beneath his feet. It smelled of lavender and myrrh, sharp enough to make his head buzz and his eyes water. David and Fritz followed close behind, though they stayed far enough back not to impede him should he have to fight.

Candles flared to life with every step, guiding them through an antechamber and into a sanctuary that was three times the size of the Cathedral's. It was a beautiful room, filled with stained glass—and a ceiling of glass, Sasha realized. But of course, the god of light would want it to shine down in this holiest of places.

Movement caught his eye just as he heard Fritz and David cry out. He froze, nearly dropping his sword when he took in the figure that took up most of the space inside sanctuary. How in the Fires had he missed it?

The beast—the Sentinel—seemed twice the size of the Great Sentinels, though that could have simply been because it filled so much of the enormous sanctuary. Its horns were each nearly as large as a man, curving inward and then back out to end in sharp-looking points. Sasha caught a hint of wings, tightly folded upon its back. Its eyes, as they slowly opened, swirled with every imaginable color.

It moved again, and the scuff and rattle of metal drew Sasha's eye to the massive manacle and chain around its front right leg. The other end of the chain seemed attached to the Citadel itself. The enormous Sentinel could not break free without bringing the entire Citadel down upon itself.

"It's the Holy Sentinel," David said, sounding awed and terrified in equal measure, eyes going wide as the Sentinel slowly rose and gave a deep, mournful sounding cry.

"No," Fritz said, dropping to his knees beside them, sobbing. "It's Drache."

Lost

Beloved, I'm sorry. So very sorry. If I could have warned you I would have. For nine hundred years I have longed for and dreaded this day. My beloved other half ...

Near-hysterical laughter mingled with Fritz's sobs. *You're the Holy Sentinel. Are we going to have to kill you as well? Grant you mercy as we did to the Great Sentinels? Why would he do this to you? To us? What went so wrong that Teufel would bring all this cruelty to people he was supposed to love?*

Drache rumbled, the sound making the Citadel shiver, and bowed his head low. Fritz trembled at the size of him—and the size of his teeth, the longest of which was bigger than his own head. *Beloved ...*

Swallowing his fear, unable to resist that plaintive voice he could not live without, Fritz closed the distance between him and the poor, trapped Sentinel that was the other half of his soul. Drache huffed at him, breath strong enough to rustle Fritz's robes. Still Fritz kept walking, until finally he was able to reach out and gingerly placed his hands on Drache's enormous snout. Fresh tears streamed down his cheeks as warmth and joy and pain rushed through him. "Drache ..." he choked out and buried his head in his arms on Drache's snout, torn between joy and pain, the agony of knowing that they were together but would always be apart.

There is yet hope. The child of chaos is here, is he not? And now that you are here with me, the spell of silence breaks and I can tell you all that I know.

Fritz swallowed his agony, forced himself to behave as High Seer, as Priest of Night and Day, and turned to face Sasha and David. "Meet Drache, my long lost other half. He says now that we are together the spell keeping him silent is broken. He can tell us all that he knows of what happened long ago."

"Where is Teufel?" Sasha asked. "He drove us here with the phantoms, so he must be close."

The phantoms always come out at the stroke of midnight and stay until the stroke of dawn. Of Teufel I have felt nothing. If he is here, he is masking his presence well.

"He says Teufel isn't here, or else he is masking his presence too well for Drache to sense him," Fritz said, grimacing.

Sasha sighed. "I like this situation less with every second that passes, but I guess there is nothing we can do about it." He sheathed his sword and gazed around the sanctuary. "This place is stunning."

"It's beautiful," David said. "I can't imagine how it must look in the daylight."

The most beautiful thing in the world, and when we sang the hymns, they could be heard throughout the city, Drache said, and as he said, Fritz could remember it: people filling the sanctuary of the Citadel, voices rising, spilling out across the city where people would pause in their work and sing along until the hymns ended and the last strains faded away.

Sasha finally looked at them again. "You said you could now tell us all that you know about Licht and Teufel."

Drache stirred, rumbles shaking the Citadel, chain rattling, the sound echoing. *Fritz ...*

Yes, Fritz said and placed both of us his hands on Drache's snout as he settled again. Closing his eyes, he poured his magic out, reaching out to Drache's. Tears stung his eyes again as the two halves of magic met, intertwined, and he felt just a hint of what it meant to be complete.

As they worked their magic, Drache's rainbow eyes began to glow brighter, the jewel-tone colors growing sharp and reflecting off the glass of the Citadel windows. Fritz drew a sharp breath as the magic took, poured through him, and then out in the shape of a shimmery, translucent image of the Drache who had always inhabited his mind—an image of the man they had once been before Teufel split Ehrlich's soul in half.

The wispy image bowed to them, seeming to flicker in and out like a candle. Fritz poured more magic into the spell, one hand still resting on Drache's snout, and the illusionary Drache seemed to stabilize.

"Welcome to the Citadel," Drache said, voice soft and whispery. "It has been too long since anyone but Teufel has entered this sacred place. I am limited in what I can do to help, but I will do my best."

"Tell us what happened," Sasha replied quietly. "Tell us why Licht tried to destroy the world."

Drache nodded. "It started small. Licht was always the most ... reserved of the pantheon. The dragons loved to play, loved to be involved in everything. The gods have always ruled as equals, but if anyone was truly in command, it was the Dragons of the Three Storms. Chaos, after all, is the foundation. But they grew too close, too involved, Licht felt. He was always of the opinion that gods should hold themselves back, observe and guide from on high. The others sided with the Dragons, living close to their children, accessible and always participating. Little by little, that blinded them to problems ..."

"I know a little of that," Sasha said. "Raz explained what the gods do know—that the dragon Raiden was willfully oblivious to the problems create by his lover, and all three dragons neglected the growing problems of their land. Raz grew bitter and cynical with the behavior of his children and turned from them until too late..."

"The Basilisk grew increasingly depressed and isolated himself while secrets and jealousy tore apart the court of the Faerie Queen," Drache finished somberly. "Everywhere Licht turned, he saw the ill effects of the way the dragons and the others had chosen to live. He tried constantly to tell them to remove themselves, to step back, to see what they were doing to themselves and their children. But they wouldn't listen, and frustration turned to anger and eventually turned to hate—and ultimately madness. I think Licht would have moved against them much sooner, save that for a long time Teufel tempered him. Neither of them had always been the terrible beings whom all now fear."

Sorrow filled his face as Drache tilted his head back. Fritz started to reach for him, feeling the pain, the longing, the centuries of sorrow. But his hand slid through the illusion, and Fritz swallowed against the raw pain. He returned his hand to Drache's snout, the scales warm and smooth, reassuring in their own way, but not what either of them needed.

"Licht was often lonely, or so Teufel once told me. Choosing to isolate himself and live apart, he did not often have company—either mortals or his fellow gods. He lived in his tower and left the running of the country to a group of priests with whom he rarely directly spoke. When he did see the others of the pantheon, too often the meeting devolved into bitter arguments.

"One day, after a particularly ugly fight with the Three Storms, Licht retreated to Gold Rock, his favorite spot in Schatten, to lick his wounds. A boy stumbled across him—a young man, really." Drache looked at David. "He was about your age, but regretfully not your maturity. Unfortunately, despite all he said, all the arguments with his brothers, his beliefs ... in the end, Licht was no better than his siblings. The willful blindness he hated in them, especially in the dragons, he fell prey to whenever he looked at that boy."

Sasha frowned. "Boy? What boy? I have never encountered anywhere a tale of Licht attaching himself, in any way, to a mortal. Licht was well-known for the distance he kept, as you've said. What mortal?"

Fritz's mouth twisted as he shared the memories that filled his mind. "The boy, whose name was Stefan, did not realize at first who it was he had encountered. He had only skipped away from his chores to have fun for a bit and found a wounded, sad, beautiful man. Stefan took the man to his home where he lived alone and nursed the man back to health. Licht, touched by the boy's kindness, went along with it.

"Licht eventually left, but could not forget Stefan. Time and again he returned to Gold Rock to watch the boy, though he kept to the shadows and had no intention of revealing himself. But Stefan knew he was there and gradually figured out who it was that watched him. One day he revealed what he knew, and Licht ceased to hide. They started out simply talking, being friends insomuch as mortals and gods can be friends ... but it was not long before Licht took the boy as his lover. In secret, of course, always in secret, because Licht did not want to admit—to himself or anyone else—that he had fallen for a mortal just as he had raged at his siblings for doing."

"They went on that way for some time—months at least, possibly years, though Teufel never told me for certain," Drache said. "I do know that others in the village become aware of Stefan's lover, saw his good fortune. Many became jealous, some hostile, and one day it culminated in a fight that led to Stefan's death. Desperate to try to hide what they had done, the townsfolk burned the body."

"That would never work," Sasha said with a sigh. "I guess the villagers never knew the true nature of Stefan's lover?"

Drache nodded. "When Licht arrived later in the day, it took him only moments to realize what had transpired. Unfortunately, Stefan's body had been burned. He could not restore him. What he did instead was capture Stefan's soul and prevent it from being reborn as a mortal. He kept the soul and placed it in his own shadow, poured his power into it to give it life, made of it a living shadow."

"Teufel," David whispered.

Sasha shook his head, looking impressed and horrified in equal measure. "Everyone always believed that Teufel was *just* his shadow. Even the other gods have never mentioned believing differently. How did the gods never realize the truth? Surely Zhar Ptitsa, of all of them, would have noticed that Teufel was, at heart, a human soul."

"I don't know," Drache replied with a shrug. "I would hazard that the soul changed so much, became Licht's shadow so completely and lost any traces of its mortal origins, that there was no humanity left for even a god to detect. Given how distracted they all were back then, it is not out of the realm of possibility that he simply never noticed the soul had vanished. Sometimes they tire of being reborn and drift back into raw chaos."

"So Stefan became Teufel," David said, looking stunned.

"Yes," Fritz said. "Stefan became Teufel, and together Licht and his shadow were happy again for a time."

"But ... " Sasha said.

Fritz grimaced. "At first, everything truly was well. Licht was so remote, so reserved, that Teufel was good for him and for Schatten. Licht had always been content to keep his distance and let his children manage themselves for the most part. The most he offered was occasionally visiting his priests, to whom he had granted the infamous power of Seeing. Once upon a time, people from all over the world visited Schatten to hear their possible fates. I would be surprised if anyone beyond Schatten remembers that."

Sasha shook his head. "I certainly did not know it. We know of the Seers, that they were admired and feared and the most powerful of magic users, but I never knew the other four countries had sought Schatten out for visions. It makes sense, though."

Drache said, "It was Teufel who found me, gave me power, raised me up to be the Priest of Night and Day. He picked out my twelve Priests, six of Night, six of Day. Together we ruled the country and told the fates of the world. Teufel helped Sonnenstrahl flourish, built up Raven Knoll after Licht gifted him with Unheilvol, made Schatten great. Licht, all the while, kept his distance, content to watch from afar like the sun to which he is bound. Always, he regarded Teufel as his moon.

"What Teufel wanted, Licht let him have. Rare was the occasion Licht denied Teufel anything. Eventually, the power began to corrupt Teufel. Licht might have stepped in if he had been around more, but by the time Teufel began to shift from shadow to darkness, the problems in the world had gotten much worse. Licht spent more time beyond Schatten, trying to make his brothers see reason ... and then later, working his plots against them. Teufel loathed being ignored and neglected. He became obsessed with Schatten, with controlling it. I think he believed that if he could not have Licht, he would have Schatten. He poured out his love and his rage on Licht's children.

"Those of us who should have better seen Licht's descent into madness, the true depths of Teufel's lust for power, the way their connection meant they were actually poisoning each other, instead kept our heads down, too cowardly or captivated to stand up and fight back. By the time we did make a stand, it was too late.

"Licht's rage turned completely to madness, which manifested as a desire for destruction, and so he set about causing it. In Kundou, he taught the Priest of Storms how to steal the power of the Three Storms and seal the dragons away. He provoked the riot that's resulted in the death of Zhar Ptitsa and manipulated the Faerie Queen into giving him a poison that would allow him to steal the destructive powers of the Basilisk."

Sasha frowned. "How do you know all that?"

"Because I Saw it," Drache replied. "My power ... what you see now, between Fritz and me, is paltry compared to the Priest of Night and Day we once were. As Ehrlich, my powers were nigh unstoppable, gifted by a beautiful shadow who once, in his own way, cared for me. The past, present, and future were mine to see, and I had the strength to sustain most of the visions. When I could no longer deny that everything was going wrong, when I felt the world scream as chaos lost its grounding, I went to the top of the Citadel and I Saw. But I acted too late, and when my priests and I finally stood against Teufel we lost—brutally, humiliatingly—and suffered cruel punishment for our defiance.

"The only good that came out of the entire affair was that the Basilisk stood strong. He killed Licht and gained the world enough time to fix itself. But the death of Licht broke Teufel, and he surrendered completely—irrevocably, I fear—to his own black heart and the madness that had been slowly infecting him because of his bond with Licht. With nothing else to lash out at, he turned on Schatten. That is when we defied him, or tried to, and there was no one to stop him when he struck. He murdered the residents of Sonnenstrahl first and bound them as phantoms just to break us. It worked.

"After that, he turned my twelve priests into the Great Sentinels, created the Great Wall, and bound them to it. Me, he saved for last, after I had been made to watch all the rest of Schatten suffer. When there was no one else left to break, he broke me—took my life, captured my soul, and tore it two. One half he bound forever as you see me now, the Holy Sentinel chained for all time to the Citadel. He cast the other half out into the world where it was cursed to be reborn again and again into a life of madness and misery."

Sasha sighed softly, face full of sorrow as he looked at the glass ceiling and the endless dark beyond. "Some loves are panacea, some loves are poison. Bad enough when an ordinary man cannot see his love for which it is. All the world suffers when the gods refuse to see the difference." He looked at them again, reaching out to gently touch David's cheek before he said, "At least we know what really happened back then. Armed with that knowledge, we should be able to figure out how to stop Teufel and set all to rights again. Which raises an interesting question: Teufel is the Shadow of Licht. He's not human; he's a human soul sharing Licht's life and power. He should have died with Licht, but did not. Why? Answering that question will tell us how to kill him, but where we can find the answer I don't know."

"Come, now, your Majesty. Are you so easily flummoxed as that?" Drawled a cold, derisive, and familiar voice.

They turned as one toward the sound of it, and Fritz's mouth gaped when he saw who had spoken, who stalked toward them like a Sentinel that had scented easy prey. Sasha immediately went for his sword—

"Enough!" The word boomed out, making the Citadel shake and groan even as it filled with brilliant, blinding, pale lavender light. Fritz screamed in pain and tried to shield his eyes, but found he could not move.

A cold, mocking chuckle filled the Citadel as the light slowly faded. "Now *that* is a Light of Truth." When the light faded away entirely, Fritz saw that even Sasha was frozen in place, gold eyes blazing with fury.

Still laughing, Killian walked up to Sasha and smacked his cheek sharply, then trailed one hand down his chest. "You tried, fire child, I will grant you that, but chaos does not mean that I lose all ability to make people dance the way I want." He drew the sword from Sasha's sheath and walked over to David.

"Killian, what are you doing?" David asked, tears falling down his cheeks.

Killian stroked his face, then leaned up to kiss the tears away. "Do not trouble yourself, pretty. All will soon be well and as it should be." He kissed David's lips, then turned away and walked over to Fritz and Drache.

Though he still appeared to be a young boy, Fritz would know those hard, frigid eyes and cruel smile anywhere. He had gazed upon them countless times when he was still Ehrlich. "Your eyes, your smile ... but you wear a different face. How?"

"Ehrlich, Ehrlich ... so beautiful and talented, in the temple and in bed. If you had but stayed obedient and willing you would not be suffering so. I could have used your help all these centuries, you know."

"We would rather die," Drache said and growled.

"You know very well I would never grant you anything as easy as death," Killian replied reprovingly. "I thought I had taken care of you, but I see that you've been very naughty, communicating with each other. I'll have to think of another way to break you to obedience."

"I wish we had defied you sooner," Fritz whispered as Drache roared in agreement so loudly that the glass ceiling cracked in several places.

Killian laughed and the sound of it seemed to make the room grow colder. "But you didn't, and here you are, still trying too late to be something other than a priest and a whore. I think a grander punishment is in order, but I have other things to do first. Until I feel like dealing with you, be as stone." He waved his hand dismissively at them.

Fritz made a strangled noise and nearly fell to his knees as the Light of Truth released him, catching himself on Drache. In the next moment, he felt hot and cold all at once— except for his feet, which had no feeling at all. The numb feeling creeped up slowly, and Fritz's eyes pricked with tears. *Drache …*

But there was no reply, as Drache too began to fall to the spell, both of them paralyzed again as the spell crawled up their bodies, turning flesh to stone.

He watched, helpless and afraid, as Killian turned to Sasha. "I suppose I should be honored that those fools sent not just a child of chaos, but the Tsar of Pozhar to stop me. How does it feel, your Majesty, to die so far from home? To die knowing that you have not just failed, but by handing yourself to me have doomed the world to return to the dark times from which it is so desperately struggling?"

"What—" Sasha's question was cut off with a pain cry as Killian abruptly plunged the sword into his gut, then viciously yanked it out again. He watched, unmoved, as Sasha fell to floor, blood pooling out all around him.

"No!" David screamed, and Fritz *felt* it when he broke the hold of Teufel's magic.

The last thing Fritz heard before the spell claimed him completely was David's wracking sobs.

Darkness or Shadows

"Why?" David asked between sobs. His tears fell on Sasha's face as he stared helplessly into dying eyes. "Why would you do this? Sasha—don't—you *can't*—"

He sobbed harder, body shaking with the force of them, when Sasha just gave him a gentle smile before his eyes lost the last of their brilliant, golden glow. David screamed, held him tighter, and begged for gods he barely knew of to do something—anything.

But Sasha remained slack in his arms and the only immortal who responded to his screams was Killian, who drew closer, standing so that he loomed over David and Sasha. David looked up at him, shivering, because Killian still looked like the boy he had always known and yet so much like a stranger. "Why, Killian?"

Killian dropped Sasha's sword carelessly to the floor, the sound of metal against stone echoing, scraping against David's ears and making him flinch. "I think, sweet David, that you know very well that's not my name. The boy Killian died long ago; I merely took his body."

"Teufel," David whispered, shuddering again, unable to bear looking into those dark, hate-filled violet eyes. "Why?" he asked, staring at Sasha's still, pale face.

"Why? You'll have to be more specific, *sweet*. Let me have that." Before David could protest, or even register what was happening, Teufel had taken Sasha's body away from him and moved further into sanctuary.

David stared, numb for a moment, then surged to his feet. He swayed slightly, feeling dizzy, but managed to regain his balance. He caught up to Teufel and grabbed his arm, forcing him to a halt. "No! Give him back. Isn't it enough you've killed him? Why can't you leave his body in peace? Leave him—" He stumble d back with a cry, holding a hand to his throbbing cheek, licking blood from his lip. "Please," he begged. "Leave Sasha alone. He's dead. Leave his body alone."

Teufel laughed. "Dead? He's not dead ..."

"What—"

"Yet," Teufel finished, and David wanted to cry all over again. "I cannot have his soul turning back into pure chaos; I need it for something else. It really was quite kind of them to give him to me." He turned away from David and continued on, moving carefully around poor Drache, whom Killian had turned to stone—

But David did not dare think about Fritz and Drache right then. He could not save them, not unless he somehow saved Sasha. Who wasn't dead yet. David barely dared to believe, certain Killian—Teufel—was just being cruel.

He followed Teufel around Drache and up several steps to a high dais where a white marble altar table rested in the very middle. Along the back of the dais were nine tall windows, each portraying what he assumed were the other gods, given what Sasha had told him about them. Ignoring the windows, David watched as Teufel laid Sasha down upon it and stroked his hair from his face with a gesture that should have looked gentle, even loving, but only made David want to throw up.

There was so much blood and only as he went to wipe away the tears in his eyes did David realize that he was covered in it. His skin pulled where it was already turning sticky on his hands. But Sasha wasn't dead, and David had to cling to that or else he feared he would lose his mind once and for all.

Approaching the altar, he looked down at Sasha's slack face. Dead, or near enough, without ever being given a chance to fight after trying so hard and losing his memories and managing to do what no one in Schatten had been able to for nine hundred years. It wasn't *fair*.

"You do have good taste, David, I will concede that," Teufel said, tracing the lines of Sasha's face. "The poor Tsar is a beauty. It's a pity his brains do not equal his features."

"He's not a—whatever you're calling him. He's Sasha."

Teufel chuckled and gave David a pitying look. "He's the Tsar. Put in terms you understand, he is the Chief of an entire country—Pozhar, to be precise. He surrendered that role to come here, but I would not doubt that it is waiting for his return. There are people waiting for him, people who want—need—him to return. The gods made him undertake this quest; he is, after all, the oh so special child of chaos. But he has a country to run—or did, anyway. Now, I am afraid he has left two countries in ruin. Not a very good Tsar in the end, hmm?"

David just stared. "I don't understand."

"No, I guess you wouldn't," Teufel said. "But it does not matter, sweet David, because the Tsar is no longer your problem. They should not have trusted that a single man could defeat me because all they have done is given me exactly what I need to get exactly what I want."

Swallowing against the lump in his throat, David just kept staring, trying to comprehend what Teufel was telling him. Chief of Pozhar? What was Teufel going to do to Sasha? And what was that about Sasha's having to go back?

It didn't matter—nothing mattered except stopping Teufel, but David had no idea how to do that. He didn't even understand why he was still alive when he was easily the most useless person present. "What are you going to do?"

"I'm going to put chaos away again," Teufel said, stroking a hand along Sasha's body, then back up to his face, giving his cheek a sharp slap before finally stepping away. "The problem with chaos is that it needs a sheath. The Eye of the Storm does a good job of stabilizing chaos, but the Eye is also bound to the dragons and so is biased. Chaos is a blade of sharp edges that does not care what it cuts and should be used carefully. Order is the sheath, but here come the gods trying to destroy that sheath once and for all. Fools them for not trying hard enough, because I can now use the pretty Tsar to my own ends."

David felt more helpless than ever, listening to everything Teufel said and not really understanding any of it—only that they had lost, and that Teufel was going to use Sasha to do something terrible.

Teufel laughed, cold and mocking, as he regarded David. "The raw power of our dear Tsar and his ring is all the power I need to take back control of the threads of the world. I can set all to rights again, undo the work the gods have done so far."

"The threads …" David trailed off as Teufel stepped around the altar table and approached him. He jerked when Teufel twined arms around his neck. "Why do you look like Killian?" David whispered, because the contrast was hard to endure, was breaking his heart. Killian, whatever their disagreements, had been his friend.

But apparently he'd never been Killian at all.

Teufel laughed again, and his breath smelled like rotted meat. "Why, to get close to you, sweet David. To befriend you, enthrall you, and save you."

"Save me?" David asked, wishing Teufel would stop calling him 'sweet'. "Save me from what?" He wanted desperately to pull away, but he was more afraid of what would happen if he did.

"From yourself," Teufel replied, rubbing against his cheek like a cat. "Come with me." He walked to one side of the altar and pushed at a panel that proved to be a hidden door.

David obeyed, not certain what else he should—could— do. He hoped, however futilely, that he would be able to discover the way to stop Teufel and save everyone. Bitter self-loathing washed over him in the next breath, however.

Him, save everybody? What could he possibly do when Fritz and Sasha had fallen in mere moments? He was a village boy who had still been running the local goods shop and occasionally assisted the village healer. He wasn't meant to be anything except that. To think he could save the day when the High Seer and Sasha had failed ... it wasn't just laughable, it was pathetic.

"There, there," Teufel said soothingly, voice almost sounding kind. If not for his foul breath and the clammy feel of his skin, David might have been lulled into thinking he really was Killian and still cared. Teufel waited for David to reach him, then slid an arm around his waist as they continued walking together down a dark hallway.

Eventually they stepped into a room of black marble threaded with veins of gold and silver. Tapestries decorated the walls, but the room was so dark David could not really see what they depicted. In the middle of the room was a large pool filled with shimmering ... David wasn't sure *what* it was, actually. Like watery milk with a rainbow sheen to it.

"Essence of Moon," Teufel purred. "It is always used by the Seers when they tell the fates of the penitents. Amusingly, if you were to ask them why they needed it, they would not really be able to say. 'Necessary to See,' and 'It's how it's always been done,' or 'it adds clarity,' perhaps, but that's all they could offer."

"Why, then?" David dutifully asked.

"It keeps them from aging," Teufel said, leaving David to move around to the other side of the pool, staring down at the Essence that gleamed and shimmered in the dark room. He stripped of most of his clothes as if suddenly unable to bear them. "Seers in the earliest days were honored because they took up a hard burden—the price of Seeing into the future is time. Seers aged faster than most because they sacrificed minutes, hours, and days that eventually piled up into months and years for their power. Licht eased that as best he could, but he did not believe in interfering too much. All things have a price, and his priests knew it when they accepted their positions.

"Then I came along and created this," Teufel said and knelt before the pool. He dipped his hand into it all the way up to his elbow, swirling it around. "Essence of Moon is ... distilled divinity, in a sense. Poured into a vision bowl, it bears the cost of life for the Seer. The only one who never really needed it, who had so much power and life he was able to bear the cost without even really noticing, was my Priest of Night and Day. Because of power I woke in him, gave to him; power he tried to use against me in the end."

David wondered if Teufel knew how bitter he sounded, how hurt. He fought a sudden, stupid impulse to say he was sorry. He *wasn't* sorry. Teufel had more or less killed Sasha, he'd hurt Fritz and Drache. He'd probably killed Killian, too. He'd kept his people isolated and afraid, and then set the Sentinels loose upon them. He did not deserve anything except the death Sasha had planned for him.

But David still felt a tug of ... *something* ... when he looked at Teufel's angry face with its shadow of sorrow. "Why?" he asked again. "Why are you telling me all of this? Why pretend to be Killian?"

Why did David matter?

Teufel did not reply, simply stood up. His bare arm was covered with the Essence, which clung like thick, shiny oil to his skin, dripping slowly to the black marble as he walked toward David.

It took whatever strength David had remaining not to recoil, not to turn and run. But he couldn't repress a shudder when Teufel caressed his cheek with an oily hand in an imitation of every precious touch Sasha had ever given him. David started crying again. "Why?" he repeated yet again, desperate for an answer. "Why are you doing this?"

"Because Licht left me," Teufel snarled and abruptly grabbed David's hair, yanking his head down and to the side, forcing David to a painful angle. "Because he wanted to remake the world so badly he was determined to kill *everyone*. No exceptions. Nothing—" his voice faltered the barest bit. "Nothing was good enough. So he set about destroying the world, and in the end, all he destroyed was himself. But it was me and Schatten who suffered the most for it. The only things he once claimed to love, he was willing to risk to obtain his goal. He left *me* to deal with the fallout of *his* mad hate. So I did—I sealed his country away and gave his people the absolute fate he desired."

David shook his head. "But the Sentinels ... the isolation ..."

"For the good of all," Teufel replied. "Licht wanted order at any price, and so I instilled order. But without him, I'm nothing. The body he gave me slowly died with him. So I move from body to body, keeping each alive as long as possible with the Essence of Moon. But those bodies were weak, insufficient. I need a body, a vessel, that is better suited to me. I have waited a long time for you to be born, sweet David ..."

"Me?"

Teufel kissed him, whisper soft, and let him go. "Even I can only manipulate the threads of fate so far. I could not prevent the birth of the child of chaos, though I tried. Neither could I speed your arrival, though again, I tried."

David tried to ask what he meant, but fear closed his throat. He shivered as Teufel released him and undid the laces of his shirt, then drew it off and tossed it aside. Teufel ran his hands along David's bare chest, one hand cool and dry, the other warm and slick, leaving behind trails of Essence of Moon. "So much dormant power in you, exactly as was in me so many centuries ago. You are *exactly* like I was back in the days when I was mortal: a quiet, harmless village boy, alone in the world, despised and envied by those around him ... born on a night when there was no moon in the sky."

The words made David choke. "The dark of a moonless night ... Anything can happen—"

"Where nothing can be seen," Teufel finished. He twined his arms around David, nuzzled against him. "It could have been easy for you."

"E-easy?"

Teufel laughed, rotted breath wafting across David's skin. "Your parents left you, the village thought you an ill-omen and simply waited for an excuse to toss you out. A life of too much work and too little pleasure. Beaten half to death for a triviality. The only man you had to call family tragically killed before his time. Only faithful Killian to love you, to stand by you when the village cast you out."

"They didn't cast me—"

Teufel dug his nails into David's back, drawing blood, making David whimper. "Do you want to know your fate? The fate woven for you if I had not changed it? Child of fate, child of the moonless night—abandoned by your parents, abandoned by your caretaker, abandoned by the village that saw you as a blight. They would have thrown you out, beaten and bloody, left you to die in the snow. But they would have feared being found out and dragged you back to burn you." His lips brushed against David's ear. "Do you know why?"

David shook his head, unable to speak, fear locking his voice and blurring his eyes with tears.

"Because you are the dark of a moonless night, where they live in oblivion, content that there is nothing they can do about it. They must wait for someone else to appear with a light, take their hand, and guide them. They need someone else to endure the light and tell them where to go, what to do, free them of that burden of choice. Sweet David, they fear you, fear me, because we embody the darkness they most want and do not want to admit to wanting. Licht knew that, understood that what people most wanted was darkness, but that they would not know it or admit it because chaos, in all its sharp brilliance, is bewitching."

"But Licht is light …"

"There must be light to give people the shadows they crave. If people do not know light, they do not appreciate darkness. But if the light shines too brightly, they flee to their precious dark. Even your Sasha came here to the land of shadows because it was a way to escape the stifling heat and light of Pozhar. He was Tsar, he was favored by a god and loved by many across the whole world, and he is the child of chaos. But he was not truly happy until his memories were snatched away and he lived in darkness."

David closed his eyes and did not fight when Teufel pulled his head down to rest in the hollow of Teufel's shoulder. His tears fell against Teufel's skin, which smelled like incense and shadow blossoms instead of like rotted meat as it had before.

"Were you not happier, sweet David, before the light drew you out and took everything from you?"

He shook his head because he'd had that fight with himself before, hadn't he? "Sasha—"

"Was never meant to be here. He tore apart your world—everyone's world. Chaos is what destroyed everything, by being uncaring, by being unable to care. Chaos is chaos and cannot be anything else. Sasha is a child of chaos. He will never stay and settle into an orderly life. The brilliance of chaos would have called him back to Pozhar eventually."

"He promised—"

"So did your parents, so did Reimund. Everyone makes promises, but even the gods break them. Licht made the same promises to me that Sasha did to you. But here we are alone, their promises in shards at our feet. In the dark, the truth always comes out. Think of all that has gone awry since Schatten was cut by the jagged edges of chaos."

Helplessly, David did, remembering the way everyone had been nice to him, the way Killian would later come and tell him of all the things they said when he wasn't around. How much worse the gossiping behind his back became after he started nursing Sasha back to health. How cold they had turned once Reimund was no longer there, how much more they disliked him when Sasha was there. The way the sorcerers were meant to protect, but would beat a man simply for being jostled in a crowd. He remembered the way the caravan had broken out in a fight just because they had no guidance and how eager they had been to keep him when he'd lashed out at them, made them behave.

As the thoughts and memories overwhelmed him, he clung tighter to Teufel, scarcely aware he did so, desperate for any sort of grounding as he battled his own mind.

"Without chaos running loose," Teufel said softly, "there would not have been nine hundred years of misery. No sacrifices, no Vessels, no Roses, no Tragedy. All those events, all those deaths, all the misery of the world because of chaos. I would still be at Licht's side, still be beloved. You would be a young man happy in his little village, madly in love with your best friend, and eager to plan the life you would spend together. Instead, you are used by a lost Tsar eager to escape the mistakes of his past—mistakes that his presence caused because he is chaos and destroys everything he touches. If you want happiness, David, stop staring into the sun and let your eyes become accustomed to the dark. Stop being a coward and accept your fate."

David swallowed as Teufel urged him to lift his head and could do nothing as Teufel leaned up to kiss him. Whatever he'd expected—not that he'd expected Teufel to kiss him—it was not for Teufel to taste sweet and warm. Like fragrant tea with a generous amount of honey. His kiss was nothing like Sasha's. Teufel was firm, claiming—conquering. David felt like a battle had been fought, but it was over before he'd ever had a chance to find a weapon.

Then Teufel's kiss changed, turned soft and gentle, soothing as if he were relaxing in a rare hot bath, or a holiday where he got to sleep for a couple of extra hours beside the warm stove. If he had been conquered, the surrender at least was sweet.

As he was drawn deeper and deeper into Teufel's embrace, images began to pour into David's mind.

A beautiful man with a long fall of sun-gold hair sitting against a boulder, covered in bruises and blood, clothes torn. Despite his obvious pain, the man had the most beautiful smile.

~

The sheets were soft against his back, but Licht's skin was softer still, his lips like silk as they slid across his body. Licht was almost too hot to touch, but that heat was so very satisfying as it pushed inside his body and claimed him.

~

His new form was strange, but in a good way. And the way Licht looked at him had not changed, except to strengthen in potency, and that was all Stefan—no, he was Teufel now—wanted as he was pulled into Licht's arms and given a hungry kiss.

~

Licht looked at him, but never saw him. Not anymore. Not unless Teufel was atrocious, did something wrong, made him angry or jealous. He hated it, but he would rather have Licht's anger than be forgotten entirely. Why was he no longer good enough when his love for Licht still shone so brightly? Why could Licht not see it?

~

Dead. He screamed in agony, the power behind it making all of Schatten suffer with him. Licht was dead and he had left Teufel behind—had not even said he might be going to his death and told him goodbye. No longer loved him enough to do even that.

Despair overtook him and turned to hate. If Licht wanted order, then he would have it, and the whole world could suffer with him.

Teufel opened his eyes, stretched and flexed in his new body, settled into it. He was pleased to finally be back in a body that was worthy of his power, would sustain him for centuries instead of mere decades.

He stepped over the husk of Killian's body and knelt in front of the Essence pool, scooping up handfuls and drinking them, adding strength to his body, preparing himself for what he must do next. Rising, wiping his mouth, he left the Essence chamber and headed back to the sanctuary to sacrifice the child of chaos and cause such a state of disorder across the world that it would be easy to take back full control of it.

When he entered the sanctuary, he glanced at the frozen halves of his Priest of Night and Day, who had betrayed him nearly as deeply as Licht. He was still pondering a suitable punishment, but he supposed there was hardly a need to rush the decision.

Dismissing them, he turned to the altar—and nearly fell to his knees, struck by pain and longing and a thousand memories he did not want.

David saw the look in Sasha's eyes, but was not sure what it meant. Before he could think longer on it, Sasha's mouth covered his. He drew a sharp, startled breath, excitement and heat rushing through him as he realized that Sasha was kissing him.

But then Sasha started to draw back, and in dismay, David leaned in, chasing after him, lips landing clumsily on Sasha's again—but apparently that was all Sasha needed to take back control. His lips were warm, slightly chapped, but moved with knowledge and, David suspected, real talent as they tasted and explored David's.

He kissed back shyly, awkwardly, hoping fervently that he was not doing a horrible job of it. His body was too hot, felt too big for his skin, and he mourned when Sasha finally drew back. He stared at Sasha, still not quite able to believe what had just happened. "You—you kissed me."

Sasha laughed and did it again, and the joy of it nearly made David dizzy. Kissing back was easier the second time, though he struggled briefly with his hands before he finally settled them cautiously on Sasha's shoulders. He curled his fingers into the fabric of Sasha's shirt as their mouths slid together. David wondered if Sasha was going to go further than kisses and wished suddenly they were not in the middle of the Shadow Forest and practically buried in snow.

~

Stefan flushed at the look on Licht's face, scarcely able to believe it really was Licht who stood before him—had been Licht the whole time. What would a god see in a simple boy like him?

"You're beautiful," Licht said, resting his hand over Stefan's heart. "Every thought, *every emotion—you're the most beautiful thing I've ever encountered."*

"You made me, lord."

Licht's mouth quirked in that way Stefan loved—amused and affectionate with a touch of tenderness. "I do not make anyone, not as you mean. I am merely in charge of seeing that chaos does not consume them."

"Then perhaps I was simply made for you," Stefan said shyly, hoping he did not presume.

"Whether or not you were, you are certainly mine now," Licht said softly and drew him in close, tilted his chin up and brushed a thumb across his lips. Stefan drew a startled breath, but before he could form words, the thumb was replaced by Licht's mouth, warm and sweet and tasting of summer.

Stefan clung tightly, kissed back heatedly, certain that he was exactly where he was meant to be.

~

Sasha's touch was dizzying, but the way he looked up at David through his lashes was very nearly David's undoing. Then Sasha took David's cock in his mouth and David thought he might expire in the best of ways. "Sasha, I can't—"

Sasha pulled off his cock to chuckle and pressed a kiss to one thigh. "Do you want me to stop?"

"No!" David burst out, then flushed at how desperate he sounded. "I mean—"

Sash nipped the soft skin of one inner thigh. David swore and writhed, not certain if he wanted more of that or for Sasha to stop. Sasha laughed again. "Do what you must, sweet, but say my name when you do it." He returned to his task, taking David deep into his mouth and light that was the most shocking—

David tried to hold back, make it last, but the heat of Sasha's mouth, the feel of it, the unreality of Sasha doing such a thing—and to him—was just too much. David came, letting out a ragged cry, fingers digging into Sasha's hair, skin hot with the realization that he had so shamelessly spent himself in Sasha's mouth.

He lay there panting as Sasha slowly pulled off his cock, heart kicking up another notch when Sasha crawled up his body, licking traces of David from his lips. David whimpered as Sasha kissed him, realizing the bitterness he tasted was himself. The thought made him moan.

Swallowing his nerves, suddenly desperate to do something in return, he loosed an arm from around Sasha's neck and reached between them to wrap one hand cautiously around Sasha's cock. Sasha startled in his arms and drew back. "Sweet, you don't—"

"I do," David whispered, hoping he was conveying that he did need to, possibly more than he needed to breathe.

Sasha closed his eyes, but the look on his face just reassured David he was doing the right thing. "Harder," Sasha said, then abruptly sat up to straddle David's hips. He wrapped his hand around David's, encouraged him to tighten his group, move his hand faster. Determinedly, David obeyed, eyes raking Sasha's body, landing on his face, addicted to the emotions that filled it, the fire that blazed in Sasha's eyes that said he very much enjoyed everything they were doing.

Then Sasha bent to kiss him, hard and deep, as he shuddered in David's hand, release spilling between them, and David had never been so pleased in his life. Eventually Sasha calmed and stretched out alongside him, held him close, and there was nowhere else David ever wanted to be.

~

Licht kissed him hard as he sank into Stefan's body. Stefan whimpered, clung to him, fed eagerly on his mouth as he was overcome with heat and need.

It had taken Stefan entirely too long to convince Licht to take things so far, to come to this after so many months of little more than kisses and teasing touches. He had exhausted himself convincing Licht that all would be well, that it was right, that there was no manipulation or advantage being taken.

That a god could love a mortal and a mortal could love a god without it all going wrong.

Every second of frustration was worth it as Licht drove into him, claimed him, his gold eyes blazing, beautiful, making the sun dull by comparison surely. Stefan clung tightly to *him and let the light consume him, crying Licht's name when he finally came apart.*

~

Sasha pulled him close and David went easily—gladly, soothed as always by the warmth of Sasha's body, how perfectly they seemed to fit together. "I'm so glad you're safe," Sasha said. "I saw that whip strike—"

"I saw you collapse," David replied. "I wanted to run back to you, but I had to keep running away. I don't like running away from you. I did that once—twice now. I don't want to do it again." He wasn't even certain what he was saying, but the words only made Sasha nod and draw him in for a kiss.

When they finally drew apart, Sasha said, "Wherever we run, we'll do it together, I promise."

David nodded, something in him easing, and he leaned against Sasha and just soaked up his warmth.

~

"I love you," Licht said softly. "I would never want any harm to come to you."

"If I come to harm, it will not be because of your love," Stefan said. "Without you, I would definitely die. Stop fretting so, my light, and just love me."

Licht took his hand and kissed the back of his fingers. "I do love you and always will. Perhaps my brothers know something after all."

"*Perhaps you can show them how to do it properly,*" *Stefan replied teasingly.*

Snorting softly, Licht said, "You need rest before I show anyone anything. Come, let us walk. The blossoms are in bloom."

"*They call them Licht blossoms, you know.*"

Licht made a face. "Flowers do not need to bear my name; they are beautiful all on their own."

Stefan laughed and twined their fingers together as they walked down the path that led from his house to the winding mountains beyond, which slowly turned from green to white as fields of Licht blossoms bloomed.

"No!" Teufel howled. "Stop it! Stop it!"

Wholly against his will, he reached out to caress Sasha's face, tracing his forehead, his eyes, his nose, lingering on his lips before gently combing fingers through his hair.

They say love overcomes everything, but the sad truth is that it doesn't. Sometimes, love just isn't enough.

Hot tears fell down Teufel's face, and he wiped them angrily away, furious that he was still succumbing to the weaknesses of the man he had just recently been. He was not David anymore. He was Teufel, the darkness that ruled Schatten. The darkness that was all that remained because love had not been enough to keep Licht at his side, to make Licht want to live.

But try as he did to fight it, the truth would not stay quelled. *I don't want to be darkness,* David's voice whispered.

Teufel sneered. *Darkness is what people want. Darkness is how it always ends. Even Licht preferred the dark in the end.*

No. Light to dark to light again. Balance. One cannot exist without the other.

"Then why did he leave me in the dark!" Teufel bellowed, causing the cracked glass of the ceiling to break free and fall to the floor where it shattered into a million pieces, the sound of it deafening. "There is no light! He left me, he died, and now there is no light and there never will be."

"Do you mean it?" Teufel asked, smiling excitedly. Licht brushed his fingertips across Teufel's face, ending at his lips. "You don't mind me making changes to your priests?"

"Our priests," Licht corrected, smiling at him, bending down to brush the barest of kisses across his mouth. "You hold my essence, my power—and most importantly, you hold my heart. I am not here as often as I want since I must contend with my careless siblings." His face clouded, but the kiss Teufel pressed to his fingers burned the clouds away. "I trust you as I trust no other. If I am not here to take care of Schatten, then I at least am able to rest easy knowing that you are doing it. So do as you will, sweet shadow mine."

Teufel sank to his knees, overcome by anguish as the forgotten memory washed over him.

You hold my heart.

He wrapped his arms around himself, wanting the pain to *end*. He was *tired*. If he had Licht's heart, then why had Licht left him?

I trust you as I trust no other.

He didn't want Licht's trust. He wanted Licht.

If I am not here to take care of Schatten, then I at least am able to rest easy knowing that you are doing it.

He hadn't taken care of Schatten, though. He had poured all his anger with Licht into it, warped Schatten into a land of dark and terrible fates, made them suffer in Licht's stead, made them suffer with him.

Teufel had never wanted to rule Schatten *for* Licht; all he had ever wanted was to help Licht, to stand beside him, behind him, to be Licht's. "I don't want to be darkness," Teufel whispered. "I just want to be a shadow."

Heat—burning, agonizing heat—tore through him, made him double over and choke on a scream. He clawed at his chest and nearly passed out as the heat abruptly burst from him and the sanctuary filled suddenly with brilliant, golden light.

Teufel shuddered, slowly looked up, and stared in confusion at the orb of light that hovered in the air above the altar. It called to him, soothed him, and made his body ache with longing and loss.

"The heart of Licht," said a soft female voice.

Looking down, Teufel saw a woman standing at the top of the stairs leading up to the dais. She was beautiful—breathtakingly so. She wore a long, elaborate dress and butterfly wings fluttered on her back, containing every conceivable color; her hair shimmed silver-gold and her eyes flickered with countless colors. She was also transparent, as though a phantom, though Teufel knew she was not one. "Faerie Queen," he said quietly, more confused than ever.

"Only a last, fading piece of her," the woman said, voice soft, faint. *"A shard of memory in the ring of chaos."*

"What do you want?"

"I no longer exist. I have no wants. The question, little shadow, is what do you want?"

"Licht," Teufel whispered, eyes drawn helplessly up again—first to the golden orb and then to Sasha.

"Then let there be new light," the Faerie Queen said. On the altar, Sasha began to glow, and the ring on his finger burst into a riot of rainbows like a crystal struck by the sun.

High above, the heart of Licht flared into even brighter light, searing Teufel's eyes, forcing him to look away. When the light finally faded, he turned back and slowly rose to his feet. At first, nothing seemed different.

Then Sasha's fingers twitched and the Citadel echoed with a soft groan.

Licht

His head felt strange—fuzzy, as if it had been heavily packed with wool before someone stored it away. He groaned again and sat up, only vaguely aware that he was even lying down. Why did he feel as though he had just woken from a very long sleep? But even as he thought it, the wool began to fall away, and the dusty, sleepy corners of his mind began to fill with light.

He tilted his head up, smelling flowers on the breeze coming in the poor, shattered windows of the Citadel's sanctuary. The sun was coming up; he could feel it like a lover's whisper in his ear. He closed his eyes and, with a thought, banished the clouds. He sighed softly as the sunlight began to overtake the dark sky—first deep blue, then a hazy gray, then ember to rose to cream until, finally, a brilliant blue morning sky greeted him.

Licht smiled and finally looked down ... and his smile slid away as he took in all that was wrong, and the memories of Sasha collided with the memories of Licht. He dropped one hand to curl over the wound in his stomach that was no longer there and slowly slid from the altar. He took a step toward the man watching him with wide, dark, tearful eyes, then another step, until he was close enough to caress soft skin. "Oh, sweet. What have you done? You should have left me dead. I am not fit to be a god, and I am not a god who should have been revived."

Teufel gave a shaky laugh, then abruptly fell against him, head buried against Licht's chest. "I made my choice. I won't live without you anymore. Don't make me."

"I won't," Licht said softly. "I'm sorry." Teufel gave another one of those horrible laughs, and Licht drew him up into a deep kiss, held him tightly. "I'm sorry," he said again as he pressed their foreheads together.

"I'm not forgiving you yet," Teufel said. Licht did not reply, just kissed Teufel's tears away and held him again.

"Fix Ehrlich," Teufel said eventually, voice sad. "There's nothing I can do now for the other priests, but do something for Ehrlich. Please."

"Of course," Licht replied, and with a last caress to Teufel's cheek he stepped away and down the altar stairs. He walked past Drache's enormous form until he reached the front, where Fritz had been turned to stone with one hand still on Drache's snout.

Licht sighed softly, sadly. "My poor priest, I am sorry this is what happened to you." His gold eyes shone and he lifted a hand, drawing in sunlight, filling the sanctuary with it. As it slowly faded away, Fritz sank to his knees and Drache opened his swirling rainbow eyes. His soft growl filled the sanctuary. *Lord Licht?*

"Sasha?" Fritz whispered.

"Yes and yes," Licht said, rubbing at his temples, willing away the deep ache of two minds merging, the past and the present, the power that was rushing back to embrace him after existing so long without him. "I am Sasha and Licht. Still two, but they are rapidly becoming one." So many names: Nikolai. Sasha. Licht. "I think, at least amongst us four, I would prefer Sasha. That is who I am now and who I will always be."

"Of course, Lord Sasha," Drache rumbled. *"It is … strange to see you back, but good."*

Sasha's brows rose at that. "Good? I cannot think, after all that I have done, that seeing me is *good.* I told Teufel he should not have done it."

"David. If you are to be Sasha, then I am still David."

Turning, Sasha watched as David strode toward him. His eyes glowed with power, and something about him looked older, more jaded. The sweet, earnest young man was still there, but he possessed Teufel's sharp edges. "Of course," he said before he turned back to Fritz and Drache, looking at them thoughtfully. "I cannot reunite you as you are," he said at last. "Your soul has been split so long and gone in such different directions that the two halves have each become a whole of sorts. If I send you on to your next life, the halves would not be able to rejoin for several lifetimes. Of course, if that is what you want, certainly it will be done. But I can also do this ..."

He placed one hand on Drache's snout and hummed softly. Soft, shimmering rainbow light poured from his hand, covered Drache's snout and then moved along the rest of his body. He shone in the sunlight like sparkling glass—and then began to shrink.

When the light finally faded, in place of the Holy Sentinel stood a tall, lithe man with dark skin and pale gold hair that fell all the way to the floor in a thick braid. Fritz made a pained, disbelieving noise. "Drache—"

"Fritz," Drache said and swept him up, and the two clung tightly to each other, crying quietly and exchanging desperate, clumsy kisses.

Sasha smiled faintly, relieved that at least one wrong was on its way to being righted. There were thousands to go, but the first step had been taken. Leaving Fritz and Drache alone, he took David's hand and left the sanctuary by way of the stairs off to the right.

They began to climb, leaving the sanctuary behind entirely and entering the Citadel tower, climbing the steps that wrapped around the outside. The spells he had woven long ago to keep people from falling had not faded in all the years he'd been gone.

He could have easily bypassed the stairs to reach the top, but he preferred the walk, steadied by the sound of David behind him. When they finally reached the top, he closed his eyes and simply enjoyed being bathed in morning sunlight, relished its loving touch on his skin.

David pressed against his back, arms twining around his waist, his sweet, cool shadow to counter the sun's heat. Turning around in David's arms, Sasha kissed him deeply, lingering, savoring the heat and flavor of his lover. Drawing back, he brushed David's hair from his face and said, "You look good this way, sweet." He stroked David's face, his hair, admiring the slight changes to his features, those sharp edges that had not been there, the power and knowledge in his eyes—and that bone-deep sweetness that nothing would ever banish. "Are you happy this way?"

"I'm happy to have you," David replied, though it was more of Teufel's resonating timbre in his voice. "I'm your shadow; that's all I ever wanted. Don't leave me again."

Sasha kissed him, holding him close and pouring everything he had into the embrace. "I promised I wouldn't. I intend to keep that promise. I *will* keep that promise. But our reunion may be short lived."

David nodded in understanding. Sasha gave him another brief kiss, a caress, then turned to stand at the edge of the roof of the tower. He looked out over Schatten, narrowing his eyes at the clouds that lingered. With a thought and a flash of sunlight, he banished them, giving all the sunlight he could to a country that had gone too long without it. Next, he broke the spell of winter and hastened the melting of the snow.

Satisfied with the weather, he turned his attention to other matters. Throwing out his arms, he said, *"Beasts of the dark, be at peace and choose your fate: beasts of light or nothing at all."* Across the land he heard thousands upon thousands of roars as sentinels threw up their heads to answer his spell. He felt it as many simply chose to die, felt as others assumed different forms, eager to try a different, happier life.

Sasha turned his gaze to the Great Wall and with a simple pulse of flashing power, turned it into dust that scattered in all directions, falling to the fields and mountains and valleys of Schatten, eventually to blossom into white and cream flowers that had been lost long ago. In the city below, he banished the tortured phantoms, tears stinging his eyes at the strength of their relief as they went into the arms of Zhar Ptitsa at last.

Looking toward the distant Unheilvol, he gave strength to his Seers, repaired the damage to the city, and replenished their depleted supplies. Reaching out to the minds of the Seers, he bid them care for the people of Schatten, send them to Sonnenstrahl when they had nowhere else to go. Minds rippled with shock, with awe, but every Seer immediately answered the summons with a quiet, but earnest, *"Yes, Lord Licht."*

Immediate concerns of Schatten addressed, Sasha drew a deep breath and reached out with his power one more time, casting it out over the barrier that had kept Schatten away from the rest of the world for over nine hundred years. One last deep breath, and as he exhaled, Sasha shattered the barrier.

He swayed as it broke, still new to his powers and ill-prepared for the backlash. David steadied him, then pressed against his side. The sound of thunder rumbled through the cloudless sky and David trembled in his arms.

Lightning flashed and the roof of the Citadel was suddenly filled with eight additional figures. Sasha slowly turned to face them.

"Kolya?" Zhar Ptitsa said, looking at him in shock.

Nankyokukai looked just as stunned. *"He's* the child of chaos you never told us about, Raz?"

"Nikolai," Culebra said softly and crossed the roof to him, reaching out to take his hands. "It is good to see you again, though I admit I never anticipated meeting you this way."

Sasha smiled crookedly. "Bright day, Highness. Well, Eminence, I suppose."

Culebra laughed. "I think my name will suffice. Meet my sister; I've told her about you many times."

Obediently Sasha turned to the fierce-looking woman who stepped up to stand beside Culebra, extending a hand in greeting. "My lady."

"Cortez works fine," Cortez said. "You're nearly as pretty as my little brother, but not as pretty as the Unicorn."

Gael snorted and rolled his eyes. "I cannot believe the Duke of Krasny is standing on the roof of the Citadel as a reborn Licht. I cannot believe you were the child of chaos. What is going on?"

Sasha shook his head. "I don't know where to begin." He really didn't. After all he had done, he had expected a cold reception at absolute best. If they had simply shown up and killed him again ...

Raiden strode across the roof to stand right in front of him as the others hastened out of his way. Even David slid out of the way as the two gods stared at each other. Raiden's eyes were as deep and dark as the sea, etched with a pain that Licht shared, a pain he wished with every element of his being that he had not caused. "I'm sorry," he whispered.

"I'm sorry, too," Raiden said. "We excelled at not listening to each other. It was easier to blame one another for mistakes we both made. I've had nine hundred years to accept that. Whatever your mistakes, Licht, you were not alone in making them. We, every one of us, did things we should not have, helped to bring our fates down upon us. That aside ..." he reached out and twined a strand of Sasha's hair around his finger. For the first time, Sasha noticed it was not the dark red it had been before, but was lighter and more of a red-gold. "You're not the same. Not a one of us is."

Sasha just continued to frown. Raiden's mouth quirked and with a nod, conceded, "That doesn't mean you won't be made to atone for all that you did, because you went too far and you know it. But you're not just Licht, you're Krasny—"

"I prefer Sasha," he cut in. "Krasny belonged to Pozhar and my home is Schatten now."

"Sasha, then," Raiden said with a smile. "Sasha does not deserve to suffer for Licht's crimes. As I said, you've changed. I cannot punish a man who is nothing like the one who tried to destroy the world."

"Do it anyway, because I'm still Licht," Sasha said.

Nodding, Raiden said, "Confinement. You will not leave Schatten until we all agree you may. How long that will be, I cannot say. And your power will be limited in scope until we feel you have earned the right to the whole of it."

Sasha nodded. "So be it," he said and winced as he felt the binding spell fall over him, locked in place by the powers of the other nine. It was a constant ache, the lack of freedom, the lack of power, as if his wings had been clipped and his senses muffled.

But it was a kinder punishment than he deserved. "Thank you."

"As to your shadow ..." Raiden continued, narrowing his eyes thoughtfully at David.

"Whatever his crimes, it was his bond to me that drove him and broke him," Sasha said, moving to stand in front of David. "And like me, he is not the same."

"That may be true, but he still must be punished as well," Raiden said.

Nankyokukai stepped up to Raiden's side, folding his arms across his chest. "Strip him off his power and his connection to the Seers and the other people of Schatten. If it is a shadow he wants to be, then let it be so—a harmless, powerless shadow that can go nowhere on its own, but must always be near that which casts it."

"So be it," Sasha said, and he tugged David close as he cried out from the abrupt removal of all the power and freedom he had possessed as Teufel. "David ..."

David pushed away enough to look up and smiled faintly; he looked slightly in pain, but happy. "I'm fine. It's more than I deserve, and I'm better off without it."

Sasha kissed him, then looked back to the others to softly say, "Thank you."

Raiden nodded and stepped away, and Sasha tensed all over again as Gael and Freddie approached him. "I'm sorry," he said again, though the words were woefully inadequate. It had been far too easy to take advantage of the Faerie Queen's jealousy and hatred. She was the only one who had gone along with him so easily, even eagerly. "I never meant— I should not have fed her pain—or fed upon it."

"She made her choices," Gael said quietly, pale eyes sad but accepting. "If you used her, she let you, and that was her choice. At least in you there is a Licht to be saved and nothing of the hateful, bitter, vengeful man who was bent on destroying all of us."

Freddie nodded. "Raiden is correct when he says you're different. The Duke of Krasny we knew—whom we *all* knew—could never be that terrible Licht. If a mortal was destined to take up that mantle, we're glad it's you, Krasny—Sasha."

Sasha swallowed, nodded. "Thank you. I will try not to fail a second time."

They each kissed his cheeks, then stepped away, and Sasha swallowed as Raz finally approached him. "I know I sensed happiness for you, my little spark, but I admit this is way beyond what I anticipated." Raz leaned up and kissed him softly. "I will miss your presence amongst my children, but I will very much enjoy calling you brother."

His eyes flicked to David and his smile widened, turning playful. "And here we have the real reason behind Sasha's rise to power and the opening of Schatten's borders." He dragged David forward and kissed him as well. "Hello, pretty little shadow. It is good to see you too have changed for the better. Take better care of him this time, hmm?"

"I will," David said. "I promise."

"Good," Raz replied and then turned with a flourish. "Then I say that, for now at least, all is taken care of here. Let us leave our brother to tend his country and set it to rights. We will trouble you further on another day."

In a rush of feathers and a rumble of thunder, the gods were gone, leaving Sasha and David once more alone on the roof.

David laughed, only a touch of hysterical disbelief in it. "I can't believe we're alive. I'm still not certain why."

"I'm content not to question it for now," Sasha said. "All I want is to restore Schatten and take my beautiful shadow to bed."

Twining around him, tilting his head up for a kiss, David replied, "That sounds like a fine plan to me, my light."

Sasha obediently bent to give the requested kiss while below them, the bells of the Citadel began to ring.

Epilogue

Soft lips pressed a lingering kiss to the back of Fritz's neck, eliciting a smile and shivers of anticipation. He leaned back against the warm body behind him, shivering again as knowing hands smoothed along his sides and bare chest before dipping to wrap loosely around his waist. A gentle breeze wafted through their room, carrying the sweet scent of Licht blossoms and the sounds of the people of Sonnenstrahl far below.

Drache nuzzled against the side of his neck, then whispered in his ear, "What do you See?"

"I See what you See," Fritz said with a soft snort, tangling his fingers with Drache's at his waist. Power rippled through them, power that grew in strength the longer they spent time together, slowly reforging their torn soul. His eyes glowed as he cast out, falling into a trance. "I See ..."

A man who understands the ways of the sky and the sea, a man treasured by the gods and the people, grown into his power and place. He guides the Land of Storms with a firm, but gentle hand and keeps calm the heart of chaos.

A sad soul is reborn into a happier life, given a chance to become the Tsar he could not find the strength to be before. He is helped by the priest with a heart of fire, and together they repair once and for all the rift between Zhar Ptitsa and the children of fire.

Respect for death and destruction, understanding spread by way of wandering priests with red roses at their throats. A land of misery ruled by one becomes a land of joy guided by two.

Two also proves to be stronger than three, and people flourish under the loving Voices of Joy and Sorrow.

The cruel grip of an untouchable Queen rapidly fades from memory, leaving life pure and strong once more.

Trust is a hard thing to earn, an even harder thing to regain once lost, but time heals all wounds and the people of Schatten slowly leave the dark to enjoy the light so long denied them. Nothing is yet forgiven, but more and more people walk the roads to Sonnenstrahl.

He broke out of the trance, let go of his hold on Drache's hands, and turned in his arms to twine his own around Drache's neck. "And I think we both know what Sasha is doing with his little shadow in Gold Rock."

"Come and do things with me," Drache said, nipping playfully at his lips.

Fritz laughed and drew back slightly. "Now? We have mass—"

"Not for two hours," Drache said. "I have not had you to myself, except to fall asleep exhausted, for the past two weeks. Sonnenstrahl can take care of itself for a couple of hours." He kissed Fritz softly, but with hunger, making him shiver, skin prickling wherever Drache's nails grazed it. "I have need of you, other half. Indulge me."

Smiling, Fritz replied, "Always." He let go of Drache enough that he could push him gently across the room and down onto their bed, the blankets still a tangled mess from hasty, sleepy fumbling in the dark. As heady as everything between them had always been in dreams, it paled in comparison with reality. Nothing was more intoxicating than being able to truly touch and taste and feel Drache, to be able to reach out and know the voice in his head was a living, breathing person, his true other half.

He looked down at Drache, noticing for the first time that his long hair was loose, a waterfall of gold against his skin and the mussed bedding. Being able to look at him, touch him, still stirred a deep ache. Fritz was not certain he would ever truly believe he was not permanently lost in a dream. Drache smiled at him, warm and fond, affection humming through the bond that they would always share. "What do you See?" he asked softly, though he Saw it for himself just fine.

Drache's lavender eyes glowed as he reached up to tug Fritz down. He flipped them, hair spilling all around, a curtain of gold that smelled like sunshine and incense. Taking a soft kiss, he then drew back so that they were only the barest distance apart, and replied, "Two as one, one as two. Night and Day. Life and Death. Chaos and Order. Harmony as far as the eye can See."

Lost God's Fin

About the Author

Megan is a long time resident of queer romance, and keeps herself busy reading, writing, and publishing it. She is often accused of fluff and nonsense. When she's not involved in writing, she likes to cook, harass her wife and cats, or watch movies. She loves to hear from readers, and can be found all over the internet.

meganderr.com
patreon.com/meganderr
pillowfort.io/maderr
meganderr.blogspot.com
facebook.com/meganaprilderr
meganaderr@gmail.com
@meganaderr

Made in United States
North Haven, CT
08 June 2022

19993896R00193